THE OPPOSITE
OF MAYBE

q

ALSO BY MADDIE DAWSON

The Stuff That Never Happened

THE OPPOSITE OF MAYBE

a novel

MADDIE DAWSON

B \ D \ W \ Y

BROADWAY BOOKS

New York

Copyright © 2014 by Maddie Dawson

Published in the United States by Broadway Books, an imprint of the Crown Publishing Group, a division of Random House LLC, a Penguin Random House Company, New York.
www.crownpublishing.com

BROADWAY BOOKS and its logo, B \ D \ W \ Y, are trademarks of Random House LLC.

Library of Congress Cataloging-in-Publication Data
Dawson, Maddie.
    The opposite of maybe : a novel / Maddie Dawson.—First Edition.
        pages   cm.
    1. Women—Fiction.   2. Family life—Fiction.   3. City and town life—Fiction.   4. Triangles (Interpersonal relations)—Fiction.   I. Title.
    PS3604.A9795O66 2014
    813'.6—dc23   2013031824

ISBN 978-0-7704-3768-8
eBook ISBN 978-0-7704-3769-5

Printed in the United States of America

Cover design by Abby Weintraub
Cover photograph by Anna Sherwin/Millennium Images, UK

10 9 8 7 6 5 4 3 2 1

First Edition

To Jim, always

[one]

They're making love on Saturday morning—almost finished, but not quite close enough to the finish line to really and truly count—when the phone starts its earsplitting chirping right by their heads.

Jonathan, who had been lying on top of her, with his face contorted in what she was sure was ecstasy, groaning, "Rosie, Rosie, Rosie . . ." now comes instantly to a halt. His eyes dart to the telephone on the floor next to their mattress, and she says, "Ohhhh, *no* you don't," and they both start laughing. They know he can't help it.

"No, no, no!" she says, and tightens her grip on him, still laughing. "Not now. Don't get up to see who it is."

"But I have to know," he says mournfully.

"But why? You *hate* the phone. And you already know you're not going to answer it."

"I know, but I have to see," he says. He bites his lip and gives her a sheepish look. "Come on, let me check it."

"All right," she says. "Go look, you big lug. But come back."

He leans so far over the side of their mattress that he nearly falls onto the floor on his head, still tangled in the sheets. And then, laughing, he has to catch himself and walk on his hands until he can pull himself out of the wreckage and get upright on the floor.

Sex as vaudeville, she thinks. This is what they never tell you about long-term relationships: how you'd just die if you were ever shown a video of yourself trying to have ordinary, household sex on any given day. And how it would *still* be worth it to you.

He scrambles for his glasses and then peers down at the Caller ID, absently scratching the hairs on his belly. Last week he turned forty-five, and when they went out with friends for his birthday dinner, he proclaimed—in a toast, yet—that he had now officially become older than dirt. (Rosie, only a year younger, had been surprised to hear this.) Raising his glass, he had laughingly announced he was losing his eyesight, his hairline, most of his optimism, and just about the last shred of his vanity.

Now, watching him as he mindlessly pulls off the condom that has been hanging on for dear life and flings it across the room to the trash can, she thinks he really might have been serious.

The condom does a graceful midair arc and lands with a splat on the lampshade on her dresser. If it had been a gymnast, the Russian judge would have given it a nine. It definitely stuck the landing.

She looks at his face. He's handsome still, no matter what he says. He has brown hair—okay, thinning somewhat and streaked with gray now—but his smooth, tanned face has hardly any lines, only a few crinkles around his wide brown eyes, which just now are scowling at the phone. That's the trouble, she thinks: in the last two years, he's looked perpetually dissatisfied. Maybe that's what he was talking about on his birthday, how he doesn't care about life the way he used to.

"It isn't Soapie who called, is it?" she says. She has to go see her grandmother later today, and it would be just like her to call up at the last minute and try to change the plan. Especially since today is the day they are going to have The Big Talk—the "wouldn't you really feel much safer with a home health aide" talk that Rosie has been putting off. She's even secretly arranged for a potential aide candidate to show up—a wonderful British woman who claimed on the telephone that she knows precisely how to relate to "women of a certain age," as she put it. So this is all orchestrated and it has to happen.

"Nope," says Jonathan. "The culprit is somebody named Andres Schultz, and he's from area code six-one-nine," he says. "Do you know him?"

"No. Not for me."

"Let's see . . . six-one-nine is . . . um . . . San Diego."

"Oh my God," she says. "Do you really know all the area codes? Seriously?"

Of course he does. Numbers have always attached themselves to him. And also, he's a collector of antique teacups—the kind from the dynasties in Asia and Europe, not from little girls' tea sets—and he's in constant touch with collectors from everywhere. It turns out there's a whole subculture of wacky obsessives just like him, always on the Internet, comparing, blogging, judging whose collections are the biggest and the hottest, and gossiping about who's been written up in the journals. It's a world she never knew existed.

By now the call has been shuffled off to the land of voice mail, but Jonathan still stands there watching to see if the message light is going to come on. When it doesn't, he says, "Shit. No message. Who could this guy *be*?"

"It might have been a wrong number, you know," she points out. She sighs. "But why don't you just call him back and find out, so we can get on with our lives?"

"No," he says. "I don't want to talk to him. I just can't believe somebody from San Diego would call here at nine thirty on a Saturday. It's six thirty in the morning there. What is he thinking?"

"I have no idea. But do you know what *I'm* thinking?"

"What?"

"I'm thinking I want you and your sweet hairy self to come back over here and resume having sex with me."

He makes a face. "I think Mr. Happy might have moved on to thinking about teacups, and you know how once he goes there . . ."

"Oh, I can persuade Mr. Happy," she says. She sticks a foot out from under the sheet and wiggles her toes at him, smiling.

"Yeah, well, maybe once upon a time, but lately he's become more temperamental. Also—well, frankly he has to pee." He frowns, looks at the phone again and then back at her. "I tell you what: I'll go have a serious talk with him, and then we'll see what he wants to do about the situation."

"Remind him that he actually likes this sort of thing," she says, and watches Jonathan's cute bare butt disappear around the corner of the bedroom door. He's humming "Born to Run," which is lately his go-to song for the morning pee.

"Hey, you know what?" he calls from the bathroom. "I bet this guy Andres Schultz is somebody answering my call for another Ming Dynasty cup. That could be good."

"Fantastic," she says.

They currently have thirty-eight teacups stacked up in their living room, nested in white, archival-quality boxes—teacups that will never again see the light of day. Apparently they have to be protected from sunlight, dust motes, and destructive air currents so they can last into eternity. Jonathan and those funny, obsessive guys he e-mails are no doubt saving the world from the problem of teacup extinction.

As Rosie has explained to their friends, every time Jonathan latches on to a new hobby, he goes a little—what's the clinical term?—oh yes, *batshit crazy*. It used to be Bruce

Springsteen memorabilia, then it was *National Geographics,* and there was a brief foray into German shot glasses.

Funny how you don't see something like this coming, and how after a while, you don't even think it's odd. As her friend Greta put it, when you've been with somebody for years, all their little insanities start to blend in with the good stuff about them, and even if you're annoyed, you find you still love the whole exasperating package.

Still, she thinks, it would have been nice if they'd remembered to unplug the phone.

He comes back and slides into bed next to her, still naked, but now holding his laptop. Evidently Mr. Happy vetoed more sex. Fine. She should probably get up anyway and do her exercises, get ready for the day, and for Soapie.

"Let me just see if Andres Schultz is one of the guys on the e-mail list. Because the question is, why haven't I ever heard of him? If he has my number, then you'd think . . ."

"Jonathan," she says.

"What?"

"Do you think my grandmother is going to eat me alive when I tell her she has to get an aide?" she says. "Because I kind of do."

This is yet another time when it would be so great if her mother were alive. Then she'd be the one to make all these arrangements and plans, take on some of the worrying. But Rosie's mother died when Rosie was three, and that was when she went to live with Soapie.

Jonathan is clicking the computer keys and doesn't answer her right away. "No, she's old," he says finally. "She knows she's got to get help."

"Yes, but she's in denial," says Rosie.

It's true that Soapie is eighty-eight, but until recently she was the Betty White kind of eighty-eight, having her hair done twice a week and going to spas. It hadn't ever occurred to her that she might have grown old. She's still busy writing her latest "Dustcloth Diva" book, telling America how to keep its refrigerators spotless and its ceiling fans dusted. And she's still cussing. Wearing makeup and peignoirs. And smoking. Possibly even driving, although she's been begged to stop.

It's only in the last few months that she's started falling down and forgetting little things, like how you turn off the stove and where did she put those blood pressure pills, and why are the keys in the refrigerator. And there are other things, too: osteoporosis, blurry vision, bronchitis, some bouts of irregular heartbeat that have led them to the emergency room more than a few times recently. And Soapie, predictably, has reacted with outrage to the discovery that she's made of the same stuff as the other humans after all, bones and blood vessels and capillaries that break down and turn rickety.

"You want to know what I really think?" Jonathan says, still clicking away. "I think she'll be relieved. She's probably deep down scared about the falls she's taken lately, and she wants somebody to suggest some help for her. I think it'll go fine. Better than you think."

He's wrong about this, of course, but it's a nice sentiment. "I just hope she doesn't hurt the home health aide too badly," Rosie says. "She's apparently a nice, cultured British lady. Her name is Mrs. Cynthia Lamb."

"Maybe you should have hired Mrs. Cynthia Lions and Tigers instead."

She strokes his arm. "Did you find Andres Schultz on the e-mail list or whatever?"

"Nope. No sign of him."

"So, how about—?"

"What?"

"You know. Sex?"

Silence, then: "All right. I think we can make something happen here." He closes the laptop and puts it on the floor, and takes off his glasses. "Wake up, Mr. Happy! We're going in!"

She puts her arms around him and wiggles into position, and he starts idly kissing her cheek, only it's not great because they're not lined up just right, and his big scratchy chin is hurting her face, and then the way he starts rubbing her back makes it seem as though he's cleaning a fish.

Finally she says, "Stop a minute. Just stop."

"What are you, the director?" He lifts his head and looks at her.

"What are you thinking about?" she asks him.

He hesitates. "Do I have to tell you the truth?"

"Yeah."

"Well, actually," he says with a sheepish laugh, "I was kind of thinking that when we're done here, I'm going to Google Andres Schultz."

She removes her arms from around his neck.

"You said the truth!" he says. "You're not allowed to say you want the truth and then get mad about it."

"You know," she says, "I think it's great and all that we're so comfortable with each other that we can have all this crazy stuff going on: the hilarious Keystone Kops falling-out-of-bed thing, and Googling people and flinging condoms about the room—but sometimes, just sometimes, wouldn't it be nice if it was . . . romantic again?" She touches his ear, the soft little lobe.

He blinks. "Romantic is overrated. Sometimes you get it, and sometimes you don't. We get laughs and realness, which has got to be better over the long haul."

"I know," she says. "But can't we shift gears? We used to be able to shift gears. I think once upon a time, the phone could even ring, and we didn't pay any attention to it. Remember that?"

He says, "There's nothing wrong with us. This is just life. Middle-aged life."

"I know, and I don't want you to take this the wrong way, but don't you ever worry about us ending up like every other couple we know? You just know that Joe and Greta are checking their e-mail during sex, and that's probably why Greta wants to kill him all the time."

Greta has been Rosie's best friend since they were kids, and even back in second grade, they promised each other that when they grew up and got married, their husbands would have to be best friends, too. Who would have thought that could actually happen? But it did. And there are two other couples in their main circle of friends, also: Lynn and Greg, and Suzanne and Hinton. The eight of them have all gone on vacation together and hung out at each other's houses for years now.

But here's the thing: even though they're all the same age, the others have loaded up their lives with what Jonathan calls all the "unsavory entrapments of adulthood": big-ass houses, SUVs, stock portfolios, riding lawn mowers, scads of children, and a considerable amount of domestic bickering.

Jonathan and Rosie are the holdouts, the crazy kids who never bothered to grow up and get married. They get teased that they're hippie artist types, and that all they do is sleep late, have lots of sex, and eat meals that all qualify as either brunch or midnight snacks. Their four-room apartment is still furnished in what Rosie thinks of as "Early Grad Student"—bricks-and-boards bookcases, an Ikea couch and table, beanbag chairs, throw rugs, and posters on the walls.

It's cozy and comfortable and has a rooftop garden and a great view of the river, and yes, they're happy here, but more than once she's felt she had to defend it against the others, as if they maybe just didn't try hard enough to get ahead. No, no, she's explained. They *picked* this life on purpose. It wasn't through laziness or by accident that they didn't get married and start collecting silver and china and 401(k)s. And children.

Every now and then she can't help pointing out that she and Jonathan actually do work very hard, and not just doing their art. Even though she did have some early amazing success and had some poems published in magazines, for years now she's been teaching composition classes at the community college and teaching English as a second language in adult ed.

And as for Jonathan, he'd once been a promising potter—awards and prizes and reviews in the *New York Times*—and the two of them had a whole life traveling on weekends and summers going to art shows and craft fairs showing his work all over the country. But then about five years ago, he was turned down for some prestigious shows he'd always gotten into, and the shock of those rejections didn't seem to wear off. She'd watched as he seemed to spiral down into a depression. He didn't call it that, of course; he called it "getting realistic." He said he'd rather have health insurance and social security benefits than creative genius, which was all bullshit anyway. He took a job in a mail-order ceramics factory, where he now makes figurines from other people's designs.

A few months after that, he'd discovered the world of teacups and pretty soon he'd started collecting them himself. Hardly a fair substitute, from her point of view: rows and rows of neat, orderly boxes in their living room, traded for the messy richness of the wet clay, and the light in Jonathan's eyes. They'd stopped traveling, too; no more vagabond trips to Mexico, no more camping.

She never would have believed things would go this way—that his love for making things from glorious, squishy, formable, tactile clay would evolve into something that's merely stewardship of untouchable old artifacts. She tells him that when he's not home, the teacups ask her to let them out; they beg to feel the coolness of wet, life-giving tea once again, or of human lips against their rims. Once she told him she'd heard one distinctly *begging* for even a Lipton tea bag.

"You're jealous of them, aren't you?" he said to her once, and he wasn't even kidding. "I think you actually see them as rivals."

"Yeah, they're little Lolitas," she'd said. "Thirty-eight little Lolitas. One of these days, you're going to come home, and I'm going to have them all out on the table, all waiting to be admired and petted."

"Please," he'd said. "Don't even joke about that."

She looks at him now across the pillow, at the deep crease between his eyebrows, the lines etched underneath his eyes, and the way his lips are pursed in slight disapproval. His life is like one big fat *NO*. And what's going to happen if they don't even have sex to pull them back together?

"Do you want to get up and go get breakfast?" she says.

Maybe he hears something in her voice, because he says, "Not yet. I want to pretend it's the past, and we don't know about Caller ID or Google." He moves on top of her and looks down into her eyes, cradling her head in his gentle potter's hands.

"Impossible—" she begins, but he puts his mouth on hers and gives her a long, slow, unlikely kiss, and with so many years of experience, of habit, the automatic-pilot part of them takes over, and somehow, despite everything, the familiar rhythms begin again.

He gets up and gets the scented oil, and the air fills with the fragrance of roses and lemons as he massages her. He sweeps her long brown hair out of the way, and leans down and kisses her cheeks and neck and that spot he loves by her collarbone, and by the time he has worked his way down, they are suffused with a drowsy passion.

Afterward, they lie there quietly, touching each other, watching the way the sun slants in, how at this time of year it's beginning to catch the glint from the river down below and flash its wavy patterns above them. In the next few months, she knows, the light will become sharper and will move all the way across the ceiling, jiggling and bouncing in the wake of the boats that will come. Another year will have gone by.

"Oh my God," says Jonathan. He sits up. "Uh-oh. You know what happened? I forgot to put on another condom."

The wavy patterns shudder on the ceiling. "You forgot?" she says. "How could you forget?" But she knows why. He's not used to them. Mostly she uses a diaphragm, but a couple of weeks ago when she was washing it, she noticed it had a hole in it, but she couldn't get an appointment for another right away, and so Jonathan said he'd wear a condom in the meantime.

She looks at him in dismay.

"Yeah. Well, *we* forgot," he says. "You could have mentioned it, too."

There's something she's supposed to do at a moment like this—go out and get some morning-after pill or something. Does she really have to jump up and hurry to a clinic? She's got better things to do. He's watching her, biting his lip again, waiting for the verdict.

"I think it's all right," she says after a moment. "One of the good things about being so damn old is that I don't think I'm in danger of getting pregnant."

"Why? When does menopause come?"

"Oh, it comes when it wants to. My periods are already weird. I think I'm halfway in menopause already."

"But you don't know?"

"You never *know*. It's all mysterious with periods. They do what they want."

"I don't know how you women cope," he says.

"Us? I don't see how you guys get along with those things flapping around on the front of you. That's way worse." She looks at him and smiles. "Oh hell. Let's just get up and go have some breakfast," she says. "Okay?"

"Okay," he says. "Could I Google Andres Schultz first, do you think?"

"Do you have to?"

He smiles at her, and yes, she sees how much it means to him that Cup Number Thirty-nine might be waiting out there in San Diego, might *right now* be sitting in a white box that will come and join the others in their living room. For a moment, she feels what it must mean to him.

She's about to say it's fine, he should go ahead and Google Andres Schultz, but then she doesn't have to. "Nah, you're right. I'll wait," he says. "Let's go eat."

[two]

Once they've walked down the hill and are sitting in their usual comfy booth at Ruby's Café, with coffee and the *New York Times* spread around them, she can't help herself. She says, "Would you possibly consider coming with me to Soapie's this afternoon? You can meet Mrs. Cynthia Lamb and watch her audition for the part. Might be fun."

"Rosieeeee," he says, making a face. "I've got things to do. I'm a busy man."

"Come on," she says. "Sometimes we have to stick together. It's family."

It's so unfair. Jonathan is from a huge family, with whole battalions of people to shoulder the burdens of life with—a mother, aunts, uncles, cousins, brothers and sisters, all of whom call him whenever they please—but she only has this one old lady. He's always ducking calls from his brothers who want to schmooze about their cars, and his mother, who likes to chat endlessly about her theories about life and death and celebrity divorces. He says that family is the real reason Caller ID was invented.

Suddenly a curly-haired toddler in a pink tutu materializes at Rosie's side and hands her a doll and one half-smashed blueberry.

"I wanna sit in the window," she says.

Surprised, Rosie lifts her up and sets her down on the cushion next to the window. From across the room, the child's mother stands up and shrugs, mouthing, *Is this okay?* over the din. Rosie smiles back at her and gestures that it's fine, suddenly noticing that the place is crawling with young families today. Babies in strollers are tucked into all the available corners, kids lean out of backpacks and high chairs, and young couples, harried from the task of keeping everybody sorted out, hand babies back and forth across the table.

"Jesus, it's like they're giving out babies with the breakfasts," says Jonathan. "Be careful how you phrase your order. I think they're doing a very loose interpretation of the word *eggs*."

The little girl looks up and claps her hands. She has a smudge on her nose that might be syrup.

"You're very cute, you know that?" Rosie says.

Jonathan shakes his head and whispers, "What, is this the one they're giving us? Don't we get to pick, at least?"

"Sssh, this one's lovely," she says to him.

"She may be damaged, though. Look at that mark on her nose."

"Would you stop? It's syrup." She laughs and wipes it off with the corner of her napkin.

He's frowning, looking at the little girl as though she's a wild feral animal.

"What if you just make a quick appearance, Jonathan? In and out. Say hi, smile at Mrs. Cynthia Lamb, tell her you hope she ends up working with Soapie, and then you can leave," Rosie says.

"I've got a million things to do today. I work all week, and my Saturdays—"

"What? Really, what?"

He's quiet for a moment, looking longingly at the sections of the newspaper strewn out across their table. They have a brilliant system for sharing the *Times* each week, which they've perfected over the years, and Rosie can see he's trying to surreptitiously locate the Style section for her so that he can shut her up and get on with his precious Arts section. She puts her hand down on top of the paper and looks him in the eye. Finally he clears his throat and says, "No, no, no. This is *not* going to be a negotiation, where I say what I'm doing and then you say it's not important."

"I already know what you're doing today. You're going to Google Andres Schultz and then you're going to blog about teacups. And no, it isn't as important as human beings, Jonathan. We have to stick together sometimes. We have families, you know."

"My name is Sega," says the little girl, getting up on her knees and tugging on Rosie's sleeve. "What's your name?"

"Sega?" Jonathan says in a low voice. "*Sega?* Seriously? After the video game system?" He gives Rosie his head-exploding look and talks in a low voice. "Do you hear this? People are naming their kids after games now?"

"Sssh," she says. "Her family is right over there."

"That's another thing. Do we look like unoccupied baby-sitters or something? Maybe we should go over and tell them our hourly rate." He looks down at the little girl. "Do you have a sibling named Nintendo?"

She puts her fingers in her mouth and shakes her head.

"You will, just wait." Just then, his cell phone bleats from his pocket, and he grabs it and holds it at arm's length so he can read it before he flips it open. His face lights up. "Hello? Yes, this is Jonathan Morrow." He leans over and mouths to Rosie, "Andres Schultz," before he takes his mug of coffee, scrambles to his feet, and heads outside with the phone. She watches him through the window as he paces around, frowning and gesturing with his cup of coffee.

Ruby shows up then holding plates of eggs Florentine, and Sega's mother comes over to get her daughter.

"I hope your husband didn't mind," says the mom. She's so young and seamless that she looks like she could be Greta's daughter, Sandrine. It startles Rosie for a moment, the realization that their friends have kids who are nearly old enough to have children of their own.

When Jonathan comes back a few minutes later, his face is so pink it looks as though he's spent time under a radiant magic light. He sits down at the table, picking up his fork very precisely, as if he's trying to keep from openly quivering.

"Well?" she says. "So does Andres Schultz have the Ming Dynasty cup that will make our lives here on earth worthwhile?"

"Nope," he says. He takes a sip of his coffee and leans forward. "Actually, Rosie, he's opening a museum in San Diego. From scratch."

"Oh." This is even more boring.

"No, no. Hear me out. He wants my teacups to be on permanent display there." He puts down his fork and then picks it up again.

"Really! The Lolitas get to go on display somewhere? Are you going to just send them off, then?"

He shakes his head. "No, you don't get it. Schultz wants *me*." His eyes are so bright they're practically shooting sparks. "I guess he was at that conference I attended in Toledo and he said that ever since then, he's been thinking of doing this museum. And he says he's now got the property and the building, and some backers, and he says he's ready for me."

"Does he have teacups, too?" She straightens her floral cloth napkin next to her plate, pressing down on its folds, thinking how it is that when your life starts to change, the surfaces of everything around you take on such meaning.

"No. He collects something else. Painted pottery, I think. Plates."

She takes another stab at her eggs, but they slide off the fork, and she doesn't seem capable of figuring out how to get them back on it. Finally she puts her fork down and puts her hands in her lap.

"Look, I'm sorry," she says. "I have to be honest. I can't wrap my head around this. You're seriously considering this? You want to move to California after one five-minute phone call? To work in some guy's museum?"

"To *start* a museum," he says. "That's the exciting part. To be in on the startup of a whole museum, and then to curate it."

"But is this what you really want? You used to be a *potter*, not some museum guy."

He starts rolling out words about all the blanks not being filled in yet, how they'll talk later, et cetera, et cetera. Museum, upkeep, expenses. Pedestals for the teacups. Not a done deal. More talks to come, gauging interest, blah blah blah.

"You seem really interested to me. You've actually turned another color. You've pinkened."

"Have I?" he says, pleased. He drains his coffee cup and looks at her, folding his hands in a steeple in front of him. "Maybe so. I feel pink."

She looks at him. "Well, Mr. Pink, so you'd leave everything and move there? Just like that?"

"Us. *We* would move there. You can get a job teaching, and I'll do this museum."

"Are you crazy? I have a life here—"

"Yeah, but we're stagnating. You've said it yourself, that we need something new," he says. He takes her hands and leans across the table. "I can't get it together here anymore,

Rosie. I'm getting old, and I feel like I'm falling in a hole. I need something big and important to happen."

"But this—I can't—"

He doesn't even hear her. "You know what? We'll get married. Let's get married!"

Marriage! She laughs a little. The last time they spoke of getting married was at Lynn and Greg's wedding thirteen years ago, in Mexico, and they were tipsy on the dance floor, caught up in the champagne and the mariachi band and the moon rising through the clouds. They'd go the next day to Tijuana, he whispered, keep the celebration going. But the next morning everybody was hungover, and they all sat together at brunch, moaning and drinking mimosas and squinting in the white-hot sunlight. As the day drained away, so did the jazzy, impromptu wedding she'd imagined. It was never going to happen, not with her and Jonathan. And really, who cared? They weren't the marrying types, so why pretend?

Since then, when people rib them about why they don't just go ahead and do it, one of them invariably laughs and says, "Omigod! Did we forget to get married? I knew there was something we were supposed to do." They don't even have to plan out a response anymore.

And now he's looking at Rosie as if he doesn't remember who they are. He's delirious, is what.

"Look," she says. "We may need a change, but moving to California is crazy. We'll be away from all our friends, and I have my classes, and Soapie needs me, Jonathan. She's frail and—"

"Oh, now don't go invoking your grandmother on me," he says. "If Soapie thought you were even thinking of giving up one single opportunity because of her, she'd run you down with her convertible. And as for your friends—there's e-mail and Facebook and cell phones."

"But I love my job," she says.

"Two months tops, and you'll love your new California students, too. Come on. This is what we need. I know it is."

He stands up and pulls her to him, holding her right there in the aisle between the tables. His face is mashed right up into hers, and his voice is low and urgent. "We can do this. Soapie doesn't want to see you waste any more of your life."

But has this been a waste? Is that the lesson of today, that they've been wasting time living this life, while they waited for some guy from California to wade in and offer up a solution?

"Please . . . don't," she says. "I have to think."

He pulls her hair back from her face and smiles down at her, and her breath catches. This isn't like him; he hates public displays. The café has come to a complete halt.

"Marry me, Rosie Kelley," he says in a rough, shy voice.

The café waits to hear her answer. He is staring into her eyes and holding her in his grip.

"Don't do it this way," she whispers.

He presses his forehead down against hers and whispers, "Say yes. Why won't you just say yes?"

"Because I *don't know*," she whispers. "You don't even know. It might not work."

"It's worked for fifteen years," he says. "It worked pretty well this morning, didn't it?"

People laugh.

His eyes are like a stallion's, and his fingertips press into her arms. And then it hits her. He has said no to absolutely everything imaginable for so long now—to sex, to parties, to pieces of pie after dinner, to creativity, even to the little girl at their table this morning. He walks through life with a big chilly *NO* on his lips, and now, by God, he has said yes to something, and he needs her to say it, too.

He's the introvert suddenly bathed in public adoration. Oh, he's a pink man today, and the whole café is watching him.

"All right. Yes," she says. She wants the moment to be over. He kisses her, and everybody starts cheering, and then Ruby is at her side, grabbing onto Rosie's arm and smiling and dabbing at her eyes with a corner of her apron, and little Sega and her mother rush over, and so do about a zillion other people. There are babies and toddlers riding on people's hips and mugs clanking as they're being toasted, and people applaud and whistle.

"Wow. Are you really getting married?" Sega's mother asks Rosie.

Rosie wants to tell her that she doesn't know. Jonathan is the kind of guy who might change his mind, or forget. But she looks at him, smiling, being the center of congratulations, shaking hands, and she says, "Yes. Yes, I am."

And she's startled to realize she's—oh, probably 99 percent happy about it.

[three]

By the time she gets to Soapie's house an hour later, she's decided she's probably 99.8 percent happy about getting married, and she'd gladly round up to 100 percent except for the worry about Soapie. But Jonathan's right: her grandmother is not one of those cuddly, needy old ladies who would put up with Rosie not living her life. And if she agrees to have a health aide, as her doctor thinks she should, then what's the problem?

A new start. Lolitas out of the boxes. California.

Rosie makes her way up the white gravel driveway to the back door of Soapie's four-bedroom colonial, lugging the bags of food she's cooked for her this week, along with the treats and peace offerings—chocolate bars with almonds, honey-roasted peanuts, and macaroons.

And then her heart stops. Through the windowpanes of the back door, she sees Soapie lying on the kitchen floor, perfectly, chillingly still. Her grandmother is wearing a lavender workout suit, and her white-blond hair is splayed across the tile floor, and—this is the horrible part—her cold blue eyes are fixed on the ceiling.

Fear rises in Rosie like floodwater. Her hands start shaking so badly she can barely balance the bags of groceries on her knee as she turns the key in the lock. *So this is the way it ends,* she thinks. *Shit.*

She rams the door with her shoulder, but even before she's managed to get inside, Soapie moves. Her lavender-clad arm is fluttering upward and then floats there in midair, fingers splayed. She looks like a woman possibly admiring her manicure.

"Oh my God!" says Rosie.

"Oh, hi," Soapie says in an oddly flat, thick voice, like someone awakening from sleep. "You're here."

"Jesus, are you all right?" Rosie says. "I thought you were dead. Are you okay?" She drops the bags on the counter and rushes over to her grandmother. Soapie doesn't seem to be bleeding from anywhere that she can see, and her color is good. Better than Rosie's just now, most likely. "Did you hit your head when you fell? Do have any idea how long you've been down here? Do you know what day it is?" She takes her wrist and holds it, but of course Soapie pulls it away.

"Stop it. I'm fine, just fine," she says, and she does sound perfectly well now, just a little sleepy.

"My heart just about stopped. How long have you been down there?"

"I slipped, is all. And now don't you go making a big deal out of it."

"But what if I hadn't come along right now? Why aren't you wearing that Life bracelet thingie?"

"Why? Because I loathe it."

"But why? What harm does it do? Someone could come and help—Here, do you want to get up? Let me help you."

"Rosie. Stop," she says. "Come sit down. Stop *twittering*. You're making me nervous."

"You're making *me* nervous," Rosie says, but she gets down on the floor next to her grandmother, inhaling her signature whiff of Jean Naté. The floor is a beautiful Italian tile that Soapie had installed last year, part of a whole cosmetic redo of the house that included nothing that might be considered reasonable for a woman in her late eighties:

things like shower chairs, higher toilets, or stair railings. No, she went for track lighting, marble countertops, and Italian tile hard as cement.

"Listen to me," Soapie says, and Rosie's almost relieved to hear that her voice is as scrappy and rough as ever. "You have got to stop worrying about me all the time. If something is going to happen to me, then it's going to happen."

Soapie's eyes are crystal blue, perhaps a little foggier than they had once been, but still fringed with mascara-laden black lashes and a span of turquoise eye shadow coagulating in the wrinkled creases of her eyelid. Rosie takes in the web of wrinkles, the sagging jawline, the bright blotches of misplaced rouge—and all of it pierces her.

"I know that *sounds* like it makes perfect sense," she says, "but how can I not worry when I come in here and find you on the floor? What if I hadn't been here? You might have died *today*."

"First of all," says Soapie, "I wouldn't have died because my yoga class is coming here in an hour, and they would have picked me up—"

"Your yoga class? How could they save you? The door is locked."

"I would have yelled to them where the key is hidden. *And*," Soapie says firmly, "second of all—I don't care."

"You don't care about what?"

"How I die. When you get to be my age, one way is as good as another. If it's going to be a fall on the floor, then that's just one way it might happen."

"Some ways, it seems to me, are worse than others. And lying here, not being able to get help—"

"Stop it. Listen to me. I'm not afraid of death. I know I'm having little strokes. I do see what's happening, and it's fine with me. Remember this. When you hear that I've died, just be grateful that I went the way I wanted to. Not in some nursing home or being kept alive by machines. Okay?"

Rosie grimaces. "Let's get up off this cold floor. Please? Can't we please get up and sit down at the table or something? I'll make you a cup of tea, and we can talk sense."

"All right. I need to get the Bloody Marys made anyhow. Pull me up, will you?"

Rosie guides her slowly up to a sitting position. "We're having Bloody Marys?"

"For the yoga class. I told you."

"Wait," Rosie says. "You have a yoga class that drinks?"

"Yes. This is one of the advantages of being so fucking old." Soapie reaches up and gathers the wisps of white-blond hair that have straggled out of her topknot and twists them back with her trademark rhinestone clip, just the way Rosie has seen her do a million times before. "You can cuss if you want to, and you get to drink when you do yoga, because it's not about enlightenment or whatever the hell makes people do that stuff."

"I think most people who do yoga are looking to tone their muscles and maybe get themselves to calm down."

"Yeah, well, we like to get drunk while we do that. It's quicker." Soapie holds out her arms and Rosie scoops her up and gently brings her to a standing position. Her grandmother is so frail that it feels as though she's constructed of chicken bones and coat hanger wires held together with Scotch tape, but she's also tough, like a wild animal that's about to bolt.

"There," Rosie says. "Lean on me for a minute. Are you okay?"

"Stop treating me like an invalid." But Rosie notices she keeps leaning against her, and after a moment she wraps her arms around her grandmother. Soapie bats Rosie's arm away. "Obviously I'm not going to die *today*. So just stop it."

"But you're falling more often," Rosie says. She swallows and plunges in. "Listen, Dr. Vance has recommended a woman who can help you, and she's coming by this afternoon to meet you. She can make sure you're okay, get your medications for you, and be a companion—"

"No." Soapie makes her way over to the sink.

Rosie follows. "Dr. Vance says she's very qualified, very . . ." What *had* he said about her? What adjective was it that was going to make this all right with Soapie? Fun? Cultured? Tolerant of old people's crazy-ass opinions?

"No! Absolutely not."

Rosie tries a new tack. "But just to have somebody here, who can help with things you don't want to do? Wouldn't that be nice?"

Soapie takes the celery out of the refrigerator. "Nope. Forget it. That's all taken care of. I've got a boy living here now," she says in a clipped voice.

"Wait, what? What boy?"

"Oh, somebody my yoga teacher knows." She puts the bag of celery down on the counter and turns to face Rosie. Her still-beautiful face is flushed. "I forget who he is. It doesn't matter. Anyway, he's staying here."

"Since when?"

"Since—oh, I don't know. A week or so, I think."

"But do you even *know* this kid?"

"I know he can pour a mean gin and tonic, and he can pick me up off the floor. Also, he's funny. He makes me laugh."

"No, no, no. Soapie, we have to get somebody from an agency, somebody who's qualified to get you the help you need. A companion who can get your medications for you, and see that your blood pressure is okay—"

"You're not listening to me, darling. I am going to live out the rest of my life doing exactly what I please, and it does not involve being cared for by some idiot *paid companion* who thinks her purpose on God's earth is to keep other people from doing what they want. No."

"But I want you to be happy—"

"No, you don't. You want me to be *safe,* and that's a whole different thing. And now that I'm a thousand years old, I'm going to start having me some fun, and I am *not* hiring some *nurse* to follow me around. If I want to drink and smoke and have sex, then it's nobody else's goddamned—"

"Sex?" Rosie says. "You're having sex?"

Soapie looks at her with amused, narrowed eyes. "Well, I really got your attention now, haven't I?" She reaches for her cigarette pack on the counter, and Rosie sighs as her grandmother lights up a Virginia Slim with shaking hands. "You're too preoccupied with my life, Rosie. I woke up in the middle of the night and it hit me, what's wrong with you."

"Nothing is wrong with me."

"No. You do have something terribly, terribly wrong with you. For one thing, you have the perfect life—free as anything, no husband, no children, no demanding job—the life I would have *killed* for, and yet you're stuck. But I think I've finally figured out why. You hang around here because you think you're sacrificing for *me.*" She takes a long drag off her cigarette.

"That's not it at all."

"It is. And it hit me how unfair it is for you that I had to live this long and keep you tied here, turning into a worrier. You're such a worried person, Rosie. So just go. Please! Go to Paris and write a book or something. Or go travel around Africa looking at lions. Take the money I'm going to leave you, and just take off." She waves her arms in the air, as if she could fling Rosie overseas.

"I don't want to go look at lions."

"Then go *somewhere*! You must have something you want to do. I don't get why you don't enjoy your freedom. Here, pour this vodka for me, will you? Eight glasses." She puts down her cigarette on the edge of the sink and starts chopping up the celery stalks into haphazard little sticks. Rosie can barely stand to watch her operating the knife. "Life is too short for this. And if Jonathan is what's holding you back, get rid of him." She stops and shakes the knife at Rosie. "No, seriously. You're still a good-looking woman, especially if you paid attention and fixed yourself up, and you could still have a fun life for yourself."

"Okay, just stop. Stop, stop, stop. I wasn't going to tell you this right now, but he asked me to marry him this morning."

Soapie barks out a laugh. "You have got to be kidding."

"No. He did. Proposed while we were out at breakfast. Big public scene and everything."

Soapie stubs out her half-smoked cigarette in one of the many decorative ashtrays that are on nearly every surface in the house. "I suppose he'd never understand that this is not what you want. We'll have to strategize about how to break it to him."

"But I—I think I do want it. I want it a hell of a lot more than I want lions."

"Oh, for God's sake, Rosie, you've lived with this man for fifteen years. Are you trying to tell me you've just been waiting for him to get down on one knee?"

"No, that's not it. We didn't even think about marriage

before now. And then today we did. And so we're going to. I said yes, and that's that." She lines up the glasses on the counter and pours a small amount of vodka into each one.

"Come on, you don't want this. And for what? Security? Ha! You think that piece of paper brings you security?"

"Soapie, why can't you be happy for me?"

"Because I raised you not to run after a man. And why the hell *now* anyway?"

Rosie sighs. "Because he's been invited to start a museum in San Diego with his teacups and he wants me to go with him," she says.

"A museum!" She snorts. "So *this* is your dream come true? Living in a museum with Jonathan's teacups? You amaze me. You really do."

"Why? Why does that amaze you? I love him, and he loves me. This is what people *do*."

The doorbell rings then, conveniently—it's no doubt the alcohol-drinking yoga class—but she and Soapie continue to stare at each other, and then Soapie shakes her head and makes a *tsk*ing sound as she makes her way down the entry hall to the front door.

Rosie hears Soapie sweeping the yoga ladies inside the living room, ordering them around, and they're all laughing and talking at once, shedding sweaters and canes, allowing themselves to be herded into place. The door closes with a bang.

Rosie sighs and puts on the kettle for tea. While she's waiting for it to boil, she loads up the Bloody Mary glasses onto a tray, and then she places them on the table outside the louvered doors. She can hear the women all talking at once, and Soapie urging them to sit down and get comfortable.

She sighs and goes back to the kitchen, where she makes herself a cup of Earl Grey and takes it with her to Soapie's office at the back of the house, off the laundry room. This is the official headquarters of Dustcloth Diva Industries, a room so cluttered and dusty that it would alarm readers and health departments everywhere. Rosie sits down in the swivel chair at the desk to drink her tea and pay the bills, as she does every month.

It's a daunting task. There are papers strewn and stacked everywhere, books flowing off the shelves, leaning in precarious towers on the floor. Letters and bills are all over the desk, and so are pages of a possible new manuscript. There's a stack of copies of Soapie's first book, *The Dustcloth Diva Tackles Dirt and Dust and Still Has Time for a Life,* ready to topple, and Rosie reaches over and steadies it. That book had sold more than five million copies. The image of a young Soapie smiles out from the cover, wearing a hot-pink blouse, pearls, and white pants and holding a martini glass in one hand and an ostrich feather duster in the other. She's been long known for her catchphrase, delivered in her deep, dry, cigarette voice: "Clean it like you mean it, darling—and then take the rest of the day off!"

On an impulse, Rosie digs her cell phone out of her purse and punches in Jonathan's number. He answers on the second ring.

"Well, I did it," she says to him. "I told her we're leaving."

"Great. So she's agreed to have that woman—um, Mrs. Cynthia Lamb then?" he says. She can tell he's looking at his laptop while they're talking.

"Well. Not so much," Rosie says. "It's way more complicated than that."

He clears his throat. "Don't back down. She's got to have someone there. You know that."

She can't possibly explain to him right then how her own heart practically stopped when she arrived at the back door and found Soapie on the floor, possibly dead. In fact, he's never understood that Soapie is exciting, maddening, and terrifying—and how it is that sometimes Rosie feels that she herself is the old woman, the person about to turn into a ghost, while Soapie is the one full of life, full of plans and ideas. Bloody Mary yoga! Sex at ninety! Jonathan won't want to hear about the "boy" living here, pouring vodka martinis and picking her up off the floor if he's ever around, and how Rosie can see how that could be enough.

While she's talking she sees some papers all balled up in the trash can and reaches down to pull them out. They are Soapie's unfilled prescriptions, for the meds she has to take every single day. And right beside them—her breath sucks in so violently she starts coughing—there's a bright, fluorescent orange speeding ticket, torn in half. She picks it up and looks at it. Soapie had gone out one night two weeks ago and driven fifty-five miles per hour in a residential zone.

"Oh my God," she says quietly, and then, despite knowing what Jonathan will say, she can't seem to stop herself from telling him.

Sure enough, he says it all: She has to take action. This stuff is only going to get worse. Soapie is not in her right mind anymore; she has to be protected from herself. And— *what?* A *kid* is staying there? Somebody who's hoping to bleed her dry, that's who! Hasn't she ever heard of scams like this, guys who show up, flatter an old lady, and then take her money? Soapie could be in actual danger.

Maybe, he says, she should call the police. He would. He *will*, if she wants him to. He can have a cop over there in twenty minutes, start getting this guy out of there. Why, just last week, there was a story on the news of an older woman—

No, she doesn't want the cops. She'll figure it all out, she says, irritated. And when she finally manages to get him off the phone, she sits there staring out the window at the terrace and the trees, the pool, the lawn.

Then she punches in the cell phone number of Mrs. Cynthia Lamb. The call goes to voice mail. She had hoped to ask her advice, but instead, after the beep she says, "Hello, this is Rosie Kelley. I've talked to my grandmother, and I'm sorry it's not convenient for us to meet with you today after all." She hesitates for a moment, then lets her voice go into a lower octave, one with authority and power. She says, "But I'd like you to start on Monday anyway. I think that my grandmother will accept the idea when she meets you. I'll be working, but I'll talk to you afterward. Just arrive at nine a.m. and tell her Dr. Vance sent you. She'll be surprised, but I think that's for the best."

This takes so much out of her that after she clicks the phone closed, she opens the bottom drawer of her grandmother's desk and pulls out the photo hidden at the very bottom, in the rattiest manila folder tucked down way in the back, the one remaining photo Soapie kept of her only child. The last picture of Serena she didn't destroy in the rampage.

Her mother's young, slightly pouty face stares back at her. Serena looks to be about twenty in the photo, with long, blond, slightly stringy hair tucked behind her ears, and giant hoop earrings—and just by the look of her scowling blue eyes and the lift of her chin and her folded arms, you can see that she's furious. It must have been Soapie holding the camera—Soapie, who has never once told a story about Serena that didn't involve some kind of fuss between them. There's no glorifying the dead with Soapie, or overlooking their teenage mistakes.

Oh, Mama. Why in the world aren't you here helping me out with her now, where you should be?

four

Serena didn't go in any of the ordinary ways young people usually pick to die: some rare, exotic cancer, or drug overdose, or car accident. Instead, she was walking down the street in New York City, going to meet a friend for a Coke, and a piece of a building broke off from twelve stories above and smashed into her head, killing her instantly.

Death by building. Seriously. What were the chances?

Rosie was three, so all she has is a shadowy memory of her mother's blond hair and flowery perfume, the feel of a lingering touch on her forehead once when she had a fever, and a couple of lullabies weaving in and out of her sleepiness, songs she's pretty sure Soapie never sang to her. Had there also been a plastic kiddie pool they splashed in, and a time her mother had read her a story about ducklings? Did these things really happen, or are they simply snippets from old TV shows?

As for her father, she never had the pleasure. According to Soapie, he married Serena and got her pregnant on purpose, thinking it would improve his chances of avoiding the draft. But then he headed for Canada anyway, leaving Serena waiting for him. Soapie's lips always clamped shut when she told this part; her whole face changed, and a person could see how the photo-destroying rampage might have sprung from a mood this deep and dark.

But then her grandmother would get that grim look on her face and switch the story back. Nope. No blaming other people. Serena had been a capable, educated adult, and no one *forced* her to be with David. It had been her stupid-headed belief in romance and melodrama, her sheer foolish girlishness. And that, young lady, comes with consequences: unintended babies, early marriage, and motherhood.

And maybe even early death if you happen to be walking next to an unstable building.

For Soapie, her daughter's death meant she was plunged into another round of child rearing. Instead of the art-filled, easier middle-age years that Rosie knew she had planned for herself, Soapie left New York City and bought a four-bedroom colonial in North Haven, Connecticut, a place where no one knew them or the tragedy that trailed behind them like a bad smell. And why not start over in a whole new place? She'd tried her best with Serena, but there was no use in pretending that things had gone well. There had been lies and fights and rebellions and mistakes, drugs, bad boyfriends, the occasional arrest—everything the sixties had to offer. And then Serena was dead, and there was a child to raise.

Luckily for Soapie, Rosie thinks, she was a well-behaved, nervous child, aware at some deep level that she'd been entrusted to someone who might not be totally able to withstand the full force of a normal American childhood. For the first years, she sat cuddled close to her grandmother on the brown couch in the den, quiet and watchful, as the cigarettes burned down in the ashtray, and the ice cubes melted in the vodka glass. Even then, she remembers knowing that this New England family dream house Soapie had bought was the wrong house for them. It was as though the house itself—with its black shutters and flagstone front walk, six-foot windows, a rose garden, a terrace, and hundred-year-old maples that arched over the lawn—expected to turn the two of them into a family, and held it against them when it didn't work out.

But life has a way of moving forward, and Rosie learned how to heat up the TV dinners without burning herself, how to answer the phone by saying politely, "Baldwin-Kelley residence, Rosie speaking," and how to soothe her grandmother by going over and wrapping her arms around her. There were hard times, times when Soapie was almost unrecognizable in her grief. One time she picked Rosie up by the shoulders and mashed their faces together and screamed, *"You will not turn into your mother! I will not have it!"* And another time, when Rosie didn't load the dishwasher correctly, Soapie pulled out all the plates and smashed them one by one on the floor in front of her.

Who could blame her, though? Rosie remembers feeling more sorry for her grandmother than scared of her. Sometimes she felt like *she* was the one in charge, the one who had to figure out the right things to say and do to keep things smooth. Years later, a therapist pointed out that it was ironic that even though Rosie was the orphan who had lost both parents, Soapie was devoured by such a big sadness that it left no room for Rosie's grief.

But—and Rosie insists on this view of things—there were plenty of good things that balanced out the bad: the times Soapie read the *Little House on the Prairie* books, every night, one after the other, and then started again, and how, on summer evenings they'd go out for ice cream, driving in Soapie's Mustang convertible down to the shoreline. Those were the times when she would talk to Rosie as if she were a confidante, forgetting she was a child. "We're going to talk human-to-human here," she'd say and then explain her philosophy of life in great detail. Rosie absorbed it all: politics (Soapie was a feminist liberal who felt the world was doomed), religion (agnostic for the most part, with a nod to the Church of Unflinching Honesty and Living with

Consequences), and sex (more trouble than it was worth). And don't even mention romance. That was for idiots who'd been brainwashed by Hollywood.

She said that Rosie was going to turn out tough and strong like her, and that people can get through anything if they put their minds to it, if they just goddamned well face things honestly and stop trying to sugarcoat everything. Life was hard, and what was needed—the *only* thing that was needed, in fact—was developing self-reliance so that you never had to ask other people for help.

And for God's sake, the human race had *got* to stop its wallowing.

"Don't talk about your mother to people," she said. "If you even bring her up, they'll always think of you as a pitiful orphan for the rest of your life."

But maybe that little speech had come after she'd risen from the couch and transformed herself into the Dustcloth Diva, after she had set up her IBM Selectric typewriter in the office off the laundry room and made housework look almost miraculously amusing—so much so that she was on all the morning television shows, waving her feather duster and winking at the cameras. She took to throwing fabulous parties on the terrace and wearing designer clothes. She was a celebrity.

There would be no more wallowing, she said, no more talk of how sad they'd been, no more talk of Serena. And that was that.

• ● •

Well. But there was other stuff going on.

At school, in ways Rosie never tried to explain to her

grandmother, being an orphan was far from pitiful. In fact, as the only motherless kid in the whole school, she had rock star status. Teachers let her help in the office, brought her treats, and allowed her to be first in line. She not only ruled several social clubs in the playground, but she had a whole posse of girlfriends who invited her for sleepovers and whose mothers viewed her grandmother as something of a glamorous, eccentric woman who, poor thing, clearly knew nothing about how to raise a happy child. At friends' homes, she was treated to birthday cakes with pink icing and taken to the kind of Disney movies her grandmother did not see as good for children.

Rosie and her best friend, Greta, spent hours writing dramatic stories about her dead mother. They knew that Serena, beautiful and angelic, would have been nothing like the real, down-to-earth, practical mothers around them— the Barbs and the Patties and the Carols, energetic mothers who insisted on homework getting done and bedtime being eight thirty. No, she would have been above all that, sharing her makeup and jewelry, letting them stay up late and dress in fancy chiffon gowns.

They sobbed as they created and acted out the imaginary scenes of Serena's life. On most days, they took out the Serena Box, the secret collection of things that Rosie felt that her mother had once touched. There was a painted china cup that Soapie once said was the last cup her mother had drunk from before she left home that morning to go into the city; a turquoise silk scarf; and a fuzzy photograph of Serena as a child with the sun behind her head shining so brightly that it looked as though her hair might be on fire. Rosie also has a hair clasp with some possible Serena hairs still in it, and the most valuable thing of all, an old cassette tape with Serena's voice on it, singing in a raspy, laughing voice, "Piece of My Heart," a song that years later stopped her in her tracks when she heard Janis Joplin do an almost identical version.

On bad nights, when she was alone, Rosie would lock her bedroom door and take these things out, fingering each one of them and calling out for her mother, who never once showed up.

By the time Rosie was in high school, she had lost interest in telling the story or capitalizing on the panache it afforded her. She had gone through all the stages of thinking about Serena. She had idealized her, worshipped her, pitied her, been furious with her, hated her, and forgiven her over and over again, and she had had enough. She put the Serena Box away and didn't take it out for years.

By the time she met Jonathan, she didn't think about her mother at all. She was okay, going unmothered. He was teaching a pottery class she signed up for, and just about everybody in the class developed crushes on him, mesmerized by his wide grin and the joy that seemed to burst out of him when he was handling the clay. She recognized his type: a shy man who became a wizard when he was doing what he loved, a god who could take wet mud spinning around and guide it into becoming bowls and pots and sculptures.

She fell for those large hands, his curly hair, the way his eyes would squint when he'd throw back his head and laugh—and most importantly, the fact that, out of everybody in the class, he seemed to choose her. What was it that he saw there in her clumsiness? He put his wet, muddy hands over hers and moved her toward her own creativity.

And then one evening—soon after they'd started going out, when it was already clear they were going to be lovers for a while—they were lying in bed together at her apartment. It was dusk and they had finished making love, and were saying those things you murmur, like *oh this was the best, the very best, you are amazing.* And then she heard herself say, "My mother died when I was three."

She hadn't told the story for many years, but it was all there, waiting to be brought out and unpacked again: the crumbling building, and the friend her mother had been meeting for a Coke, the grandmother who became the Dust-cloth Diva. She told him that things had basically worked out okay, probably the way they were meant to. She realized as she was saying it that somehow she really had survived it, all of it: her mother, her father, her grandmother, all her early romances, and the confusion that comes from feeling you belong nowhere.

He didn't say anything for what felt like a long time, but his eyes looked full of knowing, like he could see both the pain of it and the freedom of it and not judge either one. His fingertips started making soft little circles along her jaw, and then he kissed the length of her arm down to her hand, and when he got to her fingertips, he whispered, "So what do you have of her? What do you hold on to inside when you lose your mother at three?"

That was a question nobody had ever asked her before. She got down off the bed and got the Serena Box, dusty from being in the back of the closet. He picked up and caressed each object with his long, long, pottery-making fingers, and his face was as serious as she could want. She realized she was holding her breath to keep from bursting into tears.

Then for a long time he looked at the teacup, the last teacup Serena had drunk from, a little china thing with a chipped handle and a painted-on spray of violets tied with a pink ribbon, turning it back and forth and running his

THE OPPOSITE OF MAYBE ▪ 39

fingers along the gold leaf stripe around the rim, studying it as though he needed to learn all of its secrets for himself.

"So this was her last drink of anything—from this?" he said.

"I don't think they really know," she told him. "Not for sure anyway." She laughed. "She may have had that Coke in New York, you know."

"No," he said. "She didn't. This was the last."

He put it up to his mouth and pretended to take a tiny sip from it, and, seeing him do that little gesture, a thing that she and Greta had done a million times in their Serena games, something in her snapped—all that feeling, unbound.

She threw herself into his arms and knocked him over, kissing him like crazy.

"Whoa! Whoa!" he said. The cup left his fingers and flew into the air and smashed into a million pieces all over the floor.

And that was that. Out of some kind of mysterious alchemy, she knew she had let go of her mother and now belonged to Jonathan. She moved in with him the next week.

As simple—and right—as that.

[five]

Greta screams with joy and then bursts into tears on the phone when she hears the news. She needs to hear every detail, making Rosie tell her again and again about the scene in the diner, laughing each time at the idea of Jonathan turning pink and discovering the joy of being an extrovert. Then, because she's Greta and is impeccably organized, she easily shifts gears into wedding planning and dress selection, and from there, it's just a small detour into questions about Soapie's care, the résumé of Andres Schultz, and the whole rest of Rosie's life.

Luckily, before Rosie has to explain that she actually *has* no plan, Greta gets called away by one of her four kids; the baseball team has a game. "We'll shop for a dress!" she says as she hangs up. "I've been waiting for this day for—well, for forever."

It's the same with her adult ed students on Monday: they all nearly lose their minds.

"You really get married? You and Yonatan . . . married!" yells Goldie.

"Well, we're not married yet," she says, feeling shy. Then, she adds, because this is, after all, an English class: "The way to say that, when it's in the future is, '*Are* you really *getting* married?' or you could say, 'Are you really *going to marry* Jonathan?'"

"You are! You are!" Goldie says, and comes barreling into Rosie. She's a heavyset woman in her sixties, with startlingly white hair and black eyes that are like onyx beads, and she's famous for hugs so enthusiastic they're more like body slams.

And since Goldie is the ringleader, she's followed, of course, by Leena and Karenna and Carmen, who come charging around the desks to the front table, where Rosie has plopped down her bag of books and blurted out the news. For a moment she's engulfed in their mingled perfume, which is the scent of spices and flowers and lovely things from their kitchens.

Then Tomas comes in, and they break away to tell him. He looks concerned and baffled by the news, and it's not until Leo gets there and the announcement gets told once again that Tomas finally breaks into a smile.

"Oh, I see now! I think before you mean Jonathan *not* marry you but someone else. I think you crying." Tomas is young and sentimental, working as a bartender and seeking a wife. The group thinks he'll eventually meet somebody, but he says the women in the clubs are all too rude. Pantomiming with his thumbs, he shows how they text even while they flirt with him.

"Jonathan is not crazy. Of course he marry Rosie." This is from Mara, Goldie's best friend and sidekick. "It take him time, yes, but he do right thing. Finally."

Goldie winks at Rosie. "Yonatan is a man who know his own time, and Rosie let him."

"Rosie should get award for patience," says Leo, an elderly gentleman with rheumy eyes. He smells of aftershave and hair gel. "Might we see the ring for admiration purposes?"

So she explains that there is no ring, that she and Jonathan are too old and settled for anything foolish like an engagement ring. Mercy.

"No, hell no!" says Karenna. "Nobody too old. You need ring."

By then, everybody else has filed in. They have fourteen students today, which is pretty typical. Some, like Goldie and Mara, the matriarchs, have been coming for years, while the others come in and out as they get jobs. This class is her guilty pleasure, taught through adult ed instead of the community college, and although she gets the students to write papers and practice their grammar, mostly they've all become good friends, working on language problems as they come up in everyday life: filling out forms, negotiating rental agreements, outlining talks they need to have with their significant others and relatives, whatever needs doing. She's gotten people out of bad relationships and into better ones, helped Tomas buy a used car, taken Mara's soccer-playing grandson to physical therapy when he got injured, helped Goldie when her father needed to go into full-time nursing care, coached Carmen through the exam to get a home daycare license.

In return, they mother and spoil her, bring her food and recipes, knit her socks and hats, invite her over to their houses for tea and spicy coffee, introduce her to their grand-children.

"Wait. You get marry, and then you still come here?" asks Goldie suddenly. "Or you move away?"

Rosie closes her eyes. She has to tell them, then, about the museum. They know about the teacup problem already; she's made a story out of it more than once.

They're quiet, staring at her when she finishes. She ex-pects them to look upset that she's leaving, but instead she can see from their expressions that all this time they've been feeling sorry for her, and that they've always quietly won-dered if she was being stupid, living for so long with a man who clearly has some kind of decision-making disorder.

There's a certain relief that he's turned out to be a real man, someone with plans they can understand.

"Well," says Mara. "It just a disappointingness that he not do this back in time. So late for all of life to come."

"Babies, you mean," says Goldie. She smiles and shrugs at Rosie and then leans over and pats Mara on the arm. "Yonatan and Rosie have whole life together already before now. Maybe they choose no babies long ago."

"Chose," Rosie says, "and that's right. No babies. The timing here is just right. It's perfect."

● ● ●

After the class is over, Rosie walks to her car in the parking lot, already punching in the cell phone number of Mrs. Cynthia Lamb.

"Hi!" she says with a great show of cheer when Mrs. Cynthia Lamb answers. "How are things over there?"

"Well, it's quite an odd sort of situation now, isn't it?" Mrs. Lamb says in her clipped British accent. "If I didn't have proof, I would almost think you gave me the wrong address. Your grandmum is nothing like I expected."

Rosie laughs with relief. This has to be a good sign. "Really? And how is that?"

"Well, she's quite a character, that one. A charmer. Even though she didn't seem to have any idea that I was coming, they were very gracious, both she and her gentleman friend. He even made me some breakfast."

"Wait. Her what?" Rosie says.

"Her gentleman friend. Tony," says Mrs. Lamb. "He's starting a gardening business."

It takes Rosie a moment to remember. "Oh, him! No, no. He's just a kid who's staying there, somebody in need of a place to stay."

"No, dear, he lives there. Both of them have made it clear that Mrs. Baldwin-Kelley doesn't need my services."

"You don't want the job?"

"Dear, they don't want *me*."

"Mrs. Lamb, my grandmother is a mess, and I'm moving across the country soon. I need to know that she has somebody who's qualified taking care of her. That gentleman friend is just a guy that nobody even knows."

"But, Miss Kelley, I don't force myself on people who don't want to be served."

"Please," Rosie says. "Just do me one favor, will you? Tell me that man's last name, and his cell phone number, and I'll go and talk to him. Trust me. He is not qualified to be her caregiver."

There is an uncomfortable pause, and then Mrs. Lamb says, "Ask your grandmum his name. I am not at liberty to say any more about the situation."

"Mrs. Lamb." She swallows. "My grandmother won't tell me his name."

"Well, there you go."

"Pretend I want him to be my gardener. Who is he?"

Papers rustle. Rosie hears a long sigh. Then Mrs. Cynthia Lamb says, "Well, I don't know what harm it could do to tell you, but I'd like to tell you that I hope I'm in as good a shape as your grandmum when I get to be eighty-eight. His name is Tony Cavaletti. Now don't ask me anything else." And then she hangs up the phone.

[six]

It takes a few days to track down Tony Cavaletti. She knows better than to stage an ambush at Soapie's house, even though Jonathan is convinced that Tony Cavaletti is out to fleece Soapie and thinks Rosie should march in with the authorities and demand that he leave. Soapie would never stand for that. There would be nothing left of Rosie but an echoing scream and a little greasy spot on the rug. She has to be sneaky. She drives past the house at different times to get a look at his car, and when she discovers a red pickup truck parked in the driveway with a rake shoved haphazardly in the back, she knows she's got her man.

And then, on the day that Andres Schultz flies into JFK airport and Jonathan drives all the way to New York to pick him up so he can come and meet the Lolitas for himself, bingo! Rosie sees the red truck parked in front of the Starbucks in Branford—and she pulls into the parking lot, checks her teeth in the mirror, squares her shoulders, and heads inside, her heart pounding.

Which customer could possibly be Tony Cavaletti? There's a dark-haired guy in jeans and an orange Syracuse sweatshirt drinking an iced coffee and staring at a laptop screen, a couple of young women texting, an older man in one of the armchairs snoozing with his mouth open, and some guys playing chess. She gets her coffee and makes her way over to Syracuse Laptop Guy.

"Excuse me. Are you Tony Cavaletti?" she asks.

He looks up blankly and then shakes his head.

"Outside," one of the chess players calls out to her. He jabs a thumb toward a courtyard where there are chairs and tables scattered about. Sure enough, sitting at one of them is a youngish man with dark brown hair underneath a Red Sox hat turned backward. He's in some kind of intense conversation with two women sitting across from him. One of them, with short pixieish black hair, is wearing a long skirt and sitting with her knees up and she looks like she might be crying, and the other one, with pinned-up blond hair and a blue sweater and jeans, has her arms folded over her chest and is staring off into the traffic. Rosie stands at the glass window, tapping on her paper cup, unsure of what to do.

"Go save him," says the chess man, and the others laugh. Another says, "Yeah, get him away from those chicks before they make him wish he was never born."

"Are you his friends?" Rosie asks, turning to them, and they get quiet. Finally a guy in a faded green T-shirt clears his throat and says, "Nah. We don't know him. We overheard those women working him over pretty good, so we feel bad for him."

Rosie wants to ask what the subject was of this workover. Were the women yelling at him about abuse of the elderly? Toxic freeloadery? She looks back out the window and sees that now the blond woman with the jeans has gotten up and is walking away, swinging her arms angrily. The other woman turns around and calls to her, and then she says something to the guy and then she leaves, too. He watches her walk away and picks up his phone.

She pushes her way out of the door and goes outside. "Are you Tony Cavaletti?" she says to him, all business. He looks up, startled. Now that she's closer to him, she can see that his eyes are so dark they look almost black. He's also not as young as she had been expecting. Handsome, she'll give him that, but in a scruffy way—and certainly not a kid, except perhaps to somebody who's close to ninety.

"Guilty as charged," he says.

"My name is Rosie Kelley," she says. She likes the tone of voice that she's using, firm and strong; she'd practiced it in the car on the way over. "I believe you're living with my grandmother. Sophie Baldwin-Kelley."

"Did anything happen to her?" he says, and there's a flicker of alarm in his eyes.

"No. I've just got to talk to you about her."

"What'd you say your name was again?"

"Rosie Kelley."

"Ah, the in*fam*ous Rosie," he says. He puts his phone down and smiles. "I know all about you."

"Actually, it's pronounced *in*famous," she says. "Accent on the first syllable."

He looks at her for a long moment, smiling. "So what can I do for you?"

Okay. She takes a deep breath and says, "I'm afraid I have to ask you to move out of my grandmother's house." When he doesn't say anything, she throws in, "I'm sure that you most likely didn't understand the situation when you moved in there, but she is really quite frail, and she needs a trained, qualified caregiver—"

"Not just some dumb guy, is that what you're saying?" he says, still smiling.

She doesn't let herself be swayed by this blatant fishing for compliments. "I need to hire somebody official to come and take care of her. And while I'm sure that you're very nice and all"—which she is *not* sure of, not in the least—"you're simply not qualified to do the kind of care that I think is needed at this time."

"How do *you* know I'm not qualified?" he says.

"Well, with all due respect, you seem to be somebody who's trying to find work as a gardener, and considering the fact that my grandmother has all these health needs at the moment that are not being addressed, I can say with some assuredness that I need to find somebody who can do more than take care of the roses."

He's silently fiddling with his phone, so she takes a deep breath and continues, "So I would appreciate it if you could come up with a plausible excuse to tell her why you need to move out, and then I would like you to leave her house as soon as you can." She stops, having run out of things to say. It was genius on her part, she thinks, to remember that Soapie is going to need to hear some excuse for why he's leaving.

He waits for another long moment, looking at her face and then looking away, possibly checking out his image in the window of the Starbucks, which is reflecting back at them like some giant mirror giving off heat.

After a while he drums his fingers on the table and says, "So, if I may ask . . . what does your grandmother want? She say she wants me to leave?"

"Well, that doesn't really matter, because she—"

"Wait a minute. What do you mean, it doesn't really matter?"

"No. You see, she's not really in a position to judge what she needs right now. I don't know if you realize it, but she's had several *very* dangerous falls lately, and she's not taking her medications, and what she needs is somebody from an agency, somebody who's qualified to take care of her."

"Wait. Hold up a minute. How do you know?"

"How do I know what?"

"How do you know whether she's in a position to judge what she needs or not? People get to say what they need."

Rosie shifts her weight to the other foot. "Mr. Cavatelli," she says.

"Cava*letti*," he says. "The L is in the middle."

Just then a young Goth couple with hair so black it's as though they mistook the shoe polish for hair dye comes tripping out through the glass door, laughing, and make their way, stumbling, over to a table by the window. They're both wearing black capes, and the girl has on purple lipstick and earrings that look like they were made from bat wings, and to Rosie's surprise, the boy grabs at her and kind of nudges her up against the window and then starts kissing her, while they both keep giggling. It's a fascinating sight, and neither Rosie nor Tony Cavaletti can quite bring themselves to look away.

When she does manage to tear her eyes away and looks back at him, he's shaking his head. "Young love. You remember being like that?" he says under his breath, and shrugs.

"Not really," she says. "I think I always had more self-control than that."

"Well, that's too bad, *in*famous Rosie."

She's trying to remember where they were in their discussion—or where she was in her monologue, but it's hard with all the kissing noises and laughter so close to them, and then she doesn't have to, because Tony Cavaletti suddenly gives up and says in a tired tone of voice, "So bottom line: you want me out of your grandmother's house," he says. "I get it. Okay. Consider it done."

"Oh! Well, it's nothing personal—"

"No, no. I understand completely. I'm outta there. I was only gonna be there for probably another coupla weeks anyways. At the outside. It's fine."

He picks up his phone, but instead of making a call, he turns it over in his palm, staring at it like it's some kind of artifact. She waits, but he doesn't say anything else.

Go! Go now, you idiot. He said he's leaving, so just thank him and go.

"Well, thank you," she says. "For understanding. And you'll think of some reason to tell her? For why you're leaving?"

"Yeah. Don't worry. I won't tell her that you tracked me down and fired me." He looks up from his phone and smiles at her, painfully.

"I just wanted to explain what she—" she begins, but he shakes his head and waves her away, still smiling. "Thank you," she says again, and heads to the door, but the Goth couple is in her way, sitting down and making out against the door now, and she can't get by.

That's when Tony Cavaletti pipes up again. "But by the way, just so you know," he calls to her, "you may not realize it now, but I'm the guy you *want* there, believe it or not. I've picked her up off the floor like five times."

She turns.

"And not for nothin' but I'm the one gets her to eat. I cook her meals, you know."

"Well . . . thank you," she says.

"Yeah, and George and I are even getting it so she doesn't drive places anymore because she's really not safe behind the wheel, even though she won't admit it. And—"

She walks back to the table. "Wait. George? Who is George?"

He lets a long beat of silence go by, and then he looks down at his sneaker and straightens out the tangled laces. "See," he says, "I'm wondering if you really know all that much about your grandmother, *inf*amous Rosie. Maybe you've got everything all figured out, but then it turns out you don't know squat about what's going on. Like, were you the person who sent over that British lady the other day? Because that was never, ever going to work out."

Rosie feels the color bloom in her face. "Look, I try. She's a difficult woman, all right? And, just so *you* know, if you're thinking you and this George are keeping her from driving, you're certainly not doing a very good job of it. She went out the other night and was going fifty-five in a residential zone at eleven thirty at night, and *then* she threw the ticket away. What about *that*?"

"Yeah. I heard about that. That was a night when I was down in Fairfield, and the next day she tells me about it at breakfast. I'm there making blueberry waffles for her, and she's all, 'Ohhh, Tony, I got me a ticket!' "

"And are you the one who told her to throw it away?"

"No, what do you take me for? I told her to pay it."

"Uh-huh. Well, perhaps you don't know Sophie Baldwin-Kelley doesn't pay her own bills. I do that for her."

His eyes flash. "Hmm. Wonder if that could be why she threw it out. Probably didn't want you to see because it's pretty clear that would be something that would sure get you ticked off."

"I'm sure she doesn't care if I get 'ticked off,' as you call it. And by the way, she also threw out all her prescriptions, too. She's got some kind of death wish, is what I think."

"Nah, she's just forgetful. And a little bit cranky. She wants fun. And who doesn't need fun?"

"No, she told me she doesn't care how she dies. She says one way is as good as another, and she's not letting anybody tell her what to do."

He studies her face. "Well, but she doesn't really want to die. You should see her with George. She's happy."

"So tell me. Who is this George?" Rosie says. "Do I even want to know?"

"I'm surprised you don't know him. They're old, old friends, she said. His wife is in some kind of home with Old Timers' Disease."

"Alzheimer's?" she says.

He flushes. "Alzheimer's, Old Timers', whatever. Louise? I think that's her name."

"George *Tarkinian*?" she says. "He's the one who's hanging around?"

"Yeah, that's him."

"Oh my God. I do know him. But he's married. He's been married to Louise forever."

"I know. That's kinda what I meant when I said his *wife* was in some kind of home. When I used that word, it convened they had a marriage."

"What do you mean, it *convened* they had a marriage?"

"Oh, here we go. So I used the wrong word. Do you make it a habit of correcting *everything* people say?"

"I teach English," she says. "It's an occupational hazard." She sinks into the chair opposite him. "And so *he's* now hanging out with my grandmother?"

"Yeah. That's right. They're kind of sweet on each other."

"Sweet on each other? What, are you from the 1940s or something?"

"My mom used to say that. It's nice. Certainly better than saying what people say nowadays: they're *hooking up*, or they're—"

"Please," she says. "Are they—?"

"Are they what?"

"You know."

"What? You think I check up on people? That's the worst thing you've said yet."

His phone rings, making a mooing sound, and she's fascinated to see that his whole face changes when he looks down and sees the number. He flips it open. "Milo! Hey, buddy! Are you with the sitter? Did Mrs. Dolan pick you up? Good." He gets up and paces around rocking up and down on his toes, his face going through all kinds of contortions. And then he says, "Yeah, well, Mommy's on her way home. She and Dena got tied up here for a bit. They'll be along. No, no. You know I don't think you should play Angry Birds on Mrs. Dolan's phone. Why don't you ask her to take you outside?" He puts his mouth down close to the phone, like he would crawl into it if he could. Rosie looks away. "I know," he whispers. "I miss you, too, kid. Naw. Well, maybe. Maybe. We'll see. I know. I talked to her about it. I love you, baby. Yeah. I love you a million dinosaurs, too. No, two million. Okay, three million and infinity. Bye." He closes the phone and it takes a moment for him to rearrange his face back to a normal expression. "That was my kid," he says. "Want to see his picture? Here. Look at the phone here."

"Sure, okay," she says.

"Yeah. Look at that little mutt face," he says, and holds out his phone, where a young kid who looks just like him is smiling and holding a toy dinosaur. Barney, maybe? She's not sure.

"He's cute," she says.

"Yep. Sweet little Milo." He gazes at the picture. "He's five. Lives in Fairfield with his mom. We split up. She was the one who was here—one of them—"

"Aww," she says. "I bet you miss him."

He sighs. "Yep. Correctamundo. But I'm trying to work

out some stuff with her. That's why I said I might leave in a few weeks. I can't stay away from this guy." He stares down at the phone.

He reminds her of her younger students, always with domestic complications they talk so openly about, and suddenly she feels everything shift a bit in her head. Jonathan is simply wrong about this guy being out to rob Soapie. He's clearly not dangerous. And besides that, he's getting Soapie to eat and picking her up off the floor, and it's not like she has anybody to replace him with anyway. And, after all, Soapie likes him. And George is there, too.

"Tony," she says, and stops. "So listen," she says, and swallows. She lays out the plan, tells him about how she's getting married and going to California, so could he just live with Soapie for two or three weeks longer? By then, surely she can find someone more official. What does he think? She's twisting her purse strap around and around her fingers, cutting off the circulation.

He looks over at her, no emotion on his face. "What? Because I showed you the picture of my kid?"

She says no. Well, maybe.

"All right," he says slowly. "I guess I could do that," he says. He seems suddenly shy. "That'll give me time to work out some stuff."

"Well, thank you," she says.

Jonathan will have a fit, but let him, she thinks.

"Don't tell her I was here," she says. "And, oh yeah, don't let her drive. Okay?"

"You should really stop doing that to your own finger," he says. "You gotta calm down."

● ● ●

That night she gets home to find that Andres Schultz has moved into their apartment, and the Lolitas, amazingly, are perched on tables, nested in open boxes, and one of them, shockingly, is in Andres Schultz's pink, plump hand.

Rosie has to keep herself from rushing over and grabbing it back to safety, so deeply has this been ingrained in her.

"This is Andres!" says Jonathan, who has turned pink again. "And this is Rosie."

"Well, hi, Rosa," he says. Andres, a pudgy, shiny-faced guy with a round baby face, stands up and takes approximately a full minute to elaborately set the teacup on the table—and all three of them watch, holding their collective breath, as he does so. Then he exhales loudly, grins at her, and shakes her hand, and then he pulls her into a damp, exuberant hug. He smells of aftershave and airports and rumpled clothing.

"I already feel as though you're family," he says. He's in his fifties, she guesses, and intense in a nerdy kind of way. He probably sleeps on *Star Wars* sheets and stands in line at midnight for the Harry Potter movies. "You and Jonathan! It's been such a divine pleasure to meet Jonathan and to get to see up close these very, very . . ." Words seem to fail him as he gestures toward the piles of opened white boxes.

They talk, then, about Andres's flight and about the conference where they met last year, and about the daringness of what they're about to do. You'd think they were going to scale Mount Kilimanjaro, to hear the hushed way they speak of this venture. She stands, still holding on to her purse and smiling a frozen, exhausted smile.

Then Jonathan—the new, expansive, excited Jonathan—starts recounting every single second since he first laid eyes on Andres Schultz at the airport, how they recognized each other (clever Andres was holding up a cardboard teacup), and what they said at first, what they said next, and next, and next.

She thinks she might pass out from sheer minutiae overload.

"By the time we pulled out of the parking garage and started for New Haven—" Jonathan begins.

"We knew we had to work together," finishes Andres.

"And then, by the time we got on the Bruckner, I was asking if Andres wanted to stay at our apartment instead of going to a hotel," says Jonathan.

"I readily agreed. And by the time we stopped for dinner in, which was in—"

"Bridgeport."

"Yah, Bridgeport, by then we were composing our business plan," says Andres.

"We wrote it on a napkin," says Jonathan.

She feels a little dizzy. Jonathan tells her that Andres will stay for three days or so, during which they'll finish up the business plan for the benefit of Andres's backers, and then Jonathan will give notice at his job. He's got vacation time accrued, so he'll get a decent check to start out with. He rubs his hands together, red-faced, beaming. A buddy at work knows somebody who's looking for an apartment and could move right in so the landlord shouldn't mind . . . and Rosie's classes will be over in another week, right?

Ah, but she's signed up to teach the summer session, she says, and Jonathan says, "But you can totally get out of that." He looks at Andres. "We're available!"

Wait. Is she really actually doing this? Like, in the next few weeks, packing up all her stuff and . . . moving?

"Well," she says. "Wow."

● ● ●

Later, she's brushing her teeth in the bathroom when Jonathan comes and leans against the doorjamb. "So you're okay with everything?" he says.

She stares at him in the mirror. His eyes are still too bright, and he has patches of color on his cheeks.

"Well. Is it my imagination, or did our lives just start running at warp speed?" She dries her mouth on the towel.

"I think they call it momentum," he says. "The building is available, the guys giving money are itching to write the checks for some kind of write-off, and—well, I think Andres is the kind of person who gets things done."

"But you're not," she whispers.

"See? I'm trying to change."

She bites her lip. "You're not coming to bed?" She goes and turns the covers down and slides under the sheet.

He comes over and nuzzles her neck. "Andres is a talker. And I'm too excited to sleep anyway," he says.

"I wanted to tell you about meeting Tony Cavaletti today."

"Tell me now."

"No. It's too late. And you're so . . . distracted. And buzzy. You've turned pink again."

"So, hey, what I came in here to say was—well, I was telling Andres about our . . . proposal scene the other day in the diner, and then I thought, well, that was kind of weird, and I—well, I wanted to ask you the right way. So here goes. Ready?" He closes his eyes and kneels down beside the bed. "Will you marry me, Rosie?"

She laughs at his scrunched-up face. "Get up. I told you I would."

"Okay, now this. Will you marry me this weekend?"

"Jonathan! This soon? Can't we—"

"I want to do it now because things are going to get crazy.

We're leaving in three weeks, and I want to run down to the courthouse Saturday morning and do the ceremony, and then if you want, we could invite some friends over for a beer or something. Okay?" He runs his index finger along her arm, down to her knuckles, where he draws little circles.

"I think I want something a little more festive than just a beer," she says.

"Well, nothing huge . . ."

"No, no, not huge. But friends and family should be there. We could have a luncheon or something at Soapie's house, something simple—"

He blanches. "Really? Because I want us to leave for California in three weeks. We don't have time."

"Wow," she says. "You're like somebody who's put his life on speed dial or something. I want to slow everything down and think about it."

"No. No think. Just do." He wiggles his ears, a trick he can usually only be persuaded to do on New Year's Eve when he's had too much to drink.

She can feel herself caving.

"This weekend?" he says.

"Maybe the weekend after. I have to make sandwiches, you know." She looks at the indentation on the ceiling, from the time they had champagne in bed, and the cork flew up and dented the stucco ceiling. What had they been celebrating then? She can't even remember. Some pottery show he'd gotten into. It was a *long* time ago. This place, this place. *Home.* All the days, all the hours, all the memories. *Don't think about that.*

"And I need a dress. And we need a license—"

"I knew you'd get into it," he says, and then suddenly kisses her. It was meant to be a quick, grazing cheek kiss, but then it turns into one of those movie kisses, deep and real.

She puts her arms around his neck, overcome with emotion. She wants to ask him one little thing: What if it turns out that they've waited too long, and they don't know how to go somewhere new and set up a new life? What if it's too late?

Instead, when he pulls away from her and is getting ready to go back to Andres Schultz, she hears herself saying, in a casual, bright voice, "Oh, by the way, Tony Cavaletti turns out to be a really nice guy. I asked him to stay with Soapie until we go, and he said yes."

He looks back at her blankly, his hand on the doorknob. "Oh. Great. Whatever."

"He's got a little kid. And he's getting Soapie to eat, and picking her up off the floor."

"Well, that's good then," he says, as though he'd never had even the slightest objection.

"And he's very, very cute," she says, but of course Jonathan is already gone, which is fine. He didn't need to hear that anyway.

seven

"Now don't take this the wrong way, but your prospective husband is certainly going about this wedding in the most *Jonathan* way possible," says Greta, smiling, and taking dress number three off the hanger—a white satin number with a frothy full skirt that looks like it was made in a blender rather than on a sewing machine. "This is him at his *most* Jonathanish. I mean, he waits fifteen years to marry you and then gives you a week to plan it all. What the hell?"

They're in the fitting room at Landon's Bridal Shop, which is ridiculous, Rosie thinks. The only other customers are twenty-something brides being tended by enthusiastic girlfriends and twittering moms, people who are *not* criticizing the groom—not within earshot, at least. Nothing like a bridal shop to make a forty-four-year-old feel like a big, lumpy, geriatric impostor. She should have gone over to Target one afternoon when school was out and picked out something to wear, without Greta.

Rosie plows through the piles of dresses, saying no to each one. "That one would only look nice on a seven-year-old at a ballet recital . . . that one looks like it was made of fattening dairy products . . . that one with the red beads at the neck would look like I was wearing a bandage and bleeding out the top of it. Like I'd been decapitated."

"Okay. Jesus. Some brides have no sense of humor at all. This is for that zombie-theme wedding that's all the rage just now."

See? There are reasons to love Greta, she thinks. And they explode in laughter, and of course the saleswoman is instantly outside the curtain, calling to them, "Girls! How are you doing in there? Can I get you anything else?"

"No," says Rosie. She whispers to Greta, "We have to get out of here. The more I think about it, the more I think wearing white or cream is such a cliché. I think I want something red so I can wear my red cowboy boots."

"What?"

"Yeah. Maybe a nice red blouse with jeans. I'd even be willing to iron a crease in them for the occasion." She's surprised to realize she actually means this. It's the first thing today that has felt authentic.

"You are not wearing a red blouse with jeans to your own wedding, even if you are marrying Jonathan Morrow," says Greta. "I cannot risk my reputation with my children by standing up next to a bride in jeans, and I'm assuming I'm the matron of honor since I've been waiting for my whole life for this."

"So I'm stuck with you. Is that what you're saying?" Rosie is still smiling.

"You are. Who is going to stand up with Jonathan? Do you know?"

"Oh, Greta. It's not that kind of thing at all. This is . . . us, remember? This is just a quick thing. It probably shouldn't even be called a wedding, the way you're thinking of it. We're simply saying some words to each other."

Greta sits down on the spare chair, pushes a strand of curly brown hair out of her face, and looks at Rosie in exasperation. "No, you're not *simply saying some words to each other.* Listen, this is your *wedding,* and even if Jonathan doesn't take it seriously, the rest of us do and you should, too. This is what he's always doing to you. He minimizes things of importance. He makes you wait to get married, and then *he* decides on *his* timetable, and you all of a sudden have to figure everything out like it's an emergency. It makes me mad for you that you have to do it this way."

"Nope, it's not that," says Rosie. "I *want* my red boots, and okay, no jeans. I want a red short skirt with ruffles—and I want Indian food." She's surprised at the vehemence in her own voice.

"Indian food?" Greta sounds a little hysterical. "What am I going to do with you?"

"Look," says Rosie, "can't we just get the hell out of here? I can't look at these stupid white dresses anymore. I hate this."

"What, you're mad at *me*?" Greta says. "I never said you had to have a white dress!"

"But you liked them."

"I did not. I thought the zombie one was hideous. We were laughing. We were just laughing one second ago, Rosie."

"I just want to get out of here. I can't talk about this anymore." Rosie's pulling on her denim skirt and blue cotton sweater and sticking her feet into her slides. She grabs her purse.

"Fine, then," Greta says in her calm, competent, resident adult voice, and she carefully places the dresses into one big stack, and Rosie, who has flung back the curtain and is marching through the store, feels Greta walking more slowly behind her. She's no doubt fingering the fabrics, stopping to look at other dresses on the rack, nodding to the saleswoman, perhaps even apologizing for her friend who's, you know, so temperamental.

She and the saleswoman might smile knowingly at each other. *Bridezilla.*

Yes, and the older ones marrying lunatics are the very worst.

• ● •

They patch it up, though, later. Suzanne and Lynn meet them for lunch—a ladies' lunch, as Greta puts it, *not* anything even close to a bridal shower, although they order champagne and do some toasts, and then it turns out that they've brought little gifts, too. Rosie slides her eyes over to Greta, who is beaming at her: she'd arranged this whole quasi shower for her, and is now acting pretend-scared that Rosie will be mad about *that*. Which of course she isn't. She's grateful that people take this wedding seriously—she just doesn't want them to try to take it over, or to pity her for it not being exactly what they would want.

She realizes that she's actually happy. In seven days, she'll be getting married, and then in another week after that, she'll be leaving for California. She almost has to pinch herself to believe it. Everybody is smiling and laughing and yes, teasing her a little, and she is basking in it, laughing right along, even when they start calling it another episode of *The Jonathan and Rosie Show*. This started years ago, actually, when the eight of them were going on vacation together to the beach, and the rest had watched in dumbfounded fascination as Jonathan packed up the car in his crazy, obsessive way: making sure he had his water shoes, his special fiber towel, the sunscreen that has about a billion SPFs, the sun hat with the flaps for the ears and the back of the neck, his wraparound sunglasses that looked like they had been designed for Stevie Wonder. And Rosie, they said, was hardly better, with her sacks of poetry books to read and Jonathan's art books, her string bags and her lotions.

It became an episode ever after referred to as "How Jonathan and Rosie Go on Vacation," followed a few months after that with "How Jonathan and Rosie Throw a Dinner Party" (hilariously casually, without even thinking if they have enough chairs), and "How Jonathan and Rosie Get Ready for Work in the Morning."

"'How Jonathan and Rosie Put on a Wedding' is the coup de grâce," says Lynn.

The answer: It's going to be crazy! No two people have ever or will ever put on such a hilarious rendition of a wedding. The bride will wear a red skirt with ruffles and red cowboy boots, and the bridegroom will likely show up with rings he's fashioned from aluminum foil, all because he forgot to go to a jewelry store in time.

"Sorry, but it *is* funny," says Greta.

"It's hilarious," says Rosie. "More likely he will make it to the jewelry store, but then he'll decide that aluminum foil rings are more artsy and creative, so he spends so much time making them that he forgets to take a shower before the ceremony."

Lynn says, "You know what's going to be the hardest? We're not going to get to see up close the show 'How Jonathan and Rosie Adapt to Married Life.'"

"I'm quite sure our lives will go on much the same. Believe me. You won't miss much."

"Oh, come on," says Greta the expert. "You'll be surprised how it changes things."

"You'll find your fights are way more—how should I put this?—*loud*," says Lynn. "He may stop bathing altogether and start eating macaroni and cheese three times a day."

"Oh, stop. Rosie and Jonathan don't fight," says Greta.

"It's true," says Suzanne. "All the rest of us are having dramas all the time, and you guys just sail along."

It is true that Rosie has often felt that she and Jonathan were mostly audience members in their friends' lives, watching as they went through one life-changing situation after another. They bought and renovated houses. They got jobs, shifted to others, moved on, got promotions, moved on again. Children came: Greta and Joe have four kids, Suzanne and Hinton three, and Lynn and Greg two.

And oh, the crises that came up! One year Hinton had a crush on a colleague, and Suzanne almost left him. But that blew over, as did the time that Greta's husband Joe, a physician, almost died from a tick bite. And then Lynn's mother was killed in a car accident, Greg lost his job, and Joe's father moved in with Greta and Joe and grew senile there, until they had to put him in a nursing home.

Sandrine, Greta's daughter, started making herself throw up after eating, and Lynn's son was expelled for bringing a bow and arrow to school. Over the years there have been plenty of lesser emergencies, too: bad grades, mean camp counselors, sleepovers during which no one got any sleep— not to mention the bouts of flu and possible food allergies, dogs that died, unfair eliminations from soccer teams, best friends who turned into bullies, devastating eyebrow piercings ranking right up there with tonsillectomies, torn ACLs, and twisted ankles.

For years as she's watched, bearing witness, babysitting their toddlers, attending Little League games, consulting on lunch box shopping, there have been times—though not as many as her friends probably imagine—that she's tried to picture herself padding around in their mammoth houses, driving their minivans, and cuddling children, that *maybe* she's felt a little twinge. But that was it, just a tiny twinge from time to time.

More often, she and Jonathan would come back home from their friends' houses, and she'd walk through their silent apartment, its four rooms clean and plain, and find herself grateful for its smooth emptiness, for her freedom to write, for the pens neatly arranged on her desk. In the evenings, she'd smile across the living room at Jonathan, who was also reading under the lamplight, and one of them would say, "Letterman or Leno?" and off they'd go to bed, snuggled under the sheets, watching television until they fell asleep, their books, old wineglasses, and stained coffee cups balanced beside their bed.

When she moves to California and makes new friends, she'll be a whole new person, Jonathan's wife, and no one will know about *The Jonathan and Rosie Show*. No one will guess that they are adorably incompetent and eccentric. At last they'll be free to be themselves.

● ● ●

Funny, how something like a wedding can fall apart in a hundred ways.

After it happens, she rather thinks of it as like a Slinky on the stairs, picking up momentum and speed, bumping its way to the bottom, slowly and inevitably at first, and then . . . well, it's over.

Andres Schultz—he who seems to be the chief change catalyst of her life right now—stays and stays at the apartment. For some reason, on day three, which is officially the day when houseguests and fish begin to stink, Andres Schultz, not realizing he had outworn his welcome, declared he was staying for at least another week. And then another. He continued to use up their oxygen supply, continued to refer to her as "Rosa," continued to stride through the living room, bellowing into his cell phone. By then he had even commandeered the little office that belonged exclusively to

Rosie. He had backers to talk to and cajole, and apparently there were other teacup men who needed to be dragooned into participating or donating, as well. Rosie can't keep track of it all.

And why should she? Thanks to him, she's busy planning a wedding and a move, and quitting her job, announcing the news to her students and her friends, even to her grandmother's doctors and neighbors. She has to get boxes, she has to hire a caterer, she has to let the landlord know they're leaving, she has to clean the apartment so it can be shown. And she needs to figure out who will marry them; somehow she knows a guy who knows a guy who's a friendly, cool justice of the peace (because Jonathan says you can't just have *any* old justice of the peace) and this person *might* be free on Saturday, although it's short notice. Oh, yes, and big big BIG on the list is finding the right caregiver for Soapie. Are they renting a U-Haul truck for the move? Should they sell one car or should they drive separately? Where are they going to stay when they get to San Diego? Did Jonathan extend his health insurance benefits to cover him in California when he told the human resources department at his company that he was quitting?

All this has to be done while stepping around, in front of, and behind Andres Schultz, who only stops pacing and talking on the telephone long enough to offer his personal observation about the way life can *whiplash* you around, flinging you into a better place you didn't even know was there.

He has, she realizes, a bland, slow-talking positivity that gives her headaches. And, worse, he finds nouns and verbs to be interchangeable. He *meetings* with people. He and Jonathan need to do a lot of *teacupping* because, let's face it, thirty-eight teacups might not *platform* spectacularly.

Never mind the grammar, *this* was news. Thirty-eight teacups were not enough for an exhibit? In what universe is that possibly true? Thirty-eight is a *lot* of teacups.

Then, on Thursday night, less than forty-eight hours before the wedding, Jonathan comes into the bedroom and sits down on the bed and tries for a few minutes to make sounds. He keeps opening his mouth and closing it again, and then he cracks his knuckles a bunch of times. She stares at him.

"I have something horrible to tell you," he says finally.

Her hairline freezes. "What? Did you forget to go to pick up the marriage license?" She'd reminded him twenty-two times to do this.

"Nah, I did that."

"Then what?"

His face is ashen. Ashen, as in perhaps he has a brain tumor and has been told he has a week to live and is curious as to how they should spend it. Should they risk flying to the Bahamas to try for that experimental treatment sick celebrities go for, or should they hunker down in the living room and tearfully watch all the old movies they'd always meant to get to?

She sits down on the bed beside him, and reaches over and touches his face, and he takes her hands away.

"I can't get married on Saturday," he says.

"Wait. What? Are you dying or something?"

"*No*, I'm not dying. Not unless you kill me."

"But . . . then what?"

"Andres and I are flying out to San Antonio in the morning." He gives her a look of abject fear, his eyebrows becoming little tents above his whipped-puppy eyes. "I'm so sorry."

"Oh, no, no, no, no," she says. "Flying out to San Antonio?

What are you talking about?" Caterers, justice of the peace, friends, family members. No, no, no.

Teacups. A huge collection. They have to go pick them up.

"Let Andres pick them up. We're having *people* come to Soapie's house to watch us get married. There's a justice of the peace and food—"

"Andres can't do it. He doesn't know anything about teacups."

"But he knows about boxes, doesn't he? Why doesn't he just put them in boxes and fly them out to the museum?"

"He won't know if they're legit. He doesn't know the historical stuff. Believe me, I've thought of all this. I need to see them."

"Wait a minute. This does not make any sense at all." She can feel her eyes narrowing. "Why don't you go pick them up on Sunday? *Why,* Jonathan Morrow, does it have to be right now first thing in the morning the day before our wedding?"

"Has to be. The guy's house is flooding, and he's got 'em squirreled away upstairs, but he's got to get 'em out of there before they condemn the property."

"Uh-huh."

"No, it's true. There was a lot of rain in Texas—maybe you heard about it—and a big storm coming on Sunday, and this collector guy decided that he was going to get rid of his collection anyway because he's getting divorced, and he needs money—"

"So let me see. There's a previous flood, and a divorce, a house being condemned, a *predicted* flood, and teacups that may or may not be legit, even though he's a reputable collector. This is beginning to sound like a whole lot of crazy, strung-together excuses, and you know it."

"Sssh, please. Andres is going to come running in here to interfere in a minute."

She goes over and locks the bedroom door. "Let him try." Then she stands against the door, with her arms folded across her chest, staring at him, and hisses. "Why is he still here anyway? Tell me that! When is he going to go home? And what is all this *really* about? Listen, Jonathan, *you* were the one who started this whole wedding business. I was fine going along the way we were, but you pulled me into this whole thing."

"Sssh. I know, I know."

"Come on. There *is* no guy in San Antonio with two floods and a divorce, is there?"

"There is. There really is. It's all colossal bad timing. *Huge* bad timing. But this is the beauty part about being us, don't you see? We're people who can just pick another day to get married. We don't *need* to have a whole group of people standing around us to make it real. We can do it next week, on a Tuesday. A Thursday even. We don't care."

"Ohhh, so *this* is what this is about! The party. Or— oh, wait a minute. Is it about holding it at Soapie's house? Because I asked you and you said—"

"No, no, none of that. Not the party, not the house. I feel as badly as you do."

"Bad," she says. "If you say 'feel badly,' you're actually describing the state of your fingers, not an emotional state. 'Feel' is one of those words that is about how you touch things, or about how you are processing an emotion."

"Rosie," he says. "Please, for the love of God—"

"Just this once—*just this once,* I wanted us to stand up and do the thing that we said we were going to do," she says. "Our friends are going to make fun of us so much for this."

He looks at her pityingly. He would never care about that, and he feels so sorry for her that she does care about it.

● ● ●

On Friday night, when Jonathan and Andres are gone, after she makes all the difficult calls canceling everything—the cupcakes (which she will still have to pay for, so will donate to the soup kitchen) and the justice of the peace and the guests, she wanders through the dark, silent apartment, hugging herself and truly feeling the quiet with a kind of sweet, melancholy relief she hasn't felt in days.

Outside, across the river, she hears music playing and people laughing and talking, their voices drifting from a party taking place in a restaurant on the water. She stands on her darkened balcony and watches them. A woman in a red dress—and why does she have to be wearing that, if not to signal something to Rosie?—is laughing loudly and dancing around the patio, first with one man and then with another. Rosie leaves the balcony and goes into her study and turns on the light. Andres's stuff is still in there, but she pushes it all aside into a pile and sits down at her desk and starts writing a poem.

It's the first poem she's written in such a long time. She would have expected to be rusty, but the words pour out as though they've been waiting for her to get around to them. It's about this moment of in between, being married and not married, between New Haven and San Diego, between leaving and staying put. The river is in there, and the red skirt, the friends' sympathy and disbelief, and the way none of it ultimately matters. It just *is*.

I will go to California with you, the poem says, *but I'm not going to marry you.*

When she finally gets up, she stretches her neck, cracking her backbone, working out the stiffness from sitting. And then when she turns—how does it happen?—her foot trips on Andres Schultz's duffel bag that's halfway sticking out from under her bookshelf. Her ankle twists underneath her, and she sinks down on top of it, like a ballerina making a graceful little twirl. For a moment, she sits there, too stunned with pain to even cry out. She had felt a snap, and when she makes herself test it out, her ankle will not take her weight anymore.

After a long time, she manages to crawl to her room, get the ibuprofen and a glass of water from the low bedside table, but even though she can also get to the kitchen, inch by inch, once there she sees that she isn't able to stand up and reach the ice in the freezer to stop the swelling. It's too late to call anyone, and she can't think of what to say anyway, so she ends up spending the night on the little patch of rug between the kitchen and the living room, next to the Lolitas in their boxes.

She hears the party dying down, and the refrigerator motor turning on and off, the traffic on Quinnipiac Avenue dwindling as the night deepens . . . and the Lolitas sighing in the night.

So congrats, you won again, she says to them.

Oh, we will always win, they whisper back.

[eight]

The doctor said it would have been easier to treat the ankle if it had actually been broken. Instead, it's merely a bad sprain, necessitating ice, ibuprofen, and crutches. If Rosie was something of a klutz before (and she was), she's now an actual menace to herself, to others, and to the Sheetrocked walls as she navigates the narrow, dark stairways on crutches, sliding, jabbing holes in things, knocking her elbows and knees against banisters and walls.

It is pathetic. She's a wreck in so many ways she can't even count them. Her hair now strays out of its long braid and frizzes around her face in the humidity. Her period is due, but it seems to have started and then stopped again. She's had a headache for three days, and her foot is killing her, *and* she's got a gazillion things she's supposed to remember.

The good-bye business is unexpectedly hideous. Well, what had she expected—that it would be easy to leave the place she'd always lived? Her students keep taking her out for lunches and dinners, wanting to thank her in front of their family members, as if they feel she needs a succession of public tributes. She goes to three lunches and one barbecue in one week, pitifully, grouchily, and she fights back tears at each one.

It's all almost too much to bear, in addition to being furious with Jonathan, who has come back from Texas without Andres, thank God, but who is acting as though he's calm when he's actually buzzing with a kind of irritating energy.

He's doing a thing she realizes she's always detested: acting passive-aggressive, as though she is the anxious, worried person, when really he's so paralyzed by change that he can't make anything happen.

"I hope you know I'm not going to be able to carry one single box down the stairs," she says to him on the Tuesday before they're set to leave.

He greets this news with a stoic silence.

"So that means you need to get some movers. Jonathan. I'm talking to *you*. You have to get the movers. I've done everything else. I've—"

"I will, I will." Sigh, then a put-upon tone. Then he says, "Why are you being like this? Has anything ever *not* worked out for us? I mean, ultimately?"

The top of her head explodes. "Well, for starters, just looking at last week *alone,* there's the wedding! That didn't exactly work out for us."

"*That's* what's bothering you, isn't it?" he says. "Well, then, get your purse. Let's go down to town hall right now and find a justice of the peace. We'll do it right this minute." He gets up from his chair.

"No," she says. "It's not that, and you know it."

"I don't know it."

"I wanted the red velvet cupcakes. I wanted the party."

He stares at her. "We could have had the cupcakes if you hadn't donated them."

"But I can't wear the red boots. They don't fit on my foot anymore." It sounds so ridiculous, and it is, but it's the truth. He shakes his head and goes back to his laptop.

And then there is Soapie. How can she even begin to say good-bye to her grouchy old grandmother, knowing she's falling down all over the place, knowing that she's probably in more need of Rosie than she's ever been before, and yet is now even less able to admit to any of it? Is she really supposed to be able to say, "Bye! Hope you don't get seriously hurt!"—and then leave?

One morning as Rosie is hobbling around on crutches, trying to put things in boxes, Soapie calls on the phone and says, "Well, the boy is leaving me. I guess you know that."

"Tony?"

"Yes."

"Is he going back to his wife?"

"I don't know what he's doing. I have to go take a nap when he starts talking about his life. It's too complicated for any ordinary human being to follow. But that's not why I called you. He says that I should tell you that I'm having that British woman come when he goes."

"What? You're having Mrs. Cynthia Lamb come back?"

"Yes, her. Whatever her name is. She starts tomorrow."

"Oh. Well, that's great," Rosie says, trying not to show how relieved she feels.

"It's great until she tries to keep me from doing things I need to do, and then she's out of here. I won't have it."

"Of course," says Rosie, smiling. "So that's when Tony is leaving?"

But Soapie doesn't hear her. Instead she just starts in on how she hopes Rosie's not going to get maudlin with good-byes, because nobody likes good-byes. They're stupid and pointless, and they just stir up stuff that doesn't need to be stirred up.

"Well, I do need to come over and bring some of my coats to store at your house, if that's okay," Rosie says, "but I promise I won't say good-bye to you."

"I mean it. When you walk out the door, just don't say anything. Don't even let me see when you go." Soapie's voice has gotten rough. "We're not having drama."

When she gets there on Thursday evening to drop off the coats, she expects to see Mrs. Cynthia Lamb in the kitchen making dinner—bangers and mash, perhaps—and Soapie resting on the couch, downing gin and tonics. But instead, Tony's there, and he and Soapie are standing in the garden, looking at the rosebushes, heads together, conferring about something. Rosie parks the car, and as she gets out, she hears Soapie laughing.

Then Tony says, "No, no, forget it!" and he's shaking his head and laughing so hard that his backward baseball cap falls off, and he has to stoop down to pick it up off the lawn. Soapie, who's wearing a red chiffon blouse and white pants, reaches down and cuffs him on the shoulder as Rosie comes hobbling over, fighting her crutches, which keep sinking into the soft grass.

"Rosie!" Soapie calls. "Tell Tony that he needs to go over and steal some of Helen's peonies for me."

"I am not stealing peonies from somebody else's garden," he says. "You're crazy!"

"It's not polite to call people crazy. And I need them," Soapie says in her wheedling voice. "They go with these roses so beautifully. Think how nice they'll look together in a vase. Tell him, Rosie."

"I can't, I can't," he says. "You know Helen will come after me. She already thinks I'm charging her too much for gardening—which is due to *you* telling me what to ask for, by the way."

"I did you a favor. And you can tell her you're putting in overtime, pruning her peonies for her," says Soapie, and then they both dissolve again into laughter.

"It's nice to see the two of you having such a good time," Rosie says.

"Yeah, well. It's all a good time until she gets me put in jail," says Tony.

"You know what? I'm going to march over there and get them myself," says Soapie. "I've been stealing Helen's flowers for years, but usually I wait until she's at church. If she comes out, I'm just going to pretend I've gone senile. You both can come and lead me away."

"Why don't I just go and buy you some peonies?" Rosie says, but Soapie takes the shears away from Tony and makes her way across the yard. She has her mouth fixed in a serious pout, but she's clearly in danger of bursting out laughing again, and she's doing an exaggerated tiptoe walk, like something from the Pink Panther movies. They watch her slip into the flower bed and start snipping Helen Benson's glorious light pink peonies.

Rosie shakes her head. "I can't believe she's doing this," she says. "Look at her."

"Shoplifting in other people's gardens. She's bad-ass."

"Incorrigible, really," says Rosie. She looks over at him. "Hey, I'm surprised you're still here. I suppose Mrs. Lamb is in the house cooking dinner?"

He doesn't answer. He's wincing at Soapie, who is now right up next to Helen's living room window snipping away.

"Wasn't she going to start today?" Rosie says.

"Well," he says. Soapie waves in triumph from the peony bushes and starts making her way back. "Oh God," Tony says. "She's got five of the biggest flowers."

"I got greedy," says Soapie. "I have got to stop being awful, you know that?" She looks at Rosie's face. "Yes, I see you agree. Let me just get these inside before the cops get here. Tony, you were no help at all. None."

"Be sure you tell that to the cops," he says, and the

three of them go inside, and Rosie says, "Really, where is Mrs. Lamb?"

"Oh, we changed our minds about having her," says Soapie. "Find me a vase, will you? I think the big green one is under the sink."

"What do you mean, you changed your mind?" Rosie digs out the vase and puts it on the counter.

Soapie starts arranging the flowers one by one without looking over at Rosie. "Oh, she called me last night and started making up rules and drawing up schedules and talking about bedtime and the four food groups and all the *cultural outings* we'd take. *I* don't need her to take me on cultural outings, and I certainly don't need anybody telling me when I have to go to bed at night or what I'm supposed to be eating."

"But what—?"

"Tony can stay, it turns out. And we're fine, except that he appears to be kind of a coward when it comes to getting flowers. But we'll work on it."

Rosie turns and looks at him, and he ducks his head and smiles. "It's all good," he says. "Today she fell, but we got her right up and she was fine, and then we went and got her prescription filled, and she took her medicine."

"But how long are you planning to stay?" Rosie asks him in dismay. "I thought it was all settled—"

"Don't start this," says Soapie. "I'm fine, and you know it."

"I have to go," says Rosie. She feels so heavy, it's as though one of those x-ray dental aprons has been put on her chest, and she's staggering under the weight of it.

"No scenes, no scenes," says Soapie. "Make Jonathan stop every couple of hours so you can stretch your legs, and drink lots of water, and call every now and then so I'll at least know you're alive."

"Soapie, I—"

"No!" her grandmother yells. "I told you *no*. I can't and I won't. Just go *now*. Get out!"

Soapie stalks out of the kitchen, waving her arms in the air like she's trying to bat away spiderwebs. Rosie feels her eyes stinging with tears.

"She makes me so crazy," she whispers. "Why can't she just hug me and act like she's going to miss me?"

"She's just upset," Tony says. "She's already missing you so much."

"Then why can't she show it like other people?"

"You know why," he says, like he knows anything about them at all, like even one minute of their history would make sense to him.

"You seem to get along with her pretty well!" she says accusingly.

But he just smiles. "Other people's old people are always easier. That's all. She doesn't love me."

• • •

Two days later, on moving day, Jonathan gets up early and gets ready to head out to pick up the U-Haul truck. She calls out to him, "So how many movers did you hire? And when are they getting here?"

"No movers. I got our friends to help," he calls from the bedroom.

She feels her blood stop cold in her veins. She hauls herself over to the bedroom door and stands there glaring at him so hard that she hopes his eyeballs fall out of his head when he sees how mad she is. *"What?"* she says. "You are *not* calling in our friends. Don't you even know how they make fun of us? The whole day is going to be how first we didn't have the wedding we said we were going to have, and now we didn't hire movers?"

"But they're already coming," he says. "They didn't mind at all. And who cares if they make fun of us? We're funny."

"Jonathan, you are so freaking unconscious all the time! What is the *matter* with you?"

"Oh my God, Rosie," he says, and starts laughing very hard. "Is this going to end up being the red-boots-and-wedding conversation *again*?"

She is too mad even to speak.

"What's the matter with you?" he says, and his eyes are rounded in amazement that he has to explain these facts to her. "Friends help each other move. It's a time-honored thing. Beer and pizza. Laughing together. Don't you know these guys would be insulted if I didn't ask for their help?"

"Trust me. They would not be insulted."

Greta and Joe arrive first, and when they're still crossing the yard below, Rosie sees that Greta is dressed in a white sundress and sandals and carrying a tray of iced coffees—not at all like somebody who's planning on putting in a day of packing and carrying boxes. "Just think of this," Joe says loudly when they get upstairs. "This is the last time we climb up here. Brings sort of a tear to the eye."

"Well, you mean maybe after *today* it's the last trip you make up these stairs," says Jonathan. "You've got a few up-and-down trips to make today, old man." He claps Joe on the shoulder. "We've got all these boxes and all this furniture to load on the truck."

"You're kidding me, man," says Joe, and he laughs. "I'm already wiped out. How are we supposed to get all this shit down these stairs?"

"Also," says Greta, "sorry, but we've got a soccer parents'

meeting to get to this afternoon. If you don't get there on time, you get assigned all the worst jobs for the whole next season."

The other four come in then, trailed by Jonathan's younger brother, Patrick, a quiet guy in his twenties who always gets dragged into helping.

"Did you guys know we're s'posed to pack all this crap on the truck?" says Joe. He pushes his expensive sunglasses up on his head.

"As always, there'll be beer and pizza at the end of it for you," says Jonathan. "Play your cards right, and it'll have bacon *and* pepperoni. No expense spared!"

Hinton, Suzanne's husband, a scientist who always seems to be in the middle of complex calculations, says, "I don't think I've worked for beer and pizza for quite a while."

"Jesus. Not only is there the queen-sized bed and the foldout couch, but there are three dressers, a desk, and boxes and boxes and *boxes* of these crazy goddamned fragile teacups," says Joe, who's been walking around the apartment, peeking into rooms. "You're trusting us with these precious teacups?"

"I am," says Jonathan. "What choice do I have?"

Patrick, who weighs about a hundred pounds and still has acne and plays in a rock band, who has been restlessly bouncing from one foot to another and cracking his knuckles, says, "Come on, man. You and I can do this by ourselves. It's okay." He grabs one end of the kitchen table, and Jonathan reaches over and picks up the other end.

"Rosie," he says, "when you order the pizza, see if you can get them to add some testosterone to it for these guys."

Rosie scowls at him. How could he not know that his friends are all in their adult lives now, the world where men prove their manhood by hiring others to do the inconvenient tasks? He's clung to his grad student existence as though it were an ethical stance.

Lynn's cell phone rings then and she gets embroiled in a feisty conversation with Brittany, her high-school-age daughter, who wants to spend the day alone with her boyfriend.

"Speaking of testosterone," says Greg.

"Yeah, send *that* guy over here," says Joe. "In the interest of keeping him from getting Brittany in trouble, of course."

"Wow. Do they still even call it 'getting in trouble'?" asks Hinton.

"Shut up," growls Greg. "That's my daughter you're talking about. And because you have boys, you think you get a free pass from all this stuff?"

"Like hell I do. Only Jonathan gets a free pass, because he managed to keep himself unhitched," says Hinton, and then looks embarrassed. "Sorry, Rosie. I didn't mean it that way."

"Don't look at me," Rosie says. "I managed to stay unhitched, too."

"Close call, though, last week, huh?" says Greg. "That's the closest you guys've come, right?"

"Yeah, what was up with that?" says Hinton. "We were all invited to a wedding, and then suddenly we weren't?"

"Hinty!" says Suzanne. "I told you. We're not going to talk about that today. If they didn't want to get married, it's none of our business. They're fine the way they are."

"It's okay," Rosie says. "There were some teacups in Texas that needed to be looked at, so Jonathan had to go."

"Yeah, you know how it is, Hinty, when you've just got to see some teacups," says Joe. "You just have to. We've all been there."

Rosie can feel them all exchanging their amused glances. How Rosie and Jonathan *Don't* Throw a Wedding.

Joe clears his throat and says, "Married or not, the main

thing you need to be thankful for is that you don't have any kids. No kids is what keeps you two young. You're going to outlive us all."

Greta claps her hands. "Enough of this! I've made the dinner reservation for us all at Christopher Martin's for seven. Do you think that's going to give you enough time?"

Jonathan, back from loading the table onto the truck, doesn't look worried in the least. "If we can get some man-power out of these wusses, it'll be great," he says. He turns to Patrick. "Okay, bro. Let's do it. Grab the other end of this couch, will you. You other guys, why don't you sit down and fan yourselves for a while."

Patrick comes over and takes one end of the couch, and Jonathan takes the other, and then Greg sighs and grabs a part of it, too, and Joe and Hinton take the pile of cushions, and they all start bumping down the stairs, barking at one another and grumbling and groaning. When they get down to the street, they confer on how to load the things into the truck, and then Joe takes over, pointing and directing. And then they're all laughing and shoving one another and they're back to the regular guy thing, and Rosie knows that Greta and Joe won't end up going to the soccer parents' preseason meeting, and that the guys will move this whole household—teacups, tables, beds, and all of it—to the truck and get soused on beer and filled up with pizza in the process, and at some point Joe will hurt his bad knee and Greg, who's overweight, will nearly pass out from heat exhaustion, but none of it will matter because they love Jonathan, and tonight they'll all go to dinner at Christopher Martin's and drink too much and propose toasts and tell stories about how tough it is to be parents these days, and they'll be sloppy and sentimental about how much they'll all miss Rosie and Jonathan, and then forever after this will be another story that they tell, shaking their heads as they add to the legend of Rosie and Jonathan, this mythical couple who live in some kind of odd world, bumbling along but having things work out anyway. This one will be "The Day That Rosie and Jonathan Had to Be Told That Everybody Gets Old."

● ● ●

It's nearly one in the morning by the time Jonathan and Rosie get back to the apartment, to finish up and get the truck.

Joe and Greta have dropped them off, and given them tearful good-byes on the sidewalk, and then they clomp upstairs, Rosie banging around with the crutches, Jonathan in the middle of a long, meandering, whispered monologue about how he'd describe his current state: slightly buzzy but not too inebriated to get on the road and head out. He's made clear from the beginning that they have to get going in the middle of the night so they can miss the New York City traffic, which he imagines will be awful, even on Sunday morning.

"I shouldn't have had anything to drink since I'm not going to get any sleep," he says. "But saying good-bye to friends. The only way to do that is to be drunk."

"I think we should sleep a bit," she says. Her arms and legs feel so heavy they can barely move.

"No can do."

"But my foot hurts, and my head hurts."

"Rosie. The next few days are going to be hard enough, but if we get behind schedule right from the beginning, it's just going to be worse. You can prop your foot up on the dash with a bag of ice. And take some ibuprofen. You'll be fine." He looks around. "Look at all this crap that didn't get taken away. Jesus. There are *bags* of garbage everywhere." He reaches over and turns on the kitchen light, and the bulb burns out with an explosion that makes her jump.

"Oh, holy Christ! Did you see that? The fucking oven didn't get cleaned," he says.

"Sssh. We can do it now."

"But why didn't you get it done earlier? Your friends could have helped you."

"You saw how people were dressed here today. Nobody came here to clean ovens. I still can't even believe you got those guys to carry all that stuff."

"Nah, they were always gonna help me. They're my buds."

"I know, but didn't you see how mad at you they were?"

"Here's a little secret, Rosie: people are like puppy dogs. They can't stay mad." He laughs a little. "Puppy dogs. Ask them tomorrow, and they'll say that today was the best day of their lives."

She stares at him. "Wow. God, I can't get over how you just skate through life. Nothing bad ever happens to you," she says. "You always get forgiven, don't you? By the way, did you call your mom?"

"What is this? I called her on Thursday."

"But she wanted to see you. Was she mad that you didn't come?"

"She's used to me," he says. "I say it again: puppy dogs. Clearly you don't have your friends and family trained the way mine are." He laughs.

"I never even tried to train them," she says. "It's despicable." But maybe he doesn't hear that last part, because he's knelt down next to the oven and is peering inside at all its caked-on splotches.

He sits back on his heels and puts on his German accent. Sort of a *Hogan's Heroes* thing he does from time to time, to great laughter from his friends. "Dis black mark iss num-ber two thirty-seven, the Turkey Catastrophe of five years ago," he says. "And over here ve have the Cherry Pie Disaster, number three forty-five. Date still unknown. Fräulein, I am so very sorry, but ve cannot let you destroy the past by clean-ing this oven. No. *Nein.*"

"But I think we have to clean it. We need the security deposit back."

"No. No. Cannot be done. Against the rules of scientific discovery." He closes the door and comes over to her. "We're not doing it, babe. Come on. Let's go." He smells like garlic and beer and sweat. She feels a sudden sweep of anger, with her breath fluttery in her chest. She might be in danger of throwing up.

"Nobody ever holds you to anything," she says, pulling away from him. She looks back at the oven. "You've decided we're not cleaning this oven, and so if I want the security deposit back, too bad. Because you don't really care. You can really walk away from this, can't you—leave this apartment in this appalling state, and not—" Her voice is getting higher.

He laughs and looks around. "What are you talking about? This is not exactly appalling. Appalling would be if we had left dead bodies in the closets." He goes over to the closet and opens it to show her there's no such thing. She watches his expression, the flourish of his hand, the hooded look of his eyes, and then she swallows and just says it.

"Listen, I don't think I'm going with you. I can't."

"What? What are you talking about?"

"I'm not going to California." Her hairline feels suddenly freezing cold, as though it, too, is surprised by this news. She balls her hands into fists so they won't start to tremble in front of him.

"Aha! But you have to. Your stuff is on the truck. Or did you forget that?"

"It's toward the back end of the truck. The stuff I need, at least. I can take it out."

"Oh, come off it, Rosie. You're being dramatic."

"I'm sorry. But I can't."

"Goddamn it, woman, it's nearly two in the morning, and I want to get to Pennsylvania before we have to stop again. Just get over whatever this is, and we'll solve it in the truck."

"Take me to Soapie's," she says, and now she's shocked to see that she's actually calm. She's really doing this. It's the right thing.

He stands there with his hands at his sides, and then he sighs. "Look, is it the oven? Because I swear I'll *pay* you your portion of the security deposit, if it means that much to you."

"No."

"Well, then what is it? We can't clean the damn thing right now, even if we wanted to, because there's no light in this kitchen. *And* the stores are all closed, so we can't go buy a lightbulb. So get over yourself, and let's hit the road. It's been a long day."

She sighs. "No. I'm not going."

"What the *fuck*, Rosie?" He goes into the bathroom and closes the door. She hears the water running, the fan going on. She folds her arms across her chest and stares out the window at the streetlight. Breathe. Deep, deep breaths. Then after a while the toilet flushes, and he comes out and stands in front of her. "What if we compromise?" he says heavily. "We'll go spend the night at Soapie's and then leave in the morning. Okay? That what you want?"

"No."

"Come on," he says. "I don't know what my crime is, but won't you give a guy a chance to say he's sorry?"

"But you're not sorry," she says calmly.

"But this is madness! Because I know you. In exactly two days you're going to call me and say, 'Ohhh, Jonathan, I've made a mistake, and can't you come back and get me?' And the truth is, I won't be able to, because there's a deadline on turning in this truck, and if I turn around because you've got some bug up your ass, then I've got to pay a lot more money. And I'll have had to drive through Pennsylvania *three times*." His voice is rising, and he stops himself, closes his eyes for a moment, and then pats the air with his hands. "I'm sorry," he says softly. "Getting mad at you is not going to help matters, I know. But the fact is, Rosie, we don't have a lot of money. So even if you decide to come much later, it's going to be hard to get the airfare together to fly you out there."

"Then I won't come."

"So we're breaking up, then? Just like that?"

"No. Yes. I don't know."

"What's the matter with you?"

"I don't know! It just hit me, how you really are, and what this is going to be like. I can't get in that truck and drive across country with you and deal with that twerp of a man while you and he set up some museum. I can't."

"Twerp?" He laughs. "This is all about Andres Schultz again? And don't tell me, there's going to be a part about the wedding, too. And red boots! There is, isn't there?" She knows what he's doing: he's trying to jolly her into laughing, and then she will be disarmed, and then after a few more jokes and maybe some hugs and some halfhearted promises that look fullhearted, she'll willingly go and get in the truck.

THE OPPOSITE OF MAYBE • 89

She knows he thinks this. She knows it has worked for him before. But she is not a puppy dog. No more.

"Just stop it," she says.

He looks out the window and then drums his fingers on the countertop, calculating. Then he sighs and says, "Okay. Fine. You want to change the whole plan right here at the eleventh hour and ruin what we've been planning for weeks, then great. You go right ahead. I'm taking you at your word."

"Thank you," she says. She gets up and makes her way to the truck, banging her way down the stairs on her crutches, and then he comes down and unlocks it and gets in, without even once looking at her.

Riding back to Soapie's, with the wind blowing her hair, she feels as free as she's felt in a long, long time.

[nine]

Soapie's house is dark and quiet as they pull up. Jonathan drives the truck around back, and Rosie winces at the crunching sound the tires make on the gravel drive, the way the whole thing rattles and shudders when he turns the key off, and mostly at the white gleam of the headlights against the bank of kitchen windows. The sensor lights come on, and she is braced for even worse: that Soapie herself might come charging out of the house in her nightgown, demanding to know what's going on. The old Soapie would have done that. But when it doesn't happen, Rosie says quietly, "Okay, well, let's get this over with."

Jonathan, who has been grimly silent all the way over, climbs out of his seat and goes around to the back. She hears the rolling door go up, hears him plunking boxes down onto the ground. Has he forgotten that she needs help disembarking from the seat? Or maybe he's too angry to come and help her. He's ready to be done with her. Whenever she dared to look over at him during the drive, she saw his jaw working back and forth, his eyes staring straight ahead.

After a while, she opens the truck door, places her crutch down on the running board, braced against the frame of the truck, and then leans herself on it and eases her way down. Just as she's almost to the ground, though, the crutch slips out of its place, and she is sent sprawling on the gravel, landing on her stomach. She's skinned her knees and her hands, which she put down to break her own fall. And she has to stifle herself from crying out.

He's not anywhere near, thank goodness. He's carrying boxes over to the back door and stacking them up on the porch. There aren't many, really. They've agreed that he'll take all the furniture with him to California, and she'll keep only her clothing and some of her books.

She gets up gingerly, and takes the crutches and limps her way over to the back door. Through the window she sees that only the stove light is on, and she can see that the dinner dishes are still all lined up, dirty, on the countertop, with pots and the frying pan stacked on the stove. She gets out her key and turns it in the lock, ever so quietly.

Jonathan comes back from the truck with two more boxes and sets them down as she gets the door open.

"Okay," he says. "What do you want me to do with all this?"

"Just leave them on the porch."

"But how are you and Soapie going to get them in tomorrow? You're both physical wrecks, you know."

"Look, we'll manage," she says. "I don't want any more of this long strung-out good-bye. Okay? It is what it is."

"Great. The porch it is." Then he looks at her. "So, you're sure about this? You realize what you're doing?"

"*Yes.*"

"Yeah, so . . . good-bye then, Rosie Kelley." He turns on his heel and gets back in the truck, and she steps inside the cool haven of Soapie's kitchen, closing the back door without once looking at the truck backing down the driveway. She can hear the spray of gravel signaling that he's going too fast. She's never felt so honest-to-God free, except for the tiny fact that she has to go throw up.

Afterward, she goes back outside and stares at the boxes,

trying to remember which one might hold her toothbrush and her nightgown, but she has no idea. She realizes she doesn't even care. She'll sleep in her clothes, she thinks, making her way across the dark kitchen and into the hallway and up the stairs. Soapie's door is closed at the end of the hallway, and she can hear snoring. With difficulty, she goes to her old room and turns the doorknob, hits the light.

Oh God, it's Tony Cavaletti. In her bed.

"What the—? Who?" he yells, leaping up like he's going to have a heart attack. "What? What's going on?"

"Sorry," she says in a whisper. "Tony, it's Rosie. Sorry to scare you."

His hair is sticking up all over, and his eyes are squinting in the light. "What are you doing here?" he says. And then he looks afraid again and says, "Wait. Did something happen to Sophie? Did I sleep through—" and starts to get out of bed.

"No, no," she says, and holds up her hand to stop him. "I just came back here to sleep. But it's okay. I'll go to the guest room. You go back to sleep."

She turns out the light, and she can hear him settle back down in the bed.

Then he says, "Wait. Weren't you, like, moving to California today?"

"Yes," she whispers thickly, "but I didn't go. Long story."

"Is this your old bed? I'll go to the guest room if you want."

"Yes. No. I'll talk about it in two or three weeks, which is how long I'm planning to sleep." She closes the door and goes down the hall to the room that was always saved for Ruthie, Soapie's editor, whenever she would come. It's a boring, generic room with hardly any personality to it: brown mahogany furniture, a highboy, and the kind of long, low-slung dresser that was popular when Soapie was young.

Rosie pulls down the white crocheted bedspread to discover that there are no sheets underneath. She collapses on top anyway, wrapping herself up in the cover, not having the energy to haul herself out to the hall closet, search for clean sheets, and then figure out how to manipulate them onto the bed.

It's all she can do to lie down and squeeze her eyes shut, and hope that maybe she can remember how relieved she feels, so that then she won't be sad.

● ● ●

"What in the world are you *doing*? Are you planning to sleep forever? What's the matter with you anyway?"

It's Soapie, and the blinding shards of light and crack of pain are Soapie, too, because she's flung open the curtains and released the window shades with such force that they have clattered and banged their way to the top of the glass, landing with the approximate decibel level of buckshot. Rosie buries her head under the pillow and groans.

"What's going on here?" Soapie comes over and shakes her foot. "For Christ's sake, you don't even have any sheets on this bed." Rosie lifts the pillow, shielding her eyes with her hand. She'd flailed around in the covers all night long, freezing and then broiling, and she doesn't think she's really slept at all. Maybe only in the last twenty minutes or so, and now Soapie is going to keep that from happening again.

"I thought you went to California. Why didn't you tell me you were going to come here?"

"Because it was the middle of the night," says Rosie. "I decided to stay here and help you."

"Help me with *what*? That's the biggest crock I ever heard," says Soapie. "I didn't even know you were here until I saw all those boxes on the porch, and Tony told me you were in the guest room. What's got into you?"

"My foot hurts. I didn't go."

"You came to your senses, you mean."

"No, I really did come to take care of you. I'm going to stay here for a while."

"You're not taking care of *me*," says Soapie. "You can stay here for a while if you want to, but I have a *life*. Get up and come downstairs and have something to eat. Do you have any idea what time it is?"

"No."

"It's nearly noon." She works her way through the room, Dustcloth Diva–style, picking up Rosie's flip-flops and putting them down again by the closet door, restacking the magazines that are on the dresser, using the elbow of her sweater to dust off the highboy, and peering into the empty trash can. Then she shakes her head and says, "Come on downstairs. You need to eat," and finally leaves.

Rosie manages to sit up and swing her legs over to the side of the bed and consider the landscape of the bedroom in the daytime. Utterly charmless, except for the unusable brick fireplace in the corner—a nice touch by 1880s standards, when this place was built.

Well, she should see to fixing this place up. When she's better, of course. She'll help Soapie with setting things right again. And she'll make meals for the two of them—nice, healthy, vegetarian foods that will help them both feel better, and she'll serve them in the garden this summer on the wrought-iron table. And monitor the medication, mow the lawn, drive Soapie to all her social engagements. Buy peonies at the nursery. Tony can resume his life, go back to his wife, or whatever it is he thinks he's doing.

She lies back on the pillow for just a moment longer, hoping that if she closes her eyes for another few minutes, she can stop picturing Jonathan's stunned good-bye and actually feel good about what was probably the best decision she ever made in her life.

●　●　●

Later that day, she sits out on the patio with Soapie, who has insisted she at least look at a tuna fish sandwich and a mound of potato chips. Soapie, she of the elegant cheekbones and the slim ankles, is drinking a Bloody Mary, and looking serene and put-together in her khaki pedal pushers and white crewneck shirt, exclaiming about the bright sunlight and the dry air and the warm temperatures, as though she herself has managed to engineer them. Her hair is done, and her nails are painted a neon orange that actually makes her speckled hands look dangerous, as if they have pointed weapons on the tips.

"At least drink that tea. You look dehydrated," says Soapie. "God, I'm the one who's going to have to take care of *you,* aren't I? I can't believe you didn't even put sheets on that bed. You were all curled up in there, like some animal."

"Well, there was a man in my real bed," says Rosie, yawning. She cannot stop yawning. "I guess you won't need him anymore, now that I'm staying here. He can go back to his wife."

"I like him," says Soapie.

"Well, I *know* you like him, but that doesn't mean he gets to stay here and live with you forever. Doesn't he have a life?"

"He's got a complicated domestic situation apparently. There are at least two women involved and some little boy—I don't know. It's ugly, I take it. I can't fathom what happened to your generation, why none of you ever learned to cope. And what the hell is the matter with *you* anyway?"

"I don't know. I'm having an early midlife crisis maybe."

"You're so melodramatic. Seriously. Did Jonathan break up with you?"

"I may have broken up with him."

"You did not."

"I kind of did, actually."

"Was it because he wouldn't marry you?"

"No. He wanted us to get married last week. I said no."

"You did, huh? I wish I believed *that*. For God's sake, will you eat that sandwich?" Soapie takes a long sip of her Bloody Mary and then gives Rosie a long look. "So *you* called everything off, then? Well, if that's true, I have to say I'm proud of you."

Rosie shakes her head. "Thank you," she says. "It's nice to have you finally proud of me for something, even though a lot of people would see this as me being a coward. But thank you."

"Well, it remains to be seen whether you stick with it. This is a short-lived declaration against marriage on your part, I suspect."

"Yeah, probably." She takes a sip of her iced tea. "While we're on the topic, maybe you can tell me why you hate men so much."

"Where'd you get the idea I hate men?"

"Oh, maybe the fact that you never had any around, and

also maybe the thousand warnings you gave me about them. 'They're all out for one thing! Give 'em an inch . . .' Greta and I still recite that to each other when we've had too much to drink."

"I had to tell you that. It was a legal requirement back then that girls get their safety warnings." She stretches out on her chaise and massages her temples. "Actually, I like men a hell of a lot better than I like women. You don't see *men* losing their minds in the name of almighty *love* and romance. Men don't play those stupid little games women play—all that hard-to-get crap. I've watched women my whole life, and there's not any one of them that doesn't have some tragic love story they can't wait to sit you down and tell you."

"Speaking of which . . ."

"What?"

Rosie looks right at her. "I understand that your old pal George Tarkinian comes over all the time now."

Soapie narrows her eyes. "What does that have to do with anything?"

"Nothing. Just why didn't you tell me?"

"Why should I tell you? It's none of your business."

"You know, sometimes people who are related tell each other about their lives because they like to share information. It's called love and communication. Plus, I had to hear you were seeing George Tarkinian from Tony Cavaletti, and that was pretty embarrassing. He said it was clear I don't know anything about you."

Soapie actually laughs. "You certainly don't know as much as you think you know."

"So, how's his . . . um, wife doing?"

"Rosie, if you are trying to get me riled up, you are not succeeding. George and I have fun together. Okay? Don't even try to make this seem like something you can manufacture a sordid little drama out of, because you can't. His wife has Alzheimer's. She doesn't even know him anymore."

"*I'm* not looking to manufacture a sordid little drama!"

"The hell you say."

"I just wish you told me things . . . you know . . . about yourself. Why do I have to hear it from Tony, when I'm the one who loves you?" She can feel the tears behind her eyes, so she looks down and starts picking at the scrape on the palm of her hand, gotten when she fell out of the truck last night. When she looks up, Soapie is actually smiling at her. And then she leans over to Rosie and says, in a mischievous way that might be considered almost girlfriendish, if Soapie had that category to her: "He dances good. I kind of like that about him. Also—well, he's . . . ardent."

"Really now?" Rosie says, fascinated. "Ardent, huh? There's a word you don't hear much. So what do you call him? Would you say he's your boyfriend?"

"God, that's so distasteful in people over thirty, isn't it?"

"Well, what do you prefer then? Lover? Partner?"

"God, no. *Lover* is way too clinical, and *partner* makes it sound like we went into business together."

"Wow. This is big-time, isn't it? Soapie Baldwin-Kelley falls in love at long last. It's been a long dry spell since Grandpa. Good for you."

"I guess he's my main squeeze. That's it." Soapie settles back in her chair, looks at her nails for a long time. "That has the right touch of joie de vivre, I think. That, by the way, in case you haven't figured it out, is what was wrong with you and Jonathan."

"That I didn't call him my main squeeze?"

"No. That you don't have joie de vivre with him."

"How do you know?"

"Because I have eyes, Rosie. You want more out of life than he could ever give you. He's a nice enough guy, but he's *limited*. Pitifully limited."

"Well, in some ways maybe, but we're all . . ."

"No. Just look at his thing about teacups in boxes, and you'll see everything you need to know about him. He's a *dry man*. No spirit! He's like an arid desert of a human being. Now that you're done with him, I can tell you the truth. I never knew what you saw in him. I always thought you were settling."

"Come on, he's funny," Rosie protests. "Mostly. Or sometimes."

Soapie sighs and lights a cigarette. "Uh-oh, now you think you need to defend him. I just think he's not the love of your life, that's all I'm saying."

"Huh. I didn't know you believed in the concept of 'love of your life.'"

"I'm not sure I do. But you do. And you're way better off without him. Even today, with your hair like that. If you'd get your hair done, eat some decent food, and buy some decent clothes, you could start having a little fun and then you'll see what life can really be like. Get you some joie de vivre. You could have adventures."

Seriously? Rosie wants to say. *You think I should take life advice from a woman who's nearly ninety years old and after fifty dry years is only now discovering how great it is to have a man in the bed?*

● ● ●

Two days later, she finds herself in the kitchen with Tony Cavaletti, who is making a pot of coffee and a pan of cinnamon buns for breakfast. After two days of having no appetite, she has been brought to her knees by the smell of the cinnamon. She's pretty sure she can gather enough self-control to keep herself from grabbing all of them and running upstairs once they're done, but she can't promise that at some point she won't be licking the pan. She just hopes she can wait until after Tony leaves for work before she starts in on it.

He hands her a cup of coffee and smiles at her. "So if you don't mind my asking, what's the deal with you anyway? Why didn't you go with your fiancé to California?"

She gives the short version: teacups, Andres Schultz, sprained foot hurting, too much pain to ride in the truck for days and days. She leaves out: fury, dirty oven, friends being referred to as puppy dogs. None of that feels particularly significant right now, somehow.

"Now see," he says, "in a case like that, I myself would ask myself if I didn't hurt my foot unconsciously to get back at him."

"Yes, well, there might have been a little of that," she says. She pours cream into her coffee cup and stirs it. *When are those cinnamon buns going to be done?* She wants to get as many as possible and then leave the room.

"Because—well, didn't I hear something about how there was going to be a wedding here and then it got called off or something?"

She sighs. "Yes, you're right. We had this wedding all planned and everything, and then he decided he had to go to Texas to check out somebody's teacups, and I had to cancel everything."

His eyes bug out. "What? Dude didn't come to his own wedding because he had to go see some teacups?"

"Dude even had a whole story about floods and fires and

apocalyptic events that might be threatening these little teacups."

"Please tell me you're making this up."

"No, but I'm actually making it sound worse than it is," she says. "I probably should have just hung in there and waited it out. I mean, it's not like I was even all that mad about not getting married. We'd been living together just fine for fifteen years, and I didn't even care if we got married, not really. And now I'm here and he's out there, and it's all screwed up." She takes the sponge and starts wiping down the counter. "I think it was just that my foot was hurting."

"So now you really miss him." He stops and looks at her so deeply that she has to look away. "I get that," he says. "The heart is a funny little animal, isn't it?"

"It is." She feels a lump in her throat.

"It gets this idea about somebody, and then it doesn't let go, even when things go bad. Even when they go *awful*, and anybody else could see plain as day you should get out. There's your own stupid little heart just bumping around claiming, 'No, it's fine! I'm fine! It's all good!'" He does a funny little dance when he's showing the heart talking.

"Well, that's not quite the situation here," she says. "I just was *momentarily* mad. But I'm probably going out there to live with him again. Eventually. I just need to get Soapie straightened out first."

"Well, sure," he says.

"And how's your situation?" she says.

"Don't even ask," he tells her. Then the oven timer goes off, and he gets busy taking the rolls out, and she gets busy trying not to fall into a swoon over them, which requires balling up her hands and putting them in the pockets of her bathrobe.

She's not sure why she's crying.

● ● ●

All in all, the first week living back at home with Soapie turns out to be more of a challenge than she'd bargained for. As she told Greta, she'd barely survived living there the first time. Luckily there are other people with them now. Tony bops around the house and makes gin and tonics every evening for everybody and appears ever ready to pick up anyone who happens to fall on the floor. Rosie likes the way he takes the stairs two at a time and how he goes tearing out of the house each morning with his bent-up rake and an old lawn mower, ready to tackle the gardens of North Haven like he's some superhero in a backward baseball cap.

And George Tarkinian comes over nearly every night, and Rosie finds herself so pleased to see him again. She and Soapie used to go on vacation with his family when Rosie was little, and she remembers him and his sweet wife, Louise, and their much-older daughters. He had been a voice-over announcer as well as a competitive swimmer, and Louise— she suddenly remembers this—made brownies with instant coffee in them, and Soapie would never let Rosie have any because she said they would get her too "jazzed up." Of course she had sneaked in and stolen a brownie and then had spun in circles on the front lawn, laughing until she was dizzy, and George had scooped her up and carried her inside when she fell down and cried, holding her against his chest.

He still has those broad swimmer's shoulders and, as Soapie points out, all of his original teeth and most of his hair, and a rich, intimate voice that can make you want to go out and buy household cleaning products.

He smiles at her and holds out his arms. "Look at you! Let me just tell you how glad I am that you're here with us," he says.

With us. He and Soapie are clearly a couple—and yet both of them talk about Louise as though she's a very dear friend they have in common, someone unfortunate whom they both adore and wish were with them. It's the very oddest, sweetest thing: he goes to sit with Louise in the nursing home every day, and then comes to Soapie every night. The two of them hold hands and take long walks, and Rosie has come upon them practically making out in the kitchen.

Late at night, they walk upstairs to Soapie's bedroom, arm in arm, both of them holding their glasses of water, Soapie carrying her cigarette case, and they close the door and spend the night together.

Rosie has to admit that it's actually kind of wonderful.

● ● ●

At the end of her first week, Jonathan calls her in the middle of the night. She fumbles in the dark for her phone, before she quite comes awake, and then there he is in her ear.

"I just wanted to say I miss you and I love you," he says, his voice crawling up right there next to her brain.

Maybe she's dreaming. "Are you really there?"

"I am."

"I love you, too," she says, but her voice feels as if it's coming from very far away.

She flips over her pillow, which has gotten hot in the night. She's going to have to get up and turn on the air conditioner. It's stifling in this room. What time is it anyway? 3:23.

This can't be a good time to be awake. She tells him something important, but it turns out that it was a thought left over from sleep, and he says she doesn't make any sense.

Then he starts filling up the air with his facts. He knows the average daily temperature in Nevada versus the average daily temperature in Arizona for June. He's got the goods on rainfall situations everywhere. Gas prices. The cost of an average night's stay in hotels across America. He says he fears for the teacups when he goes over the mountain passes. Also, there is no good radio in the middle of the country. And it is hot already. Vicious, wicked hot.

She is silent.

"You should go back to sleep," she hears him say, and then he is gone.

After that, it's like the "I Miss Jonathan" switch in her brain has been activated. She was better off for the first few days when she thought she might hate him. In her suitcase she finds one of his T-shirts, packed there by mistake, and she takes it to bed with her each night because it smells like him. Some days now she aches for her old life: the way the river's reflection danced on the ceiling, the hibachi on the balcony, the way he held her in bed.

She finds herself trying to explain to Greta how furious she was, and how much she now misses everything about Jonathan.

"You'll end up going back with him," says Greta. "It was sensible not to ride in that truck with a broken foot. You did the right thing."

"I know," she says. "But I probably should have married him when he wanted to, two weeks ago."

"Don't worry. When your foot heals, and you get Soapie settled, you can fly out there and join him," Greta says. "Right now you can just have some drifty time. And I hate to say this, but it's probably the last big chunk of time you'll get to spend with your grandmother. It would be good if you could enjoy it."

Greta's right. After that, Rosie spends the next two weeks cleaning out Soapie's office, making piles of old files to throw out. She collects paint chips for the guest room. She spends time talking with Soapie about the possible new Dustcloth Diva book. But the whole time, she's aware that there's something wrong with her: she's tired and sad, just dragging around, really, like somebody who has a low-grade fever and probably *this minute* she's growing a catastrophic brain tumor or something. Maybe it's only that she really does miss Jonathan more than she ever thought she would, but she wakes up crying some mornings. And then, as she lies in bed debating whether it's worth the trouble to get up, she thinks that maybe she's coming face-to-face with the real lack in her life: the fact that she never really had a mother and that in a deep, fundamental way, she's always been an unwelcome addition to Soapie's life.

The horrible truth is, she doesn't truly belong anywhere and never really has.

And now, even worse, she sees that after telling Jonathan she was maybe starting menopause, she realizes that she really is. She got up in the middle of the night one night and checked the Internet, and there were dozens—dozens!—of women who wrote about going into menopause at forty-four. So *that's* what's wrong with her, she thinks as she looks at her pathetic, drawn, wrinkling face in the bathroom mirror each day: she got old and tired, and somehow she missed out on having the life she wanted. It's no wonder she wakes up crying. She doesn't even know what that life would have been.

One night George brings over ice cream, and the four of them—George, Soapie, Tony, and Rosie—all go sit outside on the patio to eat it. There are supposed to be shooting stars that night, but there's too much light to really see them, and so the night is something of a disappointment to Soapie, who says that all the major astronomical events of the century have been just hype.

"Just eat some ice cream and enjoy the evening," George says. "Listen to the crickets and the frogs. They're never a disappointment."

"We have ice cream on a hot night, so how bad could life be?" Tony says.

Then George tells a lovely story about making peach ice cream with Louise on another summer night so long ago, and how ice cream took on a whole new meaning for him after that.

"We churned it until we were both so tired and sweaty. I kept thinking this couldn't possibly be worth it, and why didn't I just go to Dairy Queen and get us some? But then—*then*," he says, and Rosie can see his eyes shine in the darkness, "then the texture, the sweetness, the real cream!" he exclaims. "You think of how people in the world are suffering, and there you are, eating fresh peaches that you've whipped up yourself in a churn with cream. It-it . . ."

Words fail him, and Soapie leans over and pats his leg, and he places his arm around her shoulders and wipes at something in his eye.

"And here we are tonight," Soapie says, "eating ice cream together, you and me, and the world for us is perfect."

Rosie, watching in the drowsy twilight, feels as though she's never known her grandmother at all.

[ten]

Three weeks after she's moved in, on an overly warm July night, Tony and George start ostentatiously cooking dinner, some concoction they are quite proud of, involving red sauce and pasta and garlic and mozzarella and every pot and pan in the kitchen. And wine. She and Soapie have been told to sit, the men will do all the work tonight—and Rosie is happy to support this. It's interesting having sweet, loud, well-meaning men around, with their flourishy cooking.

Soapie is swanning about, and having declared that it's lovely to see men working, she is seemingly unable to sit down and actually let it take place. She's made piña coladas for everybody in her inimitable Soapie way, sweeping around the kitchen in her designer bedroom slippers and Vera Wang dressing gown, gathering up the ingredients one by one, narrating her progress and asking for help as she goes and then yelling at the people who give it. The kitchen is a garlicky, olive oil–reeking mess, with pineapple odors thrown in for good measure.

Tony, still wearing his baseball cap backward and gesturing with the knife as he cuts up the garlic, is talking, loudly, about his mother, the finest cook in Hoboken, and how once she won an award for her tomato sauce, but then the prize got rescinded because some lady—and here he is using the word loosely—said that Mrs. Cavaletti stole her recipe from somebody's Aunt Toots in Mount Kisco, and it was a big scandal for a while, and Tony and his friends ended up having to TP the lady's house just to teach her a big lesson. Both Soapie and George need to hear how it is that a person can actually drape a house in toilet paper, and Rosie, who'd put a coat of primer on the guest room walls that day, gets so tired during the explanation that she has to lay her head down on the table for just a moment. When she looks up, they're all staring at her.

"I'm sorry, but my head is killing me. I think I really just need to go upstairs to bed," she says. "I think I'm coming down with something."

"What you need is red meat," Tony says. "Tomorrow I'm going to make you a big steak. Did you ever have steak with butter on it? Best thing in the world for you when you're run down."

"I don't think I'm run down," Rosie says. "I'm just old and *tired*."

"Rare is best. You like rare? With mushrooms? I read somewhere that mushrooms can cure anything."

That leads Soapie to point out that so many of those food cures are just the thing, and maybe there's a way for the Dustcloth Diva to incorporate some food cures into her next book. "Give me a pencil, George. I'm going to write down that mushrooms cure anything. We have our first tip."

"Mushrooms can't cure everything," Rosie says grouchily, "and the Dustcloth Diva can't do food stuff. It's not right. Your advice has to involve things that can be improved with dustcloths. That's your brand."

"So I'll be the Tablecloth Diva."

George laughs. "How many divas can one person be? We're already scared enough of you as it is."

"You should be scared of me, George Tarkinian," she says, and leans over and nuzzles against him. "You've done a million things wrong, starting back in 1945 when you married the wrong girl—"

"You, I believe, weren't available, my dear, having already gone and married another man," George says, and Rosie wants to hear more—really, this has been going on *forever?*—but Tony claps his hands and jumps in with, "Now, now, there will be none of that talk about the things George did wrong. The past is gone."

He shepherds them all into the dining room like they're his own personal patients, Rosie limping and ill, and the two old people toddling along with their arms around each other. Soapie goes to light candles on the dining room table and nearly catches the sleeve of her gown on fire reaching across, and Tony jumps in and shields her right at the last second and then tucks her into her seat, placing her napkin on her lap and her hands close to her plate, just so. She smiles up at him, and Rosie is surprised to see that she has the expression of a compliant schoolgirl, waiting to be given directions. Her eyes are slightly cloudy, and her hands shake as she reaches for the bowl of pasta, which he then gets for her and dishes onto her plate. Some for her, and then some for George.

"You're always saving us," Soapie says, and gives Tony a huge smack on the cheek.

After dinner, Soapie and George take their drinks and go off to the living room, pretend-bickering over whether they'll dance to Frank Sinatra or Frankie Laine tonight. George is arguing that Frankie Laine is too moody and gloomy, but Soapie claims that she can't find the Sinatra record. Tony goes and helps them turn on the stereo and look for the record, which was right on the record player, he tells Rosie when he comes back into the kitchen. She's piling the plates in the sink.

"Here, I'll do that. You rest," he says.

"I'm really okay."

"No, I insist. Go sit down. Once I've made you steak and mushrooms, *then* you can work."

She goes and sits down. "Look, you really don't have to fix me a steak. It's just that I was painting the guest room today and I got tired."

"Yeah, but you look—I don't know—like you might be sick."

For a moment, she thinks how much fun it would be to wallop him, but then she thinks better of it and merely says, "Well, I said I was coming down with something." Anybody with any sense would realize she also means, "So leave me the hell alone."

But of course he doesn't. He stops loading the dishwasher and stares at her, coming closer so he can more easily peer into her face.

"What?" she says.

"Is there any chance you could be . . . pregnant?" he says. "I mean, not for nothin', but you look to me like you got a classic case of baby-on-the-way."

She glares at him and shakes her head. "No, no, no."

"I mean, sometimes I'm a guy who can just *sense* pregnancy," he says. "I don't know why. My ex said I should hire myself out as a human pregnancy test, save people a lot of money on those home kit thingies. I knew right away when she was expecting Milo, even before she missed her period. I can just kind of *read* it. I don't know how it works, it just does."

She rolls her eyes. "You might have known about Milo, because you were the one who had sex with her. Right?"

"Well, yeah, but there've been some other cases, too. I swear it. It's a gift."

"Well, that's a nice gift to have, I'm sure, but I'm not

pregnant," says Rosie, although her voice is shaking as she says it.

He shrugs and goes back to loading the dishwasher. "Steak'll be good for you either way, pregnant or not," he says.

"Yeah, but I'm really not," she says. She's about to explain to him that the Internet thinks she's probably in menopause, but why engage him in thinking about her hormonal life at all? Why encourage him? *This is ridiculous.* "I'm just tired from painting in the heat, that's all this is. That, and I'm missing Jonathan and my old life. I used to have a very nice life."

"So why *are* you painting the guest room?" he says.

Rosie speaks in a low voice. "I'm trying to get this place in order for when Soapie can't live here anymore and we have to sell it. Her doctor said he'd like to see her in an assisted-living place sooner rather than later, because of the little strokes she's having."

"That's wack," he says. "She's in there *dancing,* for God's sake. She doesn't need assisted living."

"Well, I know it may seem that way to you right now, but the doctor's point is that she could get used to it before she really needs all the services, and she could be in the independent-living part and then get increasing amounts of help as she needs it."

He scowls. "She's fine. The best place she can be is here with us. We're assisting her with living."

"Yeah, but who knows how long we're staying?" she says. "As my fiancé points out, we need to be practical. And she doesn't seem to want to take care of herself."

He puts the plates on the bottom row of the dishwasher. "I hate this kind of talk. She just wants to have fun. Eat good food, do fun things, have a little romance, enjoy the neighbor's peonies. I don't see what's so wrong with that."

"Well, of course it's fine for *now*," she says. "It just won't stay this way. She's going downhill, in case you haven't noticed."

"But why should we rush it?" he says. He frowns as he wrestles the pots onto the top row of the dishwasher and closes the door, and Rosie can absolutely feel what he's thinking about her right then: that she's the type of person who would gladly put her grandmother in some kind of facility just so she can go out and join her noncommittal, teacup-loving boyfriend who doesn't care enough about her to marry her, even when she had the celebration all arranged. And that she's even too clueless to know that she's pregnant. Which, by the way, she is not. He is clearly the bossiest, nosiest person she's ever met, and he's given her a headache.

"It's not how you think it is," she says to him, getting to her feet. "Things aren't always the way they look, you know. That's what you learn when you get older."

She heads up the stairs to bed.

"If I were you, I'd go buy a test," he calls after her.

● ● ●

She eats the steak dinner he makes for her the next night, and she has to admit it's good, even if the sight of the mushrooms make her a little bit skeevy. All that slimy brownness. She eats them anyway, just so he won't get on the pregnancy bandwagon again—telling her how food sensitivities are just more evidence. She's armed tonight, though, with news she gleaned from the Internet: getting pregnant at age forty-four is pretty much considered a freaking *miracle*—and the odds of having gotten pregnant at that age in one accidental time of unprotected intercourse are practically incalculable. She very much hopes, though, that she will not start talking about her sex life with Tony Cavaletti.

Soapie and George go into the living room after dinner again; more slow dancing to Frank Sinatra. Rosie looks in on them, and she reports to Tony that what they call dancing looks more like standing in the middle of the room and swaying one inch in each direction.

"*Dancing with the Stars,* here they come," he says. "Gotta love it."

"It's hugging to music," she says. "I can't get over it. *The Dustcloth Diva Finally Falls in Love.* Now that's the book she ought to be writing."

"Except she's having too much fun to write it," Tony says. "Say," he says in an artificially bright voice, a change-the-subject voice. "I've kinda been wondering this. Why do you call her Soapie anyway? Is it because of those cleaning books? Because she's so clean?"

"No. Hardly that. When I was three, I probably couldn't pronounce Mrs. Baldwin-Kelley."

He looks startled. "What? She didn't want you to call—oh, you're joking."

"Well, not by much. I think she wanted me to call her Sophie, and I heard it wrong or something."

"But why not Grandma? Or, I don't know, Oompa or Nonnie or something."

"Why, let's go ask her why she didn't want to be Grandma. This ought to be interesting," she says, and she gets up and limps over to the door to the living room where Soapie and George are hanging on to each other, sidestepping to Frank Sinatra.

When the song ends, Rosie says, "Hey, Soapie! Tony here wants to know how come I call you by your name, and not Nonnie or Oompa or Meemaw or something."

"I didn't say that," he protests from behind her.

"Okay, call me Oompa then," Soapie says. She flings her hand out as George softly turns her in a spin. "In fact, call me anything you want."

"But he wants to know why you didn't want me to call you Grandma when you first got me."

"Now why in the world would I have wanted that? I was forty-seven years old. I was still cute back then." She smiles in that coquettish way she now has—the way she did when she was talking about George being ardent. The wisps of her hair have come loose from the clip, and she reaches up to capture them again.

"See?" says Rosie to Tony, smiling. "There you have it. She was too young and pretty to be my grandmother."

"She may still be too young and pretty to be your grandmother," says Tony.

"Oh," says Soapie. "I just wish you could have seen me then. You'd know what I mean. I was still wearing miniskirts and black eyeliner. And, the real reason"—she laughs a little bit and wiggles her hips in a way that Rosie sees would once have been sexy—"well, there was a man, a man who was sort of in love with me at the time, but he got scared away by everything that was happening. I remember *he* called me Grandma once as a joke, and then I never saw him again. So I was damned if I was going to turn into that. Bad enough I had this toddler who cried all the time and clung to me."

"Oh, well. Losing a mom can do that to a toddler," says Rosie in a low voice.

The album has stopped, and Soapie makes her way over

to the table, where George hands her a drink, which very nearly slips out of her hands.

"Oh, I knew why you were clingy," she says, with the slightest hardening in the edge of her voice. "But I didn't *want* a kid. And I guess I was dumb enough to think that if you didn't call me Grandma, it wouldn't be really true." She laughs and takes a swig of her piña colada and staggers just the tiniest bit.

Rosie turns to Tony, whose eyes have widened. "So there you have it. That's why."

"Let's put the music back on," says George, smiling. "I want to keep dancing." He goes over to the stereo and places the needle back at the beginning of the record. "The Way You Look Tonight" starts playing.

"But it didn't make the slightest bit of difference," Soapie says, too loudly, "because I couldn't get *away* from being your grandmother. I tried, believe me. I admit it. There weren't—"

"Sophie, darling, come on over here and dance with me again," says George.

"—there weren't any other takers showing up to claim you, is the truth of it," she says, even louder, "and I certainly wasn't going to put you in foster care. Some kid in the Bronx had just been killed by his foster mom, and it was in all the papers."

Rosie sits down on the couch. "So at least you didn't want me killed," she says. "We had that going for us."

"Come on, Sophie," says George. "I knew you at the time. Don't say this stuff. You were grief-stricken, and there was never any question that you were going to take Rosie. I remember it." He winks at Rosie. "This is all embellished. Your grandmother has always adored you."

Soapie laughs, and Rosie realizes now how drunk she really is. Her eyes somehow look both glittery and vague at the same time. "Don't start with me on this love and adoration business. I am not going to apologize for what I did or did not feel at that time. I did my duty. And I did it without wallowing, and we survived, I'll say that for us. We did it, didn't we, baby?"

"Without Rosie, you wouldn't have become the Dustcloth Diva," says George. He looks like a big teddy bear, broad-shouldered and comforting, ready to embrace all their troubles away if need be. "You did a wonderful job raising Rosie. And Rosie appreciates—"

"Oh, she does. I know she does," says Soapie, and she trips on the rug but catches herself. She makes her way over to the couch and sits down next to Rosie, and reaches over and pats her on the leg, a little bit harder than necessary. "And now *Rosie* is not going to end up writing about cleaning products just because it sells and can pay the bills. *Rosie* will have her choice of occupations, once she gets herself together."

"But you loved being the Dustcloth Diva," Rosie says, and she touches her grandmother's hand. "You got to meet all those famous people, and be—"

"You do *not* know anything about it," Soapie says. "Don't tell me what I loved and didn't love. I gave up a serious professional life to raise you, and writing that crap was the only thing I could do to make ends meet. To keep this huge house going! To keep you in My Little Ponies and math tutors and field hockey uniforms—"

"Sophie, you had a wonderful—" says George, but she turns on him, too. Rosie sees Tony leaning against the door-jamb, his arms folded, looking just the slightest bit shell-shocked. Good—let him see how Soapie can be. Other people's old people, indeed.

"Don't you start up, George. You remember that I was a journalist, so don't you be chiming in with your platitudes about how at least I was still writing, because it's not at all true, and you know it. I did it for Rosie, and now all I'm asking of her is that she give me back a promise to live her life with some passion to it. Why does everybody think that's so bad?"

"Now let's just turn down the volume on this, shall we?" says George. "It's getting way out of proportion to the facts. There's no point to this kind of talk. Come on, sweetheart."

Soapie drinks the last bit of her piña colada and stares at Rosie. "Well, none of it matters anyway. At least we have our agreement. Don't we, baby?"

"Our agreement?" says Rosie.

"Yes." Soapie's eyes are bright and glassy. "I told you months ago I was going to give you money to go to Europe and become a writer and do what you want, and you told *me* you were going to get married, and then you came to your senses and didn't. So now you'll go. Live out the dream for both of us."

"Wait. That's not why I didn't get married."

"It doesn't matter *why* you broke up with—with whosits. The important point here is that you did. And for that, I'm giving you your freedom." She flings her arms out and Rosie has to move out of the way to keep from being clobbered. "So take it! I want you to go to Paris and live like I would have done." She laughs. "Knowing me, I probably would have become a wino, and would have had way more fun than you're going to have, but that's neither here nor there. You can go . . . you can write the good stuff. For me. For both of us."

"*What* is this fantasy of yours about me and Paris?" says Rosie. George is signaling to her not to say anything. Even so, she says, "Soapie, I'm afraid that's *your* dream. I have never once talked about going to a café in Paris to write."

"No. *I* want you to do it! Me!" says Soapie.

"But why can't I just stay and teach English to people, like I want to do? I shouldn't have to live the life you wanted, just because you didn't get to."

"No, I think you owe me that. Why can't you be grateful? This is a gift, damn you! Why can't you just do what I want you to do? Just for once in your life, do it!"

"Now, Sophie," says George.

"She owes me this. I'm going to live through her."

"But you can't live through people," he says. "It wouldn't count."

"I say it *would* count." Her voice starts to wobble a little, but she just gets louder. "Damn it, I had to lose my daughter, and now this is what I want to happen. None of you has any business telling me what would count and what wouldn't count. I want Rosie to live up to her potential. I want her to goddamn *live* a little just for whatever time she has left. *Not* sit around here and dribble her whole life away."

"Whatever time I have left?" says Rosie. "What are you talking about? I'm not dying—" she says, but then she stops. Nobody's listening anyway. George has come over and pulled Soapie up from the couch and put his arms around her, and her head is on his shoulder, and Tony is quiet, probably planning his escape route if he's smart.

And Rosie, just sitting there, is having the most blinding sort of epiphany, if that's the word—maybe too pretentious, she thinks, to call it an epiphany when you realize for like the first time ever that your crazy, impetuous grandmother might be drunk and mean, but she's also right about you. Really, what *is* she doing with her life? She has nothing. Nothing. She's lived this quiet little tucked-in, halfway unsatisfying life, helping her students with their job applications, keeping her apartment clean, going out to breakfast on Saturday mornings, and sometimes babysitting her friends' kids—but was any of it what she really wanted? Hell, the most interesting things she ever did happened when she was traveling with Jonathan to art shows—and that life's been over for five years. If a film crew followed her around, what would they see? Nothing. She might as *well* be dying, for all she's accomplished. She never had a family, she never owned a house, she never even bought a brand-new car, had a disastrous love affair with an inappropriate person, or even dyed her hair some ghastly shade of red. How does this happen, that you get to be forty-four and you don't have anything— not even an ill-advised tattoo—to show for it?

And what if she *is* now in menopause—or worse yet, deathly ill?

She looks at Soapie, who is pulling away from George, and he's reaching out his arms to catch her if he needs to. This whole night is so weird and strange, this group of people together like this, and Jonathan seems like her missing home planet, on the other side of the country now, not even in the same orbit. She's lost, is the truth of it; she's somewhere out bobbing around in the atmosphere where there isn't enough air for her to breathe.

"Soapie," she says, finding her voice again, "it's *you* who wants to live for the time you have left, and you're doing it. You are doing it. You're amazing."

"It all went by so fast," says Soapie, and she looks at Rosie with eyes that are wide and frightened. "Life went by so quickly. Rosie, you can't believe it. It just goes!" She starts to cry, and George wraps his arms around her again, and Rosie starts to cry, too—and Tony materializes beside her and pulls her toward George and Soapie, and for a minute they all stand together, awkward as hell. Rosie can see that George has tears in his eyes, and then Tony does, too, and in another couple of minutes it's going to turn into a wail-athon, but then thank God Soapie pushes them all away.

"Stop it! Just stop it!" she says. "This is maudlin and it's sentimental, and we're wallowing, and we're not ever going to do this again."

eleven

A week later, Greta says that Rosie simply has to come out to dinner with her friends. Just getting out of the house and going into a restaurant, in public, will probably do wonders for her. She's been avoiding all her friends out of embarrassment over not going to California, fearing she'd have to hear about the chapter "How Rosie and Jonathan Cannot Even Move Together When They Start Over." But now she doesn't care anymore.

A funny thing has happened: it's as though some huge unspoken weight got lifted since the night when Soapie had her meltdown. Maybe it's just that it's now so clear that none of the four of them really has a life right now—that they're all pretty much wrecks, at least temporarily, waiting for the worst to happen and their lives to change—and there's no reason to pretend otherwise anymore. Tony has taken to calling them the Gang of Four.

George is sad because, as he confided to Rosie one day when they were alone, he really does love his wife who's across town with Alzheimer's, *and* he loves Soapie, too, and hates what is happening to her. Soapie is slipping more every day and forgetting everything. Rosie is a hormonal mess and unmoored from her life; and Tony—well, Tony is heartbroken over the loss of his son and maybe his marriage, too. Hard to tell because he'll talk about everything but that, and that's the worst kind of heartbreak there is, the kind you won't talk about.

They really are all like mental hospital inmates, Rosie thinks, with Tony rallying himself to be their self-appointed recreation director/caseworker, the one who makes them dance and eat. And now he's discovered that they can play Scrabble every night, so he hauls out the board and makes them play. He's probably no more intact than the rest of them, but at least he tries. He bosses them around and talks loudly, pours their drinks, and makes them the foods his mother used to make him in childhood, lasagnas and pasta fagioli and manicotti (which he pronounces "monny-goat," which he claims is the genuine Italian way). He says he knows the best way of preparing all foods.

Once the Scrabble game ends, usually by cutthroat Soapie losing and "accidentally" knocking over the board, they turn the music up too loud and sing along. Their favorite song, appropriately enough, is "Crazy," by Patsy Cline, and Rosie has to admit, they make it sound quite convincing.

But even Rosie can see that she has to get out of the house and back to polite company.

● ● ●

"So start from the time we all left the restaurant," Suzanne says once she, Greta, Lynn, and Rosie have settled into the gigantic round booth in the back of Bentara's and ordered a bottle of red and a bottle of white. Rosie is sitting on the end so she can stick her bandaged foot out. Tucking it underneath her in one position makes it start throbbing again. She's glad it's kind of dark in there, so they can't see the dark circles and bags under her eyes. "You walked into the parking lot and just broke up right then and there? Sent him packing, as it were?"

"No, we had a fight in the apartment when we went back inside," says Rosie.

"Was it a big fight?" says Lynn. "Because I thought that the whole day he was being kind of overbearing."

"Men are often overbearing," says Greta. "I believe they call it testosterone."

"I can't really say what happened for sure," says Rosie slowly. "He promised me he'd hire movers, but then he didn't, so I was annoyed he got all of you to pack. And then I just suddenly knew that I couldn't get in that truck and drive away with him." This seems like a lame reason, so then she throws in the part about the oven and how he wouldn't clean it, and then when she gets to the part about the German accent, Lynn jumps in and says that's enough for her, no one should be expected to get into a car with a man who's using phony accents.

"Especially cross-country," says Suzanne.

"In the middle of the night," says Greta.

"I'd have killed him by New York City," says Rosie, and she laughs, and then her eyes fill up *again*. "But now I miss him so much, and now I'm stuck here and I can't go." And of course she starts to cry again.

"Oh, man," says Greta, and they all dive into their purses looking for tissues. Greta is the first one to come up with one that, as she says, doesn't have kid material on it.

"We should order some food to go with this wine," says Lynn. "Pretty soon, we're all going to be crying." She flags down their waiter, and for a moment they're all busy squinting trying to read the menus, and Suzanne is asking questions about the dressing for the salads and how the chicken is cooked and what's that sauce for the beef that she had last time she was here.

As soon as the waiter departs, Greta leans over and

touches Rosie's arm. "Well, I will tell you this. When you didn't have that wedding, I have to admit that we three kind of knew right then—"

"But it really wasn't just that—well, yes, maybe it was," says Rosie. "We didn't know then. I mean, I didn't know then. I thought—"

"The fact that he could go chase some teacups in Texas over his commitment to you says *a lot*," says Greta. "I'm sorry, but it just does."

"And after fifteen years, to act as if the whole thing was just some kind of accident, that it didn't really matter! What kind of marriage was that going to be?" Lynn adds.

"The same kind of self-absorbed marriage I've been locked into for twenty years," says Suzanne, and all their heads swivel toward her. "I tell you one thing: I wouldn't do it again. And if it weren't for the kids, I'd go right now."

They all get quiet.

"You would?" says Rosie. She clears her throat. "You really would?"

"Well, sure. I often think about how it would be to be free and on my own again. Hinty doesn't ever think about anything for himself. It's like he got married to me, and then I was in charge of everything in his emotional life from then on. If I tell him to do the dishes, he will, but he doesn't *think* of it on his own. I just get bland smiles from him. Nothing. No passion, no excitement, no laughs. I'm not sure he even remembers the children's middle names."

Lynn says, "They get so . . . settled."

"Jonathan just wants to keep life shut out," says Rosie. "He says no to everything—until now, when he's suddenly gone all full throttle on this. He was in the off position for so long that I thought *this* would have to be better, but it's just as bad. And it's my fault, because I kept pushing him to do something with his life."

"It's not your fault," says Greta. "I've watched him for years. And he's wonderful, there are many great things about him, but he's just . . . limited. You didn't push him. He can't be pushed. He's limited."

"That's just the word Soapie used," says Rosie.

"Ah, the wisdom of Soapie," says Greta, and then she and Rosie look at each other and say in unison, "They're all only out for one thing! Give 'em an inch and they'll take a mile!"

Then they all go into their usual thing, which is to talk about how great it would be, if once they get rid of these men—they don't wish for harm, of course, but a nice, simple, painless, amicable four-way death—wouldn't it be nice if all the women just moved in together? Think of the peace and quiet! The time to read and think! The clean kitchens! The great food! They've been talking about this for years, while the guys talk about sports and cars in the other room. It is, in fact, their favorite fantasy.

Then someone, usually Greta, brings up the question of visitation for the men. "Because . . . well, won't we miss sex sometimes?" she says.

This gets discussed. Greta, of course, maintains that sex with Joe is still as good as it was when they first met, which has to be a blatant lie, and just the kind of hostile thing she's known to throw out during these kinds of conversations. The others have to roll their eyes.

"I think we should let the men visit," says Rosie this time. "We do want sex with them."

"I've read that after menopause, sex gets even better for some women," says Greta.

"Well, that's good news, because today I figured out that I'm right there. I'm in early menopause," says Rosie.

"God, I wish I'd get me some menopause," says Lynn. "I am so sick and tired of the whole business!"

"Wait," says Suzanne. "What makes you think you're having early menopause?"

"Oh, here we go! We can't get together without the period report," says Greta. "Come on. Out with it! We want all the gory details."

So Rosie tells them it's been weeks since she had her period, and also she's in a bad mood all the time. Greta needs to know just how long it's really been, and she, of course, doesn't know.

"Are you sure you're not pregnant?" says Lynn, and there's a silence around the table. They all look at her.

"Well," says Rosie. "I think I'm sure. The Internet says—"

"Wait. Have you had . . . unprotected sex?" asks Greta.

"Well, there was the once, but—" She has to stop because everybody around the table has erupted in hoots and yells. "Wait! Wait just a minute! I am not pregnant because I am forty-four years old, and my doctor said—well, not *my* doctor, but people say that it's impossible to get pregnant at that age, and anyway if I were pregnant, I think I'd know. I'd have this—this spiritual *feeling* about sharing my body with more than just myself—"

"I think you need to buy a pregnancy test," says Greta.

"And I don't want to upset you or anything, but that's bullshit about the sharing-your-body stuff," says Suzanne. "A fertilized egg doesn't keep you company for a long time. Like, until it's pretty much ready for preschool."

"Oh, my God, wouldn't that be the most ironic thing in the whole world?" Greta says. "*You* turning out to be pregnant right when the three of us get our kids practically launched and out the door? Also, are you still going to come live with us in the fabulous man-free home if you've got a little kid underfoot?"

Rosie feels like she might pass out. The blood is beating in her ears.

"Wait. I thought it wasn't completely man-free, it's just invitation-only," says Suzanne.

"Some men can never be invited. We'll have to vote."

"Oh, no, no! I'm not going to live in a home where I have to live by other people's votes," says Lynn. "Absolutely not."

"Okay, no votes," says Greta, "but let's just all agree you can't inflict bad men on the rest of the group."

"Well, what about kids? Our kids have to be able to come visit us, don't they?"

"Can't we vote on kids?"

"Rosie's kid will *have* to live there!"

"Okay. Rosie's kid can be an honorary grandchild or something."

"I know! We'll get our other kids to raise it! They'll be old enough by then."

"Sssh," says Lynn. "I think Rosie's crying."

Which is probably technically true, but she doesn't mean to be. She's so happy, actually, sitting here amid all this talk and clutter, even the talk about her pretend offspring. She's 99.9 percent sure this is not going to turn out to be pregnancy, but it's funny to hear them all talking this way, like she—she, Rosie Kelley—could ever in a million years be one of them, moms with regular lives and minivans and husbands.

"Tony says he thinks I'm pregnant," she says in a daze. And then she has to explain who Tony is, and how he thinks he has this mystical ability to read pregnancy in women's faces, but how he's really just a know-it-all, but thank God he's there to keep Soapie from falling down all the time.

"That's it," says Greta. "I don't know who this guy is, but we're getting a pregnancy test. Now."

"I have an empty water bottle in the car," Suzanne says. "You can sit in the backseat of my car and pee into the bottle, and we'll know the results right away."

"In case you've lost all your dignity, by any chance," says Lynn.

They nearly fall over laughing at that idea. Ambulances may have to be called to cart them off, they're laughing so hard as they get up to leave. The waiter waves them good-bye, looking somewhat relieved to see them go. Rosie loves that they walk her to the store, help her pick out a kit. And while she draws the line at peeing in the car, it even seems like ridiculous good fun, buying this pregnancy test, like they are naughty teenage girls. Didn't they have to buy one for Greta one time, when she'd had an incident in college?

She can't quite remember all the details. But that's what is so wonderful, because Greta remembers the whole thing, and entertains them with the story of Rosie waiting outside the bathroom door and cheering when the test came out negative.

Greta even remembers something Rosie had forgotten: that Rosie was disappointed just a little bit that Greta's test was negative. "Oh," she'd said, "it'll be so much fun when we start having babies together, won't it?"

So it had been a dream of hers a long time ago. Funny how she can't recall that.

She kisses them good-bye downtown, hugging and promising to keep in touch. The women say they'll put their family members in cold storage more often. Greta drives her home, all the way to the back door, and Rosie leans over and hugs her.

"Do you want me to walk you in?" says Greta, yawning.

"No, no, I'm fine," she says. "This is the first night I've had my energy back. I can't tell you how different I feel!"

"You just needed to see us," says Greta. "We love you."

"I'm not really pregnant, am I? That was just us talking, right?" she says.

"Of course you're not," says Greta. "Probably."

"Thank you," Rosie says, and then lets herself in the back door as Greta's SUV's taillights disappear down the driveway. The kitchen is illuminated only by the light on the oven and the bathroom light down the hallway. She notices as she turns the key that George's car isn't there. Neither is Tony's, but she'd halfway known that Tony was going to go to Fairfield tonight, to work on getting his ex back or whatever it is he does there.

But where is George? She goes inside, heart already pounding, as if it has run ahead and peeked and now knows all the bad news.

And then she sees what she's been so scared to see: Soapie lying on the floor. Only this time there is blood and this time Soapie isn't moving.

twelve

Soapie, gray, hollow, but still alive, goes by ambulance to the emergency room at Yale–New Haven Hospital, and once there, the hospital people kick Rosie out while they do all those horrible but necessary reviving things to her, hooking her up to machines and tubes.

The EMT, a big guy with an earring and a bald head, had been in the kitchen while Rosie stood by in shock, curling his brown hands around Soapie's head, cradling it gently after he eased her onto the stretcher, all his concentration beamed at making sure she was comfortable. Rosie had watched the stretcher being loaded into the ambulance, and even after she drove herself to the hospital, she was still shaking as she made her way to the chairs in the waiting room. It's only later that she realizes she could have called Greta back, or any of the others. She didn't need to be so alone like this.

By the time they call Rosie into the room, it's nearly four in the morning, and they've bandaged Soapie's head, which makes her look something like a jaunty sailor, one who just happens to be in a coma. Her eyes are closed, with her mouth set in a hard line, collapsing in on itself, as if behind those closed eyes she's thinking how angry she is at being yanked back from wherever she was going, thrust back into life.

Remember if you hear that I've died, just be grateful that I went the way I wanted to.

But could that truly be the way she felt? Now that she's

a member of the Gang of Four and has people cooking for her and dancing with her, now that the lamps are lit in the big, cavernous living room, now that she's singing "Crazy" at the top of her lungs every single night, did she still want to die?

Rosie makes her way to the empty family waiting area, off the ICU. CNN is on a big-screen TV, and she turns the volume down to zero and settles herself in a chair to wait. There's a *People* magazine there, and an *Architectural Digest,* some postcards about ailments, in case you want to be entertained by the symptoms of diabetes or osteoporosis while you wait.

At 7:13, according to the big clock on the wall, she's startled by a man striding in, wearing blue scrubs and carrying a clipboard. She'd been dozing. And drooling. She sits up, wipes her mouth, tries to smile.

The attending, Josh Grimby.

He shakes her hand and then puts one foot up on the wooden arm of the chair and frowns down at the papers he's holding. Her eyes take him in, traveling up from the large hands, the stubbly chin, tight mouth, close-cropped hair, small eyes.

He lets out a sigh, says what she would have expected, like a doctor in a TV show reading from a script.

Broken hip. Needs surgery to put a metal plate in. Surgery soon, maybe today. Managing the pain. She's knocked out. We'll know more in a few days. Get some rest. We'll take good care of her. We'll call you when we've got her on the schedule. Or if there's a change.

Can I kiss her good-bye?

Of course.

Is she going to be all right?

We'll know more in a few days. Surgery later. She's

knocked out. Get some rest. We'll take good care of her. We'll call you if there's any change.

"Well, thank you," she says.

● ● ●

She doesn't remember the pregnancy test until she gets home. And frankly, the only reason she remembers it then is because Tony Cavaletti is down on his knees, wiping up the blood from the floor and the test is on the table next to where he's kneeling. He gets up, eyes huge and brown, his hair sticking up everywhere.

"What happened?" he says. "I've been calling you. I've been out of my mind—"

"I had to turn my cell off. She fell and broke her hip. But she's alive. She's stable. They're keeping her in the hospital. Doing surgery soon. They'll know more in a few days."

"That's what they always say."

"I know." She goes over to the sink and fixes herself a glass of water.

"How does she look?"

"She looks like a person who's unconscious and who has a bandage on her head. She looks kind of like a drunken sailor, actually—with that bandage."

"Were you here, when it happened?"

This is the hard part to tell him. But she does, the whole bit of it.

His eyes bug out. "She was *alone* when this happened? Even George wasn't here?"

"No. No one was here."

"Well, where was everybody? She needs to be watched. You told me that yourself, that somebody needed to be with her—"

"Yeah, but none of us knew the others weren't going to be here. You see? It's just impossible, taking care of somebody the right way." Oh, hell, she's starting to cry again. "It's my fault. I shouldn't have gone out for so many hours. But she's been doing so well. I should have checked with you and George to see if *somebody* was going to be around. I let her down."

He stares at her. "Look, look, it's okay. I'm sorry, I'm sorry. I woulda been here if I'd'a known. Don't blame yourself for this. Nobody can do it all. And you've got a ton on your plate just now. You got a baby coming." He nods toward the pregnancy test.

"No," she says. "It's just a pregnancy test. I didn't take it yet."

"You should take it," he says.

"I—I will. I'm just waiting."

"What are you waiting for? The contractions to start pushing the kid out?"

"It's not going to be positive," she says.

"Yeah, well," he says.

"I'm too old." But even as she says that, she's feeling sick and clammy. Oh God.

"When you're too old, nature takes away the privilege, is the way I always understood the way the system works. I think you should take the test, see if Mother Nature thinks you're too old."

"Okay," she says. "But I think I want to be alone."

He actually laughs. "Come to your senses, woman. Gah! You think I'm gonna sit there with you while you pee on a stick?"

[thirteen]

And then two pink lines bloom on the stick.

Right away, bold as you please.

Hi, they say. *Guess what.*

She checks. Yes, the back of the box is pretty definite about the meaning of these two lines. She reads all the text, the fine print, the manufacturer's information and address, everything.

Huh. She feels a kind of preternatural calm, like maybe she really did know this all along and had just been fooling herself with all the thoughts of menopause. Or—here's another possibility—perhaps she's just in shock.

Not menopause? Not menopause!

She looks around Soapie's bathroom, at the pink tile walls with their white grout, at her sandals kicked off and lying sideways on the fluffy pink rug over the mosaic tile floor, the white sink with stripes of turquoise toothpaste smeared on the side, her leggings, her sleeveless sundress with its blue dancing print, the one she put on last night, which seems like years ago now—and everything has changed. She can hardly take it all in. She looks up in the mirror at her unkempt hair coming loose from last night's braid, her wide blue eyes with their dark circles, and at her white, white face, the O of her mouth. Lips, tongue, teeth, all there and accounted for. Her hands, unbidden, fly up near her face, smooth out her hair, tuck a strand behind her left ear.

She hears Tony bounding up the stairs and knocking at the bathroom door. "Well?" he says. "Can you open the door?"

She puts the test strip down on the counter and opens the door. He's standing outside, with arms outstretched, and she goes straight into them, sniffling, limping, melting.

"No, really, how did you know?" she says.

"How did you *not* know?" he says back.

● ● ●

So this, *this,* is what her body has been doing, while she's been running around, eating inappropriate foods and crying, breaking up with a man and then regretting it, trying to exist in her old childhood home, trying to understand the maniacal woman who raised her. *This?* It has been busily making life, this crazy old body: churning out cells as fast as a little factory, putting together a human being.

It was nine weeks ago that Jonathan flung the condom across the room and then asked her to marry him at the diner. Nine weeks of cells spinning out their hopeful little destiny inside her.

Damn.

The next few days, she drifts around in a kind of fog. She lifts her shirt and massages her abdomen as much as she can. Poor little geriatric reproductive organs, she thinks, thinking it was their chance at last to do what they'd been made for. So misguided of them. She actually feels sorry for them.

She pictures the one little egg all dolled up, a cartoon ovum in a sexy red dress, sashaying her way down the Fallopian tube and luring Jonathan's sperm over to join her. "Come on, boys, it's almost too *late,*" says this little ovum in a Mae West voice. And then one of Jonathan's slacker, teacup-loving, obsessive-compulsive, sarcastic guys stops leaning against the Fallopian tube wall, tosses out his cigarette butt, and decides what the hell. He lopes over, takes her hand.

Never mind it's *years* too late. These two don't care.

"How Jonathan and Rosie Prove They Are Even More Clueless Than Ever."

"How Jonathan and Rosie Mess Up Their Lives."

She starts to laugh out loud. She might be out of her mind.

Tony says, "It's an amazing thing, isn't it?"

What does he know about it? He and his wife were in their twenties when Milo was born.

She lays out the facts for him, in case he has any illusions. It makes *no* sense to have a baby at her age. She's single, she's old, she's unemployed, she's ... well, she's unequipped in every way measurable: financially, emotionally, physically, psychologically, spiritually, probably even pharmaceutically. She doesn't have the slightest idea about prenatal vitamins, just for starters, or how you get babies to not spit out their liquid antibiotic drops. And fluoride: is it an evil killer, or did it save the world's teeth? She can't even remember.

He smiles.

But amid the shock, the dread, the deep knowledge that she can't have, you know, an actual baby, because she's so old and ill-equipped, there's something else. Three mornings in a row, she wakes up watching the sun beaming through the curtains, and she discovers that in an odd little way—before she lets the practical side of herself wake up fully—it's fun to think about it.

Truly—what a thing to have happen! Scientifically speaking, it really is a statistical miracle, just like the Internet claimed. *One* slipup with birth control—one teeny tiny mistake at a time in life when anyone sane might expect that she's entering her infertile years—and *bingo!* She's pregnant. She's like a champion in the fertility sweepstakes. Her endocrine system could give lessons to other endocrine systems. She wants to alert the Internet, with all its gloomy talk about fertility rates and menopause and impossible statistics.

Here's something else that's surprising: the clinic she calls to make an appointment calls it a "procedure." She hadn't expected such linguistic bashfulness in the face of something they see every day.

And another surprising thing: they can see her on Friday for a consultation. Just two days away.

"Will you be doing the *procedure* then?" she whispers, and the receptionist, a cheery woman with a warm voice, perfect for this job, says, "Oh, no, honey. You have to meet with the health care provider first. After all, we have to make sure you're really pregnant, don't we?"

One *not* surprising thing: it's so easy *not* to tell Jonathan.

Another surprising thing: it makes her cry when she realizes life is so mean, giving her this *now*.

She wants to issue an apology to the cells that are growing and dividing inside her, to beg their forgiveness because she's not able to let them keep going. *So sorry,* she would say. *So very, very sorry.*

● ● ●

She goes to visit Soapie, who is in a regular hospital room now that she's post-op. Somehow, during all the pregnancy test drama, the hospital staff managed to go about its business as needed, putting a plate somewhere in Soapie's hip or thigh bone or wherever, and now they say she has to get out of the bed and walk every day, even if she goes inch by inch, millimeter by millimeter.

It seems like cruel and unusual punishment for an old lady, but Rosie goes and helps hold on to the IV pole as she and Soapie shuffle down the hallway, eyes straight ahead before them.

And every day when Rosie goes to see her, Soapie seems more confused.

"Not to worry," says the doc. "She'll go to rehab for a while, and do some occupational therapy, and then we'll see how much comes back."

"How much comes back?"

"Well, she's quite elderly . . ." He pats her arm. "Let's hope for the best, shall we?"

Later, Soapie motions Rosie over to the bed. "I . . . must . . . tell you this. Serena didn't really die," she whispers. She raises her eyebrows to show great significance. "Hiding."

Rosie, startled, draws back.

"Sssh. I saw her today at Kohl's. Cashier now . . . manager soon," she says, and shrugs. She makes a big show of swallowing and then, after a sip of water, she manages a long sentence: "I thought she'd do more with her life, but I guess it's good they're promoting her."

The doctor, when Rosie tracks him down, explains it. No, this isn't part of the symptoms from the broken hip, the surgery, or the medications they have her on. Sad to say, there has been a little unforeseen problem with her grandmother's sodium level. It's dropped way down, interfering with brain function.

"She might do and say strange things for a while," he says. "We're working on bringing it back up."

But it would have been so nice to believe in her words,

she wants to tell him. This had been her fantasy, too, that one day she would simply be approached by a woman stepping out of the crowd—and why not the cashier at Kohl's?—and the woman would smile at her and say, "Hi, Rosie, I'm your mama. I've been trying to find you for years."

When she gets back to the room, though, Soapie has forgotten all about it.

Instead, she flutters her gnarled, big-knuckled hands over the bedspread, as if she's trying to scoop up words and use them. She's smiling, but it's not her real smile. It's as though somebody else is behind her eyes, somebody vague and uncertain.

Rosie sits next to her, holding her hand, long into the night, watching the flicker of the television set, and waiting for another bulletin about her mother. Tony and George come for a visit, pat everyone's hands, say nice things, and leave. But Soapie just dozes, wakes up, and dozes again. So Rosie waits.

● ● ●

A woman is beaming and telling the television audience that she was forty-five when she had her twins. In vitro, but it all worked out fine. Easy C-section delivery, normal babies, everything perfect. Two adorable, towheaded moppets come out from behind the curtain, and the audience roars its approval and leaps to its feet. The mom's face has broken into a million sunshine beams, and the host of the show, an Asian woman, dabs at her eyes.

Rosie, tearing up, too, wishes the television had a button that allowed you to get a true close-up. She needs to see if the woman is exhausted. Can you see pain and suffering in her eyes, or is she really, truly happy that she had these babies? Maybe if Rosie Googles her name, she'll find that the woman keeps a blog where she reveals the *real* truth: *My life is a living hell. I cry day and night, and my husband wants to leave me.*

Jonathan calls on her cell phone, and she takes the phone outside and down to the cafeteria to talk to him. It is midafternoon, and she, George, and Tony had been playing Scrabble in Soapie's room, but Rosie is glad to get away. It kills her to see the blank, pleasant look on Soapie's face as she watches them play without even once insisting that she wants to join in. So much territory has been lost. Rosie even misses Soapie's cheating and the way she used to knock the board over if she hated her letters.

"Hullo," Jonathan says. "So here's the latest. You know those little cards that museums have that tell you all the historical features you're looking at?"

"The what?" She squints at the sun coming through the atrium windows. Around her, people in scrubs are carrying trays to tables.

"The cards. Did you ever really notice those?"

"Oh. Yeah. I guess so."

"I'm spending my days writing those now. I love this job!"

"Well," she says. "That's nice." She feels queasy from all the food smells around her, so she sits down in an orange plastic chair and contemplates the crumbs left on the table.

"This is really going to be a freaking teacup museum!"

"That's great," she says. "I already knew it was going to be a museum."

She means that she knew it was a museum because she's heard little else from him for two months now—from the middle of May until now, nearly the end of July—but he takes it to mean that she's always believed in him and the teacups. He thanks her for that.

Then she tells him about Soapie's broken hip and the low sodium, and how it looks like she'll have a long stint in rehab. He listens and then says that he knows this is hard, but it's the way things are going to go. Sad to say, but she's not long for this world, most likely.

"I'll tell her you said hello and sent your best," she says coldly.

"No, no. Did that sound awful on my part? I didn't mean it to. But, babe, she's nearly ninety. People don't last much longer than that, especially when they have a broken hip. Me, I'd be thrilled to get to that age."

"So you're saying she should be so busy being grateful she got old that she shouldn't feel bad that she hurts and that she's confined to bed all the time and can't live her life?"

"I'm just *saying* that it's *realistic* to think—" he starts, and then he sighs and stops talking. "I'm sorry. I'm being horrible, aren't I? This is your grandmother, and she's suffering. Please tell her I love her and I hope she gets better."

She's taken off guard. "Well, okay, I will," she says.

"I'm working on not being such a negative asshole," he says cheerfully. "Public relations 101: don't tell people they should be happy with their lot in life when they're not."

"Well—"

"Like next time, when you and I go to get married? Even if there are a thousand teacups in a flood in Texas, and even if they all need saving—I'm going to get married to you *before* I go to pick up the teacups."

"Ha," she says.

"And, if you sprain your ankle, I won't say that you can just wear any old shoes to get married in when you wanted your red boots," he says.

She's quiet.

"Even if I don't see the point of the red boots, they mean something to you, and I should accept that."

"Have you figured anything out about the oven?" she teases.

"No. A dirty oven is an abomination and is worth nothing."

For one tiny moment, perhaps a fourth of a nanosecond, she toys with the idea of telling him about the pregnancy, but then she knows it would be the wrong thing. She has to just do what she needs to do, she has to endure the fear and the dread all by herself; she doesn't think she could bear hearing his panicky voice, the resounding *NO* he reserves for anything that might be risky.

"I really do love you," he says before they hang up.

"Me, too, you," she says, which is what they always used to say to each other, back when he used to refer to the two of them as a couple known as "Rosiethan."

They were like Bennifer or Brangelina, he had said.

But that was a long time ago. He probably doesn't even remember.

Little losses everywhere. And some too big to even imagine.

● ● ●

"Okay, let's review," says Tony on Thursday night, the night before the "procedure" itself. She had seen the doctor the week before and had the pregnancy confirmed and the date set for the abortion. And now she just has to get through one more night of waiting.

It's beastly hot outside, and Tony's just come home from

fertilizing the rosebushes of everybody Soapie knows, he says. He's taken a shower and put on nonsweaty clothing and come back downstairs with his hair all slicked down and his Red Sox cap on backward as usual. Rosie is frightened and anxious—no, she's *beyond* frightened and anxious. She's become mentally ill, sitting there huddled in the living room, with only one lamp on, and even that one lamp giving off only the most depressing, pale puddle of light. He gets a bag of potato chips and brings it in and holds it out to her.

She shakes her head.

"No, you gotta eat salt. If what happened to your grandmother has taught us anything, it's that salt is very important."

She doesn't think that salt intake has anything to do with what's wrong with Soapie, but potato chips are good, so she takes a handful and he goes and sits down on the ottoman across from her and watches her. He has a way of sitting with his elbows resting on his knees, his hands dangling down, and his back hunched over that makes him look as though he's about to be spring-loaded into the air.

"God, it's dark in here," he says. "Can I turn on another light?"

"I don't care."

He doesn't move. "Ohhhh. You're having a really hard time, huh?"

"I'm scared out of my mind."

"Yeah. Listen, about that, can we just have a quick review of the facts as we now know them? Could we do that?"

"What facts?"

"The fact that you are currently pregnant, for one. And second, you're hormonal as all hell while you try to make the hardest decision of your life."

"I made the decision, and it wasn't that hard."

"Did you? I wonder," he says. "I think you have a whole lot of mixed feelings, and I think you should know that if you want the baby, it's not too late."

"It doesn't matter what I want," she says. "If things were different, if I were younger, if I were married, if I hadn't been so screwed up in childhood, if I'd saved up more money . . ."

"That's just the fear talking."

"Well, so what? The fear is real. Just give it up, Tony. I don't know how to do it. When other little girls were playing house and rocking baby dolls, you know what I was doing? I was holding séances and trying to talk to my dead mother. I didn't want to have a baby. I wanted to *be* the baby. *I* wanted to be the one being taken care of."

"Maybe you have to give yourself some credit for taking care of *yourself*," he says.

"But I didn't. Look at me! My life is a mess. I tripped and hurt my ankle so I left the man I love, all so I could stay here with Soapie, who *then* got seriously hurt because I wasn't home and watching out for her, because I was out with my *friends* trying to have some fun, which I did not deserve to have anyway—and then I find out that because I was so stupid, I got pregnant, *and* all my friends with kids all have regular, great lives, and I never even owned a house, or a new car even. I don't do things the right way, don't you get it? I need somebody competent to move into my brain and take over. I need a brain transplant at the very least."

"Whoa. If I could just interrupt for a minute, I'd like to say that you do not need a brain transplant. That guy left *you*. Maybe it's just me, but I myself would not have gone to California leaving behind the woman I love who couldn't come with me right then for whatever reason. The guy's a moron."

"I made him go. Also, he'd rented the truck already."

"*And* I don't think your job was ever to keep your grand-mother from falling down every single time," he says. "How you gonna do that, huh?"

"But I wasn't even here—and I stayed behind specifically so I could keep an eye on her, and then I wasn't here when she needed me the most. She could have bled to death here."

"So all this means in your head that you can't have a baby? Are you some kind of superhero that you always gotta save everybody all the damn time?" He shakes his head. "You think anybody on earth knows more about it than you do? People figure it out as they go along. Nobody's got some magic ability to know what they're gonna do."

"But I'm old. My eggs are probably like those dried-up eggs you'd buy from Ocean State Job Lot in the bargain bin."

"Lots of people are old when they have a baby. And sometimes they're too young, or too broke, or too busy, or too sick. But they do it, and sometimes it works out great."

"How old are you?" she says.

"I'm thirty-three."

"Well, see, there you go. I'm forty-four, and when my baby is fifteen years old, I'll be sixty."

"Yeah, you will."

"And Jonathan and I agreed we wouldn't have children."

"Yeah, that, too."

"And when Greta had her first baby, she wouldn't even let me go near the kid by myself, because everybody could see that I dropped things all the time. My best friend, and *she* even knows I don't know what I'm doing."

He puts his head in his hands and then takes off his cap and rubs his hair up and down, like he's trying to remove something that's stuck to it. When he stops, he just looks at her. "Greta is sorry about that. You don't drop things. You take care of things."

"You don't even know Greta."

"But I know you."

She starts to cry. "I can't do it, Tony. I have a bad track record. I do break things. Jonathan wouldn't even let me hold his teacups, and then he met Andres Schultz, and he let him take them out of the boxes first thing. Ten minutes in our apartment, and Andres is holding the teacups."

"Rosie, you are making me so tired. Let's get some dinner so you can shut up while you're filling your pie hole. I'm not trying to talk you into anything. Okay?"

"Okay, but you are ignoring the fact that babies have breakable parts, and then they grow up and they can get ruined so easily," she says. She gets up and follows him into the kitchen. "People can be mean just by accident, and then there are bullies who are mean on purpose, and you said it yourself—there's no way to protect people and keep them safe. And why do I want to do that to somebody else? I would just be so hopeful that this little kid could have a good life, and I couldn't stand it if anybody hurt it. And *everybody* would hurt it, Tony. You know that's true. Look at your own little boy, how he can't be with you, and you don't get to see him grow up every single day. How do you bear it, Tony, when something bad happens to him and you're not there to help him? How does *he* bear it? How do you let him have a broken heart about it?"

And then she does shut up because when she looks up, Tony Cavaletti is crying. Oh my God. She is so mean and hopeless that she's made Tony Cavaletti cry.

● ● ●

They barely talk after that, and once she gets in bed, she can't sleep at all. She keeps turning over in bed and then getting up and going to the window and looking out. She can hear Tony rattling around in his room, and she hovers outside his door, wondering if she should go in and apologize. But what if it's just the wind making all that noise, and she ends up waking him up? She is a terrible person, and life is too hard, and probably this clump of cells she's carrying, if it has any consciousness at all, is so grateful not to have to go any further into life with her as its caretaker.

"Look, I've gotta tell you something," Tony says the next morning. They're in the kitchen, and he's making coffee and not looking at her. "Maybe this isn't the time to bring this up, but I want you to know that Milo is fine. His heart isn't broken."

"Okay. I'm sorry I said that. I don't know anyth—"

"No," he says, and his voice sounds hoarse, like it's all clotted up in his throat. "You do know stuff, but you don't know this. His heart is not broken. It's not as bad as I've made it out to be," he says. He won't look right at her, and his voice sounds as though he's reading from a speech. "He is loved, which is a lot more than you can say for a lot of kids. His heart is not broken. In case you have become misled by things I have told you, which I should not have done."

"I'm sorry," she says. "I shouldn't have said that." Criminy, he's now said the kid's heart isn't broken three times in barely thirty seconds. She doesn't dare tell him how unconvincing he sounds. "So where are you working today?" she says. Neutral subject.

"And now I need to tell you something that I didn't want to get into, just so you know," he says, taking a deep breath. "The reason—the reason that my ex-wife won't take me back is that she's gay. *Okay?* That's why we're not together. Because she's in a committed relationship with another woman. So. Now you know."

"Oh," she says. Somehow this was the last thing she had expected to hear. "Oh, well, then." Then she says, "Oh, so it's *that* woman, then? The one I saw?"

He nods and pours himself a cup of coffee, not looking at Rosie. "Yes, that one. Which is cool. It's fine to be gay. Only it might have been a little better if maybe she knew that before she got married to *me,* you know what I mean?" He tries to pull off a smile, and fails. "Listen, do you want a cup of this, too?"

"No, thank you. I can't have anything by mouth this morning."

"Oh, of course you can't," he says. "Here I am going on about all this stuff, and we've got to get going."

"I'm taking myself."

"You can't take yourself. Didn't they tell you anything that day at the clinic?" She's looking at him blankly, so he taps his forehead and says quietly, "You can't drive home, remember?"

"Oh, yeah," she says. "I can't, can I?" She smacks her forehead.

"So you should get your things together, because I think if you're supposed to be there at nine, we should leave."

"Okay. Well . . . thank you. I feel bad you have to do this, though."

"Don't think anything. No problem."

When they get in his truck, he says, "It would be very nice of you, and I would consider it a personal favor on my behalf, if you would please not give me that it-sucks-to-be-you look, okay? That's what you're thinking, and I hate when people feel sorry for me. My wife and her partner are nice people, I like them, and I'm used to it by now." He turns the key, and the engine roars to life, like a warning to her to be quiet. Motors are in charge now.

"Okay," she says, studying him and trying to figure out how to change her facial expression. There are a million questions that come up in her head, and most of them would probably hurt his feelings, so she says, "You know, Tony, this is very nice of you, but you can drop me off, and I can call Greta to come and pick me up."

"Yeah, well, we'll see," he says. "You do know that everybody else there is gonna have a person with them, don't you?"

"No, really," she says. "This is my punishment. Going through it by myself."

"Rosie, you are a piece of work, do you know that? That's not how this works—there's no punishment."

It's gray and drizzly and he drives his red pickup truck along the wet roads with one hand resting on the top of the steering wheel. She's surprised how clean the truck is. There's a kid's booster seat jammed in the back behind the passenger seat, tilted on its side. He taps on the steering wheel and then turns on the radio and turns it off again with a big sigh.

"Both Annie and Dena are excellent mamas," he says after a while. "They're good people, and they take good care of Milo."

"Sure," she says. "That *is* good."

"And what you don't know is, I stayed around as long as I could," he says. "I thought I could stay with them forever. Hell, when they . . . when they came out, and when I saw it was real, I even let Dena move in with us, and I stayed in the house with them, all three of us, just so's I could be— well, so's I could *be* in their lives. We all lived together. For a whole year. Crazy, huh?"

"So . . . was your wife then—like, kinda with both of you?"

He looks startled. "What? No! Of course not. She was with Dena."

She can't seem to help herself. "Wow. You lived in the house with them, while they were lovers? What are you, a masochist or something? You just had to leave your bedroom and go sleep in the other bedroom by yourself?"

"Well, yeah. Pretty much." He puts on his turn signal and slows to a stop at a red light and doesn't look at her. "I didn't let myself think about it. I just had to be there for Milo," he says, and then clears his throat. "A lotta people don't know that you can just turn your brain off when you need to."

"You can't just stop your thoughts."

"I was Superman," he says quietly. She's surprised by how firm he sounds. "You just want something else bad enough that you forget about the bad parts. I wanted to be there for Milo when he woke up in the morning and when he went to bed at night, and I wanted to take him to the playground after he came home from preschool. I wanted to see the backs of those little knees going up the stairs at bedtime, and I wanted him to know my mom's pasta sauce, and not just on special occasions, but on weekdays. Annie can't make sauce for shit."

"So, who is this other woman? Dena? Did you know her before? Not that it's any of my business."

"Nah, it's okay." He sighs. "She and Brian were our best friends. We all used to do stuff together, go camping and to clubs. Couple friends, you know. And then one day—well, Annie and Dena, they just sit us down and tell me and Brian that it's all changed. They're in love. They want to be together."

"Jesus. What did Brian do?"

"He waited it out some, but then he split after a while.

Went to D.C. and met somebody else. He and Dena didn't have kids. That made it easier." He turns and looks at her. "You think I'm crazy, I know, or some kind of wimp. But I said to myself every friggin' day, 'Annie is now like a sister to me, Annie is now like a sister to me,' so that I wouldn't go all apeshit. Anybody can control their thoughts. You just have to remind yourself of what's important. What's really important. I wanted her to be happy. That's what loving somebody is. It's not just the easy parts."

She looks out the window, through the raindrops dotting the window, watches one little drop make its way all the way down to the bottom. She clears her throat and then says, "But, Jesus, Tony, I mean, why didn't you just take Milo and leave? Maybe you could have gotten custody."

"Now see, I'm sorry, but that's a very nonparent thing to say," he says. "If you had a kid, I bet you'd think different. How you wanna break the hearts of three people just to get what *you* want? She couldn't help how she felt. So I'm gonna take her kid away? For what? She's a good mom. She's a great mom. I wasn't gonna fight her."

She shakes her head. "You sound like you're running for sainthood."

"Well," he says. "I just had the right priorities. We all worked on raising him. I kept the cars running, we all cooked together, and we all got along, and we kept the kid happy together. I can't describe why it worked. They're nice people. I'm nice. We liked each other."

"Also, you're Superman," she says. "So what happened? Why aren't you still there, Clark Kent?"

"Well, the Kryptonite came," he says. "Dena—mind you, the one that's *not* Milo's mom—she takes me aside one day and she says to me that she and Annie are getting kinda serious. They want to see who they are as a family, but they can't very well do that if the ex-husband is there, being his understanding, fabulous self."

"She said that—your fabulous self?"

He pulls into the parking lot of the clinic. The lot is full, but she's relieved to see that no one is picketing out there today. She watches a young woman walk quickly to the door with her head down, trailed by an older woman, probably her mother.

He turns off the engine and looks down at his hands. "Yeah. She meant it, too. I was—I am—fabulous to her and to both of them. I get it. I *get* them, I swear to God. I'm not in any way trying to break them up. And so when she asked me to just leave the situation, to give them their shot, just for a while, I could see it. She cried, I cried, we all cried. They says to me they need this, to be on their own for a while. I'm the *ex-husband* and the father. When you look at it that way, it is crazy that I was there at all. You know? And they deserved their shot to be their own family, and not to have somebody looking on while they figure stuff out, being the know-it-all."

"But how can they ask you to leave? Wasn't it your house?"

"Nah. It was Annie's father's house. He left it to her."

"Why didn't you just get joint custody?"

"Well," he says. "Dena's a child expert, a psychology type, and *she* says that when children go through a big change, they can get confused. It was confusing for Milo that his mom and dad didn't sleep in the same room, she says, and he was always asking them questions, like why didn't Dena just leave? And so . . . well, she said I needed to give them time to . . . well, to be the main family, so that he'd see it that way."

They get out of the truck, and as they walk to the door of

the clinic, he says, "Think about it. Maybe she's right. And anyway, what good does it do for me to fight her? I need them to be good to my kid. She actually said my Y chromosome was getting in the way."

"Well, Milo has a Y chromosome, too, and I'll bet it misses having yours around for company."

"It's not forever, you know," he says. "When they're all settled . . ."

"You'd go back?" she says. "You're kidding."

His tone is sharper than it had been. "I don't know what's going to happen, Rosie. It's life. It's unpredictable. You of all people know that."

By then, they're at the door. He pulls open the glass door, and once they're inside, she squares her shoulders and goes over to check in at the little glass window in front of the desk, smiling so they will be nice to her. Yes, all her paperwork is done. Yes, she understands that they're running a little bit behind this morning. The receptionist motions to the roomful of women—and Tony was right, everybody seems to have a companion. People are perched on the chairs, either texting or reading magazines, or staring into space, or huddled together, talking in low voices. It's a tense place. Tony has already found two seats in the far corner and is sitting down with a magazine, and he motions her over. He could be her boyfriend, she realizes; everyone here must think that he's the unlucky, unhappy father. She almost feels compelled to make an announcement: *No, it's not him. He would never do this if it were his own baby.*

She goes and sits down next to him and whispers, "So are they letting you see him, at least?"

He leans toward her, so close she can smell his aftershave. "I can see him once a week for four hours at their house. That's the agreement."

"Once a week? You've gone from living there with him to seeing him once a week for four hours?" she says too loudly, and then puts her hand over her mouth when everyone looks up at her. "Why did you ever agree to that?" she whispers.

"It makes things more stable, Dena says."

"This isn't right. How do you stay away?"

The nurse comes to the door and calls the first names of four women—Ainsley, Tina, Mary, and Heather C.—and everyone tries not to watch as the four of them get up, hoist their bags over their shoulders, and are admitted into the other room.

Tony looks over at her and whispers, "I don't. Some days after work I drive to Fairfield when his day camp lets out, and I watch him in the playground with the other kids. Sometimes I have to hide because I see Annie or Dena go and pick him up. But on the days he goes to a babysitter after camp, I call him on my cell phone. He doesn't know that I'm just outside in the car, and that I can see him talking to me through the window of the babysitter's house."

"This is breaking my heart," she says.

"Well, I just thought you should know," Tony says. "This is why I'm Superman."

The nurse is back at the door. "Heather W., Brittany, Heather B., and . . . Rosie," she says. Rosie stands up, and her heart immediately starts beating faster. Her palms feel clammy.

"Just so you know," he says, "you could be Superman, too. Just don't make the mistake of giving up before the Kryptonite even gets here for you."

[fourteen]

The nurse leads her to another waiting area and tells her to get undressed and put on the gown, open in the front, and that someone will be in to get her soon.

"We're running a little bit behind," she says.

Twenty long minutes pass before time surrenders and officially starts to go backward.

Rosie sits there, in the airless, windowless changing room, which some sadist has painted a claustrophobic bubble-gum pink and stacked high with outdated *People* magazines.

After twenty-one minutes, her phone beeps. She reaches over and answers it, and it's Soapie, who says in a quavery voice, "Are you Rosie?"

"Soapie, wow! You're able to use the phone?"

"Are you Rosie?"

She stands up, feeling herself smiling all over. "Yes! I am Rosie. I'm so glad to hear your voice. How are you?"

But Soapie is all business. "When you come today, will you bring me my photograph album? The doctor here thinks I need to relearn my relatives so I can come home." Her voice sounds stilted, each word enunciated just so.

"You need to relearn relatives?" says Rosie. She almost laughs. There are no relatives to be relearned, she wants to say. Soapie doesn't have any people, just this one on the phone.

We're the only two people we're related to, she says. But

yes, she'll bring photos of George and Tony, and maybe even Helen Benson's peonies. And maybe the photo of Serena from the bottom desk drawer.

And as soon as she clicks the phone closed, she sits there for a moment. Then she stands up, puts on her clothes, folds up the little gown very neatly, places it on the chair, and walks out into the hallway. Nobody's there; they're all behind closed doors, and she can hear voices, encouraging, chatting, giving directions, and the hiss of machines, a buzzing noise, and she just walks quickly away, her arms down by her sides, walks down the hall, and then out through the waiting room.

She doesn't stop at the receptionist's desk, because no one is there anyway, and why wait to talk to somebody who just might say, "Oh, no, you can't go! You signed up for this, and now you really have to go through with it!" Would they say that? She can't be sure. She'll write them a nice note tomorrow, thanking them, and explain that she simply changed her mind.

The top of her head feels like maybe it's missing; the air seems to blow in through her and around her. She's almost giddy with relief.

"I changed my mind, I changed my mind," she says as she walks all the way outside, where it's no longer raining, and the hot summer air hitting her air-conditioned frozen face feels so good it should be illegal. She's realized that if she says that over and over, like a mantra, it keeps her from having to answer the big question, like how the hell is she supposed to live her life now?

She's about to call Greta when she sees Tony out of the corner of her eye. He unfolds himself from sitting on a bench near the side of the building and smiles tentatively, questioningly, as he comes over to her. "That was quick," he says.

"I thought you were gonna be gone," she says.

"Nah. I stayed."

God, what has she done? She feels so weird, clammy and breathless. She walks quickly over to his truck, and he unlocks the doors and helps her get in. He thinks she's had the procedure, she realizes, by the way he's holding her elbow and searching her face.

He goes around and gets in the driver's seat and looks at her.

"Please," she says. "Drive away fast." She just wants to get far enough away that the staff of the clinic won't see her and come and yell at her. She should have stopped at the desk, she should have told the nurse, she shouldn't have run out that way. They might be worried about her. She's being an idiot.

"How are you? Was it bad?" he says softly. But at least he is moving the truck, backing it up, then turning the wheel, exiting the parking lot. He has to stop for a car to pass.

"Hurry," she says. "Please hurry."

He shifts into first gear, and the truck lurches out into traffic, caught up in the flow of other cars. *Safe,* she thinks.

"I'm having the baby," she says, and then looks out the window of the truck.

When she looks back, she sees him smiling.

"I have to. We don't have enough people in our family," she says. "The doctor says Soapie needs some relatives. Also, can we stop at the hospital and say hello to her, do you think?"

"Yes," he says. "Yes, we can." After a moment, he shakes his head and pounds on the steering wheel. "God, life is so interesting, isn't it? Wowie zowie."

● ● ●

The next Monday, Soapie is taken by van to the rehab center, which is much nicer than the hospital. More laid-back and informal. It's easier for all of them to visit her there, and so most evenings Rosie, George, and Tony go have dinner with her in her room. Rosie brings a basket of food and some of Soapie's favorite treats—macaroons, chocolate-covered walnuts, lemon bars. George manages to charm the nurses into allowing him to set up a music player in there, and he plays tapes of Sinatra and Frankie Laine to cheer her up.

"It won't be long before we're up and dancing again, sweetheart," he tells her. It's been hard on poor George, having both loves of his life hospitalized. He sits, smiling through his moist, teddy bear eyes as Soapie sits propped up on pillows, wearing a pink peignoir and smiling at all of them placidly. It would be great, that smile, if it weren't so disturbing. It's as if her essence has dissipated along with her sodium, and they just have to wait for Soapie's natural saltiness to come back.

Rosie and Tony go down to the cafeteria so they can let Soapie and George be alone. Tony drums his fingers on the table and watches her wrestle open a box of chocolate chip cookies.

"So," he says, "have you told Jonathan yet?"

She grimaces.

"So that's a no," he says. "I think you might want to practice."

"Okay, let's practice," she says, and swallows her bite of cookie, which is divinely chewy and nutty all at once, with lots of gooey chocolate bits. "Jonathan," she says, "I have something I've been meaning to tell you."

"No. More casual-like," says Tony. "Don't sound like you're announcing a tragedy."

She sits up straighter. "It's hard, Tony."

"I know. That's why you gotta do it just right. You don't want to have a million convos on this with him. One and done!"

She watches as a woman on crutches sinks down at a table by the window, and then she turns back to Tony and makes a pretend phone with her thumb and little finger. "Okay, how's this? Hi, Jonathan! How's it going? Listen, are you busy? Because I thought I'd just give you a call with some news—Jonathan, I'm pregnant."

"That's good. I like the way you dive right in."

"Yes, I'm pregnant. No, *of course* you're the father!"

The woman with the crutches looks up, startled.

"Maybe you should be a little quieter, so you don't give the nice people here heart attacks," Tony says. "Also, he wouldn't say that."

"We don't know what he'll say. This is all new territory."

He leans forward. "So had you two ever talked about having children?"

"Only to decide we didn't want them. He's a great guy, but he just isn't father material, you know? He doesn't even like his own family."

"Okay. Whatever."

"He's artistic and creative. He lives in his own head, which is where he also stores a bunch of numbers and statistics, and that's why he can't really do the family thing like other people. It interrupts his head space. He's actually probably quite brilliant."

"Okay. Get to the next part, about how you're going to have the baby."

She activates the finger phone again. "Jonathan, I'm going to have the baby," she says, and falls silent.

"Now what do you think he's going to say?"

"Nothing," she says after a moment. "I think he just dropped dead."

Tony rubs his face with both hands. "Just do me one favor when you tell him, and don't do the girl thing. Do not ask his permission."

"The girl thing?" She laughs. "Did Annie do 'the girl thing' with you and ask your permission to start sleeping with her friend?"

"I wish. I'd have said no way."

"Well, then, what girls are you referring to, exactly?"

"I know how you girls are," he says. "I've watched you people for years. You ask permission when you don't need to, even when you don't care what the other person thinks, and you're going to do what you please anyhow."

"Tony, you do know that you kind of irritate the hell out of the other humans with all this know-it-all stuff, right? I think after we get my life squared away, we're going to have to work on your style."

"Fine. Beg him to let you keep the baby. What do I care?"

"*Fine.* You go plot the takeover of the world."

"It's not the world I'm interested in taking over. Just my one pitiful household."

"Hmm. I may have some insights for you on why that isn't working so well."

"By the way, you know you've got to start going to the doctor, right? You're officially a prenatal person now. The medicos might take an interest in that box of cookies you just devoured."

"They won't know."

"Oh, they'll know all right," he says. "God. Am I going to have to manage *everything* with you?"

• • •

She can't get a doctor's appointment for two more weeks.

"Even though I'm a high-risk pregnant woman?" she asks the receptionist, a woman named Pearl, whom she actually knows from her years of going to this OB-GYN practice, the same woman who had *finally* back in May okayed the renewal of the prescription for the diaphragm, even without an office visit. Talk about locking the barn door!

"Why are you high risk?"

"Because I'm way *old*."

Pearl laughs. "You're not all that old. As long as you're not having any problems, we can wait to see you in two weeks. Dr. Stinson can call in a prescription for prenatal vitamins."

"I'm already taking those."

"Well, then, you're ahead of the game. See you on the twenty-seventh."

Rosie hangs up. She'd expected just a little more fanfare from the medical establishment, thank you very much. Perhaps a modicum of concerned hand-wringing, even if it had to involve a bit of theater.

Then, a week later—the week that the Internet pregnancy sites tell her that her baby has ears and is now the size of a Brussels sprout—she's on the phone to Jonathan, and he's going on and on *again* about how the museum is having a "soft opening," whatever that is—it certainly sounds like something that would apply more to her situation than to his—and she just snaps and comes out with it: "Listen, you," she says. "I'm pregnant."

Funny how all the rehearsing and worrying just leads to this moment, like the vast universe flying from everywhere and coming to rest in one microscopic dot. She feels the words go out over the huge, intercontinental network of wires and lights, traveling so fast through the stratosphere of their relationship, landing on him, like a blanket of prickly, hot little stars. She waits while it hits him.

He doesn't seem to catch it at first; he's still talking over her, and then a beat or two later he says, "You're *what*? Did you say you're pregnant?"

Direct hit. And she hadn't even told him to sit down first.

"I did. Yes."

"Is this a joke?"

"This isn't my usual joke material, so no."

"How in the hell did you end up pregnant?"

"I believe there was sex involved. And you."

There's a long silence. She waits him out. Tap, tap, tap.

He sighs. "Hold on." She hears him put the phone down and close a door somewhere, and all the background noise—construction sounds—disappear. "How did you get pregnant?"

"You know how sex works, right?"

"Don't be sarcastic."

"Well, there was that time . . . you remember . . ."

"*That* time? That one time? You got pregnant *then*?"

"Well, it was unprotected sexual intercourse, so apparently yes."

"I thought you told me you were in menopause."

"I didn't *promise.*"

"You didn't *promise*? That's your excuse here?"

"Jonathan. I told you I didn't *know.* No one knows about menopause or . . . any of this stuff apparently. It's all mysterious. Anyway, if we're assigning blame here, you were the one who threw out the condom."

"Yeah, but you—oh, never mind. It's no good arguing about this. You got pregnant." He sighs again. "God, this is heavy."

"It is."

"So what are you going to do about it?" He says this as though the words are actually painful to utter.

"Well, Jonathan, I'm going to have a baby." She squeezes her eyes closed and waits.

He's quiet for a long, long time. She silently counts to thirty. Then, just as she's thinking he really might have dropped dead, he lets loose with a massive expulsion of sighing, and he says, "Have you thought this through? I mean, no offense, but you're kind of old for this, aren't you?"

"Believe it or not, I've thought of very little else for a long time now."

"Oh, yeah. Thanks for reminding me that I'm just an incidental part of this. Of course you've known for a long time. And shouldn't I technically have been part of this decision you've apparently made on your own?"

"It was something I needed to think about by myself first."

"So basically it doesn't matter what I say, is that what you're telling me? You're having the baby, and all I can do is just stand aside?"

"You can help me. It's your baby, too."

"Rosie, *why* are you doing this to us? Why now? I mean, what the fuck?"

"To tell you the truth, every time I think of doing anything else, I just can't. I actually signed up for an abortion, and I went to the appointment, and then everybody there was a teenager, and they put me in a room by myself to get ready for the thing, and then Soapie called wanting to look at pictures of her relatives, and all of a sudden I knew that I wasn't going to even *have* any relatives after she died, and so I put on my clothes and drove away."

"I don't think you should do this."

"I know. But I am."

"Jesus, God in heaven. How far along are you?"

"About twelve weeks."

"You—Rosie, I don't think you really want this. I know you. Sweetie, you're not and I'm not—parent material. We aren't."

"Jonathan, be very, very careful what you say to me right now, because all this is going to be stuff I remember for our whole lives. We're both going to remember it."

"I don't care if we remember it. I want us to remember it. Listen. Hear me out. You know us. We're the uncommitted do-nothingers of life. Sweetie, we're Gen Xers! Go ask Greta and Joe. Look at all our friends, as a matter of fact. We didn't want that life. On purpose we didn't want it. You can't just change your mind right now and decide to go after something that didn't even make sense twenty years ago, and now is probably certifiably insane."

"I can change my mind, and I did."

"Rosie." He's quiet for a long time. Then he says in a level voice, "When you went to that—that clinic place, did people try to talk you out of an abortion? Is that what this is about? Did you look at their evil pictures or something?"

"Nobody tried to talk me out of anything, Jonathan. That's not what this is about."

"Well, then, what the fuck *is* it about? Why are you ruining our lives?"

"I'm not ruining our lives. Jonathan, this happened to me, and I can't let it go. I just can't."

"Listen to me: You are ruining our lives. This is the definition of ruining your life. You can't change the rules for your life like this. Get it?"

She hangs up on him and, for good measure, throws the phone at the wall. All that happens is that the back comes off and the battery lands under the bed. She wishes the whole thing had splintered apart so it could never get calls again, and she considers hurling it one more time. But she's too tired, tireder than she's ever been in her whole life. It's like her arms and her legs simply have decided to shut down operations. She lies down on her bed, in the fetal position, staring into the darkness.

Fine. Fuck him. She'll do this alone. She can change the rules for her life anytime she wants.

● ● ●

For Greta, who knows how to organize things and run a household of four kids and a busy physician, mobilizing an unexpected pregnancy is a piece of cake. She brings over a box of early-pregnancy maternity clothes, a load of books (including a very premature one on baby names), a chocolate cake made with flax seeds and health-giving carob instead of chocolate, and a list of instructors for Lamaze classes. And then she sits across the kitchen table from Rosie and says a bunch of comforting things, ticking them off like they're in a list of The Etiquette of What You Should Say to Your Unexpectedly Expectant Friend.

"I know you can do this . . . you were always meant for motherhood . . . it's going to be *great*," she says, but none of it sounds at all convincing. Rosie has made the two of them a cup of pregnancy tea (also brought by Greta), and they sit drinking it together on the patio with the summer sun beating down on them.

"I know, I know," Rosie keeps saying without any conviction. "I can do it."

"Oh, hell. You've got to be scared out of your mind. So what does Jonathan think?"

Rosie doesn't answer just right away. She's busy tracing her forefinger along the water track left by her cup of tea. She allows two grains of sugar to join the trail, and she imagines they are grateful.

"Oh, God, he's being a dick about this, isn't he?" says Greta. "I was afraid that might happen."

Rosie is sick of the Jonathan-bashing their friends do, but she can't think of anything to say in his defense. They've been right about him all along. So she just sits quietly, feeling herself cut off like she's building a barrier of sandbags around her heart. She doesn't look up.

Greta's cell phone rings, and she answers it and then gets her Official Mother voice on, having to explain to Sandrine how to start the chili recipe—"No! Don't turn on the burner before you start chopping up the onions!"—and then she hollers about how Marco shouldn't ride his skateboard without his helmet, and at one point she actually gets so worked up that she has to stand up and pace with the phone while she shouts down a child who's determined to perform some other death-defying action. Perhaps it's Henry inviting zombies for dinner, or has he outgrown that phase? Rosie doesn't know.

She sits and waits for the storms of mobile mothering to subside, and then she gets up and goes inside, to the refrigerator, and pulls out some leftovers to heat up for dinner. She can't remember if Tony will be home or not. Maybe this is a day he goes to secretly stare at Milo while he talks to him on the cell phone just yards away.

Greta follows her. She finally closes her cell phone and looks at Rosie. "Does this just scare you out of your mind when you see what you're truly getting into?" she says. "Look at what I've turned into."

"You love it."

"Yeah, but it's scary. And you're going to be doing this same thing. I can't wait to hear these sentences coming out of your mouth."

"Not me. My child is going to behave itself and never turn on the burner before it chops the onions."

That's when Tony comes in the back door—he of the shaggy hair and the backward Red Sox cap and the hoodie sweatshirt with the sleeves ripped out of it. Greta's eyes widen, and Rosie lamely makes the introductions while Greta is telegraphing Rosie little sparky-eye messages the whole time. Tony, of course, has never looked more Tony-ish, like an exaggerated version of himself, brash and young, and talking in his put-on New Jersey accent, telling about traffic all the way back from Fairfield.

"So you're staying here?" Greta says to him coolly.

"Yes. He's kind of the caregiver for Soapie," says Rosie.

"Kind of? I am the king of caregivers for Soapie."

"He is. That's his official title: king of caregivers for Soapie."

"And what? So, you're the BFF?" he says to Greta, and she smiles. It's the condescending smile she'd give to one of Sandrine's friends, Rosie realizes.

"So what do you think of this baby bump, huh?" he says. "Quite a little surprise, huh?"

"Actually," she says, "I always knew that Rosie had this in her. She just liked to make us think she wasn't going to do it."

"Oh, yeah, she's gonna be amazing at this!" he says. "You can just tell. Look around the eyes—that's where you see it the most. Like—see? I look at you, and I see you've got a whole bunch of kids you love. Are you a teacher, or something?"

"No, I've just got four of my own," says Greta.

"Four!" he says.

"Yeah, I'm like a baby factory," she says and gets up and gives Rosie a hug. "I'm going to go save my family from imminent destruction. Be careful with yourself, okay? And if you get freaked out when you realize that you're going to need a father figure for this little kid, just remember that you have lots of friends who are out of their minds with happiness about this. We'll all help you."

She puts her hands on Rosie's little pooch of a belly and closes her eyes. "I'm your Auntie Greta, you little pumpkin," she says. "Don't worry about that father of yours. He's going to come around."

"You bet he is," says Tony. "Nobody can resist a baby."

[fifteen]

The next week, on a hot, humid day, she goes for her first prenatal visit, and she's so nervous in the morning that Tony asks her if maybe he should drive her there. "I don't have to be in Fairfield until school lets out," he says. "I could take you if you want."

She rolls her eyes at him. "I should drive *you* to Fairfield," she says. "Then I could have a talk with Annie and Dena. Get them to come to their senses."

But then, when she's sitting in the waiting room, she really does wish he were there to keep her amused. He'd no doubt have a little routine to do about the other fathers: the thin guy who keeps checking his cell phone while his pregnant wife glares at him, and the man who looks like a trucker and keeps falling asleep on his wife's shoulder.

Dr. Stinson takes the pregnancy news with the right amount of gravity.

"Well, this is certainly a surprise," she says. She's been Rosie's no-nonsense gynecologist for the past twenty-five years. Each year an annual visit, an occasional bladder infection necessitating antibiotics, one or two conversations about feminist politics, a discussion of how women don't really need to be married to be fulfilled, that sort of thing.

"To me, too," says Rosie, and Dr. Stinson laughs dryly.

"You might have done this just a tad earlier if you were going to do this," she says. "But, whatever. We have good outcomes anytime. Congratulations," she says flatly, push-ing the rolling stool away from the examining table.

She snaps off the rubber gloves and smiles. She's got crinkles now around her eyes, and her brown hair is shot through with gray.

Rosie sits up and moves down to the end of the table, covering herself with the gown. "But you do think I'm going to be okay, right?"

"Define 'okay.'" Dr. Stinson scoots over to the sink on her stool and washes her hands. "There's most likely going to be a baby in your life. Is that what you mean by okay?" She stands up and yanks paper towels out of the dispenser.

"Tell me the truth: am I too old?"

"Old, schmold. Actually you're not even the oldest woman I've delivered this year. Most women your age have problems becoming pregnant. But once the pregnancy is started, most of them do come to term. Especially when they've passed the nine-week mark, which you obviously have."

"So I can do this?"

"Your *body* can do this. I don't know about the rest of you. What kind of support are you getting? How does Jona-than feel about this?"

Rosie is surprised that Dr. Stinson remembers his name, although they have mentioned him every year—his pottery, then his disenchantment with the creative life, and then the teacups. She doesn't say anything.

"Oh, I see," says Dr. Stinson. "So you're going this alone?"

"Yeah." Rosie looks down and starts ripping at a little edge of the paper on the examining table.

"Well," Dr. Stinson says. "They used to call this a change-of-life baby. Lots of women have made this mistake. But then I guess it's only a mistake if you think of it that way. It might even be considered a blessing in some cases. Is that how you feel about it?"

Rosie laughs. "I'm still too scared to consider it a blessing."

"Let's listen to the heartbeat, shall we? Lie back down."

Dr. Stinson goes and gets a little wand thingie and smears her belly with gel, and then hooks everything up. The sound that comes out of the speaker is loud and whooshing. It sounds like the wind blowing intermittently through a tunnel.

"That's it," says Dr. Stinson. "You hear?" She smiles. "That's your baby."

Rosie suddenly can't speak.

"I know," says Dr. Stinson. "It gets me every time, too. It's amazing, isn't it?"

"Listen, can I tell you something? I wasn't sure at first, you know. I hope I didn't jinx it or anything, but I didn't know if I could handle it, and I made an appointment for— you know. And then I walked out."

Dr. Stinson looks at her mildly. "Well, sure," she says. "That happens, too."

"Do you think—I mean, do you think I somehow communicated to the baby that—well, that I didn't want him or her? Is that bad, do you think?"

Dr. Stinson looks at her very seriously over the top of her glasses. "You're allowed to have doubts, Rosie," she says. "Reasonable people do. The fetus doesn't know from thoughts. It just goes on nutrients. But if you're still not sure, then we have to move fast—"

"No, no. I'm sure now."

● ● ●

Driving home, Rosie suddenly has a hit of fresh energy and heads for a bookstore, where she buys ten books on pregnancy, nutrition, labor, delivery, breast-feeding—and just for good measure, one that promises to tell everything anyone might need to know about six-year-olds, for Tony.

Then she goes to the YMCA and signs herself up for a prenatal swim class and a prenatal yoga class; and then she drives way across town to an organic food market in New Haven, where she befriends the cashier, a young woman named Leila whom she overhears talking about her own pregnancy, which is just at the same point as Rosie's. Leila is also manless, and they get into a spirited talk about how good they're going to be at doing this all on their own.

Then she stops in at a maternity shop, looking for pants she can fit into, which normally would have been something that took a whole morning and would find her in the dressing room gnashing her teeth in distress, but which is now pure pleasure. Bring on the big pants! She tries on five pairs of loose, stretchy yoga pants, and then two body-glove-type shirts that show every pregnancy curve.

She takes stock in the three-way dressing room mirror, which gives her a bit of a shock. To be honest, she still looks more like somebody who has just let herself go to seed, rather than the radiant pregnant woman she had hoped to resemble. The only thing that's really dynamite is that she now has huge, outlying breasts that seem to be straining against all fabrics, as though nothing can hold them back. It's too bad really that Jonathan isn't around to appreciate how impressive her breasts have become. She thinks of them as two old aunties who thought they were going to spend the rest of their lives in a retirement bra and had given up on keeping themselves nice anymore, and now they find themselves looking like porn stars.

She buys them an industrial-sized maternity bra (the kind with gigantic cups and six hooks!) just because the elderly, friendly bra fitter assures her that she'll be much happier with her postnatal breasts if she gives them the support and love they need right now when they're working so hard getting ready.

"You want to nurture these hardworking girls and show them some extra love. They need a lot of coddling and support at such an important time in their lives," she says, and it's hard for Rosie to believe they're still just talking about the strap width on foundation garments.

● ● ●

When she gets home, Tony is in the kitchen, pacing around the room, talking on the phone. "So what kind of dog can jump higher than a building?" he says. He cups his hand over the phone. "Did you get to hear the heartbeat?" he whispers. "Everything okay?"

She nods, and he smiles and gives her a thumbs-up.

"Any dog!" he says into the phone. "Ha ha! Buildings can't jump." Then he's silent for a moment. "No, no . . . you see, the joke *sounds* like the building would be jumping, but—okay, okay, you get it. Talk to you later. I love you. Five million dinosaurs today. Yeah, extra because I like the way you laugh." He does a hundred smooches into the phone and then flips the phone shut and turns to Rosie.

"So! Tell me, tell me! Did you get a picture from the ultrasound?"

"No ultrasound, just the heartbeat." Rosie puts down her stack of pamphlets, brochures recommending breast-feeding, and the samples of prenatal vitamins—really an overwhelmingly frightening amount of baby propaganda, all plastered with photos of gurgling, fat infants and serene young mothers. She's already starting to fantasize about deformities and miscarriages.

"Damn. I hoped to see a picture. No ultrasound? What kind of doctor doesn't let a new mom see a picture of the baby? You'd think he'd want to see for himself that everything's coming along hunky-dory."

"It's a she." She gets a glass out of the cabinet and fills it with tap water.

"The baby?"

"No, the doctor."

"So why didn't she do the ultrasound, do you suppose? That's the moment—that's the moment when you *see* the baby all forming in there—you almost want some time-lapse photography, so you can see the little arms and legs forming and growing fingers and toes." He draws a baby in midair, and wiggles his fingers and toes to show all the growing that's going on. "Wouldn't that be something? I don't know why she didn't let you see it."

"I don't know. Maybe next visit. Maybe she doesn't even have an ultrasound machine."

"Huh. I think with Milo, our doctor let us see him at the first." And then he is off, reminiscing about all the prenatal visits—the first time he saw Milo's little feet and his rib cage—oh, the rib cage! And that little heart, thumping away there like a beacon—

She looks at him and thinks that he really should be doing so much more with his life. His hair, for instance, is really nice, and he maybe shouldn't hide it under that baseball cap all the time. And really, he should be thinking about moving along. Getting his own place, finding somebody to go out with.

"I don't mean to be rude or anything," she says, "but—"

He grins. "But you're going to be?"

"I just want to know why you're not dating anybody."

He bursts out laughing. "That's what you want to know? Look at me! Who's gonna want a date with a guy like this? A guy who's got a kid he's gotta go look after all the time."

"Well, that's another thing," she says. "I think you need to just call up Annie and Dena and say that you want Milo to come down here and visit, and that you're living with very nice people who want to meet him, and tell them they have to agree."

He shrugs, and suddenly she just loses her mind.

"How long are you going to stay stuck like this, going and spying on your kid like you're some kind of criminal? You talk about him all the time, and yet you don't do anything to help him. What the hell, Tony? You've got to go and reason with these women. You've got to try. These are days you're going to wish you had back."

"It won't work," he says.

"Tony," she says, "you've got to *make* it work. I can't stand it anymore! I didn't have a father, Milo doesn't have a father, and this baby of mine isn't going to have a fa—"

"Milo has a father!" he says, and his voice is fiercer than she's ever heard from him. "He has me!"

"Yeah, four hours a week. What does that tell him?"

"Stop it, Rosie! Milo has me." His eyes are suddenly furious. "I'm sick of the way you act as though I'm doing the wrong thing. I love him, and he knows it."

"Then you should be there!" she says. "You shouldn't just be doing domestic espionage. Why do you let them do this to you?"

"Well, it's not what I *want*, but—" He stops talking and

narrows his eyes. "Oh, I get it. This isn't about me at all, is it? This is about Jonathan, isn't it?"

"No, this is all you," she says. "What are you teaching this kid? That your rights don't matter? That his wishes don't matter?"

"Stop it," he says in a voice so low it's almost a growl. "This conversation is over." He walks out of the kitchen and slams the front door.

She stands there with her hands at her sides, balling up her fists. Now she's done it. What, is she going to become some pain-in-the-ass parenting expert now because she's had her first prenatal visit? And really, what does she know about Tony Cavaletti's little kid up there with two mommies? Maybe his life is just peachy keen without a dad.

And maybe her baby's life will be perfect without Jonathan, too. Who needs these fathers anyway, with their cowardly fears of commitments, their inability to stand up for themselves or anybody else? Superman! Ha!

She'll do this without Jonathan and his pinched-off, tiny, ice-encrusted soul. At least her child will have *her*, somebody who loves it and wants it and is thrilled to be getting this second chance at a real life. This baby will be so much better off than Rosie was. She'll make sure it's better.

[sixteen]

Her students can't believe their eyes when they see her at the first class of the new fall semester. She's sixteen weeks pregnant, and you would think, she tells Greta later, that the Pillsbury Doughboy himself showed up to teach the class, by the way they react to her size. She can feel herself actually doubling in volume as she stands there before them, explaining that no, no, she's fine; she's just *pregnant*. Goldie and Mara smile knowingly, worriedly—and then everybody wants to hear the story of the wedding cancellation, which they had all known about, as their invitations had been rescinded. But why didn't she go to California? Start new life? Did Yonatan realize stay right here? Did teacups go alone?

She sighs. No English will be taught this day, that's for sure. The administrator comes in for a moment for a first-day welcome, with his officious little clipboard and his bow tie, but he soon realizes they are all consumed with Woman Talk, and so he backs out of the room and closes the door, so that at least the middle school won't be contaminated by such goings-on.

She keeps trying to move the class to a lesson about subject/predicate agreement, but they would rather know what she's eating, how her nausea is, the due date, possible baby names, and does she know the sex. They surround her, petting her, hugging her. Goldie dabs at her eyes when she hears that Jonathan has gone away and that he is not thrilled about the baby. Rosie didn't mean to tell that part, but of course they weaseled it out of her.

The class settles into a respectful, tragic silence.

"So," she says, taking a deep breath. "For next time, I would like you all to write about a time in your life when something happened that at first seemed bad, but then turned out to be such a good thing. Because that is what this is for me."

Nobody writes the assignment down. They just look at her like maybe they know what she's in for.

"This is good thing?" Leo asks.

"It *is* a good thing," she says. "Go, go, write it."

● ● ●

Then the next day she has to go have amniocentesis, the thing she's been dreading ever since she first found out she was pregnant. She's fine, there's no suspected problem with the fetus, it's just that she's way freaking old, and Dr. Stinson has been quite firm that she has to go through with this. "You have to know if there's anything you're up against," she said, and so Rosie agreed to do it, even though it's been her successful lifelong policy not to voluntarily have needles remove stuff from her belly.

There is no day quite as fraught as this one, she thinks. She's read everything in the chat rooms, she's polled her friends, and hardly anybody thinks it's as bad an idea as she thinks it is. Seriously? A needle—next to the *baby*? What if they accidentally stab it and kill it? Rosie is of the opinion that this baby would prefer to live and isn't going to think highly of a sharp intruder coming in to steal some of its valuable amniotic fluid. She just hopes it doesn't blame her.

Greta says the people wielding the needles know what they're doing. Not that she ever had one. She was smart and had all her babies before she turned thirty-five.

Tony, the self-appointed expert on obstetrical procedures and chief of medical transportation, goes with her. He tells her he has to, that he's a sucker for fetal heartbeats, for ultrasounds, and he can stand up to amnio as well. They've been careful around each other since their argument. She hasn't brought up Milo, and she's stopped talking to him about his domestic espionage surveillance tactics. Most evenings they hang out with Soapie and George in the rehab center, and very slowly, they can see that Soapie is getting better. She's actually started complaining about things again, instead of being so overly pleasant. That, they've decided, is a good thing.

"You know what I hate? All these medical procedures I have to do," Rosie says in the car on the way to the hospital clinic. "Why does having a baby give people the right to stick you with needles all the time?" A week ago, she had to go get a four-hour glucose tolerance test. And before that, there were endless other blood tests. It's awful for a person who mostly doesn't even like to acknowledge that she has bodily fluids.

They're stopped at a red light and she sighs and looks out the window at the line of cars waiting through the Dunkin' Donuts drive-through, and then at two women walking down the street, and she is suddenly, horribly certain that something is going to be wrong with this baby and that she was a fool to think it could be otherwise. She is trying to trick nature somehow, having this kid when she is too old and too broke and too messed up. They are going to poke it with a needle, and then they are going to find out some terrible disease it has, something that will consign it to a life of unspeakable horror and pain. And then she will have to sit there and say quietly, "I still want the baby. It's my baby," while they look at her pityingly.

She has always been the wrong sort of person—unmotherable, ungrateful for even the smallest morsels of human feeling thrown her way, always needing more, more, more. She has been greedy for love, and now she has done the greediest thing of all, asked for another human being to come to earth, one who will *have* to love her, even though it might live a wretched existence, twisted, painful, unable to walk or talk or grow brain cells. She takes in a ragged breath.

"I see what you're doing over there," Tony says. "You there, being so quiet."

"But what if the baby is all messed up?"

"The baby's not messed up. Don't even worry about that."

"But once you ask the question, 'Is the baby messed up?' then you have to wait for the answer. Did you think of that?"

"It's gonna be fine. We'll wait. It's fine."

"Tony," she says, "for God's sake, will you call Annie and tell her that Milo has to come and stay with you?"

"Why is it," he says calmly, "that when you're anxious about your own stuff, you always go back to worrying about my life?"

"Your life is so . . . fixable," she says.

"No. *Your* life is fixable," he says.

●　●　●

When they get there, Tony doesn't even ask if he can come in with her. After the nurse calls her name, he just stands up and walks down the hall with her, and then throughout the procedure he stands by her head and holds on to her hand.

Funny that no one asks who he is, or why he's there. After a while, two doctors come in, and one of them smears gel on her belly and then hooks her up to the ultrasound machine, and on the screen there's a little blurry picture of a lima bean, with parts that the doctors and the nurse and Tony point out to her, as if anyone could recognize that this is the head, these are the little vertebrae, and *this* now is the heart, this beating thing.

"Look at the ribs, Mom, and here's the heart," says the doctor, and she tries. She really tries. This is another thing that might be wrong with her, that she can't even recognize her own baby's body parts. Just the thing that's round and in profile—that's surely the head, isn't it? She doesn't want to ask, in case they think she's already unfit.

And then she really sees it: the beating thing, giving off its fast little pulses.

"Oh!" she says, and the room sways a little bit, and Tony squeezes her hand and leans down next to her face and smiles with her at the screen. It's more intimate than sex, his being there this way. He wipes at his eyes with his free hand and then laughs in embarrassment when she sees him.

"I'm just like this," he says. "Don't mind me."

But she is crying, too.

The second doctor, the one who wields the needle, peers at the ultrasound, and the first doctor puts a little mark on Rosie's stomach, right near her belly button, and then the other guy sticks the needle in and draws out some fluid. Rosie closes her eyes, but it doesn't hurt, not really. Just a pinprick, and a little bit of a cramping sensation. They told her that might happen.

And then it's over. After a few minutes, they unhook her and wipe all the gel off her belly, and Tony lets go of her hand.

"Now, Dad," says the doctor, "make sure she rests for the rest of the day, and call us if there are any complications. Everything looks good from here. And we'll have the results in about a week or so."

Rosie says, startled, "Oh, he's not the dad! Goodness. He's just a friend."

Tony says quietly, "I'll make sure she rests." He puts his arm around her shoulders while they walk out to the parking lot. "Did you see how cute that little baby is?"

"It reminded me of a bean," she says.

"Little Beanie," he says. "With little sprouts for arms and legs. And a classic, classic profile."

● ● ●

It's a terrible, no good, very bad night. She keeps feeling as though the end of the world has happened, and that she has to stay awake to keep the zombies from reaching the house or something. Also she has a bit of spotting, which sends her into a full-blown panic, and she's got slight cramps, both of which she was told might happen and that she was not to worry. Just keep calm and carry on. Call if it goes on too long. Of course, no one knows what "too long" means. Fifteen minutes? Fifteen days?

So she's up and walking at 2:20 in the morning, and that's when Tony comes out of his room and says to her, "Oh my God. What can we do to help you get some sleep?"

"I'm bleeding."

"Just spotting?" he says. "Or more?"

He knows the word *spotting*. She can't believe that.

"Spotting," she says.

"They said this might happen. I don't think you're losing the baby. That little bean was in there pretty good if you ask me."

"But how do we *know*?" she says. "I've never been here before. I don't know what's supposed to be happening. And I went on the Internet, and it said—"

"No, no, no. No Internet," he says. "That's the sure-fire way to get yourself all full of agita. I'll stay with you. Let me just get my pillow and blanket and I'll come in with you."

She thinks that probably isn't a good idea, but her cup of chamomile tea hasn't helped, and neither has tossing and turning in bed. So she goes back to bed and pulls the covers up around her, and he comes in and puts his pillow and blanket on the floor next to her bed.

"That can't be very comfortable," she says.

"It's fine."

"If you want, you could get up here. I could scooch over, and there'd be room."

"No," he says. "I'm fine."

But then the next night, the spotting is still going on, and so he sleeps there again. And then, without even asking, he comes the next night, bringing with him a blow-up mattress that he places next to her bed. When on the fourth night, she nearly trips over it when she gets up to pee, he moves it to the foot of the bed. But then he hits his head on the legs of the desk, and besides that, it's pathetic to have a grown man sleeping on the floor, so the next night, she says he should sleep on the bed with her.

And then—well, the next week is the hardest week of all, waiting for the results to come, and so every night they fall asleep on her bed, lying side by side, and when she wakes up in the middle of the night, she's startled to see that he's still there. And then, as she's turning over trying to get comfortable, she feels something fluttering inside her, and so of course she wakes him up.

"Tony, Tony. Something's happening. Either there's a colony of butterflies flicking me, or Beanie moved," she says.

He moves up close to her. She thinks she is going to stop breathing altogether when he puts his soft, sleep-warmed hands on her bare skin, closing his eyes while he waits.

He laughs softly. "Ah, now I remember about babies on the inside," he says. "They come to a complete halt when they think you're waiting for them."

"Well," she says after a while. "I guess it's gone back to sleep. And so should we."

She gets up and goes to the bathroom, and when she comes back, he's returned to his own room. She stands there for a moment, looking around the room, which suddenly feels so empty, and then she climbs back into bed.

The doctor's office calls the next day, and the woman on the phone says she has good news. The baby has no chromosomal abnormalities.

Rosie feels herself come back to life in a way she didn't even know was possible.

"Would you like to know the sex?" the nurse asks.

"Yes," she says, barely able to breathe.

"You're having a girl."

A daughter! She has to sit down then on the floor with her head on her knees. This clump of cells has decided which gender it wants to be. And it picked such a good one.

She's going to name her Serena, she thinks. Serena the Bean.

seventeen

The next Tuesday afternoon, two months after Soapie had her fall and when Rosie is nearly eighteen weeks pregnant, Soapie gets sprung by the rehab center. It's not that she's healed or anything. Her sodium levels are very nearly normal, and she's been through lots of occupational and physical therapy, but it's undeniable that she's lost a lot of ground, the doctor says. This is just as good as it's going to get.

"You don't break your hip at this age and go live in a rehab place and expect to bounce back to where you were before," he tells Rosie. "It's possible she's having some more small strokes, or that the sodium problem left its mark. She *is* eighty-eight." There will be good days and bad days, and the bad days will soon outnumber the good by far. He gives Rosie the laundry list of disabilities plaguing her: macular degeneration, some evidence of liver damage. Osteoporosis certainly, arthritis. Weak heart. A bit of emphysema. Dementia, worse at some times than others.

"In other words, she's giving out," says Rosie, and he says, "Exactly. It's what happens to the human organism, unfortunately."

When she goes to bring Soapie back home, she finds her in the lobby, dressed in her lavender workout suit, sitting primly on a wingback chair with suitcases stacked around her. This is where she's insisted on waiting, docile and smooth, like anybody's darling grandmother, her hands folded in her lap. She's wearing lipstick and rouge, and even her drawn-on eyebrows seem to be in the right spots, which has not always been the case. Her white hair is swept up the way she has worn it all her life, except for this recent period when she's been in the hospital, when it spread out across the pillow in a thin, wild, defiant tangle, like the wind had been whipping across her bed. Rosie would work on it some days, urging a comb through its knots and brambles while she sprayed it with a detangling solution.

Rosie smiles at her. "You look—you look kind of wonderful," she says. "Your hair—"

Soapie smiles, almost wincing. "They sent over a beautician," she says. "You're a very nice lady, but you're no hairdresser. Here, let's get my things and get out of this place. I can't take it here one more second."

"Do we have some signing-out stuff to do first?"

"No. Let's just go."

But then a nurse in blue scrubs is hurrying over, waving some papers, and sure enough, there's a little bit more to it than that. Soapie purses her lips, stares off at an elderly couple who are making their way to the French doors out to a courtyard.

The nurse, whose name tag reads *Lorraine,* hands Rosie a whole pile of papers to sign, and Rosie flips through them, signing and taking back responsibility for her grandmother once more, saying she understands about the medications, follow-up visits to the physician, et cetera.

"I guess you saw I have a walker now," says Soapie. "A contraption."

Of course Rosie has been watching Soapie use the walker for weeks now.

"Yes, Mrs. Baldwin-Kelley, and we want you to use it," Lorraine says loudly and slowly, as if she's talking to a kindergartener. "Much, much safer that way."

"Well, we'll see," says Soapie. "At home, where there's carpet, I expect I won't."

"Well, we think it's always a good idea," says the nurse.

"Well, *I* hate the goddamned thing."

Rosie brings the car around to the little turnout by the glass entry doors and loads the suitcases into the trunk, while Lorraine helps Soapie inch her way over to the car. The walker is a gleaming red thing, the kind with a seat. Soapie pushes it in front of her almost defiantly as if she's planning to fling it off away into traffic, but Rosie notices that she does seem to lean on it.

"I think I got a little crazier in there, being around crazy people," Soapie says, once they've gotten her settled and buckled into the front seat, with the walker folded and put in the back. Rosie starts the car and edges it through the turnaround, out past the welcome sign with its cheerful little daisies.

"You know, that can happen, don't you?" Soapie says. "Catching crazy. Take me to Burger King. I've been craving a Whopper for five months. Is that how long I've been in there?"

"No, not nearly. Does it seem that long?"

"I don't know time anymore. Let's just go eat burgers and be happy I got out before I went completely bonkers."

So Rosie drives to Burger King, and Soapie eats her hamburger in the car in the parking lot under a shady tree, insisting that they share the cardboard container of fries.

"You're putting on weight," Soapie says.

"Am I?" She feels herself flush a little, but then Soapie doesn't seem interested in pursuing that. Instead she crumples up the wrapper of her hamburger and wipes her chin with it. She pushes away the napkin that Rosie scrambles to offer, and then she says, "This is as good a time as any to have the talk I've been wanting to have with you. It's good we're not at the house when we do it."

"Why?"

"Because of those men we seem to have there. Why do we have men now, do you suppose? We didn't always have men."

"I don't know. I thought we kind of liked them."

"What's the young one's name again?"

"Tony."

"And do you remember just how we got him?"

"Ah, I believe you hired him to come pour your gin and tonics."

"Oh, right." Soapie swallows, looks out the window, and sighs. "Okay, listen to me good because I made a paper for you. Of my wishes."

"You made a paper of wishes?" Somehow this sounds so nice, like something a child might create, and yet Rosie knows it's not going to be good.

"Yes. Here it is." With difficulty Soapie reaches down in the pocket of her sweatshirt and pulls out a lined piece of paper, folded into eighths.

"Did you want me to read it?"

"No. I'll read it to you. We're going to discuss."

Rosie can see that the first word on the paper, written in a spidery script, is *Death*.

"First order of things: I am dying now, Rosie," Soapie says.

This conversation again? Rosie stares out the windshield at the oil change place just on the other side of the parking lot. A man is getting out of his car, and the attendant is rushing over with a clipboard. Just beyond that, there's a Walgreen's, and the sign with its big red letters is advertising Tylenol for sale, and bottled water. All the parked cars in that lot are silver. What were the chances of that?

She drags her eyes back to Soapie's face. There's a buzzing

sound from somewhere. Soapie is saying, "So in six months I want to go into one of those places, a home."

"What are you talking about? You just got out of one, and you hated it."

"You have to listen. In six months, I want to go back in there. And in the mean—"

"But this isn't what you ever said you wanted. Not one time."

"Will you just listen to me? This is a new plan. I'm doing medium fine *now,* but it's not going to last, and I know it. I'm not going to be able to take care of myself forever, and I know that now. I saw myself dead in there, you know."

"You saw yourself . . . dead?"

"I couldn't tell what was now and what was then, and I didn't know people anymore, and I was just . . . locked away somewhere in my head. That's dead, if you ask me."

"Oh, Soapie."

"Maybe I'm like . . . George's . . . wife."

"Louise? No, she has Alzheimer's. You don't have Alzheimer's. You just forget things sometimes." Rosie reaches over and strokes her grandmother's arm.

"But I wouldn't know if I did, now would I?" She pulls her arm away and waits, looks at Rosie steadily, head-on. "I wouldn't know when the time came. Did George tell you that he came, and I thought he was Eddie, my husband? Eddie, right?"

"Yeah, well, that was when your sodium was too low—"

"George is nothing like Eddie. And I sat right there and called him Eddie for one whole day, and I actually *thought* he was Eddie. Dead Eddie! And the point is—what was the point? You've made me lose it again. Just be quiet and let me finish." She stares out the window, takes a listless sip of her Coke. Rosie can see her mouth muscles twitching;

a rivulet of Coke runs down her chin. There are tiny black hairs around Soapie's mouth, hairs she's never noticed before. "So. Anyway. I now see the wis—the wis, the *good,* in going where they look after you. I don't want to be alone with the stove. I think I've got only a little while left. End of the year is what I'm thinking. In January I want to go to a nursing home."

"But, Soapie, honey, I'm going to stay with you. You don't have to be alone. Let's get you home and settled in, and—"

Soapie frowns. "No, damn it. Why won't you let me tell you the best part?"

"There's a best part to this?"

Soapie waits, tapping her hands against her polyester pants, closing her eyes while she summons the words up from the depths. "You and I—we have the fall. Before I go to the home." She turns to Rosie, and her eyes are almost wet with need, with begging. "So let's go to Paris, just you and me. We'll sell the house and then go and live in Paris until it's time for me to come back and go into the home. We'll travel all over France and have ourselves a time! George and I went there on our honeymoon, you know."

Rosie feels like she did the day she went on the Tilt-A-Whirl five times in a row. She would like to quietly get out of the car and maybe throw up politely on the sidewalk. "George? You mean Eddie?"

Soapie makes a fist and pounds on her hand. "Eddie. Of course, Eddie! Eddie, Eddie, Eddie. Why can't I keep it straight?" She looks at Rosie. "I can show you so many places. You can write in the cafés, and I can just *be there* with you. I can show you things."

"Oh, Soapie—"

"We could do it. It could be our trip. Our last trip."

"No, no, don't. Please. We can't. We could never manage

it, with your broken hip and . . . trying to get around . . . oh my God, the walker and stairs and maps . . . the trains . . . Jesus."

"And I could die there, and then I wouldn't *have* to go into a nursing home. I bet Paris is a good place to die."

"No. No, we can't do that."

Soapie's eyes are glowing now. "Stop saying no! Yes! We *can* go there! You're always selling yourself short. We can make a big change if we want to! It's the thing I've always tried to get you to see, and you never want to take any chances. Let's do this! Our final thing. It could make the difference for us, for our whole lives." She's talking louder now, and she starts beating one hand against the other, in a karate chop, over and over.

"Soapie, no, no, listen to me. I'm pregnant. I'm having a baby in five months. In February."

There's such a long silence that at first Rosie isn't sure for a while that Soapie understands. But then she sees the precise moment that the news lands. Soapie's face undergoes a range of expressions, everything from shock to anger to surprise, landing somewhere near defeat before she looks down at the crumpled-up hamburger paper in her lap. "This can't be what you want."

"It is, yes."

"You're going to tie yourself into a thousand knots, doing this, you know."

"I—"

"You're way old for this nonsense, don't you think?"

"I am. But I'm doing it." She strokes the baby, making sure it's real. "I'm the age you were when I was born. And you did it. You raised me."

"Why are you doing this? What are you trying to prove? You'll hate it, and then it'll be too late."

"It'll be different for me," she says calmly. "This will be *my* child." She tries to say it kindly; she means it's not some burden, some grandchild who's an orphan, but Soapie turns and looks at her with such a flash of anger that everything in the car wobbles for a moment.

"How dare you say that to me? How dare you? Listen— no. Just take me home, okay?"

"What? I meant that—"

"No. I know what you meant."

"I meant that because I'm choosing—"

"Take me home."

"Okay. Okay. I'll take you home."

Rosie starts the car. She's humming under her breath. She's thinking that she withstood the abortion room, she withstood Jonathan's fury, and she can withstand Soapie's continued disappointment in her, too.

"No. First throw away this bag. There's no sense in keeping junk like this around. I never let my car get all cluttered up the way you do."

"I know. Here, give it to me." She takes the bag and steps out of the car and walks down the parking lot to the trash can. Her heart is pounding, so she makes herself stop and take in a good, deep breath.

When she gets back to the car, her grandmother is shrunken down, leaning against the door with one hand resting against her head, her eyes closed.

[eighteen]

Leila, the pregnant cashier at the health food store, is Rosie's new BFF. She confides in Rosie that no one thinks she should be having a baby either, especially since her boyfriend left her. So now they high-five each other and call each other "BFF" whenever Rosie comes in for her weekly supply of organic kale and chia seeds and all the rest of the stuff the Internet says she should be eating. (These are definitely the kinds of foods you'd like to see your baby composed of. Your better humans all have internal organs composed of kale these days.)

She and Leila are getting so friendly that soon Rosie is sure they're going to do a belly bump right there in the store. And it's so great to have someone to compare symptoms with. Even though Leila is age-appropriate for pregnancy and will not be receiving her AARP card in the next few years, she still feels just as alone and scared as Rosie does most days.

Leila has a boyfriend who's nothing but trouble, to hear her tell it.

"Big mistake, that guy," she says. "But he's gone for good. I think. For a while it was on and off, off and on, but now I think he's pretty much decided to split. Which is fine. I said to him, dude, either help me or get out of my way. And I think he picked *out of my way*."

Rosie can't for the life of her think why talking about all

this is fun, but it is. She tells Leila about Jonathan and how freaked out he got when he found out. Fifteen years together, and one condom fail, and now he's decided he's not going to play daddy.

"Men!" says Leila. "How nice for them, that they get to rethink the whole thing, huh?"

Then they get to listing their various ailments and aches and pains since they saw each other last. Laughing, Leila tells her that the manager is about to move her off the cash registers and to the back room, where she can supervise the high school employees and serve as their model of what not to do.

"You've heard how if you can't be a good example, you just have to be a cautionary tale? Well, that's me," she says with her eyes shining. "The managers want me to whine about pregnancy all the time, how hard it is, how much my back hurts. Isn't that brilliant?"

It isn't until Rosie's back in her car with the groceries that it hits her. Leila and Tony would make such a great couple. She's so cute and young, and he's so enamored of pregnancy—they'd be delightful together.

She thinks she'll go right home and announce that she's met his future wife—except then, luckily, she realizes in time that would never work with him. Even as lonely as he is, he would just balk. No, she'll have to think of a much more subtle way to get the two of them to meet. By accident.

As she's falling asleep that night, she hears him get up and come out of his room and go down the hall into the bathroom. The door closes with a soft click, and then opens again after a minute or so, and he walks past her room again. She holds her breath and stares at the ceiling. It is possible that she might be missing those nights when he slept next to her. His bare warm hands on her belly, waiting for the baby to move. How had she managed not to turn to him and start madly kissing him?

She squeezes her eyes closed. She has to get him a girl-friend. For everybody's sake.

● ● ●

A week after Soapie comes home, she and Rosie are walking slowly down the path outside by the rosebushes, Soapie inching along with her walker and frowning at how hard it all is, and Rosie is talking about the baby and how pleased she is. And then she swallows and says, "Soapie, I am really so sorry that it didn't work out about us going to Paris. I know that's something you really wanted, and I would have loved to be able to do that with you. If only our timing had been a little better, you know?"

Soapie looks up at her in complete bafflement. After a while she says, "Who's going to Paris? What are you talking about?"

It hits her like a body slam, how much has gone and in such a short time. She has to turn away.

There's no mistaking the difference in Soapie now. They're not the amusing little Gang of Four anymore, dancing and singing and cheating at Scrabble. George's eyes look shiny all the time, like he's holding all his tears right there behind them. He has that smiling-through-adversity deal down perfectly, which makes him seem almost patho-logically sunny and optimistic, like the singing orphans in *Oliver Twist*. He flits back and forth in his little double life, as Tony calls it, looking like a vaudeville performer who's just about to grab a baton and break into a song-and-dance routine.

"George, my man George, now he's living the dream! Two ladies in his life, and they both love him to death!" That's what Tony says.

"And neither one has an ounce of her right mind left," says George, and it makes them all laugh, even Soapie. They do this riff nearly every day now because they all enjoy it so much.

In an odd way, life seems even better than before, the way a warm, sunny day in winter might catch you by surprise in between snowstorms.

Rosie and Tony cook each night now, and the four of them eat together just as they used to do, except now Soapie is easygoing and quiet, and the rest of them hover around her, cutting up her food, patting her hand, stopping to give her kisses. There is, Rosie thinks, a kind of surprising sweetness in the house that she never felt before, when she can be still enough to let it in. It's the sweetness that comes when something can't be permanent; it comes attached to an ache.

One day, eating at a Chinese restaurant, she gets a fortune that says: "Be happy in the middle because the end will crack you open."

Greta, who is sitting across from her, says that's the best description of pregnancy and childbirth she's ever heard.

But Rosie knows that the fortune is really about Soapie, and that where they are now, *this* is the middle, and she is responsible for noting all the possible happiness while she's passing through here. There are worse things.

At night, after dinner, they all still try to play Scrabble, but as she says to Tony, it's Scrabble for Idiots, perhaps bordering on Scrabble for Those in a Vegetative State. No-body would dare come up with a hard word. They used to be so hilariously competitive, mostly because Soapie said they had to be, but now they only form baby words and they happily give Soapie loads of extra time when it's her turn. Usually, that's when Rosie goes and does the dishes, and Tony brings in another beer for him and George. People lie back on cushions, change the record from Mel Tormé to Michael Bublé. The plants get watered. E-mails are answered.

Then Soapie says, "Damn it, you people, you know I need that book," and someone goes and gets the large-print dictionary that is sitting on the floor not two feet away, just where it was last night when Soapie needed it.

And then after another long time goes by, she yells, "Okay! I got it! Zak. Huge points for that."

"But what is a zak?" says Rosie.

"Oh, hell, Rosie. It's one of those big hairy animals," says Soapie.

"That's a—never mind." She sees Tony and George frowning at her and shuts up.

"They're in the north," says Soapie. "The big north maybe. You've probably never seen one."

"Great word!" says George, and Tony's eyes crinkle up as he pats George on the back. They both start humming "The Way You Look Tonight," which was playing an hour ago on the stereo, both of them probably not even realizing they're doing it. And then George breaks into song as he leans down and studies his tiles for his next turn.

"Someday . . . when I'm awfully low . . . la la la la *la*."

Rosie looks up at the table, and for a moment she sees the scene before her go all blurry, as if it were an Impressionist painting. She's like the cameraman on one of those movie cranes, looking down and backing up at the same time. There is the brightly lit living room with its rows of bookshelves and its low-slung modern birch-colored furniture, the butter-colored walls, the dramatic color of the red geraniums in blue pots near the French doors. The dark of the night just beyond, and the reflections of all of them right there, bending over their tiles, frowning or smiling. Oh, these faces. All this feeling.

We're all such pitiful wretches, she thinks: Tony battered from his trips to Fairfield, where he still goes a few times a week to stealthily watch Milo talk to him on the phone; Soapie, fading away so fast, like some big cosmic eraser is following her around, disappearing her life; and George, dear, placid, adorable George, who just keeps plodding along with the wet, sad smiles behind his eyes.

How is it ever going to be bearable? And what is she doing, bringing a baby into this world? Are these people glad they were born? Is there anyone who says, "No, I wish it hadn't happened to me"?

"I've got to go to sleep. I'm exhausted," says Rosie. It's not true, but she's always the first one who wants to turn in these evenings, since just looking around the living room at the lined, sad faces of the old people, and at Tony's strong arms and hands, makes her want to weep—and how can she, when everyone else is smiling instead.

Grief is always such a surprise.

• ● •

"I'm going a little crazy here," says Tony one night, two weeks after Soapie comes home. "Let's celebrate October by going out and seeing a flick or something. Once we put the old people to bed."

It's actually wonderful being out. They go to the Cineplex, not even knowing what's playing, and decide to watch a thriller because the only other films are romantic comedies, and she refuses. "I don't believe in all that stuff, and I don't want to be made to laugh at it," she says.

"What do you mean, you don't believe in it?" he says. "Of course you do."

"No, I don't. I think romantic love is just some kind of bullshit Hollywood tries to make us believe so we perpetuate the species."

He laughs and pays for the tickets to one of the Bourne movies. Car chases and Matt Damon, maybe. "Who do you think you're kidding?" he says as they walk to the theater, right past the snack bar, without even stopping. "Look at you, all pregnant and having a baby! That's romance right there. You have to believe in romance to have a kid."

"What? They come repossess the baby if you don't?" she says. "This baby didn't come from romance, it turns out. It came from somebody forgetting to put a condom back on and now he's very, very sorry about that lapse."

"Aww," says Tony, and he follows her up the steps of the stadium seats all the way to the back row, which is where she always likes to sit, so people don't kick her seat. "Really? This was a condom fail situation?" he says when they're settled.

"Yes. Failure to have one on in the first place. Possibly due to a kind of premature senility."

"You know what they say about those babies. Meant to be, then."

"No. Not according to him."

He laughs. "Oh, Rosie, Rosie! When did you get to be such a hard-assed cynic?"

"I believe it was back in May."

"But you're not fooling me one bit," he says, grinning. "How could we not believe in romance when we get to see Sophie and George every night acting it out for us, even through all the trouble and sickness?" He rests his hand lightly on the back of her seat.

"Soapie and George?" she says, moving slightly forward to avoid his touch. "They're another tragedy."

"Well, that's what romance is sometimes. But they're the real deal. George told me they'd been at this for forty-something years. But she was tied up with raising you, and he's Catholic so he couldn't get a divorce."

"What? He's been seeing her all that time? That is such a waste."

"Well, maybe not *seeing*, like you're thinking. But he loved her."

"Jesus. What some people do to themselves! And you call that romance?"

"Sssh. The movie's gonna start. But yes. It is."

"It makes me mad," she whispers. "All that wasted energy. And here's something else: all those years, she never told me about it at all. She always acted like she didn't need men or sex or fun or any of it. She told me *nothing*. Nothing that could help me with life or men or anything! Do you know how much I hate that?"

"She's a pipster, that's for sure."

A pipster. That makes her smile. "I'm going to sit here and try very hard to forgive her."

"Okay. You do that. And I'm going to sit here and try to forgive my ex."

After a moment, she leans over to him and whispers, "Don't even tell me that she still won't let you see Milo."

"Sssh!" says a man down the row.

They're quiet for a bit, watching the fourth and fifth trailers.

"I'm going to go get some popcorn," says Rosie. "I'm starving."

"You shouldn't eat that. Popcorn has too much fat."

"I won't get it with butter. Not that it's any of your business."

"Even without butter. You know what they pop that stuff in? Pure grease. Lard."

"But it's fiber. Fiber wins over lard. Like rock wins over scissors."

"Would you please be quiet?" the man says again.

"It's just the trailers," Tony says to him.

"I don't care. I *like* the trailers!" says the man.

"I'll be right back," says Rosie.

"I'm coming with you. I'm paper. Paper wins over rock."

"No. Stay here. Save our seats." She stands up, facing him, and slings her purse over her shoulder.

"Oh my God!" he says out loud. "Look at you! You're really, really pregnant!"

"Oh, for God's sake!" says the man. "Maybe you two shouldn't have come to the movies. Go out to dinner if you want to talk. Or go back home and make another baby."

"We already ate dinner, and you can't make another one, sir, when one is already in the oven," Tony tells him, and Rosie says, "Come on, Tone. Let's go get the popcorn."

But once they're out in the hallway, he says, "I didn't want to see that movie anyway. Not with people like that in there. They ruin it for me."

"Ruint? Is that what you said? Ruint?" She laughs. "That guy thought it was our baby. Did you catch that?"

"Yeah. That happens. Not a lot of pregnant women go out on dates with another guy. Come on. Let's go play the video games."

"Video games? You're kidding, right?"

"No, this is better than a movie because I'm gonna beat your ass on these machines. I'm the champ."

"I don't care. What I want to say is, the time has come to invite Milo to come and stay with us." She stops walking.

"Stay with us? Are you crazy? Annie and Dena are never going to go for that," he says.

"For a weekend," she says. "Who knows? Maybe they'll like having some time to themselves."

"They'll say no."

"I'm on to you," she says. "You're a wimpasaurus of the highest order if you continue to let Dena keep you from getting to bring your kid down here to visit us. You are no threat to Dena and Annie's relationship, and it's time they let your kid out of their sight."

"Wimpasaurus?" he says. "Did you really just call Superman a wimpasaurus?"

"I believe I did, Mr. Clark Kent. Give me your phone," she says. "Come on. Punch in Annie's number and hand me your phone."

"Rosie, Dena is a freaking child life specialist. She knows stuff. And also I don't want to hurt them."

"Tony, you are three thousand kinds of a nice guy. We get that about you. Now give me the phone. This is too important."

"What are you going to say?"

"I have no idea. I'm going to explain that I'm also a nice person, and that everything will be okay. I'm going to talk in my teacher voice, maybe. Just give me the phone, and then disappear. Go buy some popcorn."

He punches the number into the phone, and then he hands it to her. And goes outside. She can see him pacing in front of the theater, hands jammed in his pockets, walking back and forth amid the teenagers, looking over at her with a hopeful grin every now and then.

"Annie?" she says. "This is Rosie Kelley. You don't know me . . ."

nineteen

Milo comes the next Saturday, and he is adorable—with Tony's glossy dark hair and huge brown eyes and a smattering of Annie-given freckles across his nose. He looks both sturdy and frail somehow, Rosie thinks, in his khaki pants and blue striped polo shirt. He clambers into the back of her Honda, where Tony has put his booster seat. She admires his SpongeBob Band-Aid, but he brushes off the compliment.

"This is a baby Band-Aid," he says. "I hafta take it off before I go to school on Monday."

"Why?"

"Kids laugh."

"Oh," she says. "That's too bad."

He shrugs. There are more important matters to discuss, apparently. "Did you know that you can make diamonds out of peanut butter?" he says. "My mom says you can't, but this guy at school says his uncle did it."

"Huh," she says to him. "No, I didn't know that."

She also didn't know there was going to be a conversation about childhood cruelty followed immediately by a science exam right off the bat. Also, there seems to be another kind of exam going on, too: how to get the damn car seat installed in her car. She is leaning over him, stretched beyond all comprehension, reaching so hard her belly is far into the backseat—why, why, why does she have a two-door?—to thread the seat belt into the little plastic slots of the car seat, which would be difficult enough for any normal non-gymnast to do, but is nearly impossible for a normal non-gymnast who's also twenty weeks pregnant. Plus, Milo, already in the car seat, is about two inches from her face, and is studying her solemnly, disconcertingly. He breathes through his mouth, directing a stream of little boy-breath as well as the smell of his pancakes-and-bacon breakfast right at her.

"Are you my dad's girlfriend?" he asks.

"No," she says. "We're just housemates."

"Housemates? What the heck is that?"

"We're friends, and we live in the same house."

"Did you know he used to live at my house?"

"I did know that." She smiles at him, and he looks back at her solemnly.

"Now I live with Mommy and Dena. S'posed to be two mommies."

"Nice," she says.

He shrugs. "It's okay. But Rachel says you can't really *have* two mommies. Only one person can be your mommy, and one person can be your daddy. That's the way it is."

Now biology and ethics.

She looks out the back window of the car. Tony is standing on the lawn, his old lawn, talking to Annie. His body language says things are going about as awkwardly as possible: he's got his thumbs tucked in his armpits, and he's rocking tensely back and forth on his heels, going so far back he looks as though he could easily topple over onto the walkway in a moment. Annie, who has short, spiky black hair, is wearing a purple tank top, jeans, unlaced combat boots, a yellow lace scarf, and about four intriguing string necklaces with shiny rocks on them. She has her arms folded across her chest. She keeps turning and glancing back at the house, a cute little Cape painted lavender, looking at it with such regret and fear that it's as if she expects that it's going to possibly blow up.

Rosie knows from the five—yes, *five*—phone calls she's had with her this week that it's because Dena, the expert in all things child-related, never really did think it was a completely good idea for Milo to go off with them.

She's just ultracareful, Annie had said. It's on account of her work—she just knows too much about childhood trauma and confusion. Also—she had lowered her voice and laughed as if she and Rosie were conspirators—Dena just doesn't *get* male energy. She claims half the planet has testosterone poisoning, whereas Annie likes men and gets along with them just fine. "When Milo and Tony really get going with all the roughhousing and stuff, she just gets really annoyed," she says. "It's not her fault. She grew up with sisters."

"So she'll get to have a weekend alone with you," Rosie had said. "That should be wonderful for you guys."

"Well," Annie had said. "Yeah."

"You'll have fun, I bet," said Rosie. "And I promise that Milo will have fun, too."

Annie had laughed nervously. "But not too much fun, or he won't want to come back! Just kidding!"

Milo is swinging his legs and watching her. "His uncle did it in the microwave," he says. It takes Rosie a moment to realize that they are back to talking about making diamonds from peanut butter.

The seat belt finally allows itself to be threaded into the proper holes, and she is able, through superhuman strength—thank you, second-trimester adrenaline!—and a bit of grunting, to snap it into place. Milo is, for the moment, safe. She straightens up and bumps her head on the roof of the car. He is still staring at her.

"We could get a microwave oven and try to make diamonds," he says. "We could *see* if it works."

Tony is motioning to her. "Annie wants to know if Milo is going to need his bathing suit."

"That is *not* what I said," Annie says. "I said that I hoped you weren't going to take him swimming because Dena thinks that one of us has to be with him when he swims since sometimes he can try to go too far out in the water," she says. "And he tries to look like he can swim, so sometimes the lifeguards might think he's safe when he isn't."

"Jesus Christ, Annie, I'm not going to let my kid drown."

"I know, I know. I didn't say you were," she says in a low voice. "Come on, Tony. She didn't want me to allow this, you know, so I'd appreciate it if you could just take it easy and follow our rules this time."

"He's *my kid*," says Tony.

"I know, I know. It's crazy. Just whatever you do, bring him back on time. Let's not scare her. Could you just do that? Please? Rosie?"

Actually, Rosie hadn't planned to be a part of this weekend at all. But Annie had said she had to assure Dena that Rosie was coming along, too. At one point, perhaps in phone conversation number four, Annie, who has a surprisingly high, thin voice, had actually laughed her tinkly-sounding laugh and said that Dena is always paranoid that Tony is going to try to take Milo away—as a way of getting Annie to come back to him. "Ha ha ha—kidnapping. I mean, WTF?" she says.

"Kidnapping?" Rosie had said. "Tony?"

"I know, I know. It's crazy," said Annie. "But I think it's because she and I got together—you know, from cheating. We were both married, and all four of us were best friends,

208 • MADDIE DAWSON

and then over time she and I sorta kinda realized we didn't
love those guys *that way,* and then we knew we loved each
other, and it was all messy and complicated. And when you
do that—well, the price you pay is that you always know the
other person is capable of doing that. Of breaking somebody's heart. And the next one could be yours."

"But here's what I don't get. Why does she think Tony
would take Milo away from you?" Rosie asked. "First of all,
he's not like that. And second, it seemed like what he really
wanted was for all of you to live there together. He didn't try
then to get you to come back, did he?"

Annie lowered her voice and said, "Rosie, I don't know
if you know this, but Tony spies on us. We see his truck all
over the place."

Rosie said, "If he's in Fairfield, isn't it possible he's working there? I don't think he's spying on you."

"Well, it doesn't matter what you and I think. Dena
thinks he's about to make a play for me and Milo, and that's
why I needed to assure her that *you're* a good person who
won't let him do anything like that. I told her you were his—
well, his girlfriend now."

Oh! "Well, but I'm so much older than he is. If Dena ever
sees me, she'll know that can't possibly be true," Rosie said.
"Plus, the fact is, I'm five months pregnant."

"Tony loves pregnancy," Annie had said. "Dena will totally
believe that. He's like a pregnancy groupie or something."

● ● ●

It starts to rain, so they go to Kid City, an indoor amuse-
ment park with room after room filled with toys and instruments and slides. Kids, trailed by their parents, are running

in the hallways and hiding in all the little nooks and struc-
tures, picking Velcro apples from painted-on apple trees,
driving cars and spaceships, going through mazes, playing
with marbles. The place even smells like little kids, Rosie
thinks: sweaty and warm and yeasty, like soap and paste and
sunlight.

Milo runs around the music room, banging on percus-
sion instruments, and then he takes them to the space room
and he drives the spaceship, and then prances off to a place
where Ping-Pong balls are floating in midair, suspended on
air currents.

Rosie watches all the people loaded down with backpacks and diaper bags and strollers with a new interest. She
is going to be that woman over there, the one wearing a front
pack and hurrying with a baby into the restroom. Or the one
whose daughter has just flung herself to the ground because
she heard it was time to leave. She might be—no, she *will*
be, she can feel it—she'll be the woman over there who is
alone with her shy, ostracized, sniffling little kid who can't
get any of the other kids to play with him and so is trying
to bury his head in his mother's neck, like maybe that's the
pathway back to the womb.

Oh my God. Can she do this? Does she know what to
say to a child? Her eyes swerve over to Tony, who is kneeling down next to Milo, listening and smiling at something
Milo is saying—and just the way Milo is resting his hands on
Tony's face, the way he mashes his nose up against Tony's—
she wants to run over and start taking notes. *Press nose
against child's cheek. Smile reassuringly. Give pat on back.*

"It's okay," Tony is saying.

Say it's okay.

She's grateful when finally, hours later it seems, Tony
beckons her over and they go to the pretend diner, where she

can sit down. Milo insists on serving them a lunch of plastic food: eggplant, watermelon, a rubberized fried egg, and a chicken leg.

"Wait, wait, does this stuff even go together? Plastic egg-plant hurts my feelings," Tony says. He turns to Rosie to explain as Milo starts to giggle. "One time when Milo was two, we served him oatmeal for breakfast, and he said that oatmeal hurt his feelings."

Milo laughs.

"Not me, I'll eat anything," says Rosie. "Oatmeal, the plastic eggplants . . . you name it."

Tony looks at her closely. "Wow. I think we've got to get you some real lunch," he says. "We should go."

"But I don't want to go yet!" says Milo.

Tony smiles at him, and says to him in a low voice, "Nah, you know what? This lady we brought with us? You know something about her? She's gonna have a baby, and that makes ladies really, really hungry. And I think if we don't feed her soon, she's gonna start eating this plastic food, and then we'll be in real trouble."

But Milo looks sad, and so Rosie says, "No, no. Really, Tony. I can totally wait. Let him play."

Milo heads off to the room where kids run a pretend fish factory. It's intense in there, little kids running around with baskets of rubber fish, looking like they're all corporate-raider CEOs dealing with union bosses as well as fish thieves and the board of health.

"Come here for a minute," says Tony in her ear, and he takes her by the hand down the hallway into an empty little room with a window seat, where kids could look at books—if they weren't all busy sharpening their skills of being ruth-less capitalists in the next room, that is.

He gives her a funny smile, and then he pulls her over

to him and wraps his arms around her and looks down into her eyes. And then he kisses her. His mouth is warm and insistent on hers, and she feels herself buckle, as if she'd never had a first kiss before. She puts her arms around his neck, and she kisses him back. That's the most surprising, remarkable thing, she thinks, the way she's just willing to let herself slide right into this with no fight to her at all. But in her own defense, it *has* been so long since anybody has kissed her, and she has been watching him for so many days and weeks—his arms, his hands, the way his hair flops. His eyes. Oh God . . . and she has such rampaging pregnancy hormones.

When he releases her, he laughs a little and says, "Wow. I hope you're not mad at me, but I just had to do that."

She is looking up. "I—" but then she's not sure what words she had arranged to show up after that first one. She wants to reach over and touch his lips with her fingers. But he's pulling away.

"Shh," he says. "I know all the reasons that was a bad idea. You don't have to tell me."

It's crazy, but if it were up to her, she'd close the door of the book nook and start ripping off his clothes. How long would they have before the Kid City authorities would come barging in and make them stop? He smiles gently, like he can read her mind, and reaches down and touches her nose with his forefinger.

"Hmm. My goodness, enough kissing for you," he says, and laughs. "We have to go get the kid."

Luckily she's still got her wits about her and can recognize reality when it asserts itself. This was just fatherly exuberance, nothing more. Really, who would be hot for a woman in her sixth month of pregnancy, anyway? This was just gratitude to her for making the phone calls that made this day happen. He grins at her and takes her hand and Milo's and they head for the car. Milo is talking sixty miles a second, about how when he grows up he's going to invent a special meatball, and inside the meatball will be all the pasta and sauce.

"I could totally go for that meatball right this minute," she tells him.

Maybe it's the mention of the meatball, or maybe it's because she's sitting down in the car after walking so much, but once they're riding again, the baby starts kicking and doing somersaults. She thinks for a minute that she'll tell Tony, but she knows what would happen. He would swerve over to the side of the road and start feeling her up, and be just as joyful as anyone could possibly be. He would beam at her, and invite Milo to join in—and it's just not right.

She has got to get it through her skull that Tony is not her person. She's having this baby by herself, and there are going to be a lot of things that she is going to be experiencing alone. Someday this little girl is going to take her first steps and say her first words, and chances are, Rosie is going to be the only one there to witness that, too, and she needs to get used to it.

Was that what it had been like for her mother, too?

She puts her hand over her abdomen and just rests while, inside her, Serena the Bean turns somersault after somersault. She has no idea.

● ● ●

Once they get home, she takes Milo on a tour of the house. He immediately seems to know it's a house meant for kids to slide down the banister and to throw as many objects as possible down the laundry chute and then race downstairs to the laundry room to see where they land. He is stunned—*stunned*—by the claw feet on the upstairs bathtub, as well as the window seat in the dining room and the fireplace in the guest room.

When he gets to the kitchen, though, he elbows Rosie as they're standing in front of the counter. He points to the microwave and whispers, "That's where we could make our diamonds."

"I'm not sure that's a good idea."

"But a kid did it with his uncle. Don't you *want* a diamond?"

She does not really want a diamond, as a matter of fact, and she really doesn't want a diamond that she makes in the microwave, but looking at him makes her laugh. She says she'll think about it and watches his face darken.

"That means no," he says.

"How do you know it means no?" she says. "Maybe it means that I am really going to think about it. Anyway, why don't you ask your dad?"

"Oh, he wouldn't do it," Milo says.

Tony comes down just then, having liberated a tent from the attic. He and Milo are planning to sleep in the yard like the manly men they are. "What wouldn't I do?" he says.

"Nothing," says Milo, and he gives Rosie a meaningful look.

"Nothing," she says.

They cook hamburgers and hot dogs outside on the grill after Tony gets the tent put up, and Soapie and George come out, too, and they all eat at the picnic table, even though it's slightly late in the year for this, and Tony ends up running inside and fetching everybody's sweatshirts.

Soapie, weak and frail, keeps getting confused about who Milo is and has to have Tony's marital situation explained to her over and over again. Milo tells Soapie that he has two mommies, except that you can't really *have* two mommies, you can only have one.

George finds that a riot.

Soapie looks at Milo. "You are very, very cute, young man. Now *who* are you again? And why are you here in my house?"

"Now, now," says Rosie, and she explains everything again.

"I don't understand children," says Soapie. "Never did, never will."

"And soon there's going to be one around here full time," says George. He had been so pleased when Rosie told him about the pregnancy, and now he smiles at her. Maybe, just maybe, he can be pressed into service as a great-grandfather figure. It's occurred to her she may need to start lining up family members in advance. She maybe should get a sign-up sheet.

Tony gives Milo a bath in the claw-foot tub, and after they go outside to get settled, Rosie gathers up extra blankets and pillows for them.

It looks cozy in the tent, with the lantern lit and the sleeping bags all unfurled. Milo, in his pajamas now, is getting ready to play Go Fish, with his wet hair all slicked back just like Tony's. Tony is lying on his back with his arms behind his head, looking contented.

"Is this just the greatest thing, or what?" he says. "I don't know why I haven't slept here all summer long."

"Rosie, you should come sleep here, too," says Milo.

"No, I can't," she says.

"But why why why?"

"It's too crowded," Tony says quickly, like maybe he doesn't trust Rosie not to accept. "And besides that, remember when I told you Rosie was going to have a baby? She needs to sleep in a soft bed so she can be comfy."

"Oh," says Milo. He looks at her. "What if you bring like seventy-five pillows? And you could have my sleeping bag."

"Thank you," she says. "But the tent is just big enough for two, I think."

She walks back to the house slowly. This is what is crazy hard and keeps breaking her fool heart over and over again every time she thinks of it. She and Leila might laugh and do belly bumps and high fives all they want, but right underneath the surface is the sad question: is her baby ever going to know the presence of a gentle, involved father willing to sleep in a tent outside on an early-fall night?

It's optional, she knows. A lot of people are missing worse things than that. She missed it, for instance, and turned out mostly all right. But right at this moment, closing the door to her room, it seems like such a horrible thing to have to miss out on, like not having the color red or chocolate ice cream.

And once she's gotten in her bed and turned out the light, there's no way around the wild grief that comes. She's going to be doing it alone, and that's all there is to it, and she puts the pillow on her head and cries with her fist in her mouth until the dark overtakes her and she doesn't know anything anymore.

[twenty]

The phone wakes her up later that night. She struggles to see what time it is and is shocked when she sees it's only 11:05. She feels as though she's been in a deep sleep for hours—the hard, cracked sleep of the cried-out—and her heart starts thumping like a tennis shoe in the dryer as she grabs for the phone on the dresser top, knocking over her glass of water and her set of silver bracelets.

She punches the button, still not fully awake. "Hullo?"

"So," says Jonathan, "are you still speaking to me?"

"I dunno," she says, and flops back down on the pillow. "Depends."

"On what?"

"On what you have to say."

"Well. Maybe I'm in luck because I'm calling to say I'm sorry and to ask if you're still pregnant. Did I wake you up?"

"Yes. Both."

"Oh, sorry. Should I call you back tomorrow?"

"No, it's okay," she says. She heaves herself over on her side and tucks the phone under her ear on the pillow. "I'm pretty much awake now."

"Why did you go to sleep so early? Nothing's wrong, is there? You sound like you have a cold."

"No. Just tired. Long day. And eleven isn't early."

"Well, I—uh, I've been worried about you a little bit. I was reading that the chances of miscarriage are kind of high with these pregnancies."

She's wide awake now, irritated as hell. "What do you mean by '*these* pregnancies'?" she asks. "I'm only having one pregnancy, and it's doing fine, thank you very much. *And* I'm hanging up now."

She hears him swallow. "Wow," he says. "So touchy. Let's go back to my apology, okay? I'm sorry about what . . . well, what I said before. And maybe that wasn't the best way to begin, but what I'm trying to say is that I'm worried about you."

She stays silent.

"I shouldn't have told you that you can't handle this, because I know very well that you can," he says, clearing his throat.

"I think I don't want to talk to you until you can talk to me better than this."

"Better than *this*?" he says. "Like what? This might be my best stuff. What am I supposed to say?"

"How about, 'How *are* you, Rosie?' 'How are you feeling?' Or try, 'Do you need anything? What can I do to help you?'"

He does an exaggerated sigh. "How are you, Rosie? How are you feeling? And wait, what was the last one?"

"Never mind," she says. "Forget it. I'm fine. Just stop worrying about me."

"See? How can we have a conversation if you're not going to give me any more than that? How are you really? What's going on there? How is Soapie?"

In short, clipped sentences, she tells him then that Soapie's just come home from rehab, and it's taking all of their best efforts—hers and Tony's and George's—to take care of her.

"And who are Tony and George?" he says. "Wait. Am I supposed to know who they are, or have I missed a couple of chapters?"

"Well, Tony is the caregiver guy she hired, the one you said was going to steal her blind, but so far he hasn't, and George is her lover."

"Her what?"

"Yes. Soapie has a lover."

"Even in her state?"

"It makes it even more romantic and beautiful, or so I'm told."

"Well," he says. "Huh." Then his voice changes, gets all serious, and he says, "I just want to say that I'm really sorry about what I said before. I love you, you know, and, well, I also was thinking that, well, if you're having a baby, then I want in on it."

"You want in on it? Nice of you."

"You know what I mean. Come on, Rosie. I'm trying to say the right thing here. I want to be with you. It turns out I love you."

"How interesting of you," she says. "That hasn't been especially evident lately."

"And I'm so sorry I didn't marry you the way you wanted me to—"

"Wait a minute. The way *I* wanted you to?"

"No, no. What I mean is *in the manner* that you wanted it to happen. With the party and all that. The red skirt and the boots. All that."

"Because if you're trying to say that *I* was the one who thought we should get married—"

"No, no, no," he says. "It was all me. Listen, where do you get these ideas that I'm the one resisting? I *love* you. I'm the one who begged and begged you to come out here with me. You're the one who walked out on me. Remember that?"

"I *limped* out on you," she says. "As I recall, I couldn't

very well walk back then. But you're the one who drove away in the truck."

"Yes," he says. "It was all very unfortunate."

She tucks the phone under her chin and fluffs her pillow and props it against the wall. "But, Jonathan, never mind the wedding, I haven't talked to you for—how many weeks? Six? Seven? I can't even remember. The last I heard from you, you were telling me I'd ruined our lives."

"I know. And in my history of telling lies and being a general fuckwad, that may have been the worst overstatement I've ever been guilty of."

She doesn't say anything.

He sucks in his breath. "So what I'm calling to say is that I'm so sorry about that, about all of it. Listen, in my defense, I'm old and crotchety, and I don't do well with change, and that's a problem I have. And you *did* make a unilateral decision about our lives without even consulting me."

"It *is* my body."

"Fair enough," he says. "But it's more than your *body* we're talking about when we're talking about a baby. And you can understand that *the father* might like to be included on the ground floor of these momentous discussions."

"You were just going to say no."

"And you had made up your mind, I know," he says. There's a silence, and then he says, "Anyway, I don't want us to get stuck back in that loop. I'm calling because I want us to be together. The wedding with the red boots, the red velvet cupcakes, the impending baby, the furnished apartment, family, you name it, the whole nine yards."

She closes her eyes and stretches out on the bed, rubs her belly, her new talisman. What is she supposed to say? The baby thumps. *This is your father,* she beams to it. *I am sorry to tell you that he needs a lot of rehabbing before he'll be any good to either of us. He is possibly a hopeless case, and I'm sorry you have to hear any of this.*

He clears his throat again and says in a low voice, "Listen, you. I've thought of little else but of the stupid mistakes I made. One, I should have insisted on us getting married when we were supposed to. And two, when you told me you were pregnant, I should have realized that if you want a baby, then I shouldn't just look at my own selfish . . . self. I should trust you and go with it. I should always trust you and go with things. You've been right over and over again."

She tries to stifle the laugh that comes up from out of nowhere.

"I mean, I myself will most likely be a klutz and have no idea what I'm doing, but maybe you do, and if you do, we can probably muddle through. I admit, it's taken me longer than most to get used to the idea—"

"Seven weeks actually," she says.

"Okay, it took me seven weeks because I'm extra-stupid and hardheaded, but I—I think we can do this. If you say we can, then we probably can. What more can I say to convince you? Because that's all I got."

She turns over in bed and waits, thinking.

"And may I add that if you say yes, this time I'm going to marry you so long and hard that we're going to stay married forever. Nobody will be as married as you and me. Ever."

Blame it on hormones, but something is lumping up in her throat. Damn it, she's touched by his words. She doesn't want to be, but she could hardly be in a more vulnerable state of mind. She's been pretty much marinating in fatherhood for this whole day—fathers coaxing children, taking them to the bathroom, comforting them, cheering for them as they flew on spaceships, walking them through mazes, running after their wayward Ping-Pong balls. Sleeping in a tent in her very backyard. Kissing her in the book nook.

And now here is a man on the phone begging for his chance to be one of these creatures. Awkwardly. And a guy who has no shot at knowing what he's in for, true. But who *is* in fact the other half of the DNA profile of this trampoline artist who has taken up residence inside her. This is, after all, a guy who has a stake in the outcome, even if he is a reluctant novice. He could learn. *Maybe* he could learn.

She winds the phone cord around her index finger. And also, frankly, there's the sex to take into consideration. They had such good, good sex for such a long time. And they could—might—again. Put clinically, here in the cold bracing reality of a lonely night, who else *really* is likely to step up to the plate and be interested in her that way again? Even Tony's one-off sweet kiss was just a token of thanks.

"I don't know," she says, although she does know. She's already caved. She's like one of those YouTube videos showing the thawing of the Arctic ice caps, all that crashing and melting going on.

"It could work," he says. "If you let it."

She's quiet for a moment. "The baby's a girl," she says softly.

"A girl? No shit!"

"Yep."

He says, "Holy shit! You know it's a girl? For sure?"

"I do. I had that amnio thing."

"Rosie, listen! We should be together for this pregnancy. What would it take to get you to come out here now? I have us an apartment. We'll set things up, get a crib, buy a decent couch, have this baby. You know. The wacky American dream and all that."

"But aren't you busy with the museum? And tracking

down teacups? I wouldn't ever even see you. And I've got so much to do here, teaching and taking care of Soapie."

"I'm busy as hell, yes, but I'm a person, too," he says. "Man does not live by teacup museum alone, believe me. I miss you like crazy."

"You've managed to not call for weeks. How is that missing me?"

"Missing is cumulative," he says. "I don't understand how love works. It just does. I love you. And I want to be with you. Don't you want this?"

"I've been mad at you."

"But now?"

"Jonathan. Have you told your family about the baby?"

"Are you kidding me? Of course I haven't."

"Well, why not? See? This shows how—" She gets up out of bed and paces back and forth.

"Listen. It shows nothing, all right? It shows that I was trying to protect you from my mom's meddling while we figured out what we were doing." He sighs. "Listen, this is all the more reason to come. If we stay apart much longer, you're just going to keep getting madder at me for things. When you get here, you can manage my horrible social skills the way you always did."

"Soapie's agreed to go to a home of some sort in January. I can't come before then."

"Okayyy. And when is the baby coming?"

"February twenty-second."

"Well, that's cutting it awfully close. Can't Soapie go in earlier than January? What difference would it make to her if it's now or months from now?"

"Listen, that is not going to happen. *You* need to come back *here*. Just leave the teacups with Andres Schultz and let him run the museum for a while. And then you can be here when we have the baby, and we'll get Soapie taken care of . . . and then . . . later, we'll all go back. The three of us."

"That's four months from now! How can I leave the museum for that long? It's just getting started, and I'm committed here. *You* come. Before you get any more pregnant."

And then they go back and forth, and it's rather aggravating actually—who should come to whom, when it should happen, what it all means—and then he puts an end to it by saying that he'll work out things with Andres Schultz and come to her at Christmas. Just for a visit, though, just to behold her in person because he can't stand not being around her. And then that's when they'll tell his family about the baby. In the meantime, she'll find an assisted-living place for Soapie, where she can be cared for all the way up to the end. And she'll put the house on the market.

And that, she says, is plenty. More than plenty for someone whose belly is now blocking her view of her knees most times.

"So," he says, once the deal has all been hammered out. "How do you look, pregnant? How is that whole thing going—the bigness and all? Are you huge?"

She laughs. "Oh my God, I'm so huge now. You wouldn't believe how I look, and how hungry I am. All the time. It's so weird. It's like being invaded by an alien species."

"Really," he says.

"I'd send you a photo, but I'm not sure you could really handle it."

"Yeah," he says. "I mean, I can."

"I'm not sure. I look way different. I mean, I think it's sexy in a way. My boobs are magnificent. But my stomach is now catching up to them, so it's not so interesting anymore."

"Please," he says. "Do you have to use the word *boobs*? It's so disrespectful."

Oh, yes. She'd forgotten that, his sensibilities about sex slang.

"And it's so weird—I have a brown line going down the center of me now—it's some kind of pregnancy thing."

"Jesus God in heaven," he says.

"Yeah," she says. "See what you're missing? Are you sure you can handle all this?"

"Handle it?" he says. "Handle it! I'm all over this stuff. Ha ha. I love the brown lines."

"I'll send you some books," she says. "So you can learn about the whole process, too. It's a whole new world. Oh! And Jonathan—I feel the baby move now. She just leaps around. May be something of an acrobat."

"Yeah?" he says.

"Yes! At first, she was like the tiniest little butterfly ever just hitting against my stomach. Or like a little tiny cricket thumping there. So weird."

"Maybe you're having a female insect. Did they test for that?"

She feels suddenly magnanimous. "I haven't told anybody else about the movement," she says. "Just you."

Which is such a lie. But she wishes right then that it were true. She thinks of Tony's hands on her belly. That can't happen anymore.

After they say *I love you* four times each, back and forth, like singing a round the way they used to do, she hangs up, and she sits there, staring out the window for a while, running her hands across her stomach.

It's dark down in the yard, but she can see the moonlight shining down on the metal tent poles, glinting there like some kind of little beacon.

• ● •

She is practically singing the next morning as she and Tony make breakfast for everybody: apple cinnamon pancakes and cups of hot chocolate piled with whipped cream. Milo is telling her about all the noises he heard in the night, and his theory that when you sleep outside, you get different dreams than the ones you would have gotten in your bed.

"Your reg'lar dreams look for you in your room," he explains with that vague making-it-up-as-he-goes-along way that children have, "but they just have to sit and wait for you to come back, because you're outside getting the animals' dreams instead."

The animals' dreams. Rosie likes that. Tony says he didn't get the animals' dreams; he claims he had dreams that he was in a medieval torture chamber being stuck with swords, and when he woke up, he realized his air mattress had deflated and there was a rock sticking in his back.

Rosie laughs. Everything seems so wonderful this morning. She doesn't even get scared when Soapie seems confused yet again about why Milo isn't staying permanently and says, "But I thought he was the reason you were painting the room. I can't keep up with anything."

"It's fine," says Rosie.

"But I *want* to stay," Milo assures her, and then looks over at Tony with hope in his eyes.

"Not this time, buddy," Tony says. "In fact, we have to get on the road. I told your mama I'd have you back by noon."

Rosie can feel how nervous Tony is all the way back to Annie's house. He's made sure that Milo's face and clothes are clean and that everything is packed into his little suitcase just the way it was. He doesn't want her to have one tiny thing to object to.

As it turns out, it's Dena who happens to be at home when they arrive. Rosie remembers her from that glimpse at the Starbucks so long ago, the woman who got up from the table abruptly and walked away. But this Dena, rosy and blond with a tangle of curly hair, looks relaxed and pleased, and she greets Tony and Milo with hugs and shakes Rosie's hand.

"Oops, wait a minute," she says. "I have to make sure this is the very same boy we gave you, and that you didn't give us a different, inferior one." She pretends to search in Milo's ears and in the crooks of his elbows, while he laughs and tries to squirm out of her reach. "Okay," she declares. "I'd know that wiggle anywhere. It's the same boy. Did you have fun, sport?"

He tells her all about Kid City and sleeping outside, jumping up and down while he talks. Rosie expects that Dena will look irritated at all this boy energy, but she doesn't. She smiles at him and then mouths to Tony, "Our time off was wonderful."

"You see?" Rosie says to him when they're back on the road. "A great precedent has been set. Everything is working out great. You can probably now get Milo anytime you want."

"Soapie's not going to put up with him being there a lot," he says.

"Soapie? She thought he was living there permanently," she says.

"You're sure in a good mood."

So she tells him then about Jonathan's phone call and how he's reconsidered his whole position on fatherhood and the baby.

"Is he coming back?" Tony wants to know.

"Well . . . no, he can't come back," she says. "He's coming

for Christmas, but then, once Soapie goes into a nursing home, I'm going to move out there. Like I was before."

Tony stays silent.

"It's just that now I know the baby is going to have a father around. I have to tell you, I was so sad last night after you guys went in the tent. I was thinking my baby will never, ever get to have that kind of experience. With a dad."

"And now all that's changed?" he says.

She laughs, trying to picture Jonathan sleeping in a tent with their child. "Well, it's better," she says. "I won't be by myself at least."

"He's a mensch, all right," Tony says.

"Are you being sarcastic?"

"No, no. Lots of guys take seven weeks to decide if they're going to stand by their girlfriend when she's having their baby. I'm sure he's even ahead of schedule from some guys."

"Come on," she says. "It's progress."

"I know." He reaches over and pats her knee. "I shouldn't be this way. It's great. He's going to end up being a really good father. I can tell."

She looks at him.

"No, he is. Truly. You and Beanie will do your magic on him. This guy's toast." He doesn't say anything else for the rest of the ride home.

[twenty-one]

"I have an interesting idea," says Tony one morning about a week later. They are standing in the kitchen, fixing breakfast. She's making a kale omelet with goat cheese and sun-dried tomatoes, and she is explaining to him how this omelet alone is going to provide, like, four hundred nutrients that her baby needs. And he is pouring a cup of coffee into which he proceeds to load three tablespoons of sugar and, oh, nearly a half cup of whipping cream.

"I don't really like the taste of coffee," he explains when he sees her looking at him with her eyes bulging out. "Try not to be jealous."

"And you try not to be jealous of my kale omelet," she says. "Unless you would like me to make you one, too."

"Um, no thanks. I may have to eat a jelly doughnut later, just to confer for having been in the same room with this omelet."

"Come on now. You've gone too far. You know *confer* doesn't go in that sentence."

He laughs. "I know. I'm trying to butter you up so you'll go along with this idea. I want you to come with me to Fairfield."

"No, no, no, Tony! You don't need to go spy on Milo anymore. I told you that the two mommies have seen your truck."

"No, it's to a teacher conference. Totally on the up-and-up."

"But why do you need me there?"

"Because—okay, I didn't want to tell you this. But Annie called me up, and she said she's going to file for divorce, and—"

"Oh, no!"

"No, it's time. We're not reconciliating, I know that," he says. "But she's worried that I might try to get custody or something, so she said Milo can't come here anymore on a regular basis. She says Dena wants it to look like they have the house and the stability, as if I'm just some kind of unsettled guy. At least that's what I think she said. My head was exploding while she was talking to me."

"Oh my God. But she was so nice, when we took him back! And then she goes and does this? What do you think happened?"

"Nothing happened. That's the way this goes. It's Dena, just trying to stake out her claim. And so they went to the teacher conference already, and God knows what they said about me to that teacher, and I need to have my side represented. And if you come in with me, looking like a good English teacher and a stand-up member of the community with your nice pregnant belly—well, I think she won't think I'm such a dumb guy. Also," he says, "teacher conferences are gonna be something you might need to know about. Since you're gonna have some in your future. This could give you a real leg up."

"Ah."

The conference is scheduled for right after school. Can she make it? Actually, she can't, she tells him. She has an OB appointment at four thirty. But he'll do fine, even without her there.

But this just makes him open his eyes wide and stand up straighter. "Perfect," he says. "We'll do the teacher thing with Milo, and then zoom back to New Haven for the OB visit. I haven't gotten to meet your OB yet. And George says he can be here all day with Soapie."

"No," she says. "You aren't meeting Dr. Stinson. That is unnecessary."

"Just kidding," he says. "I'll wait in the waiting room. Unless, if they were going to do an ultrasound for any reason, in which case, I would be happy to be invited in."

"There won't be an ultrasound this visit. And no just getting up and coming with me into the exam room like you did with the amnio."

"Wasn't that nice, though, that I was there? Didn't you end up really needing me?"

"I did," she says. "And it was nice."

He makes a pleading face at her.

"Okay," she says with a sigh. "I'll go with you."

• • •

The elementary school that Milo attends is just like the one Rosie had attended: a nice, low-slung, concrete-block suburban school with a big green lawn, playing fields, a circular driveway, and white-and-tan tile floors and mint green walls all decorated with bulletin boards and posters about how fun reading is. From the gym, they can hear a whistle blowing and the sound of kids laughing and running.

"This place gives me the willies," Tony says as they walk down the hall. "Listen, the real reason I want you here?" he whispers. "I don't want to get all explainy about my stupid life, you know, how I used to live there with the two of 'em, you know? And how I drive to Fairfield all the time, okay? And how I don't have a real job right now. If you hear me start to say inappropriate things, will you just interrupt or something?"

"I'll try," she says.

"Good. I just want to look respectable, like good dad material."

The kindergarten room has a bank of windows with construction paper autumn leaves stuck on them, and little tables with chairs for eight children at each. There's a circle area with a rug, and a felt board with a sun, a rain cloud, snowflakes, and raindrops, all ready to be pressed into their meteorological duties. And best of all, there is Miss Minton, according to the sign on the board, striding toward them wearing leggings and a long red sweater, with her black hair cut in a sharp angled bob.

"Come in! Come in!" she says, smiling like a girl in a shampoo ad, Rosie thinks. "You're Milo's dad, and . . . ?"

"I'm just Rosie, a friend."

"How nice," she says. "I met Milo's mom and her partner last week, and I'm always so glad to meet the other pair, as well."

"Oh, no, we're not—" she begins, but Tony has already plopped himself down in one of those ridiculously little kindergarten chairs Miss Minton is pointing to, and is leaning forward, tenting his fingers and tapping his thumbs together. "Must make for a lot more conferences these days, what with so many kids having two homes," he says.

"That's true," says Miss Minton, still smiling steadily. "But I really don't mind. It's important for me to understand my students' lives and everybody who's important to them. Shall we?" She brings out a folder of work that Milo has done, including a portrait of his family. "So, you've been divorced for how long?" she asks. "If you don't mind my asking."

"Um, well, it's complicated," says Tony. He licks his lips. "We're just separated now. But she just told me she's filing the papers. So . . ." He shrugs. "Who knows what's up for us? I told her that I won't fight her on things, but that I want to make sure she gives me a lot of time with my son. Which hasn't been happening so much, so I really wanted to be here, you know, to see how he's doing and stuff."

Rosie slides her foot over to his and nudges his sneaker, and he shuts up.

"These things are always complicated," Miss Minton says, and waits to see if he wants to say more. When he doesn't, she opens the folder. "Well," she says, "he's clearly adorable, and he's very smart, and he's energetic and engaged here. He seems to like coming to school, and he's making lots of friends. The other kids like him."

"But?"

"But what?"

"I hear a *but* coming. Is something wrong?"

"No, no, nothing's wrong. It's all new to him, that's all. It's a breaking-in period. First weeks of kindergarten, we're just trying to get them all comfortable."

"And is he?"

"Yes, I'd, ah, say he's more or less comfortable. Mostly."

"What's the matter then?"

"Tony," says Rosie.

"No, she's acting like something's wrong, and I know something's wrong, and I think I know what it is, but I don't know how to fix it."

Miss Minton opens her eyes a bit wider. "If there's something . . ."

Tony leans forward and puts his elbows on his knees, letting his hands fall. "Look, I gotta level with you. It's tough right now. His mom, as you know, has this partner who's kind of . . . well, she's a child life specialist or something, and she thinks that they've got to prove they're the main parents. She doesn't want me around much."

Rosie clears her throat, but he pats her knee to quiet her and goes on.

"Now, I myself like both of them. They're great moms, but I'm trying to have a relationship with my son. A real relationship. I've supported them and helped them, and I respect them for what they're trying to do, but it's getting all legal-ish, and I don't want to lose out on getting custody of my son. I want a place in his life."

"Tony," says Miss Minton. "It's okay. You absolutely need a place in his life."

"And I just don't know what to do anymore."

"You have to have a place in his life. It's very important that he knows how much you love him."

"I call him every day, and I—I'm on time for visitation, but just this past week—well, that was the first time all summer they'd let me take him away from their house, and even then it was because Rosie here made all the arrangements. It's like I'm gonna steal him or something, and I'm not. I just—I just—"

"Look, look," says Miss Minton. She opens the folder and shows him the picture Milo drew of his family. There's a picture of Annie with spiky hair, right in the center, and then a picture of Milo himself, standing right next to her, and then next to Annie on the other side is Dena, with squiggly long lines for hair. Way off to the side, and drawn in a tiny, spidery way, is a stick figure with a big rectangle next to the round head.

"That's you," says Miss Minton. "See? You're in the picture. That's you on the phone."

"That's how he sees me? I'm that little wavy guy on

the phone?" Tony says. He looks away, unable to speak just then. Rosie wants to reach over and touch him, but she doesn't dare.

"But here's the thing you should know," says Miss Minton, looking at his face. "He talks about you all the time and how you call him every day. He adores you. When he was going to visit you last weekend, he told everybody. Even the lunch ladies knew he was going to stay at his dad's house, and then that Monday when he came back to school, he talked about sleeping outside in a tent and how you let him have apple pancakes. It was a big deal. A really big deal."

Tony's nose gets red. He looks up at the ceiling.

"A lot of these kids don't even get to talk to their dads on the phone," she goes on in her silky voice, like she's somebody who doesn't know she's got a guy just about to burst into tears right in front of her. Or maybe she doesn't mind seeing grown men cry, Rosie thinks. "A lot of dads don't even get included in the family portrait! Really. Sometimes it's because of divorce, but a lot of times it's just that they're working so many hours and they don't have time to see their kids," Miss Minton says. "Milo is one of those kids who knows he's loved, but he misses you a lot."

"He misses me," he says flatly.

She nods. "Yeah. He's a little sad, I think."

Tony hits his fist into his other palm and gets up, taking a ragged breath that Rosie is sure will turn into a sob if they stay any longer. "Thank you, Miss Minton. Thank you very much."

"Call me Amelia. And listen," she says quickly, "life is messy for kids, and that's just the way it is these days. And it's okay. The important thing is that you give him lots of love and that he knows he can count on you. That's the whole secret to parenthood: showing up. Don't give up. If you have time to volunteer in the classroom, that could be another way you get face time with him, maybe."

"Okay," he says. "That would be better than what I do now, which is driving around seeing him in the playground. But then I can't talk to him because I'm in the car."

Rosie reaches over and touches him again, more insistently this time. Miss Minton turns to her. "And Milo talked about you, too. He said you and he were going to make diamonds? In the microwave?"

"You are?" says Tony.

"Well," says Rosie. "I'm afraid I'm not a permanent person in his life. I'm just a friend, while Tony is taking care of my grandmother who is dying . . . long story short, my boyfriend lives in California, and I'm supposed to join him, but then for the longest time he wasn't sure if he can handle having a baby, because we sort of never talked about it, but now . . . well, he thinks he can . . . but we weren't sure with my grandmother dying, only now she's going into a nursing home, and now the baby is coming, but now it looks like I'll be leaving . . ." She stops talking and wipes her nose, which has started to drip a little, and says, "Yes. Diamonds in the microwave. We're using peanut butter."

● ● ●

"Wow! Well, I think we did superbly," she says to Tony on their way out to the car. "We didn't reveal anything odd about our personal lives whatsoever! Clearly we're totally sane."

"I was afraid you were going to tell her about the condom breaking in another minute or so," he says.

"And I was afraid you were going to be sobbing on the desk in another minute," she says. "Also, for the record, it didn't break. Don't you remember? He forgot to put one on. I told you."

He opens the car door and slides in. "Not for nothing, but how does a guy forget to put a condom on? Not that it's any of my business, but there just aren't that many responsibilities guys have, and if they don't want kids, that's pretty much job one."

"Long story," she says. "Oh my God. I feel like I've got to call Jonathan right this second and tell him how important he is to our kid. I had no idea! He's got to step up his game like a thousand percent."

"Yeah," says Tony. "Fathers. We're what it's all about."

"Jesus."

"So," he says after another minute, "so that was our dry run. When we get to the OB office, we'll try to hold it together better."

"Ohhhhh no, you are so not coming in with me."

● ● ●

But of course, before he can drive out of town, he is constitutionally incapable of *not* driving by Milo's babysitter's house just so he can make sure Milo got there all right. And sure enough, they get a glimpse of him in the backyard, standing next to another boy, a little red-haired kid. The two of them are looking at a shrub, and they have something in their hands.

"Are they pissing on that bush?" Tony asks. He starts to pull the car over.

"No, no. It looks like they've got a magnifying glass. This is very good, scientific exploration they're doing here. No worries," says Rosie.

"I just got to drive by another time," he says, turning down a side street.

"This is what you do, all the time then?" she says.

"Yeah. I drive around the block a few times, and then I park sometimes across the street and eat a sandwich and just watch him to make sure everything's okay."

"This is, what? Parenting by car?" she says.

He pulls up across the street from the house. "Too bad we don't have a sandwich."

"Really, Tony," she says after another few minutes have gone by. "You have to get a handle on this custody stuff with Annie. You need a lawyer and a plan. This is ridiculous. You can't just watch your family through the car window. You can't."

"Don't you think I know that?"

"We've got to get you out of the car. You need a regular visitation schedule, where he comes to you."

"How'm I gonna get Dena to do that without pissing her off?"

"Maybe you can't. Maybe lawyers can do it, though. Whatever. You just have to."

"You can be my lawyer. You handled the first thing great. Now we just need to do it again."

"You know what? I'm gonna invite them to Thanksgiving dinner. In fact—here's a great idea—let's you and me have a huge Thanksgiving thing, invite everybody we know, decorate the house, cook a bunch of food, have a big blowout. Really! We'll go for broke."

"Really?" He looks at her sideways.

"Yeah. Let's do it. I've never cooked Thanksgiving dinner before. Jonathan hated the whole idea. Oh, wait. Feel right here. The baby's kicking."

He reaches his hand over, and it's large and warm and

when he moves it around, searching for the kicks, she almost moans. "What's the dude got against Thanksgiving?"

She pulls herself together. "Oh, I don't know. Something about how he doesn't want the American culture dictating anything about what he's supposed to be doing or thinking, up to and including eating turkey and mashed potatoes," she says. "Really, though, it's about how he hated having to dress up and act special for anything. Called it enforced fun."

He looks at her and shakes his head. "Well, didn't you have a say? Wow! That was a big kick. I felt it." He moves his hands away.

"I guess I did. I mean, I could have. But what fun is it if you always have to drag the other person to do what you want?"

He shrugs. "What fun is it if you never get to have it your way?"

She gives him a pointed look. "You may have had some experience with how sometimes it seems easier to just give in than to argue."

He looks down at his hands. "Ah, yes."

"Yeah. That's why we'll have them for Thanksgiving and we'll be so good and kind and love them so much that they can't say no. The charm offensive."

● ● ●

It's supposed to be just a quick pop-in visit for a weight and blood pressure check, but then Rosie remembers that Dr. Stinson doesn't know yet about Jonathan's conversion to fatherhood and family, as she's come to think of it, so she tells her the whole thing, and how this means she might end up giving birth in California instead, and would that be a problem?

"Well, you can give birth *anywhere,* but I'd prefer it obviously if you were here, where I can monitor things," she says. "I like to see my patients through to the end. Just a personal preference of mine. Why doesn't he just come here for the birth? Why do you have to be the one who travels?"

So then she starts explaining. Or trying to. Museum. Commitments. Trying to make things easier for him. He's always been a little unsure about things, so if she can do this one thing to make it easier . . .

Dr. Stinson stares at her. "Rosie, you're the one having the baby."

"I know, but by then my grandmother will be in the nursing home, and Jonathan feels that we should start our new life together. He actually wants me to come *now*."

"Well, that's frankly more sane from a physical standpoint than going at the very end," says Dr. Stinson.

"But I can't leave my grandmother right now."

"But, playing devil's advocate here, is it going to be easier to leave her when she's just gone into a nursing home?"

"I don't know! I don't know what to do!"

Dr. Stinson sighs. "Well, whatever. People do strange things when they're pregnant. I can't tell you how many of my patients move in that last month. Usually not across the country, but somewhere."

Then she checks Rosie's blood pressure and frowns.

"It's high. Probably because of what we were talking about. I want you to rest here for a bit and then we'll take it again," she says. "Sit here and think nice thoughts. And drink some water."

In ten minutes, though, when the nurse comes to take it again, it's still high. Maybe higher.

They do a urinalysis to see if there's protein in the urine, which would apparently mean she has preeclampsia, which is very bad, but when that's negative, Dr. Stinson just tells her she has to relax a little more.

"Should that adorable guy in the waiting room come in and cheer you up?" she asks.

"You know about him?"

"Yeah. He's been asking about you. He's had the nursing staff laughing out at the desk."

"Yeah, sure. Send him in," says Rosie.

He comes trotting back, his eyes shining. "It's been so long since I've been back in one of these rooms," he says. "Wow, look at all this stuff. You know? If you were from another planet and landed in here not knowing anything, you'd probably think this was all for torture." He indicates all the instruments, the speculums, the little hammer they hit your knee with, the huge light.

"You can't make me nervous now," she warns him. "If my blood pressure doesn't come down, I don't know what kind of punishment I'll have to have."

He wanders around the exam room with his hands in his pockets, making faces at all the equipment. And then he goes over to the shelf where the birth control device samples are on display and picks up the diaphragm.

"Whoa, look at this," he says, and makes a little hand puppet out of it. It reads aloud from *People* magazine and dances around a bit. And then—hearing footsteps—it flies over and jumps back on its shelf just as the nurse returns to take her blood pressure again.

Which is now fine.

They walk out to the car, in the gathering darkness, not saying a word. And when he goes to unlock her car door, he takes her head in his hands and kisses her again. "Tony . . ." she says, but then she leans against the car and just lets it happen, knowing that she shouldn't, but not wanting to

think about that right now. The day has been too complicated, and somehow these kisses feel lifesaving.

She gets into the passenger seat, and he goes around to
the driver's seat, and she doesn't let herself look at him until
they're all the way home.

Which, coincidentally, she decides, is also the moment
that will kick off the first day of the rest of her life, the day
when she really, really, really gets her life under control.

[twenty-two]

By the time Thanksgiving comes around, Rosie is huge with plans. She lies in bed in the mornings, making lists and menus, seating charts, invitations. She wants cranberry relish; fluffy dinner rolls with whipped butter; a roasted turkey with chestnut stuffing. Not only that, she wants faces around the table, lots of them, all illuminated by candlelight. She wants conversation, someone to say the blessing, the good china and crystal, the "little table" where the kids will congregate, and slabs of pumpkin pie with whipped cream piled high.

Greta says she's crazy to think this way. Thanksgiving is a migraine of a holiday, she says. No one's family behaves. Nobody even agrees on the best way to thicken gravy or whether to cook the turkey right side down or right side up, or whether to just chuck the whole thing and go out to dinner. Most people dislike the cranberries you so heroically prepare, and vegetarians (her two older children included) want something called Tofurky instead of the real thing. Men huddle around the television, while women do all the work. People are expected to iron *tablecloths,* even though gravy is probably going to be spilled on them.

"Great!" says Rosie. She wants it—all of it.

The two mommies agree to come, because it's just that kind of fever dream: everyone can come. She invites Carmen and Tomas, from her class, after they happen to mention that they aren't going to be having a Thanksgiving celebration.

Then George says he was hoping to bring Louise out of the nursing home for the day because it's so sad to have her there alone, and Rosie hugs him and says of course she can come, too. The next day, shopping at Edge of the Woods, getting some Tofurky for Greta's kids, she has the best idea she's ever had in her life. She can't imagine why she didn't think of it before. She asks Leila to come for Thanksgiving, too. After all, Tony will adore her, she's so pretty and young and pregnant, and that will make Thanksgiving so worthwhile, just to see him light up in love. And Leila will probably fall in love with Milo right away, and the two mommies will approve, and when Rosie goes off to California, no one will have to be sad.

● ● ●

"You can plan and plan, and something won't work out," Greta warns. "You know that, right? And when that happens, and you find you want to drive your car through the dining room wall and take out the entire guest list, just remember that you have to take a deep breath, and everyone is fine, and we all still love you. Okay?"

"Okay," says Rosie. What she's thinking is that she's got Greta down for two pies, an apple and a chocolate cream, and that Carmen is bringing a relish dish as an appetizer, and Tomas is bringing some wine and beer, and Leila— what is Leila bringing? Not that she has to bring anything. Rosie has been stocking up on vegetables and baking bread and making two other pies, and she's pretty much gotten everything figured out. She'll make garlic mashed potatoes. With the skins on. And green beans with almonds instead of those fried onion things. This—putting on parties—just may have been her calling all along, and she wishes that people would stop warning her that everything just *might* go wrong. It won't.

"I'm also doing a little bit of matchmaking," she confides to Greta. "I think that Tony needs a girlfriend, and I've picked Leila, from Edge of the Woods. She's pregnant, and her baby daddy is some kind of rat."

Greta stares at her. "More evidence, I'm afraid, that you have gone insane. You can't run a dating service for pregnant women."

"I'm not," Rosie says, laughing. "I'm running a dating service for Tony, and the woman I picked just happens to be pregnant."

"You know, I've been meaning to ask you why he's still living there."

"Because—because he just is, that's all. Why shouldn't he be?"

"Well, didn't he supposedly come to take care of Soapie? And now you're there, so why doesn't he go back to his regularly scheduled life?"

"I don't know. I guess he's just between things in his life right now. His wife hooked up with another woman, and he's kind of in need of family. He's waiting."

"Oh. Drama," says Greta. "Why is there always drama?"

"We're all just waiting in that house," says Rosie. "We've become sort of a weird, makeshift, temporary family. All of us are people on the way to somewhere else."

Greta looks at her a little too long, starts to say something, and then closes her mouth firmly, for which Rosie is divinely grateful.

● ● ●

Rosie gets up at five on Thanksgiving morning to start the turkey. It's dark and cold in the kitchen, but she puts on the teakettle and basks in the quiet. How this kitchen used to intimidate her, this room in which she and Soapie made their TV dinners and then devoured them at the kitchen table once the beep had sounded. It was never home. It was the room that seemed to epitomize the coldness that enveloped her life with Soapie.

She catches a glimpse of herself in the dark window, her hair all piled up on her head, her face rounder than it has ever been, her eyes so black with excitement they look almost triangular. *Oh my God, just look at me,* she thinks, *standing here in this crazy, temporary life.*

Soon enough, act two will begin—but for now, in this day, she can stand off to the side, watching all the players line up for her Thanksgiving show. Later, she watches Tony, dressed up and not wearing his baseball cap, setting the table and getting the extra chairs in place, and George hovering so sweetly over Louise, who is sturdy and smiling, and willing to simply sit in a chair and watch everything going on. Periodically Louise claps her hands, such as when Milo and the two mommies arrive with a flurry of coats and bags and confusion. And then she claps again when Milo, jumping up and down exactly like there's an invisible pogo stick underneath him, loudly exclaims that he wants to give them a special tour of the house, to show them the room with the fireplace where his dad sleeps, and the special bathroom with the tub with "cool, claw feet" and then outside where he and his daddy slept in a tent one time.

The two mommies keep reaching over and touching Milo as if to calm him down, but also smiling—Rosie is pleased to see—in that way parents do when they're really quite happy to see their kid excited. Dena, plump and gorgeous, looks nervous, like somebody is going to ask her for her credentials soon, and Rosie, who knows just how that feels, goes over and thanks her for coming, and tries to steer her into a conversation about how terrific Milo is.

But just then Soapie, who was not at all sure that having such a huge Thanksgiving was something anyone needed, erupts in some kind of minor diatribe over how it's too cold in the house with the door opening and closing, and then, in a non sequitur, she calmly says that nursing homes may not get much right, but they do make people like Louise appreciate how life on the outside is a goddamned cabaret. "And this, my dears, is my last Thanksgiving on the outside, so it's a cabaret for me, too!"

Rosie leans down to Dena and says cheerfully, "Oh dear. The old people may have forgotten to bring their insanity filters today. You may have to be called in professionally at some point."

And Dena laughs.

Carmen arrives with Tomas, and after they get introduced all around, they are happy to go on the tour that Milo is confidently leading, and although Rosie can't remember if she truly cleaned the upstairs bathroom to withstand all the scrutiny it's probably getting, she decides that's just another thing this costumed, play-acting version of herself doesn't have time to care about.

"And *this* is the rug with flowers on it so it doesn't show the dirt, Rosie said, and *this* is where they keep the towels!" she hears Milo crow from upstairs, and she goes off to baste the turkey. "And sometimes my dad told me there are mice in the attic, and you can hear them at night!"

Soapie says, "Did we hire that child to sell our house or something?" and Tony laughs and starts passing around drinks. It's alcohol time.

The party really gets started once Greta and her crowd arrive. They come marching across the lawn in their finest dress clothes, Greta holding one pie and her sixteen-year-old daughter, Sandrine, holding the other. Joe is checking his phone, and the three younger kids—all mop-haired boys looking as though they'd been recently chastened, walk with their heads down, kicking at clods of grass. Tony, who is being the host, flings open the front door and introduces himself to a startled Joe, who may not have been informed about there being a man of the house. He shakes hands with Tony and then looks Rosie over, as if she's a medical anomaly, and smacks his forehead.

"How did this happen to you, my sweet little flower?" he says, kissing her. "Are we to organize the brotherhood into going out to California and teaching that cad a lesson in personal responsibility?"

"Oh, he's aware."

"Well. Perhaps all we need to do is write to the cad in question and let him know that a hunk of manhood is now hosting your dinner parties, and he might want to get home and take care of that," Joe says, and Greta looks embarrassed and says, "No, no, Joe, now stop it."

"I'm here taking care of Mrs. Baldwin-Kelley," says Tony, and Joe claps him on the back.

"But he does attend amniocentesis sessions and doctor visits," says Greta. "So he's already better than seventy-five percent of the expectant dads out there. And I hear that—"

"Oh, please, stop it," says Rosie. "Come in and have a drink."

Greta tries to force her kids to sit in the living room and make polite conversation with the adults over the appetizers—even the adults who are not quite so mentally intact—but finally it becomes clear by their droopiness that the children have lost the will to live, and Rosie releases them to the outside. Sandrine grabs her iPhone and scampers upstairs, and the little boys file outside with Milo. Fortunately, it's sunny, and it's not long before Rosie sees them running around the yard, Milo leading the pack as though he's been anointed head sled dog.

All their sports jackets are in the dirt. She can't say why this makes her happy.

● ● ●

Things don't start to fall apart until much later.

First, Greta goes upstairs and finds Sandrine cross-legged on the bathroom floor, smoking a joint, and the two of them have a slight freakout everybody can hear from downstairs, until finally Joe has to go upstairs and separate the two of them. (Is it wrong that Rosie smiles, remembering when it was Greta and Rosie smoking the joints and Greta's mother freaking out?)

Then Carmen gets a text from her mother in Spain that makes her cry great, heaving sobs. Her collie, the dog she'd grown up with, has died in his sleep—and nothing anybody can say helps. People start telling their own dog stories, which makes Carmen cry harder, but then Rosie realizes it's the good kind of crying—the crying you do when people are being kind to you when you're upset. One of the children is sent upstairs to bring down another box of tissues. "*Not* Sandrine!" says Greta, and that makes everybody laugh.

Then, in another part of the living room, Soapie runs over Louise's toe with her walker, and Louise howls just like a toddler would, with big tears spouting out of her eyes.

But all this gets fixed somehow. Joe is stalwart and comforting, and Sandrine, defiant and red-eyed, watches the party going on around her, and after a while Greta slowly stops looking as though the end of the world has come. Tomas holds Carmen's hand and listens as she tells stories about her sweet old dog. And George, bless him, manages somehow to soothe both Soapie and Louise with his patient smiles.

And then Leila arrives, hours late, thin and willowy despite her round belly, and everything starts to go to hell all over again.

She is accompanied by a surprise guest, her off-again but now on-again boyfriend, a guy named Clem, who is disheveled, unshaven, and in a bad mood. Rosie can't believe this bad luck. Also, the guy turns out not to be the most perfect Thanksgiving add-on guest. For instance, when he follows Tony into the kitchen to get a beer, he discovers what he calls "the brutally murdered turkey" resting in the pan after being roasted, and he delves into a full-scale lecture about the conditions in which turkeys live and die, and also a description of the many turkey parasites that a lot of people might not know about.

"Also," he says, loudly enough for everybody to hear, "I'm sorry, man, but why would anybody have to kill something, when you already have Tofurky?" Leila, cheeks flushed, comes over to subdue him by patting his arm, but he shakes her off. "Leila, you told me they were vegetarians! I mean, what the fuck?"

"I'm so sorry," Leila whispers to Rosie. "He just showed up as I was leaving. He's the . . . you know, my baby's *father,* and he said he didn't have anywhere else to go. Maybe we'll just leave."

"No, no, it's *fine*," says Rosie, perhaps with a tad too much vehemence. "You relax and don't worry about a thing. We're glad you're here."

But once they're all seated at the table, Clem, now with some beers backing him up, wants to discuss the political party system, specifically whether there's enough difference between the two parties as to make elections even worthwhile. And that leads the two mommies to explain that, as a matter of actual fact, the Democrats have made gay marriage possible, which is wonderful.

They sit there smiling at each other, and Rosie's heart sinks, knowing what's coming next. And it does.

"As a matter of fact," says Dena, sliding her eyes over to Annie, "we'd like to announce that we're going to have a wedding very soon."

"As soon as one of the brides gets divorced," says Tony in a low voice.

"They're what?" says Soapie. "Did they say they're getting *married*? How is that a good idea?"

"Shh. Girls can marry girls now," says George. "It's a good thing."

"But is it a *good idea*?" says Soapie, undeterred. "Marriage is highly—"

"Yes," says Rosie. "It's a good idea." She turns to Annie and Dena. "My grandmother doesn't believe *anybody* should get married. Ever."

But all this leads Clem, bleary-eyed but passionate, back into his *real* beef with life, which is that government shouldn't have any say whatsoever in how people live their lives in the first place.

Rosie tries to beam a thought over to Tony: *Talk to Leila. Turn to Leila and talk to her. She's wonderful.*

But he doesn't. People start earnestly passing dishes

back and forth and eating their food, but now Louise's Alzheimer's starts acting up, possibly because Clem is talking loudly again and waving his arms, reflecting on the plight of the Native Americans.

George goes all Greatest Generation on Clem and tells him that he *must* settle himself down some, and that makes Joe leave his seat and come over to take Louise's pulse, which triggers some primordial fear in her, and she jerks back, and her water glass falls over, as well as one wineglass, which spills into the Tofurky, possibly making it even more ruined than it already is.

But it's all okay. That's the thing to remember, that this dinner is going to end and that they will all survive it. Soapie stands up and starts dumping the salt shaker over the tablecloth, quoting herself from the first Dustcloth Diva book, looking pleased.

" 'To get red wine out of a tablecloth, you need to pour salt over the stain,' " she says loudly. " 'And then let it sit overnight, and rinse it out in the morning. Of course, pouring white wine over the stain also works, but better you should drink the white wine while you wait for the salt to do the work.' " She beams at them all, and then says, "I should write another book. Rosie, weren't you going to help me write another Dustcloth Diva book?"

"We tried that," says Rosie. "It didn't work, remember?"

"Wait, you're the Dustcloth Diva?" says Dena. "My mother had all those books!"

"Oh, thank you, dear! We *were* going to write another one," says Soapie. "This one would have stain tips as well as information about not wasting your life on cleaning all the time. Where is that book, Rosie?"

"The editor changed her mind," says Rosie.

"What are you talking about? I've got all the notes."

"It's okay," says Rosie. "They said they'll just release the first one again." This is a lie, but she's proud of thinking of it on the spot like this, and Soapie smiles, confusedly placated.

But then there's Clem again. "I'm not sure red wine goes with Tofurky," he says.

Tony laughs and says, "No color of wine goes with Tofurky, man. Beer is the best Tofurky can hope for."

Rosie's heart leaps up when she sees Leila smile at Tony and he smiles back at her, but then he claps his hand across Clem's shoulders and says something in his ear that makes them both laugh.

Rosie feels that the universe is really missing one of its better chances to make something good happen. Really, how hard would it have been for Clem to get mad and insulted and leave the premises, to have Tony and Leila get to talking, for them to both realize how much they needed each other? Here she is, months from giving birth, and he's over there suffering because the two mommies have just dropped a bombshell on him. And instead of getting to know her, there he is, talking instead with the bad boyfriend, and Leila isn't even looking their way.

The children come into the dining room just then and say they want pumpkin pie, and Greta goes off to the kitchen to get all the desserts. Carmen and Sandrine start clearing the dishes away, and Tomas asks if he can put the coffeepot on.

Rosie looks around the table, feeling as though she's an anthropologist watching the native species through binoculars from very far away. Leila, between the two mommies, is talking about pregnancy, and Dena says that she'd like to give it a try herself, and they're thinking of looking at sperm donors soon. Tony, heading to the kitchen with a handful of wineglasses, seems once more like a truck has hit him, and he gives Rosie one of his looks, like a man drowning in feeling. She touches her fingers to her lips and holds them out toward him in a comradely salute.

George adjusts the napkin draped across Louise's chest, and as his fingers lightly brush her magnificent, dowager bust, Rosie has a sudden image of the two of them as young lovers decades ago, Louise bright and shiny and bosomy, and George, eager and ardent—isn't that what Soapie said?—without that shadow behind his eyes. Back when he was full-tilt happy.

Soapie looks over at them and smiles fondly, a crooked, generous, stroke-patient smile, and Rosie sees something she never realized before, that they all three once had a story for this little three-way dance they're in. And maybe the story was that George just had more love to spend than he could give away and everybody was fine with him having two women, or maybe they'd all been jealous and mean and secretive. Who knows?

Rosie feels tears spring into her eyes.

We all tell ourselves such ridiculous stories, she thinks, true and untrue, all the stories piling up like leaves along the curb. Carmen and Tomas are a couple, already writing themselves a romance. And Tony, bruised and unable to move on with his life, might any minute turn and look at Leila and see that she needs rescuing from Clem, and his story might get rewritten starting tonight. And if he doesn't? Will Leila decide to keep going on with Clem, or might she find the courage to tell herself the story of how she and the baby don't need him?

Soapie and Louise and George will die.

Rosie's baby, propelled by a force quite outside herself, is going to live.

Rosie will resume her life with Jonathan, both of them changed now, and he'll get used to the idea of what it means to be a father, and his heart will expand exponentially.

Dena and Annie will marry; Dena will have a child, and she and Annie and Milo will be cemented together in a way that will wound Tony, who simply has got to find his own story.

Greta and Joe have lived in the thick of family life and busyness, but now their kids are spinning slowly into their own orbits. Already Sandrine, with her alienated eyes, her marijuana, and her defiant chin, is mostly an adult, and the boys—who have left their sports jackets out in the dirt in the darkness—are not far behind.

And all of it—all of it—will someday blow away, like dandelion fluff, with only the remnants of the stories of love and trouble remaining, if anybody sees fit to pass them down.

She can't figure out why this makes her so happy—or why she feels her eyes filling up with tears. Maybe it's that she now feels she has a part in this huge circle of stories. She's part of a chain, in a way she never thought she'd be—she and Soapie and Serena and the new baby, who kicks gleefully inside her.

[twenty-three]

The next week, after Rosie and Soapie have had tea and toast and have watched *The View,* and then watched the rain running down the windowpanes, Rosie takes a deep breath and, unable to help herself any longer, says, "Do you remember anything about my mother? Is there anything you can tell me?" Just saying that takes so much effort that she has to stretch out on the sofa. She is so hungry for a fact about her mother that she can't even get herself to look at Soapie.

Soapie says, after a moment, "Oh, Lord. I really don't remember much about her anymore."

"But you must remember some things. Was she—when she was pregnant with me—was she happy to be having a baby?"

"Oh, I don't have any idea. Honestly. Why do you ask that? I suppose she was. Any woman might think it was going to be a great adventure."

"What about my father?"

"What about him?"

"What was he like, Soapie?"

She lets out a loud sigh. "He was one of those men who knew how to get what he wanted. He talked your mother into things."

"Like having me?"

"Oh, I don't know about *that.*"

Rosie looks over at her. Soapie has closed her eyes, gone away somewhere. "Listen," Rosie says softly. "You think it doesn't matter, because I lost them so young. But they always exist for me. They're—they're like these people-sized holes in my heart. *You* knew your mother and father. But can you imagine what it would be like if you knew hardly anything about them, and yet there was a person right there with you who actually knew them but who wouldn't talk about them?"

"I don't remember much about them."

Oh, God. She's going to cry. "But you must remember some things. Tell me what they liked to do."

"Oh, Rosie! What do you want from me? I'm old and I'm tired, and I can't give you what you want. She wanted you. Everybody loves their own kids, right? They weren't together long. He had long hair and he laughed a lot. She was one of those girls who didn't talk much. She was moody."

"She was shy, you think?"

"Probably. I don't know."

Rosie sits up. "Listen, I kept a box—I still have it—I kept a box of things that might have belonged to my mother. Objects that you—that you once said might have been hers. Did you know that?"

Soapie opens her eyes and stares at her. Her face is all contorted with something—pain, maybe, or fear. But she's watching.

"Here, I'm going to get it for you."

"What do you mean, you kept a *box*?"

"I did. I kept a box." She goes into her bedroom and finds the box, which has been stored at the back of her closet. She brings it back into the living room and sets it down.

"Here," she says. "Let's look at this together."

"No. I don't want to drag all that stuff up from the past."

"It's not going to be bad. Here, it's just some things. Look." She starts taking out the photographs, the scarf, the hair clasp, the cassette tape, and laying them out on the table, looking at Soapie's face. "I just picked these things up. Some of them, you mentioned . . . I thought they were things that she'd—that she'd touched."

Soapie is looking at her, alarmed. "Where did you get this stuff? I didn't want any of those things around us! Just poisons things, keeps people from starting over."

"But we did start over. That's done. And I know that's how you saw it, but I just always thought maybe I'd find a little bit of her . . ." She stops talking because her throat has closed up. Then she begins again. "I kind of remember her, a little. I think she sang me a lullaby, one time."

"She did. She sang." She pushes the box away, as if it might be full of snakes. "I don't think looking at this stuff is going to do either of us any good. It just makes us sad after all these ye— Christ sake. What do you have here, anyway? These weren't hers, you know." She peers in.

"No? Are you sure? I guess I just needed something back then. I told myself they were hers."

"No. That was *my* hair clasp. And that scarf—well, maybe she wore that. I can't remember."

"There's a tape of her singing. Would you like to hear it?"

"No. God no. Put this stuff away, will you?"

"Did she—did she love me?" Rosie can barely say the words.

Soapie looks up from the box and something shifts in her eyes. "Oh, don't be silly. Of course she loved you. What the hell does love mean anyway?" She stops and swallows and lowers her voice. "All right, I'll tell you what I remember. But it won't do you any good, just stirring all this up. She loved you just fine. But it ruined her—you know, with *him*. Your father not sticking around. Because of the—because of the . . . the times . . ."

"The draft?"

"Yes. He could have done other things, I don't know, gotten a lawyer, got out of it. But he takes the coward's way out and goes to Canada. And he tells her he can't come back. Not ever. So she wants to go there, too, but he says no. He's got some other plan for them, he says. Keeps putting her off and asking her to wait. And so she's living with me and saving money and planning to go. Anybody could see what's happening, but not Serena. No sir. She could be so stubborn about things." Soapie closes her eyes. "I don't want to talk about this anymore."

"But did he ever know what happened? To her? Did you tell him? Did he ever try to be my father?"

Soapie is silent. Her lips clamp together tightly. "I can't, I won't," she says at last. "It doesn't do anybody any good. All that hurt dragged out again."

● ● ●

One day, after Rosie is tired of looking up local assisted-living facilities for Soapie that will allow a person to have both overnight visitors and alcohol, which Soapie is still insisting upon—she types into Google "diamonds from peanut butter."

And holy bling! It turns out that there are lots of sites that say you *can* turn peanut butter into diamonds—but that to do it right, you'd need the pressure of fifty elephants for one square inch of peanut butter, and a temperature source that could get to two thousand degrees.

Or a microwave you don't care anything about, and the courage of Superman. She watches a YouTube video that makes her put her head in her hands.

"Totally not worth it," she reports to Tony, who has also

looked it up and, being Superman, of course wants to do it. "You've got to do it outside, and it involves fire and electrical cords and, if it goes wrong, you probably won't have any eyebrows for the rest of your life."

He says, "Hmmm."

"The two mommies will have a fit when they hear about it," she says.

He says "Hmmm" again, like somebody who can pretty much do anything he wants. He's been out painting a house all week, and it looks as though his house-painting business is taking off. A real estate agent called him and said she's going to recommend him to all her clients who need to get their houses in shape before they go on the market, and he's thrilled.

She argues just the same, knowing she can't win. It's dangerous . . . lighter fluid? . . . blow up a microwave? How is this sane? Also, any custody matter that later comes up will be sure to mention the day that Tony lost his mind. Judges, she points out, are always looking for that sort of evidence.

He laughs. He tells her he visited the kindergarten class, and every one of the nineteen children in the class *and* Amelia Minton were talking of nothing else but Milo's peanut butter diamonds.

Like that matters, she says.

And then when Milo comes over to visit the following Saturday, Tony says, "Get in the car—we're heading out for a secondhand microwave, a jar of peanut butter, some charcoal, and a bottle of lighter fluid! The Cavaletti men are going for broke!"

When he and Milo get back, they set up everything on the patio, snaking a long cord out there so they can plug in the microwave.

Milo is so excited he's like somebody on a pogo stick. Soapie and George are in the house, peeking out the window, and Rosie goes outside and helps Tony smear the briquettes with peanut butter. Milo does a somersault across the yard, and then another and another.

"Can we sleep outside again, Dad?" he calls.

"It's winter, you crazy," says Tony. "Come and look to see if you think this is enough peanut butter." He holds up a huge, messy chunk.

Milo runs over to inspect it and declares it needs a little more on the side. So Tony coats more on, and then puts the two briquettes into a glass microwave-proof dish and slides it into the microwave and closes the door. It has to cook for one hour, according to the Internet.

"Here goes!" he calls, and Rosie and Milo both come over and stare through the microwave window at the dish turning around and around. Tony shivers and lifts Milo up in the air and runs around the yard with him, with them both yelling and singing at the top of their lungs. When they make a lap close to where Rosie is, she can tell they're singing, "You're a Rock Star."

Every ten minutes, Tony runs over and turns off the microwave for a bit. Just to keep the thing from blowing up, he says. Every time he opens the door of the thing, smoke comes pouring out, and Tony claps his hands. "This thing is really *smokin'* now!" he yells. He and Milo do jumping jacks, play a game of checkers, do some Angry Birds during their ten-minute intervals, and while the smoke clears each time, they run victory laps around the yard.

"This, ladies and gentlemen, is science at its best!" Tony crows at one point, with black smoke billowing in the background.

Soapie totters over to the door and says, "What kind of

fool nonsense is this?" George joins her, and Tony explains to the two of them that diamonds are being created here. George is interested and comes out and peers (from a safe distance, arms behind his back) into the microwave and declares this to be a scientific marvel, if it works.

Rosie is cooking supper for all of them when the sixty microwave minutes are up, and a whoop of celebration comes from the outside. Tony takes the dish in his oven-mitted hands and walks it over to the barbecue grill, where, amazingly, he pours lighter fluid on it and sets the whole thing on fire. Milo goes wild.

"We did it! We did it!" he squeals, coming to the kitchen and pogo-ing himself through the doorway. "Now we just need some spatulas and a calendar."

"A calendar?"

"You know, to poke the ashes through the holes," he says. "We're gonna get all our diamonds now!"

She laughs and gets him the colander.

"Are you, by any chance, related to Mr. Tony Cavaletti?" she says, and chucks him under the chin. "Are you happy?"

He doesn't answer, just grabs the colander and the spatulas and zooms back outside.

In the end, it's not so much a beautiful diamond that surfaces through the black ashes as a lump of some stone that looks—well, kind of yellowish and unclear.

"It looks—it looks kind of like an old toenail," says Tony. "Wow."

"It does not!" yells Milo. "It's the best diamond in the world." Then he screws up his little face and says, "What is a diamond anyway?"

She can't stop laughing and eight hours later, when Tony takes her into his arms in the darkened hallway and kisses her soundly on her mouth, she buckles under the weight of what is clearly an overflow of joy. Sometimes, a kiss is just laughter being expressed in a different form, and even though she dimly knows she's supposed to be pushing him away, she's so happy, too, and she can't.

That's it. She just can't.

● ● ●

She's no better at pushing him away when he kisses her two more times the next morning when she's making pancakes for breakfast, and then once after lunch when he comes upstairs to use the computer and finds her already there.

She's messaging with Jonathan about Soapie, and then suddenly she's not typing anymore. Tony has put his hand over hers on the mouse, and just his touch makes her go all swoony—and then there they are, kissing again and she's out of her mind.

When she opens her eyes, the cursor is blinking, and Jonathan has written: "So I made my airline reservation. Be there on 12/20. Can't wait to see you."

She and Tony both look at the screen. His hand is still dangling on her shoulder, and she knows that if she shifted just slightly, his fingers would be closer to her breast, and that he would look at her questioningly, and then all it would take is for her to close her eyes slightly and he would get her signal, and that would be that. The truth hits her: he is no longer kissing her out of gratitude, or exuberance, or sympathy. He's not put off by the fact that she's nearly seven months pregnant and that right now there's a baby kicking inside her. He wants her as much as she wants him.

"Tony," she says softly, summoning from somewhere that other tone—the one that says no. She shifts her body the other way, and he pulls his hand back. "We can't," she says. "You know . . ." She tilts her head toward the computer screen, where it seems the world of Jonathan and the baby and the plane trip and California and all the rest of life are watching her from that cursor.

He gets up quickly. "No, you're right," he says. She doesn't see his face because he's already out of there. She hears him in the hallway and then going down the stairs, taking them two at a time.

She shoves her fist in her mouth and clenches her eyes shut, and then she takes a deep breath and types to Jonathan that she's looking hard at nursing homes, but she can't find the right one yet.

"But are there any truly great nursing homes?" he writes. "Maybe you just have to pick one."

There's no way to explain to him how outlandishly grim most of the places seem—how the smells are the first things to assault her: the oppression of boiled vegetables, tired old people, disinfectant. But the sounds get to her, too: the sadness of metal walkers plunking against the tile floors, the slippered feet sliding down the hallways, the earnest sing-song voices of the staff members urging, cajoling, encouraging. The way the residents first look hopeful when they see her coming toward them, and then how they go blank with resignation when they realize she's not there for them, that she's not the much-loved daughter who can do something to change their day, that she, in fact, doesn't even know them. And who will Soapie have to greet her in the hallway? No one, that's who. No one will be coming for her.

And how can she possibly explain to him the rightness of Soapie's demands—for alcohol, for George spending the night, and for a garden, a screened porch, and room for a king-sized bed and throw pillows, Sinatra music?

"Look, she's an old lady," Rosie types. "I want her to be comfortable."

"No place is going to be good enough," he writes back.

She sits and looks at those words for longer than necessary, and then she writes, "And I know you mean that in the nicest possible way. Gotta go. What time is your flight again?"

"Red-eye flight. Gets in at eight a.m.," he writes. After a moment he adds, "And I do mean it nice. Just so you know."

But then, later that day, she hears about the Harbor View Assisted Living and Elder Care Home, which seems, on the phone at least, to be a cut above. Spacious rooms, a dayroom with lounge chairs and tables for playing games. The units have their own screened porches looking out over a courtyard with plantings. It also has a pathway outside for walking, and some inviting benches near a pond, and a garden that has large maple trees and shrubs and rosebushes, just like home.

And best of all, the woman on the phone reassures Rosie that independent-living residents are permitted to have overnight guests—there's even a foldout couch, not that George would ever sleep on *that*—and that having alcoholic beverages is perfectly all right. In fact, it's thought that it helps keep up people's appetites and spirits—as long as there's no history of alcohol abuse.

"She can do things for herself, right?" asks the woman, and Rosie assures her that Soapie can shower and dress herself. She just shouldn't cook. Or drive. And someone needs to make sure she takes her medication.

And then, filled with a mixture of relief and trepidation and hope, she makes an appointment to go see this wonderful place, where maybe, maybe, maybe Soapie can spend the last of her days with George at her side and a gin and tonic in her hands—and a nurse standing by if the worst should happen.

● ● ●

On the morning she's to go, it starts snowing, and the radio says the roads are slick and that there have already been a couple of spinouts on the highway. She's drinking the last of her green tea, tapping on the side of her cup while she thinks, and looking at the snow out the kitchen window when Tony comes banging downstairs and pours himself a cup of coffee from the pot George has made.

"Where are *you* going?" he says to her.

So she tells him about Harbor View, and before she even finishes, he says he'll take her there.

"No, you don't have to," she says. "I'm fine."

"Rosie. Your car doesn't have snow tires yet. I said I'd take you, and frankly I'd rather drive you there than worry about you. Also, I have something I want to talk to you about."

She sighs. She hasn't seen him much lately. He's been working long hours, painting some guy's addition, but she knows that he's also been avoiding her and finding reasons to stay out of her way. There's a heaviness between them that she hates. And it seems so unfair, too, if this is just about the kisses she turned away from. After all, he's the one who talks about how important fathers are—and what's she supposed to do, just reject Jonathan's attempts to get back into her and the baby's lives? How would that help anything?

They ride mostly in silence, until he asks her about Harbor View and why she likes it. She turns down the radio and tells him all its good features and why she thinks Soapie might be reasonably happy there. But then she runs out of things to say, and he stays quiet. She looks at his hands drumming on the steering wheel.

"Listen," she says finally. "Did you have something you wanted to talk to me about? Because I just want to say that I'm sorry about everything that happened."

"Don't be," he says. "You did the right thing."

"Well, then, can we be friends again?"

"We're fine, Rosie. It is what it is." He takes in a big inhalation. "I guess I'm just pissed off lately. Dena has asked me to be her sperm donor."

"What? When did this happen? What did she say? And it was Dena? Not even Annie?"

"Well, Dena's going to be the one who gets pregnant this time. You knew that."

"Well, I *knew* it, but I didn't know she wanted you. Holy God."

"Yeah, right? This is a bad, bad idea. But Dena said it would be just great because then at least the children would be *related*. Milo would have a real *sibling*, you know. The kick in the head is that they're asking for full custody of Milo, and yet it was like we're all together in this fucked-up little family or something, like I'm supposed to be thrilled that I'm creating this band of children for her pleasure. That's the part that really got me. It was like, 'Oh, Tony, I just think you're so wonderful, and I want to have another child that I can keep you away from.' And then she said we could sit down and draw up contracts. Contracts! Babies don't come with contracts."

"Ideally, no."

"Well, they shouldn't. That's not who I am. I'm not a contract guy. Jesus Christ! And all I could think was then there'd be another baby whose life I'd want to be part of, but I'd still be just pushed out. I mean, what's the deal? Do I look like somebody who's just got a bull's-eye painted on his dick?"

"I wouldn't know about your dick," she says.

"Well, apparently there's something there that says, 'Kick me.'"

"Wow. You've got to get that removed."

"Yeah, well, I'm supposed to be so flattered. They're like shocked that I'm so negative. That's what they said. 'When did you get so negative? You're such an upbeat kind of guy! That's why we want you to be the father of our new child. You've got the happy genes.' Then they both get on the phone, and Annie is begging me to do it, saying that we're already all family, so why not just continue that? And I said, 'Sweetheart, you two pushed me the hell out of your family, and were pretty goddamn firm about it, too!' I'm not doing it. I can't."

"You said that?"

"I did. I don't want to be part of their family anymore. That's the killer thing. I'm done. And she's all about maybe they won't ask for full custody if I agree to this new baby situation, and I'd be a real stand-up guy to do this for them, and it would be good for Milo. I said no way."

"This is stupendous!" she says. "Look at you! Up on the hind legs! First the derring-do with the microwave and now saying no to being their dick-boy!"

He smiles at her for the first time, and she feels as though she's gone back into the sunshine after being in a cave. "Did you just call me a dick-boy?"

"No. I believe I carefully said you were *not* a dick-boy."

He pulls into the parking lot of Harbor View, a massive place with pillars and a fence and large pine trees, all frosted with snow. She cranes her neck and can see a fountain spraying up from behind the hedges. His hand rests on the back of the seat as he backs into a parking space next to a haphazardly parked Saab wagon. She looks at his tanned hands, one on the seat and one on the steering wheel while he's concentrating on steering the truck backward. God, she loves those hands. Two days ago he had put his arms around her and touched her face with those hands as he brought his lips to hers, but she's not going to think about that now.

"Hey," she says. "Here's something I never told you. This is funny. Did you know that I invited Leila to Thanksgiving because I thought you two might hit it off? Guess I was sensing the impending change in you."

"Who's Leila?" He frowns. "Oh, that pregnant chick?"

"Woman, but yeah."

"The one with the maniac boyfriend. Thanks a lot."

"Yep. Of course I didn't know she was going to bring the maniac with her, but I figured she could dump him and you could get over the two mommies, and the two of you could go off and raise her baby together and live happily ever after. It seemed like such a good idea at the time." She's saying all this in a lighthearted tone that she knows he'll realize is funny any second now. Instead, he goes so ominously quiet that it's as though a soundproof wall has come up between them.

He turns off the motor. She looks at the sidewalk by the entrance lined with potted evergreen trees, being slowly decorated with snow. "I'll wait here for you," he says in a weird voice.

"You'll what? No, please come in with me. You can help me decide if this is a good place."

"No. I want to wait here."

"Tony! Oh, come on, Tony! I need you in there."

"I don't feel like it. I'm sick of being needed right now. Okay? You go in there and figure it out for yourself."

"Come on. Are you mad that I tried to fix you up and didn't tell you about it?"

He's silent.

"Is it that I used the highly offensive term *dick-boy,* for which I owe you a huge apology?"

"No."

"So, um. You didn't like Leila?"

"I liked her fine. It's you. You think you can manipulate everything to your liking. Don't you even get what's going on? What thought process made you think it was your job to set me up with that woman? Tell me that."

"What are you talking about?" She can feel her eyes widen. She hears her heart in her ears, drumming like hoofbeats.

"You *know* what I'm talking about," he says in a low voice. He turns to face her, and she wants to hide from the expression on his face. She should just get out of the car right now, not hear what's coming. "Listen, I gotta tell you this," he says. He looks full-bore right into her eyes, refusing to even show a flicker of hesitation. "You know full well that every single breath I take is all about you, and that it takes everything in me to keep from throwing myself at you every single minute. And that you think you can just play God and set me up with somebody else—when you know how I feel— well, it's offensive, is what it is. And you know it."

"What?" she breathes. "I—I didn't know it."

"Rosie, don't be ridiculous. People in other time zones can see how I feel about you! People in other *galaxies* get this. Insects and one-celled organisms know it. I am in love with you. Okay? Do you hear this now? *I love you.* You, you, you."

"I didn't—"

"Yes, you do know, and you know how you know? Because when I say your name, it's not like when any other person says it, because when somebody loves you, it's like your name is *safe* in their mouth."

She stops breathing and puts her head in her hands.

"I love the way you look in the morning when you wake up and you're all discombed and walking around, rubbing your belly. And I love how you walk across a room. And I love how you laugh, and how you take care of Soapie, even when she's horrible to you. And how you eat those stupid kale omelets and pretend you like them, even though no one could because kale was only meant to be a decoration on plates and not something people really eat. And I love how you talk about your students, and how you miss your mom, even though your mom has been dead for so—"

She looks up. "Wait. Kale is good—"

"—for so many years and you never even knew her, but how you think she's right here with you. And kale is not good; it tastes like stems and grass. But that's okay, because it's nice to see you pretending. And, Rosie, I love how brave you were that day you went to have the abortion, and then how much braver it was when you didn't have it—and the way your eyes filled up with tears when we saw the baby's face on the ultrasound, and how you think you can turn Jonathan into a father, and how hard you're trying—"

"Tony, Tony, you're going to be so sorry you said all this to me. We can't. We just can't." *How is it that he doesn't have the filters and shields that come as standard equipment on most of the other humans?*

"I'm not going to be sorry." He smiles at her. "I thought I'd be sorry, but I'm anything but. This is me, Rosie, falling at your feet. Ka-boom."

"But I've got to be with Jonathan. He's the dad, and if you've shown me anything, it's that fathers are important. I see you with Milo, and how you're starting to fight for him, and I'm so freaking proud of you for that, and I've got to give Jonathan that chance, too."

"Rosie, all that is very interesting, but it doesn't have one single thing to do with who you love."

"Yes, it does—"

"No, no. Don't you get it? We don't get to pick who we love. The heart just goes on doing what it does best, falling in love and opening itself up, and it doesn't give a shit about who we're supposed to be with. It's just happy to go on churning out all this love."

The snow has made the car into a cocoon. He takes her hand and squeezes it, and she knows that they could so start kissing right then and not stop for a week, but he doesn't even lean toward her. "All right," he says. "Now let's go into this nursing home and see if it's any good."

"You'll come with me?"

"Yes." He closes his eyes. "Apparently I will always come with you."

They get out of the car, and he comes around and takes her arm so she won't slip on the pavement with her off-balanced, front-heavy self. Walking up the path to the front door underneath the pavilion, he's smiling and whistling like he's the freaking Dalai Lama of love or something. It must be exhausting having to be him and have all those emotions all over the place. Nothing like Jonathan, who of course has feelings, but he's so much more able to bear them. Even this—even though she's just told him that she doesn't love him, he's walking along beside her, humming a little bit and (she can tell) he's having feelings about the potted plants in their giant concrete tubs, about the spray of the fountain just ahead and to the left, about the woman

272 • MADDIE DAWSON

wearing long braids and wrapped in a plaid wool shawl who is wheeling herself in her wheelchair toward them as though she's in a race.

There's nothing else for Rosie to do but plod along beside him, holding on, concentrating on not falling.

● ● ●

Harbor View is pretty damn good, and, miraculously, it has an opening for the end of January for a room with a porch, far enough away from the dining room that no boiled vegetables will come wafting down to depress anyone. No one looks deranged, and there's no click of walkers because there is soft carpeting, no hooded eyes looking blankly into her own. Rosie signs the contract pending Soapie's approval, and later—just because they're on a roll—they head to Tony's real estate agent friend and put the house on the market. And they try not to think about how this is the start of everything coming to an end.

[twenty-four]

The next day, Greta calls and says they have to meet for lunch, away from home. So they go to Chestnut Foods in New Haven. Rosie puts on her best sweater, the long turquoise one that does not have any toothpaste droppings across her middle. She actually applies lipstick and mascara, puts her hair up in a ponytail, and grabs one of Tony's coats, which still fits around her middle. She looks pretty fabulous, if she does say so herself.

Greta's late, and she comes flying in, all business and consternation, apologizing, harried.

"Here, sit down, breathe," says Rosie. "What's the matter?"

"Everything. My life. Our men. Joe. Jonathan. Did you order yet?"

"No." Rosie feels a flicker of fear. "What's wrong with Joe and Jonathan?"

"Let's get some paninis or something. Sorry, I don't have a lot of time, so I have to get to the point. I caught Sandrine smoking pot again, and now apparently, there's also a *guy,* so I'm insisting on picking her up every day from school myself. I really don't even have time to eat."

"See? This is why I won't even let my kid out of the womb."

"Yeah, that's probably what I should have done," says Greta.

"Next time you'll know," says Rosie. "So, what's with Joe and Jonathan?"

Greta goes over to the food case and orders them egg-plant and arugula paninis with melted mozzarella without even asking Rosie if that's what she wants. Short on time; no time to ask. Rosie folds her napkin and tries to arrange her face into a pleasant, open smile. Fortunately she likes the eggplant and arugula paninis; otherwise she would have to murder Greta.

"Okay," Greta says as she comes back. "I've gotta tell you this: Joe woke me up in the middle of the night and said he just figured out that you're sleeping with Tony. And this is Clueless Joe, who has never detected sex in his life, up to and including when it was happening to him."

"Is that it? Trust me. I'm not sleeping with Tony."

"Well, *I* know that. When he told me what he'd been thinking, I told him all the reasons that you *weren't* sleeping with Tony, which are . . ." She pauses for a moment, seeing if Rosie is going to jump in and fill in the reasons, but when she doesn't, Greta sees that having come this far into the sentence, she now has to go on—"which *are*: he's too young; he's kind of . . . well, he's not your real *type*; also, he's got a seriously complicated home life; *and* he wouldn't really fit in with the other guys in the posse. Which is important after all these years." She sits back. "There. Did I miss anything?"

"I don't believe so," says Rosie coldly.

Greta peers at her. "So are you and Jonathan . . . all right? I mean, I know it must be awful being separated like this—I can't even imagine how lonely you must be, going through all this. And Joe was really upset with me that I wasn't see-ing enough of you. He said that I was your best friend, and that he and all the rest of us needed to step in and support you during this time, while you wait to go join Jonathan and all."

"We're all right," says Rosie. "I mean, as you recall, it took him a little while to come around to the idea of family and fatherhood."

"Well, sure. I mean, this is Jonathan we're talking about. He's cautious. And babies aren't like teacups, let's face it."

"But he's into it now," she says.

"Well, that's good," says Greta. "Joe's calling him tonight, in the name of the sacred brotherhood and all, to tell him how he has to step up his game. Antlers, you know. When one female is thought to be perhaps falling out of the pack, the other males circle around. Or something. I don't know what I'm talking about."

"No," says Rosie.

"This is just Joe's fantasy life probably. Forget it. Listen, though, more importantly, I've found a woman who gives Lamaze classes in her house. Same person I used way back when, she's still giving classes, thank God. You don't want to just take the hospital course, trust me on this. It's four weeks, and I can go with you because it's in the evening, and Joe has said that he'll watch the kids."

"How very nice of you."

"Yes, it'll be our weekly outing. I'm looking forward to it."

The sandwiches show up just then, and they get busy eating.

"How old *is* Tony anyway?" says Greta with her mouth full.

"Oh. Nineteen," says Rosie.

"Stop it. Okay, I deserved that. So I take it that he and that pregnant woman at Thanksgiving didn't hit it off, huh? The one you were fixing him up with?"

"Not so much."

"Tough when her idiot boyfriend was there. Man, that

guy was a piece of work, wasn't he?" She puts down the rest of her sandwich and starts wrapping it up in the paper to take along. "Hey, so Lamaze starts this week, on Wednesday night. I'll pick you up?"

"Okay." Rosie feels like a sullen teenager, like Sandrine must feel. Really, she'd like to maybe take the kid out for a Coke and they could compare notes about Greta.

Greta is studying her. "You look good, you know that? That color is nice on you. I wish I had your freedom right now, I'll tell you that. It's just run, run, run all over the place lately." Then she stops and lowers her voice and leans in. "Rosie. Do not fuck him. I remember how pregnancy hormones are, and I saw the way he looks at you. Joe might not know what he's talking about, but he *is* on to something. I know this guy might look good when Jonathan is so clueless, but you can train Jonathan. And here's the big one: Jonathan is the *father of your child*."

• • •

The Lamaze teacher, Starla Jones, is about the same age as Rosie, but of course her children—she has five of them— were all born long ago, and, according to her speech at the start of the class, their births were joyous, calm, almost religious experiences. She is firm in her spiritual conviction that a person can breathe her way through pain. In fact, she tells the class—a motley assortment of five young, hugely pregnant couples and then Greta and Rosie—that *pain* isn't even going to be a word they use. Ever.

"Do you know what word we're going to use instead?" she says.

"Discomfort?" asks one of the pregnant women, who

has a long blond ponytail and looks as though she's possibly going to deliver a hippopotamus in the very near future.

Starla Jones frowns. "No, our words are too powerful to use them so negatively," she says. She looks around, one eyebrow arched, and raises and lowers her arms slowly, as though she's parting the Red Sea. "We'll just call them *openings*. We're opening to our new lives. We'll develop mantras and focal points to help us through."

The class meets in her condo, and once all the women are lying on the living room floor with their pillows and their massive bellies sticking up, Rosie thinks the place looks like a balloon factory showroom. Children's artwork is everywhere, tacked up on the walls. Down the hall, they can hear the sound of kids squabbling, and periodically a deep male voice issuing a command for quiet.

"Does this really work?" asks one man in a squeaky voice, and the rest of the group laughs.

"Does it *work*!" says Starla Jones. "Does it work! I could show you my home movies of every single one of my births, and you'd be convinced."

Oh, please no, Rosie thinks. She and Greta widen their eyes at each other, which makes Rosie laugh. She's grateful, really, that Greta is going along with her to the Lamaze classes, even though when she told Tony about it, he pointed out that he remembers every single thing there is to know about Lamaze. She stretches out on the floor in Starla Jones's living room and follows the directions, relaxing her left side, then tensing her muscles, and then relaxing her right side.

"Breathe," commands Greta in a soft voice close to her ear, and she does.

"Why is there a *For Sale* sign in the front yard?" Soapie asks her one morning.

They have been over this about a dozen times. "Because we are selling this house, honey," Rosie says gently. "You said we should sell the house, because you are going to live at the Harbor View. Remember the nice apartment there? It's going to be available at the end of January."

"The end of January? Why do I have to wait?"

Rosie looks at her. There is no telling when they start these conversations exactly which way they're going to go. Sometimes Rosie finds herself talking to the Soapie who wants to move immediately, or sometimes it's the Soapie who can't remember she's going at all. So far, at least, she hasn't had the Soapie she'd dreaded the most: the one who says she's not going after all. Sometimes there seem to be storm clouds behind her eyes, but she never argues or complains about it. It breaks Rosie's heart, this bravery.

"We have to wait because that's the date they're going to have your apartment ready," she says.

"And you're really going to California?" Soapie asks, as though this is just a normal conversation they might have once had on the pros and cons of moving. "Where is Tony going?"

"He's getting his own place."

"And George?"

"George will be coming to see you every day."

"Will he spend the night?"

"I expect he will. If you want him to."

"What I want is for us to go to Paris," says Soapie, swiveling her head over to Rosie and fixing her with a filmy-eyed stare. "That is the only thing I believe I ever asked you for."

"It's true, you did ask for that," says Rosie.

"It was too much to ask," says Soapie, and she looks away.

Her face these days has changed. It's lost a lot of the tension that used to hold her muscles in place and sags now, as if everything on her is simply tired of holding itself together. Rosie hopes that the promises she's made to her can really come true—that she'll truly be able to live independently at Harbor View, that George will be able to visit, that there will be vodka and dancing—and that she won't have to go so quickly into the more restricted nursing home unit. Sometimes, though, it seems as if door after door is quietly closing in the room of Soapie's mind, never to be opened again.

Oh, it is all so hard.

The baby rolls around inside her now, flipping over like an acrobat. Tony calls her a prizefighter baby. Sometimes she has hiccups, which is so interesting—as though after Rosie's gone to sleep, the baby has gone clubbing, and now the two of them together are experiencing the hiccupping. Also, there are times now when Rosie's belly gets tight like a basketball and hardens there, gripping hold of the baby. Braxton-Hicks contractions, says Starla Jones. Practice for labor.

It's good, that practice, it shows that even her old and inexperienced body seems to have the idea of what it needs to do: fire up those uterine muscles and get them ready to push the baby out. Start the milk-production mechanism. Cue the maternal hormones that never dreamed they'd be called into service. But here they are, showing up for active duty, standing in formation, saluting her.

● ● ●

She and Tony go get a Christmas tree together. He is supposed to be simply there to lug it to the car, but then it turns out he has a million thoughts about trees. He likes the big, showy ones and the kind that smell good, and the kind with needles that don't hurt. She has allotted approximately fifteen minutes for picking out this tree, which she explains to him. She is in the mood to look at exactly one tree and then buy it on the spot.

"And here's why this doesn't matter. We're all about to move out," she says to him, standing in the drizzly parking lot of Home Depot, where the plastic-covered Fraser fir trees behind the chain-link fence remind her of recreation time in the prison yard. "It's crazy even to *get* a tree. I'm supposed to be spending all my time throwing things *out—*"

"If we don't get a tree, we might as well just throw in the towel on life," he says. "Come on. Where's your Christmas spirit?"

"Tony," she says, "look at us. We're all pathetic. It's the end. The credits are running."

"That's when Christmas spirit comes in the handiest," he says. "Let's get this eight-foot one. It's Soapie's last tree. Think of that."

"Soapie," she says, "never did even care for trees. She has no Christmas spirit to her, that woman. She wrote Dustcloth Diva columns on how to *avoid* the mess of Christmas. If you could keep a tree out of your house, so much the better."

"I like this huge one," he says, as if he hadn't even heard her.

"But it costs so much. Look at it."

But he just laughs. "This is the biggest one here. We're getting it even if we have to go get a bank loan."

"We don't have enough ornaments."

"We'll cover it with lights. That's prettier anyway."

"White ones? I only like the white ones."

"Nope. Colored ones. And icicles."

"But those are so gaudy and they make such a mess. Tony, please. I have so much to do. And now I'll have to both put up a tree and take it down."

"Oh, Rosie! It's Christmas. By the way, I don't know if you know, but you cannot have any eggnog this year. Raw eggs are not good for you."

"I hate eggnog."

"Well, then, you've got that going for you." He goes and tells one of the workers that this is the tree for them, and the two guys drag it over to a machine that puts even more net on it. She stands on one foot and then the other. It's cold, and she left her gloves in the car, so she tucks her hands inside the sleeves of her coat. Jonathan has never once argued about Christmas trees with her. She wonders if he even bothered to pack up their ornaments, or if he just threw them away.

When their tree is finally loaded on top of the car, Tony drives to the drugstore and turns the car off. "I'm going in for lights and icicles, and while I'm gone, you should do ten minutes of stage one breathing, and then if I'm still not back, go into the hee-hee-hoo breaths. Okay?"

She laughs. "I can't believe you remember all this just from Milo's birth."

"Rosie," he says seriously, "Milo's birth was a turning point in my life. Of course I remember everything about it."

He gets out and then comes to her side and raps on the window. "And don't forget the cleansing breaths," he says when she opens it. "You always forget those when we practice, and I don't know what's going to become of you if you try to go into labor without the cleansing—"

"O-*kay!*" she says. "Go get your lights. I've gotta pee."

He comes back with ten boxes of colored lights—ten!— and a bag full of silver icicles, a Christmas candle, and a can of spray that says it smells like fir trees, since he doesn't think this tree has quite enough of a fragrance for him.

They do hee-hee-hoo breathing all the way home, even when she starts laughing so hard that she loses all semblance of bladder control.

He just looks at her and laughs. "God, you're a hot mess," he says. "Never mind. All those muscles are relaxing. You're getting ready for the baby."

"No one ever told me about the humiliation factor," she says.

"Yeah, well, you'll be fine," he says. "Everybody survives. Most people."

He turns up the radio—"Have Yourself a Merry Little Christmas" is playing, which she tells him has got to be the most melancholy Christmas song around, and shouldn't have even qualified for being a holiday song. When it gets around to that part about being together again if the fates allow, he joins in singing.

"From now on, we'll have to muddle through somehow," he sings, extra loud, with feeling.

"What kind of a Christmas carol talks about muddling through somehow?" she says. "What about decking the halls and all the joy we're supposed to feel?"

"Nah, this is about the real Christmas," he says. "We have to muddle through to *make* the joy ourselves. That's why we got the biggest possible tree." He looks at her. "How is it you don't know this?"

Her phone rings, and she reaches over and turns down the radio and takes the call. It's Greta, all harried, saying she can't make the Lamaze class tonight—a teacher conference has been changed and changed again, and now this is the very last time she can schedule it.

"Joe says he's going to go with you," says Greta.

"Joe?" says Rosie, and Tony mouths to her, "I'll go." She tells Greta Tony's going.

"*Tony?*" Greta says his name as though Rosie has just said that she'll pick up a hitchhiker to take along to Lamaze.

She laughs. "Yes, he has a child, remember?"

"Oh, yes. I remember. Well," says Greta, "I suppose it makes sense. Give my regards to Starla, will you? Do you think I should call her and let her know that I can't come?"

"I think Starla can probably cope with running the class without you, just this once," she says, perhaps a little more sarcastically than she means to, and when she hangs up, she says to Tony, "God! That woman is driving me absolutely crazy! She and Joe are worried about . . ."

"Me and you?" he says.

"Well," she says. "Actually, yes."

By now they've arrived at the house. He cuts the engine and turns to look at her. "Okay, I've been dreading saying this to you all day long, but I gotta say it before we go and do more stuff together."

"What?" she says.

He drums his hands on the steering wheel. "I got my own place, and I'm moving out this weekend."

"What?" she says. "But I need you!" She can feel her breath high in her chest, fluttering like a bunch of insects have taken over.

"No, you don't. Jonathan's coming for Christmas, and he doesn't want me around, I'm sure. Also I can't—I really can't keep doing this. For me and you."

"You just talked me into a gigantic tree," she says. "And what about helping me with Lamaze? Jonathan doesn't know anything about Lamaze."

"I'll still do Lamaze with you when Greta can't. And I'll help you with the practices, because you gotta practice. It doesn't come completely natural, even though they call it natural childbirth."

"No, okay, fine," she says, and looks away because tears are dangerously close to the surface.

"Aww, don't be that way," he says. "This is just the hard part, now."

She wipes at her eyes. "What about Soapie? What's going to happen? How are George and I going to pick her up off the floor?"

"She doesn't fall anymore since she got the walker," he says. "She doesn't need me, and you and Jonathan certainly don't need me around." He touches her arm. "This is for the best, believe me."

She would like to point out that Jonathan isn't coming for another ten days, but she can't bring herself to beg him to stay. Heartsick and numb, she goes in the house and heads upstairs. She can hear him bringing in the tree and setting it in the stand she set out. He's talking to Soapie and George, and maybe he's even got them helping him put the icicles and the ornaments on. The stereo is playing Christmas carols, but she doesn't come back down until it's time to leave for Lamaze, not even when she can tell he's at the bottom of the stairs, bellowing out "Have Yourself a Merry Little Christmas" with all his might.

twenty-five

Greta had said once that Christmas is like a giant art project competition that everyone is working on, and that the whole reason it gets stressful is that everybody is imagining that the projects happening at other people's houses are even more elaborate, more perfect, and far more harmonious than those at one's own house.

And, looking at it that way, Rosie knows she had been doomed from the start. She doesn't know how to put on a Christmas any more than she knew how to put on a Thanksgiving. She and Jonathan were only good for low-key holidays—a tabletop tree and an optional wreath, maybe one string of white lights strung along the window panes—and now Tony has dragged this giant *monstrosity* into their lives and decorated it with gaudy colored lights, strung pieces-of-aluminum-foil icicles across its branches, recorded a bunch of Christmas music CDs, and then moved away.

Rosie thinks she never knew such an angry, unreliable person. What kind of man saddles you with a huge tree when you'd told him you wanted a tiny one, and then leaves?

She also feels like she may have a limb missing.

"I know why he had to go," says George, "but I wish he'd waited until after Christmas. This is feeling just the slightest bit gloomy."

Tony, in fact, has gotten a job bringing Christmas to others. He told Rosie he's taken a job in a nursery, helping people decorate their houses. The service is for people who are too busy to put up their own trees and holly wreaths. But she can't help but picture innocent people coming home to find every inch of their homes strewn with tinsel and colored lights, all blinking and singing Christmas carols. They are likely going to get more Christmas than they bargained for when they bring in Tony Cavaletti.

She looks at their monstrosity of a tree, draped in silver tinsel and colored lights. True to the song, he's put a star on the highest bough. It makes her want to cry.

"Let's go to Paris," says Soapie. "That's where we belong. Paris, Paris, Paree."

This makes Rosie cry, too—from regret, from guilt, and just because anything at all can make her cry. But then she wakes up one morning and knows that if she has to do this massive art project, she'll make Soapie's last Christmas a Paris Christmas. There'll be croissants, of course, and crepes, champagne, chardonnay, chicken Francese, perhaps some escargot. Some *chocolat*. No, a *chocolat fondue*! She actually starts getting excited by the idea. She finds a three-foot statue of the Eiffel Tower in a junk shop and drags it off to her car. It'll make a wonderful centerpiece, right in front of the tree.

"We're bringing Paris to us," she tells Soapie, who looks pleasantly baffled by the idea. "No, *non, madame, c'est magnifique*! You'll see!"

French music, French movies—she looks up and downloads everything she can find. One day she's about to order a French flag for the front of the house and comes to her senses. Instead, she orders a large poster of Paris twinkling in the evening and hangs it in the front hallway.

Jonathan arrives on the red-eye five days before Christmas. When Rosie first sees him at the airport, pushing his way through the crowd, head and shoulders taller than the rest of the people, she feels so giddy that she thinks her knees are going to buckle. He's wearing jeans and his nubbly Irish sweater that some aunt of his had knitted him (he has so many knitting aunts that he never could keep straight which one), and he's carrying his leather jacket and a duffel bag, and he hasn't shaved, and his graying hair looks so distinguished and his face so rugged and grown-up—well, how could she have forgotten how handsome he is? The baby jumps in her belly, like she might recognize him.

Okay, so it would be nice if he would hold her at arm's length and shake his head in wonder at the beauty of the fulsomeness of her, if he would need to perhaps wipe a tear from his eye at the whole remarkable miracle that is taking place right now inside her. She is building his child, for heaven's sake, and the least he could do is to smack himself in the head and grin and marvel at her talent in pulling this off. Not just any forty-four-year-old can do it; the ultrasound nurse says that every time.

But he doesn't. He doesn't have that in him. Instead, he simply hugs her and kisses her on the top of her head—he's never gone in for those dramatic public kisses, except for that one time, the day of the proposal. Now he is as cool and unruffled as ever, a tall drink of water of a man striding across the airport next to her while she hurries to keep up.

"Look at me!" she says, and twirls around for him in the parking lot, and then nearly falls over her own feet because she's now so pregnant she's swaybacked and her balance isn't what it used to be. He looks her over and says, "You sure look plenty ripe," but then later, on the way home, when they stop at a diner for breakfast, he looks into her eyes and manages to say the right things. Jonathan style, at least. He says that she looks radiant, that he's missed her terribly, and that she'll be a wonderful mother, and that Andres Schultz says the baby is welcome at the museum anytime at all, as long as it doesn't tip over the displays.

"You do know what babies are, don't you?"

"Not really," he says. "I've heard rumors that they're a lot of trouble," and she says, "Yeah, well, I don't really have much of a clue about them either," and he says, "How did we get into this mess, again?" and it's crazy, but just the fact that he said *we* instead of *you* makes her heart soar.

Then they go to Jonathan's mother's house, and it's *really* fantastic there. Edie, his mother, shrieks in joy at the sight of the two of them—and she comes over and rubs Rosie's belly just as though she's met the Buddha right then and there. Then, when she's had her fill of rubbing, she goes over and smacks Jonathan for not telling her sooner, but she's laughing and wiping her eyes, and anybody can see she's not really mad. She sits Rosie down and insists she put her feet up, and then yells at Rosie that *she* should have told her about the baby, even if Jonathan didn't: after all, this is the grandma she's talking to! But it's okay, she says. She knows how weird her son is about telling news. And then she gets on the telephone and calls at least ten of her closest friends and announces that she's going to be a grandma *again,* made possible by the least likely of her children. And when she gets off the phone, she starts swatting Jonathan again, and then kisses him all over his face, and brings the two of them cups of hot chocolate. Jonathan sits there and rolls his eyes, but he's smiling with his faraway, crinkly eyes, and Rosie thinks, *This is what family means. Someone to be happy when you tell them you're adding family members, and mad at you for not telling them sooner.*

It's different, of course, when they get back to Soapie's house, which they have to do soon because Tony isn't there anymore and Soapie can't be left alone. George has stayed home from visiting Louise in the nursing home today just so he could watch out for Soapie, and Rosie finds the two of them in the living room sitting on the couch, drinking Christmas martinis and listening to Christmas music on the stereo.

George has his face arranged to be welcoming to Jonathan, and he jumps up from his chair in his charming old-man way, but Jonathan doesn't even meet his eyes.

"Now, Jonathan, *this* is the amazing George Tarkinian," Rosie makes a point of saying, and steers Jonathan right over. The two men shake hands, and George keeps looking up at Jonathan with his bright eyes all fixed with the expectation of being regaled with witty stories and observations and maybe even appreciation for being there during Rosie's pregnancy. But there's nothing coming back. Jonathan, stiff and uncomfortable, doesn't know how to play that game.

It's when he goes over to hug Soapie and she searches his face and says, "So where have *you* been?" that he looks truly pained.

"I'm in San Diego now, Soapie," he says. "I've got my own museum."

"Yeah, well," she says, peering at him. "Is it the teacups? People pay money to come see those things?"

He laughs a little. "Yeah, they do. Not enough. But some." He shoves his hands down in his pockets and glances around the room, looking like he's a prisoner of war and expecting the torture instruments to come out soon. Rosie remembers that he's always hated this house, that he thinks of it as the epitome of a suburban nightmare. A WASP nest, he called it once. A place that traps guys, hands them lawn mowers and hedge clippers, and turns them into automatons or something. Strips them of their manhood.

Soapie turns to Rosie, looking so artificially and pleasantly addled that later Rosie wonders if she wasn't being mean on purpose. "*Where* is that Tony, do you think?" she says. "Is he here?"

Oh, it's going to be a long afternoon. Rosie explains again that Tony has his own apartment now and then dashes into the kitchen to get snacks. George asks Jonathan to help him bring in wood for a fire, and then everybody tries to settle in and make polite small talk over drinks.

George tells about how Louise is doing (not so well, and yet not so bad either), and what the nursing home does for the residents at the holidays (they give them stocking gifts), and how the weather has been (milder than you'd expect, could be global warming). Jonathan tells a few things about San Diego and about the museum (the price of admission is $8.50 for adults and children, the same price because they don't *want* children in there, actually, so why give them a discount) and Rosie talks about her students, all of whom want to give her a baby shower. Conversations keep trying to make it aloft but then keep running aground. Eventually it's time for her to get up and make dinner, and the only thing that keeps her going is that soon she will get to have sex.

She and Jonathan will lie in her bed, with his hands cupping her enormous breasts and her even more enormous belly, and she'll close her eyes while the baby kicks and divebombs her internal organs, and then she'll open her eyes and smile at him, and he'll . . .

"Whoa. Is this even safe?" is what he says when they finally get to bed.

"Of course. Here, don't you want to feel the baby move? Put your hands here."

"Um . . . well, okay."

"Come on, it's so cool! It's the best part of everything." She takes his hand and places it against her belly, and he leaves it there and closes his eyes. She moves against him, starts to undo his belt.

"Rosie—"

"It's okay."

"No."

"Jonathan, you're driving me crazy. It's *okay*. Pregnant women can have sex. It's even good for them."

"It's—it's . . . I can't."

"Why not?"

"I don't know. It's freaking me out. There's a *person* in there." He laughs. "It feels too public, somehow."

"Public? Did you say it's too public? This is a fetus, not an audience. It doesn't know."

"But what if—I don't know—what if it *does* know?"

"What if it does know?" she says. "Yeah, what if it does know? What then? You think it's going to mind? It's fine. Trust me on this. You're grossed out by me, aren't you? That's the truth of it. You don't like me this way."

He does not deny this. Instead he says, "It's just so . . . different. Also, I wouldn't even have the slightest idea how to even . . . you know, fit . . ."

"You can fit."

"Rosie." He bites his lip and looks at her. "I can't, okay? I can't."

"Is it my stretch marks? Because we can turn out the light—"

"No, that's not it. Please don't feel that way. It's that you're too—too delicate."

"Call Joe," she says. "He's a doctor, and he has four kids. You think he didn't fuck Greta for the total of three years she's been pregnant in their marriage? Call him. He'll tell you it's doable. Everybody does it. You know what my Lamaze teacher said about how long you can have sex while you're pregnant? She says it's a good idea to stop when the contractions are five minutes apart, so you can go to the hospital. Get it? All the way up to the last moment!"

But he won't, even when she is nearly in tears. He asks her if she'd rather he sleep in another room under the circumstances, and she cries and says no. And she asks if he's seeing someone else in California, and then they have a big fight, because he's *not,* and how can she not trust him when he loves her and begs her—has begged and begged—for her to come and join him? And there's no one else, never will be, never has been, and then they have part two of the big fight, which is about why they didn't get married when it was scheduled, and he says he will marry her in the morning if she wants, that's how sure he is, but he will not stick his penis anywhere near that baby. She cries and throws a pillow at his head, and he says he hopes that makes her feel better, because it certainly made him feel better. And now could they just go to sleep?

So they do, somehow. She on one side of the bed and he on the other, clinging to the edge of the mattress for dear life. The next day she calls up Greta and tells her what's going on—or what's *not* going on—and says that if Joe has an interest in saving this relationship, maybe he could find a way to put that medical degree of his to practical use and just step in. And so Joe takes Jonathan out for a beer and explains the facts of life to him, and the next night, Jonathan pulls her to him in bed, and they do it.

It's not the best sex anybody ever had, especially between

people who basically love each other and have been apart for seven months, but it's a start.

· She wakes up at three fifteen, hot, tangled in the covers, and needing to pee. When she comes back from the bathroom, she sits on the bed and watches him sleep. He's lying on his back with his mouth open, one arm flung across his forehead, and, seeing him there sprawled across the bed, she knows that this is all a terrible, terrible mistake.

Jonathan only *thinks* he wants them to be together, but for him it's just an abstract concept. He's actually just fine walking through the world all by himself, gathering up his teacups and his numbers and measuring his successes in ledgers and blog posts. He's just fine without all the messiness and bother of making love, of having a baby, even of having to interact on a deep level. All this time apart, and he's been basically, fundamentally fine—while she's been the one changing and discovering things about herself, creating this baby, figuring out what she wants out of life.

She doesn't know why she didn't realize this before. He doesn't need her and the baby. He doesn't even require more of a life than the one he's got. She reaches over and touches his arm, and he snuffles something from sleep and turns toward her. She lies down, plopping her stomach into place. The bed shakes and he opens his eyes, looking frightened. "Oh," he mumbles. "Christ. I thought this was another earthquake."

"No. It was just me. Moving. That's what it's like when I move lately."

"Ha." He laughs and turns over, away from her. "You two keep it down over there, will you?"

"Jonathan," she says. "Do you ever think your heart isn't big enough for a baby?"

After a moment, he rolls onto his back and looks at her.

"Oh my God," he says. "Have you been awake stewing about stuff all night?"

"No," she says. "But I really want to know."

"My heart is fine," he says, rubbing his eyes. "What's going on?"

"We have to talk."

He groans. "Ohhhh. You're saying this because I didn't want to have sex with you last night. Because tonight I thought everything went great . . . You came, didn't you?"

"That's not what this is about," she says. She reminds him about the little girl with the blueberry in the diner, and about the times when their friends with kids have needed them to babysit and Jonathan has never wanted to go. "Our lives," she says "are going to get so much bigger than they are now, and I know you're not with me on it. I always try to pretend that you are, but you're really not, and now I'm so scared because I'm going to be doing this all by myself and trying to pull you along, and I can't. I can't make it interesting for you, or compete with the teacups or the museum. I can't even compete with Andres Schultz."

"You don't have to compete with Andres Schultz, believe me," he says, and laughs uncomfortably.

"Don't laugh at this. It's real. We haven't lived together for seven months, and every single thing about us has changed. I don't think we even know each other anymore."

"Whoa, whoa, whoa," he says. "You're giving me the 'we don't even know each other anymore' speech? Please. Come on. Can't we just go back to sleep and talk about this in the morning?"

"Why did you call me up and tell me you wanted to be with me and the baby?" she says, and leans over and turns on the light. He blinks and puts his hands over his face. "What were you thinking this was going to be like?"

"Okaaaay," he says, and sighs. "So I guess we are going to have this conversation now." He sits up and rubs his hands over his face. His voice sounds miserable. "I told you I wanted to be with you because I missed you. You and I have been with each other for nearly sixteen years, and you're the one who knows me best, and who keeps me going, and I love you." He turns and looks at her, and his face is full of feeling. "And mostly I realized, being away, that everything was just emptier and sadder without you there. Every day there were things that happened that I wanted to tell you about, but you weren't with me anymore."

She looks at him. "That's it?"

"What do you mean, 'that's it'? That's what love is," he says. "And I strongly believe that once we live together again, everything's going to be fine. Our feelings are the same." Then he takes her hand and looks at her closely. "At least mine are. Don't you still love me?"

"Of course I do," she says, but then she tells him that even before all this museum stuff came up, she had always hoped he'd find his way back to being creative again, and how she felt the teacups just sapped his energy and took him from being a potter to being some kind of Internet wonk. "Just today, you've checked your phone about eleven thousand times—and those are just the times I saw. When you went to the bathroom, you probably added another five thousand to the total."

"I did. Five thousand more at least. So what? Rosie, I'm a businessman now. Don't you get it? Does that mean you can't still love me?"

"I do love you, but I need you to open yourself up."

"For Christ's sake," he says, "look what's been thrown at me. I haven't been here with you for all this pregnancy stuff. I'm new at it. You've got all those maternal instincts kicking in for you, but I don't know what's going on here. I'm trying."

"You're not trying. You couldn't make conversation with Soapie and George, you couldn't even touch me. How are we supposed to make everything good again when you're just so bound up?"

"You've got to let up on me. I'm not *Tony*."

She can tell her face has changed expression by the way the world tilts just a little bit.

Luckily he's not watching her. He's reaching over to look at his phone to check the time. "Yeah, Joe told me everything that's going on. That there's this guy who has the hots for you, even though you're . . . clearly spoken for, from the obvious look of you."

"He has nothing to do with this," she says. "This is between you and me."

"Joe says he's got a kid and some kind of crazy domestic life with his wife going rogue on him. So I get it: that's the attraction here. He's already got a kid, so he can be the big man around here. But it's not fair of you to compare me to him, when I'm new at this." He looks at her. "You don't have *feelings* for him, do you?"

"No, of course not," she says quickly. "I'm trying so hard to make things work with you, but when you act like you can't touch me and you act so uncomfortable around me, what am I supposed to think?"

He sighs. "It's going to take time," he says. "Look. You may think I'm not good about thinking about the baby, but you don't care one bit about the museum either, and you don't see me complaining about that. How can you care about it, when it's all so new?" He pulls her to him and kisses the top of her head.

"What are you talking about? You tell me every single detail of the museum," she says.

"So then you should tell me everything," he says grimly. "No detail is too small. I want to know all about your pregnancy. Every minute of it. And if I get bored or grossed out, call me on it. Yell at me. Make me be a part of things."

"Make you?" she says.

"Yes. I love you, you crazy. And I'm this kid's father."

"All right," she says. "But, Jonathan, I have to ask you a very, very serious question, and your answer to this is going to determine everything. That's why I'm warning you in advance. Will you come to the Lamaze class with me?"

He blinks. Yes, okay, he'll come. And then: "And what is Lamaze again?"

● ● ●

And so this is how it happens that she attends the final Lamaze class with yet a third person. She hadn't been able to bring herself to go to the third class the week before; she wasn't about to call Tony to ask him to take her, and Greta was tied up once again. She's sure the other smug couples look at her and think she can't even manage to get one person committed to her.

There is Jonathan, giant Jonathan, curled up in Starla Jones's living room with the pillows and the tennis balls and the other husbands and the even-more-pregnant-than-ever women, with their larger-than-ever bellies. One woman, it is reported, has already had her baby, and the class applauds at the news.

Starla has what they all want (everyone but Jonathan, that is): she has the facts about the birth. "She was in labor fourteen hours. First sign was the expulsion of the mucus plug, and then her water broke all over the bed, and she and her husband got up and they walked through the streets while she did stage one breathing . . . at the hospital, four centimeters . . . fetal heartbeat slowing . . . then by transition . . ."

Rosie looks over at Jonathan and sees him fanning himself. He gives her a wavery smile. He doesn't blanch even when they start talking about tightening the pelvic muscles. When they describe the rare complication of baby poop in the amniotic fluid, he looks forward, smiling bravely.

"So what did you think?" she asks him on the way home. He did well through the whole class, even chatting up the other husbands and carrying the pillows. She was proud of him. He was also by far the handsomest of the fathers, and the tallest. He looked artistic and debonair, not scared out of his mind.

"I've been thinking. There's one question I have for you," he says.

"Yes?"

"Why do you think Tony moved out so suddenly? Was it because he didn't want to meet me?"

She stares at him. "Oh, who knows? I thought you might have a question about Lamaze, about the childbirth process, Jonathan. That's what we were there for."

"I think he didn't want me to see how he feels about you," he says. "Joe says he's pretty far gone on you, really."

"Joe's clueless most of the time," she says. "Just ask Greta."

"Well, I think we should invite him for Christmas. I've decided I want to get a look at this guy."

"We are not inviting him for Christmas," she says. "He

has a child, remember, and he'll be spending Christmas in Fairfield, I'm sure . . ."

But then, wouldn't you know, Tony shows up anyway, and everything unravels, in the way it seems to Rosie that holidays are always just waiting to do. They love unraveling more than anything.

[twenty-six]

On Christmas morning, sitting next to the tree with a fire blazing away in the fireplace and coffee percolating in the kitchen, Jonathan gives her a silver ring inscribed with their initials, with a space for another initial—for the baby's name, he explains. "This jeweler I met in California made it," he says, and smiles at her, and she feels herself melting a bit. He was actually thinking about *them*—the family they're making—when he bought her present. She puts her hands up to his face and kisses him.

She'd been thinking of their family when she bought his present, too: some original editions of Winnie the Pooh that she'd found on eBay, and a book of poems about fatherhood.

She puts the ring on her finger, but it's way too small. "This is it, the end of the line," she said. "Now even my fingers have gotten fat."

"Your ring finger will go back to its regular size," Jonathan said, as if he'd ever had any clue about what size her regular ring finger might have been. "If not, you can always wear it as a pinky ring."

"This isn't a wedding ring, is it?" says Soapie from the couch, and George smiles and pats her on the arm to quiet her.

"Well, it could be, I suppose," says Jonathan. "But for our purposes now, I'd have to say no. We're holding off on that."

That's when the doorbell rings. Rosie is closest, so she unfolds herself with only a slight degree of difficulty and answers it. And there stand Tony and Milo on the doorstep, holding a bag of presents. Her breath goes a little jagged. Milo is jumping up and down, on his usual imaginary pogo stick, and Tony is squinting, looking past her into the hallway. He's got three wrapped presents under his arm, one of them a giant box.

"Oh!" she says. "Wow. Merry Christmas."

"Hi," says Tony. "Merry Christmas. Just wanted to say hello and bring you some gifts." He shuffles about a little bit, ruffles Milo's hair, and doesn't meet her eyes. "So. Everybody in the living room?"

She steps aside. "Yes. Come in. Soapie is going to be so glad to see you." In a low voice, she says to him, "I have some presents for you guys, too, but really, you couldn't have warned me?"

"I like the element of surprise," he whispers. "Where is the father-to-be? Living room? He behaving?"

"I brought the diamond to show you! I brought the diamond to show you!" Milo says about five thousand times in a row. She leans down and hugs him and admires the diamond, and he tells her about Christmas at his mom's, how he got a bike and a helmet. And then he says how his dad picked him up, and they decided to come over, and and . . . Tony shrugs and looks at her with a beaming smile.

Her chest gets so tight she's sure she's going to stop breathing, but she leads them into the living room, and Soapie, next to George on the couch, starts making cooing noises and flapping her hands. "Our Tony!" she says. "And the diamond boy!"

Rosie makes the necessary introductions, and Jonathan gets up out of the easy chair and greets Tony. And as they shake hands, she sees such a naked delight in his eyes when he sizes up the competition and realizes that he's the taller of the two. Advantage: Jonathan.

But Tony, unabashed at being shorter, keeps pumping Jonathan's arm, talking loudly (just a shade too loudly perhaps) about how happy he is to finally get to meet him. After all this time! Too bad you've had to *miss* so much of the exciting developments here, eh? Yeah? Doesn't she look wonderful? Congratulations, man.

Jonathan looks over at Rosie, as though seeing her for the first time. She does, she does, he says. He shakes Milo's hand, too, for good measure, just because Milo is standing directly in front of him with his hand outstretched. He doesn't see, of course, that Milo is really trying to show him a peanut butter diamond. Rosie has to point that out.

"We made this, me and Rosie and Dad," says Milo, when Jonathan finally notices. "It's from peanut butter. Not many people know that you can make a diamond from peanut butter, but you use a microwave, and that's what we did, me and my dad and Rosie."

Jonathan looks suitably baffled that this object is a diamond, but before he can say anything, Tony says, "I hear you're in teacups, man," and George gets up and hurries off to make drinks. Alcohol may be needed, he says. Jonathan mumbles something about the number of teacups he is currently showcasing, and Tony says he personally just uses teacups to drink out of, but he can't wait to see a whole museum of them. Maybe someday, eh?

Soapie explains to Milo that they're really in Paris, France, today, and when he asks why, Soapie looks up at Rosie blankly. "Why are we doing this?"

Rosie is grateful to have a reason not to watch the two men, who now seem to be emotionally circling each other like prizefighters. "I don't know," she whispers to Soapie and Milo. "It just seemed like a good idea."

"Because we like Paris, and we couldn't go. I think that's the reason," says Soapie. "We're *pretending*."

Jonathan has now gone to his comfort zone—numbers—and is giving some powerful mathematical data, such as how many ancient teacups he hopes to have by the end of the year, and the number of visitors the museum has had thus far, and how much it costs to buy a ticket to the museum.

Tony, always a master of subtlety, reaches over and ruffles Milo's hair and says children are a blessing that just can't be underestimated. "You're not gonna believe how it changes you, man," he says. "Just the getting ready alone—it lets you be part of a whole chain of humans. The preparation now, that's of *parliament* importance."

"Parliament?" says Jonathan, and Rosie flees to the kitchen.

"Oh my God. How did my life get to this?" she asks George.

He laughs. "I think you should relax and enjoy it," he says. "How many pregnant women get a day when two men are having a pissing contest over them?"

From the living room she can hear Jonathan saying, "Yes, we have an apartment, and Rosie is going to decorate it when she gets to California." And Tony is saying, "Really? She's going to do that and give birth all in the same few weeks?" And Jonathan says, "Man, you know her. She would have hated anything I picked out. Believe me, this is best. Even if it doesn't get done, at least it won't be stuff she'll yell at me for buying."

She eases herself down into the nearest chair and does her Lamaze breathing. They don't tell you in the course that it's going to be good for so many things in life.

● ● ●

Jonathan says, on the way to the airport two days later, "Well, I'm not so worried about you and Tony anymore."

"Good," she says.

"He's not at all what I pictured, from what Joe said. You know?"

"No?" she says.

"No. I mean, I think when I heard he was Italian, I pictured a kind of Italian stud, I think. This guy—I don't know— he's short and not really much of an intellect, you know? I mean, he's nice enough and all that. And that kid of his. What chance has he got, with the home situation he has?"

"Please," she says. "We don't know—"

"You're right. You're absolutely right. What do we know?" He looks out the window of the car. "Anyway, we got ourselves on track, didn't we?" He takes her hand across the seat. "We got a lot of things established."

"It was great," she says.

"Only casualty was the ring not fitting. But it still might, once you get that bundle of joy off the front of you."

She smiles and looks at her pinky where the ring is.

"So are we all right?"

"Us? Sure."

"No problems? We've survived the long separation, haven't we?"

"Yes," she says. She switches lanes, gets into the fast lane.

"But I noticed we don't do that love-you-me-too-you thing anymore, do we?"

"I guess not."

"Well, maybe we'll start it up when we get back together."

"Yeah, I'm sure we will."

"And you're going to get the rest of the house packed up, and get it sold, and come to California once Soapie is settled in?"

"Yes." She closes her eyes. So much to do, so many fraught things lying ahead of her.

"You can do it, you know," he says. "You don't have any doubts, do you?"

"No. I'm fine. I know I can do it. It's just going to be . . . hard. Saying good-bye to Soapie and all."

"But you know it's the right . . . well," he says, stopping himself. He looks out the car window for a moment, and she can feel him trying to come up with the right thing to say. "Hard stuff, but then we'll be together. And you're going to love San Diego. I just know you will." He leans over and squeezes her arm. "I love you, you do know that?"

"I do."

"Hey, did you find a doctor in California yet?"

"My doctor has contacted one."

"So all is good on that front."

"Yes."

"One thing we haven't really talked about much. I'll still have to work a lot of hours. But we can handle that, can't we? You're going to be plenty busy with nursing and . . . all that."

"Sure," she says. Then she has one of those moments when she can't quite believe how her life is going to change. She's going to have a family. She'll be able to flip her hair and toss off sentences that start with "Oh, yes, well, *my daughter* . . ."

"It's going to be okay," he's saying. "You'll have the baby and I'll have the museum. Funny how we didn't ever *need* a baby or a museum either, for that matter, but it's going to work out for us. We both got something that'll keep us busy."

Is that the way it is?

"I might have needed a baby and just didn't know it," she says.

● ● ●

"I have to break all the rules and ask you out on a date," says Tony on the telephone a week later.

"What rules are these?"

"The rules I made for myself, that I am going to stop throwing myself at you," he says.

"And where is this date taking us?"

"First tell me if you like surprises."

"I'd have to say no."

"Okay, then, we're going to a party at somebody's house, and it's really a baby shower for you, and so I've been told I have to make you come."

She laughs. "Oh, God. Is this one of Greta's productions?"

"No. I don't believe so. This is from your students."

"My students?"

"Yeah. Carmen and Tomas called me." He explains that it's being held at Goldie's condominium, and all the students are coming, and so are her friends, just possibly anybody she's ever spoken to for longer than three minutes through her whole life. And he would have kept it a surprise; he himself *loves* surprises, but he figured there was a good chance she might not come if he didn't let her know in advance. So could she please look surprised?

Okay, yes, she can.

So, Friday night. Eight p.m. sharp.

He'll pick her up.

"Practice in the mirror," he says. "If they find out I told you, I'm a dead man."

● ● ●

"Want to hear something kind of crazy—something you never expected to hear me say?" Rosie asks Soapie on Friday afternoon. They are in the den, next to the big windows that overlook the backyard. It's a gray, threatening-snow sort of day, and George has gone over to see Louise before the snow comes, he says.

"What did you say?" asks Soapie. She reaches down and picks up the grilled cheese sandwich Rosie has made her. It's been one of her extraordinarily good days. She's had an appetite, and she's been focused. They watched *The View* together all the way through, and Soapie laughed at all the funny parts. Usually she gets upset when the women are all talking at once, but today even that didn't bother her. It's been the kind of day that gives Rosie hope that the transition to the nursing home won't be so hard on her—and even though that date is fast approaching, she still can't picture it herself, how she's ever going to be able to simply walk away. Best not to dwell on all that.

"My friends are throwing me a baby shower tonight," she says. "Wanna come, too?"

It's a joke, because of course Soapie can't come to something like that. But she tilts her head, as if she's thinking about it. Funny how even two months ago, the news of a baby shower would have sent her off on some diatribe about outdated, sexist social customs for women. Now, she just smiles benignly and says in a small voice, "You look like her, you know. The way she would have looked if she'd gotten older."

The light, coming through the big windows, is filtered. It looks soft, almost pearly gray. Rosie stops, takes a deep breath, as though this were a moment that could skitter away like a frightened animal if she weren't careful.

"Who?" she says. "My mom?"

"Yes. It makes sense, I guess. That you'd be like her. Here, put my Coke here on the table, will you?"

Rosie moves the glass from the tray to the table next to her grandmother. Soapie is tracing her index finger on the brocade of the arm of the chair. "Lately when I sit here in the afternoons, I think about her."

"Really?"

Soapie leans forward and says in a loud whisper, "Don't tell George, but she talks to me sometimes. Come and sit by me. I want to tell you something."

Rosie smiles and pulls the armchair over, sits down, and looks at her grandmother. "Does that feel good, getting to sense her presence again?"

She sees her grandmother swallow, with difficulty. Her eyes, which seem clearer today, drift over to the window and then come to land on Rosie's face. There's an urgency in them. She swallows again. "Ahh, Rosie. After all these years, I think I know now why she did it. Hold my hand."

"Why she did what?" But it's so weird, the fact that she suddenly knows what Soapie is going to say, how the hairs on the back of her neck stand up.

Soapie sighs. "Why she killed herself. I know why. I remember now."

"But she didn't kill herself. A building fell on her," says Rosie, but even as she's saying it, she suddenly knows that building story can't possibly be true. What were the chances of a piece of a building falling on a woman? It is one of those things that has *never* made any sense. Why hadn't she ever stopped to think about that before? It's not true. It never was true.

Ka-boom.

Soapie looks at her sadly. For a long moment, she doesn't

speak, and Rosie holds her breath. A piece of herself has run away and is hiding. She can feel the shock in her fingertips. Maybe she doesn't want to know.

"No. No building, sweetie." Soapie's eyes are on her, piercing but kind.

Rosie closes her eyes. "Tell me," she says. Her voice is tinny.

"She wanted him too much, and he said he wasn't coming back," Soapie is saying, but there's a ringing sound in Rosie's ears. She can barely hear. "She was here with you and me, and he was up in Canada somewhere and this is the part I just remembered. He wrote her a letter and said he didn't want her and he didn't want a family. He changed his mind, Rosie, and it just killed her."

"But what about *me*?" she hears herself say. "Didn't she want to be with me?"

"She just went crazy. It felt like she forgot who she was."

"But I was just a little girl, and she loved me, you said."

"Nothing was enough." Soapie looks out the window. "Nothing was going to help. I tried to get her to go talk to somebody and get some help, but all she wanted to do was try to track him down in Canada. Which was impossible, of course."

But what about me? Rosie wants to shout. *You said! You said she loved me. Any mother loves her child and doesn't want to leave her that way.*

When she finds her voice, she says, "But you . . . why did you tell me about the building? Why did you lie to me?"

"You were too little to know," she says. "Who's going to tell a baby what really happened?"

"I haven't been a baby for a very long time," says Rosie. "You let me go on thinking that that's how she died. Why didn't you ever tell me the truth?" She can feel her voice rising. She feels like that little child again, smothered in not-knowing, sitting in the stuffy, stale-smelling den, missing her mother so much that her whole body trembles with the longing for her. She starts to shake. "All those years you wouldn't ever let me talk about her, and the whole time you're letting me believe this lie."

Soapie is quiet a long time. Rosie watches her hands worrying with the fringe on her blanket, pulling and tugging at it. Finally she says, "I know it was bad to lie to you. But I wanted to protect you, I guess, and I couldn't think up a better story. If I said she was sick, you'd want to know all about the disease, and if I said she got killed in a car accident, you'd be scared of cars always."

"But a building," Rosie says again.

Soapie's voice is irritated now. "Oh, who cares about that? The point is that love can be so destructive. My beautiful, beautiful daughter gave up everything for that stupid boy she loved, a useless, careless boy, and look at the lives that one act wrecked. Look what he took from all of us! I hated him then, but now I guess I don't have the energy to hate him anymore. I don't even know if he's alive. But I let him ruin our lives, Rosie."

Rosie wraps her arms around her stomach, as if she needs to protect the baby from this.

She watches Soapie's hands flutter up to her face. Rosie hears herself say, "It's okay. You did what you needed to do," but anyone could hear that she's speaking from very far away.

No building fell. No piece of masonry. You can go back to feeling good about the laws of physics.

No cruel trick of fate. No Coke with a friend in the city for a girls' day out.

Oh, but acceptance is going to be harder than this. She

knows that when she gets up and goes to the bathroom, when she forces herself to move her arms and legs. No, this is going to be hard knowledge to have. Her mother chose to die when she had Rosie to live for, to care for. It's not the lie or the fact that love can hurt—she's known that for some time. It's that she, her three-year-old, innocent self, couldn't save her mother; that Serena, who never showed up at any séance, never heeded any call, walked toward death on purpose. And how is Rosie supposed to live with that?

She stares at herself in the bathroom mirror, sees this new knowledge in her eyes that look almost smoky from the hurt they hold. It's a different mother she holds inside herself now.

When she goes back to the living room, she watches Soapie's hand, with its large veins, its thick nails yellowed in places, the liver spots thrown randomly across her mottled skin, trembling as it reaches for the glass of Coke. Just as she grasps the glass, there's a little twitch of her nerves, and the glass falls on the carpet and spills Coke all over the place.

"How did she do it?" Rosie asks quietly as she's scrubbing the carpet.

There's such a long silence that she thinks Soapie didn't really hear her. "Pills," she says at last. "She swallowed a whole bottle of pills."

"And where was I?"

"With me."

"I wish I didn't know. I wish you didn't tell me."

Soapie looks at her sadly. "I know. I wish I didn't have to tell you either."

"Maybe I should have never known. Why did you tell me now?"

"Sometimes we have to know things just because they're

true. And you can handle it now. We both can. It had a hold on us long enough."

Her grandmother sounds so tired, and it is so sad and dark in that room. Rosie gets up and turns on the lights and wraps her arms around herself. The snow has started outside now, and the heater hasn't kicked on in a long time. She goes and turns up the thermostat. It's good to keep moving. She notices that she keeps folding her arms across her chest.

She will have to stand off to the side of this story, where she's stood for so many years now, the place where her mother is just a shadowy figure who doesn't really, truly matter in any kind of daily, real way. Nothing has changed. Nothing has changed. Nothing has changed, except that where your mother was one kind of victim, now you know she's another, and it's worse. You think your heart has broken, but it hasn't really broken—not any more than it already was. You just notice it because it's got one extra crack in it right now. But that's so the light gets in. Somebody said that: the light comes through the broken places.

twenty-seven

The last thing she wants is to go to the baby shower. What a stupid idea: a party on this of all nights.

But if she doesn't go, she would have to make up some excuse. And then, worse, she would have to stay home with Soapie and George. So she drags herself upstairs and puts on her best red maternity dress. It looks like something you could buy at L.L. Bean and invite a family of four to move into with you, but she doesn't care. It also probably brings out her reddened eyes. She doesn't care about that either. She knots her hair up in a twist and sticks a sprig of holly in it, and then she practices her surprised face. She hopes it's not going to be one of those parties when people jump out and yell, "Surprise!" That's ridiculous. Who would jump out and scare a pregnant woman?

And how is it that it feels as though her mother died just today? But it does. She has to shake out everything she's ever known, touch all those objects once again, think of this woman whose life had become so unbearable that she took a bottle of pills.

"You're awfully quiet," Tony says on the way over to the party, which is in Branford by the water. Who would have thought that Goldie would live by the water? She seems like somebody who would live in the sort of village-y neighborhood where people danced outside in the square and brought each other covered dishes.

"That's because I look like Clifford, the Big Red Dog. My dress speaks volumes tonight, so I don't have to."

"Wow. A child's toy reference. Somebody's been studying for parenthood, I see."

"Tony. I think everybody who's conscious knows Clifford."

He turns into the condo complex, where there's hardly anyplace left to park. "Are you going to look really surprised?"

"Yes, of course."

"Let me see."

She makes her mouth go round.

"No, that's like rigor mortis." He gazes at her, and she thinks that if he didn't have such good manners, he might tell her she looks tired or weepy or whatever she looks like, which she knows is not good. But he doesn't. He says, "You look pretty tonight. Although you also look like you might burst into tears." She almost tells him then, but she doesn't. He looks at her for a long moment and then says, "I'm looking forward to this party. I haven't been to a party in ages—unless you count Thanksgiving."

"I just hope I don't fall asleep on the rug," she says. *Or start weeping into the punch bowl.*

And then she doesn't, of course. The place is filled up with people she knows and loves—all her students and then her usual friends, all of whom look perfectly happy to be there and non-shocked that she's walking in with a non-Jonathan man. Perhaps Joe and Greta have warned them that Tony is her handler these days. That's what Greta called him the last time they spoke about the Lamaze classes: "Oh, well, Tony can be your temporary handler."

There are bright lights and a punch bowl with red punch, and music playing. There is an endearing pile of presents wrapped in pink wrapping paper—all for her. There are a lot of people she doesn't know, too—Goldie's sons and their wives, and her single daughter, Alessandra, and Alessandra's friends—and some folks from the condo. The music is loud, and everybody is dressed up and dancing. It's the kind of party where the food is everywhere, so people cluster in all kinds of spots.

She dances—first with Leo, her dapper older student, and then with Joe, who tells her that this time next year her new child will be teething and crawling about. Then he looks stricken and says, "Oh my God, but it's hitting me. Greta and I won't be there to see her, will we? She's going to grow up a California girl," and she feels a pang. But it's just one pang, and she adds it to the pile of pangs she's already experienced today. The pile is getting quite large.

Head up. Keep smiling.

Greta moves over to her side. "Okay, so what's wrong?" she says.

Her eyes fill with tears.

"Oh, I know. Moving away, Soapie, all your students being so kind, the fact that you're going to miss me so bad you can't even fathom it . . ."

"Worse."

Greta steers her into the bathroom and closes the door and hands her a wad of tissues from the vanity. "Tell me."

"It—it's the worst. My mother killed herself. Soapie told me today."

"Oh, baby! Oh, honey!" Greta wraps her arms around her and sways with her, but Rosie can't get comfortable, really, with her belly in between them, and she pulls herself loose.

"All those times, Greta! All those séances we did, remember that? And the times we wanted to *be* her, and then she had just left me that way! Just threw me away, like I was

316 · MADDIE DAWSON

nothing. How did she think I was going to turn out okay after that?"

"Oh, baby, it wasn't about you. I don't know the facts, but I know that she wasn't thinking when she did that. She must have been so depressed, so unhappy to . . . to do that."

"But I was her baby!"

Greta's eyes are black with shock, but then she does what she has always done: she shifts gears into social worker mode, and takes Rosie by the arm over to the sink and runs cold water and gives her a wet washcloth. "Here, wash your eyes. And then listen to me, because this is important. This doesn't change anything about your life. Not really."

"But it does!"

"No. You're grown up. You're not that child anymore. Your parents were of a time when the whole world felt crazy. There was a war on, and there was all this political upheaval and turmoil, and so few options for people who didn't be-lieve in the war. And your father got caught in that, and he did what he needed to do to save himself. And maybe he did or maybe he didn't love your mother enough. But whatever, it doesn't matter. Because you are fine. You grew up, and now you're going to have your own baby, and you're going to mother yourself in the process."

"But what if I'm crazy, too? I think I am. Sometimes I don't know what I'm doing."

"You're not. You're as solid as they come. You're going to go and live with Jonathan and have your life now. It's all okay."

But that's so easy for Greta to say, Greta who has a per-fectly good, sane mother who stuck around and helped her kids in every way she could. And then Greta, armed with all that unconditional love, grew up and married a nice man who also stuck around and made babies with her. How can she ever understand what it means to have this hole inside, this huge shadow that is suddenly gaining on Rosie and threatening to swallow all the light that's near her?

Someone knocks at the bathroom door. "Is Rosie in there? Somebody says it's time to open the gifts."

"Just one sec," Greta calls. "Here, dry your eyes. We'll talk about this later, okay? I think your public is getting restless. Come on. We have to do this." She opens the door, and they reenter the fray, making their way through the smiling people, to the pile of gifts.

The presents are awesome—a stroller, lots of baby onesies and bibs, blankets, a kit of baby equipment. When she sees the tiny clothes, she laughs and holds them up. Somebody calls out, "All those years of buying those for everybody else—and now they're yours!"

She finds that she can smile. There is going to be a baby, and it is going to be a little girl . . . and somehow her mother killed herself and will never know about this. But somehow, maybe there's something of her left inside Rosie, something strong, even though Serena didn't have that strength herself. But how could that be? Goldie materializes at her side, clearing away all the wrapping paper, and she just wants to turn and bury her head in Goldie's shoulder.

Instead, someone turns on the music, and Tomas takes her hand and pulls her out into the middle of the living room, and even though she feels very far away from her real self, she does a salsa dance she remembers from two years ago when Carmen taught them all to dance one winter afternoon in class. Someone hands her a glass of nonalcoholic red punch, making a big deal about how she can't drink, and she finds herself in a conversation about winter weather, and whether Johnny Mathis is overrated, and then that conversation leads to one about snowfall amounts and the time that she needed rescuing by her students when her car wouldn't start—and then she's watching herself dance again, and it's been forty-five minutes since she's remembered that her mother committed suicide, and then she goes to the bathroom, where for a moment she thinks she'll cry again, but she doesn't, and when she comes out, she sees that Tony is dancing a slow dance with Alessandra, Goldie's beautiful ringlet-haired daughter, and that's when the world goes black.

She might be broken after all.

She goes over to the punch bowl and pours herself a glass of punch, with a shaky hand. So stupid! Then the song ends, and instead of just walking away from each other, Tony and Alessandra stand there in the center of the room, talking, and he takes her hand and then he leads her over to the table toward where Rosie is standing, and so of course she has to leave before they get there. She goes, awkwardly, to the other side of the room, where she sees him pour the two of them a glass of red punch. And they continue to stand there. Looking at each other. He tilts his head back and laughs at something Alessandra is saying. She shifts her weight to her other hip. It's a slim hip, too; there's not an inch of fat on her. And by the way, there is no earthly reason that a woman like her should be hanging out at her mom's house on a Friday night in the first place. She should have like a million dates.

Rosie can't breathe right, which is the thing that makes her the maddest of all. Tony's laugh rings out across the room. She hears him mention something about Milo. *Milo— he's telling this woman about his son?* Then she gets hold of herself. This is good, actually. He needs somebody, he does. And wouldn't that be ironic—if he ends up married to the daughter of one of Rosie's favorite students. But then she remembers that she won't have either Goldie or Tony in her life, and certainly not Alessandra. Nothing that happens is in her control or even any of her business.

She wishes she could just go into labor right this minute and be whisked out of here, preferably by an ambulance. And then it occurs to her: she could actually just leave, even without an ambulance. She's opened the presents, after all; she's been social and has let herself be overwhelmed with love and hugs and good wishes. She's lamented the fact that she has to move to California; she's filled everybody in on all the tellable details of her pregnancy and health. And now, as a pregnant person, she can just . . . leave.

She goes into the bedroom and takes out her cell phone and calls a cab. And then she goes to the kitchen, where Goldie has her hands plunged into a sink full of soapy water while she's talking to Leena, who is leaning against the counter and smiling.

"Listen," says Rosie in a low voice. "I don't want to make a big deal of this, but I've really got to go. I'm so exhausted. I just get so tired now at the end of the pregnancy . . ."

"Oh, my dear!" says Goldie, and she turns off the running water and grabs for a dish towel. "Let me drive you!"

"No, no, no," says Rosie. "I called a cab, and I don't want anyone to know. I just want to leave quietly and not interrupt the party. I'm actually fine, just really tired."

"But wait. You came with Tony, didn't you? We should tell him . . ."

"No!" says Rosie, and something in her tone of voice makes both women just stop talking and stare at her. "No, it's fine. Let him have a good time. He's always having to quit doing fun things because of me."

And then she just leaves, even though Goldie and Leena are bustling around her, packing up snacks and treats, suggesting alternatives for her. But she just kisses them both, closes her eyes, touches her fingers to her lips and blows them a kiss, and slips out the back door into the night, where a warm cab is mercifully waiting in the driveway. She turns off her cell phone and gets in. It hurts—everything—hurts so much. And the worst of it is that she has no right to feel anything that she's feeling.

She belongs to Jonathan, and he is patiently waiting for her so they can start their lives as parents.

● ● ●

She's riding on a motorcycle with her hair all tangled up and blowing behind her, and she knows she's not supposed to be doing this—it's so unsafe to ride a motorcycle with an unborn baby on her *back,* but she's doing it anyway, because there's a fire where she's coming from, and she's got to get herself and the baby to safety. People are chasing her, telling her to stop, and she wants to turn and explain to them that she has to keep moving, don't they see the danger, but for now she's just got to keep going. She feels the baby kicking her, but somehow the baby has moved back to the front of her, thank heavens, only it's kicking hard, making a noise with each kick like somebody knocking on something solid, and now it's also talking to her. "Rosie! Rosie, can I come in?"

"Come *in*?" she wants to say to it. "But you're already in!"

And then she opens her eyes in the darkness, and sees that the moon has made a parallelogram of silver on her bed. Her mouth feels thick, like her tongue doesn't really fit in there anymore. And she's not on a motorcycle, and that's not the baby talking to her. It's Tony. She can't think of anything to do but get out of bed, make him stop talking in the hallway.

She opens her bedroom door, and there he is. The hall light is on behind him. He smells like snow and the outside and cookies. He just stares at her. "What the hell—?"

"What are you *doing*?" she says. She leans against the door jamb and starts to cry.

"I've been trying to call you," he says angrily. "Why couldn't you have told me you were leaving the party?"

"I don't know," she says. "Like you cared anyway."

His eyes widen. "What are you talking about?"

"I saw you. You were dancing and laughing—"

"I was dancing *and* laughing?" He looks at her closely. "Oh, Rosie, Rosie! Are you sure? Not just dancing, but laughing, too?"

She glares at him. He doesn't even see that the blackness is filling her up.

"Listen, I expected to take you *home*. I didn't realize I wasn't allowed to talk to anyone else while I was there."

"That's not it. Don't be mean."

"Well, what the hell? I go looking for you, and Goldie tells me that you'd left an hour ago. You couldn't have even told me you needed to leave? Do you know how freaking worried I was?"

"Oh, that's interesting right there. It took you an hour to realize I'd left?"

He shrugs at her.

"Forget it. I had to get out of there. And you didn't seem like you'd miss me much."

"What are you talking about? I called you like a million times."

"I turned off my phone."

"I see that. But why did you do that?"

"Just go away, Tony Cavaletti. It's not any of your business why I do what I do. And it never was any of your business, and I'm going to move to California soon any-way, and you and I aren't going to see each other ever again, which is good. I can't take it anymore."

"Wait," he says. "You can't take what?"

"So just go away."

"I will, but first you have to tell me what this is about."

"No, I don't. Just go."

"I'm not going."

She gathers herself up and yells as loudly as she can, "Get out of here!"

There's a bump of some sort from Soapie's bedroom, and then silence.

"Go! Go! Go!" she says. By now she's crying so hard that she can't see anything through the snot and the tears, except then she sees his face up close to hers, and he wraps his arms around her, and holds her to his chest. He guides her back into her bedroom and closes the door, and then just stands there holding her against him. His kisses, when they come, are so soft against her hair, and she can feel his heart thumping underneath his sweater—that nice red sweater that he wore on Christmas, which is obviously his best holiday at-tire, and she knows he dressed up tonight for her shower, too, and knowing that for some reason makes her want to run and scream and tear her clothes and kick the wall and throw the china out the window.

He doesn't say *What's the matter,* or *You've got to stop this now,* or *Just try to calm down,* or any of that stuff. She would bite him if he did, she knows she would. It's just enough that she's letting him hold her. If he so much as tightened his grip, she thinks she would start screaming again. But he doesn't.

She says, "I don't want you to love other people while I'm right there. All right?"

He kisses the top of her head. "You were jealous?" he says.
"No. Yes."

"I don't know why, but I find that kind of sweet."

"Shut up. Can you just get me a tissue, and then will you lie down with me?"

He nods and walks her over to the dresser, where he leans over and grabs her a tissue, and then he walks her over to the bed, and they lie down. She feels him kick off his boots, hears them land on the floor with two thunks. She can tell by the sound that they landed and then fell over. The sheet is cool, and she tries to pull the blanket up over them, but it won't come. Her heart hurts at that. He reaches down and untangles it and it falls over them so softly, with a poof of air. There's a bright moon in the window—the same moon that was there the night he camped down below with Milo—and she stares at his face close to hers. She runs her finger along his jawline, feels his heartbeat just where his jawline meets that soft indentation, that unprotected little spot beneath his ear, soft and pulsing. He is perfectly made, full of life, and she is so broken and crazy right now, all jagged, red-hot edges.

"My mother killed herself," she whispers, and places her fingers over his mouth.

Don't say it's okay. It's not okay.

"When I was three. She couldn't stand being away from my father, raising me without him, so she left me," she says. Her voice is very steady. "Stupid me, I believed all these years that somehow a building happened to fall on her head. But really she took her own life. She left me."

He is quiet, kissing her fingers.

"I don't know who I am," she whispers. "I'm the person that everyone leaves, and I don't know why. I'm not enough."

"Oh, Rosie," he says. "No, no, no. You are enough. You are beautiful and good—"

"Only Soapie has stayed," she says. "Isn't that ironic? The one person who stayed yelled at me all the time and didn't share things with me, and lied to me about my mother."

She takes her hand away from his face while she's talking and starts unbuttoning her flannel pajama shirt without taking her eyes off his. He blinks in the silence. She says, "Help me take this off," and he does, and when it's gone, she presses against him. "I want to touch your skin," she says, and lifts his sweater. He takes it all the way off, which means that he has to sit up for a moment, and she closes her eyes against the wretched aloneness when he leaves her for that moment, but then he is back, and there are their two bodies, skin to skin. He leans down and puts his mouth on her breasts, kisses her collarbone, strokes her shoulders.

This, she thinks. *Now.*

She's kind of terrified that in a moment he's going to start asking her questions, like *Are you sure,* and *What are we getting ourselves into here,* and (the worst one of all) *Is this just because you're upset?*

But he just keeps kissing her slowly, his whole body a question: *Here? And here?*

Yes.

Pants are next, tougher to manage. Her leggings need to be tugged, but he is up for the challenge, and then he takes off his jeans. She hears his keys jingling when he drops them on the floor. He kneels beside her and runs his warm, soft, big hands all over her, those hands she's been staring at for months and wanting to feel touching her everywhere.

She feels beautiful underneath his touch, not ungainly, not swollen. Everywhere he touches her makes her body breathe its way into him. She reaches down and feels him respond to her. She'd forgotten what a rush of feeling all this could be, and when he enters her, first making sure she's in the right position so it won't hurt her, she throws her arms around his neck and stops remembering anything else.

There is then the holy darkness moving in her. He looks into her eyes and she feels the shuddering build throughout her body, the heat spreading everywhere. He holds her as she loses her mind, kisses her face, buries himself in her hair. And then, afterward, they lie together, holding on just as tightly.

"Oh, my goodness," she says when she can speak. She starts to cry again. He kisses her along her jawline, all the way along up to her hairline, and then down the other side, and then he takes care of the collarbone and both her arms down to every single metacarpal.

"Tomorrow," she says, "I don't want us to have a conversation about what all this means. Okay? Don't say tomorrow that we shouldn't have done this. And please don't try to get me to talk about my mother, not yet. Just hold me. And if this seems like a lot of commands and rules and instructions, I'm sorry. It's just that I got broken today."

"No, you're not broken," he says, and kisses her hair. "You're the real, perfect, beautiful you right now. And I love you."

"Maybe we shouldn't use the word *love*," she says.

"I know I'm not that good with the words and all, but I don't think there's another one that does it justice."

"So we won't use words. That's better anyway."

twenty-eight

He is a gift she is giving herself. A time out of time. And why not? Can't you just have a time of wow? An interlude that has nothing to do with your so-called *real life* (she does the air quotes for herself) but is just a break from all that ordinary, rotten stuff?

Of course you can. She's going to do the right thing eventually. She's committed to all things that are good and important and citizenly in this world, and by God she is going to be an upstanding, ethical human being, and a *mother* and a *wife*, but not just yet.

For now, she is allowing herself a little vacation from what her real life is going to be, that's all. Nothing serious. She doesn't even have to feel guilty about it. What did the Cole Porter song say about this—something about "a bell that now and then rings"? Yes! This is a bell that has been unrung too long, and now that she is forty-four goddamned years old, it has finally started clanging away to anyone who will listen to it. But she knows all too well that it will go silent again.

Sometimes in that first week, watching Tony Cavaletti sleeping beside her, she knows exactly what he means to her. He is merely an infatuation, just somebody funny and fun and gorgeous and kind and gentle, and God knows he seems to have her number when it comes to sex—and what is so bad about having this in her life right now on a temporary, consenting-adults basis?

And then there are the other times. Times she gets a jolt right through the cerebral cortex, when she can't look at his eyes looking back at her, or feel his hand touching hers, or hear the lovely, funny way he has of mispronouncing words, without wanting to just drag him off someplace forever. It sounds so ridiculous, but it's as though his body is a magnet, and when she's anywhere near him, she has to be even closer. She has never been like this before. She didn't even *know* about this. She is in love, silly and ridiculous, crazy-mad love—the kind that everyone knows, from literature and the movies, is going to end badly.

Well, but she has outsmarted that. It's going to end all right, but she knows exactly when. And it's not going to end because of despair or a huge fight or any of those other endings you read about in Shakespeare or watch on soap operas: your duels and your middle-of-the-night recriminations. It won't be heartbreak. It will be clean and simple, an inexorable path toward parting, known full well from the beginning.

In just over two weeks—sixteen days—she will put away this glorious vacation of love, this foray into living in the present, and she will simply pack up her life and leave for California. It is so simple. She wishes everyone in the world had had this opportunity. She tells him it's like going into the Peace Corps—the Peace Corps of the heart, where you get to be your own sweet caseworker, ministering to all the hurt and ruined places, rebuilding the infrastructure, and soothing the natives, teaching them about irrigation and communication and how to stop crying inside.

And then, bingo, you're healed—maybe not completely, but well enough, certainly better than you were before it all happened, and so you can resume, carry on with your regularly scheduled life. Love with eyes wide open.

She would like to stay in her room, healing herself with him all the time, but of course that's impossible. They have Soapie to take care of and monitor. Ever since the conversation about Serena, Soapie seems more checked out than ever, content to simply stay for long hours in the den, looking out the window at the birds or talking with George. She doesn't want to play games anymore or watch television. She sits in her chair, running her hands along the brocade armrests and looking peaceful.

Time seems to stand still, as though it's all just a string of moments illuminated and electrified by the fact that they're limited. When Rosie and Tony aren't making love or lying in her bed talking, they have taken to cooking divine meals, the more outrageous the better: lobster dinners with pots of drawn butter; cheesecakes dripping with strawberries and cream cheese; puddings that you can dig both hands into. She bakes bread with raisins and cinnamon, and they eat it while it is still hot, pulling it apart in chunks because they can't wait until it's cool enough to slice.

They can't wait for anything. They are greedy for everything: food, love, talking, sex, experiences, textures, kisses. Kisses and more kisses.

On Wednesday he brings home meatball subs, and they eat them on the laundry room floor, and then that leads to making love on the pile of quilts that had just come out of the dryer. Laughing and whispering, so Soapie and George, just two rooms away, won't hear them.

"Why would they start hearing things *now*?" whispers Rosie.

At night he sleeps next to her, curled around her; spoons. She has to get up at least twice each night to pee, and he waits for her, sliding over to keep her part of the bed warm for her, so that it's not such a shock when she comes to get back in. One night she is sick and throws up, and he goes with her into the bathroom and holds her hair back, and when she's finished, he puts toothpaste on her toothbrush and stands there holding her while she brushes her teeth, and then tucks her back into bed, into himself.

She gazes at him, touches his face. Then she closes her eyes and sleeps and sleeps.

● ● ●

Soapie and George never mention anything about the new arrangement, even when things get really crazy, when they are all but kissing on the living room dance floor after dinner.

And then one day when she's helping Soapie into her chair downstairs, Soapie looks right at her and says, "You've got to stop this, you know."

"Stop what?"

"Your men. This sloppy life."

Rosie laughs, but for a moment she feels as if she's been slapped. Then she puts her chin up and says, "I know. But it's not sloppy if you're learning something about yourself, and I am. This is like a college seminar for me, actually. It's part of my education."

Soapie snorts. "Well. But you have to pick. You've gotta get you some joie de vivre. Don't sit around and let your whole life dribble away. Find what makes you happy, what gives you passion. Why can't you ever get that through your head?"

"It's going to be all right. Don't worry about me."

"I do worry. I'm leaving you. I want things to work out."

"Yeah, but what would working out mean to you? You thought I needed Paris, and it turns out that all I needed was—well, this."

"I know. You need this baby. God knows why, but you do."

"Yes."

Soapie's tired out, and she lolls her head back on the chair. "Move this fleece thing. I'm cold. You've never taken my advice, but I have one more piece of it for you. Pick a man, goddamn it, and make it work. Doesn't matter which one, but it's for your girl. And also, don't glorify the past like you do, when I'm gone. I'm just your old, used-up family."

● ● ●

On Friday Tony says, "I've been thinking about something. What if everything is unfolding exactly as it's supposed to? Did you ever think of that?"

"What, all of it?" she says.

"Yeah. All of it. What if even your mom lived life for as long as she was supposed to, and then she left when she was done, and maybe it had to be that way so a whole lot of other stuff could happen in the world." He takes her hand and holds it against his lips and thinks. "It wouldn't keep it from being sad, but maybe when bad stuff like that happens, maybe it's because something else big needed to happen and it couldn't get started. Like . . . well, what if Soapie had to raise you, or you wouldn't have turned into the person you are? And then you wouldn't have had this baby, this very person that's right here in between us."

"Kicking us," she says.

"Beanie the prizefighter baby."

"But how would we know that?"

He kisses each of her fingers. "Oh, well, we wouldn't. But what could it hurt, thinking that way?"

"Soapie said my mother ruined our lives."

"But she didn't. She only ended her own, if we look at it this way. Your life isn't ruined."

"And so you and me . . . me and Jonathan . . ."

"Well, let's not go too far," he says, and laughs. And then he kisses her again. "But yes. It takes away the agita, if you think it's all okay," he says. "You just let it exist alongside everything else about you. You don't let it reach in and grab your happiness."

"Even if it kind of sucks?" she says.

"No, no suckage. It's perfect so it can't suck anymore. It's what I do, with the two mommies. I say to myself that this is the way it was supposed to be. Love for everybody. There's always enough."

"Yeah, well, that might be the craziest thing you've ever said," she tells him, but she can't quite explain why his words make her heart start beating harder. She closes her eyes.

"Clearly you need to work on this a bit more," he says.

● ● ●

Jonathan calls the next day. She chats with him, surprised only slightly at how easy it is to talk and to listen, how a different part of her brain seems willing and able to take over. It's the usual stuff: teacups, museum ticket prices, patrons' remarks at seeing the displays of teacups. Context, he tells her, is everything. You might not think so . . . you might think it's all about the cup itself. But no. It's context.

"Oh," she says. "That's really so interesting." And the funny thing is, she means it.

Then suddenly he switches gears and says, "So, just so you know, I sold the *National Geographics,* and I bought us a crib." He says, "It's just an oak crib. I hope that's okay. No frills or anything. Nice, sturdy lines." He's striving for nonchalance, but she can hear in his voice a shaky pride in himself, for his sacrifice.

For a moment she can't take this in. The *National Geographics*? The obsession before the teacup obsession is now gone. She didn't know they could disappear. She thought the obsessions just piled up, climbed one over the other, vying for prominence.

"You still there?" he says.

"Yeah."

"Is that okay? I mean, I know it's *okay.* I wanted to let you know that I'm—I'm part of this. With you. I'm in."

"Wow," she says. "I'm really pleased."

He says, "If it's seemed like I wasn't, you know, fully engaged, it's because I think I was angry before that—well, you didn't tell me about all this until it was too late for—well, for us to do anything to stop it. That really was a kick in the head, you know. But then I guess I started thinking about it, and I realized that I wouldn't have told me about it either." He laughs a little.

"What are you saying?"

"That I've been selfish, and I'm sorry. I thought about what you said, how life's been all about me. I've been a shit. So—well, I sold the magazines, and it didn't kill me." He laughs again. "I was never going to read them again anyway. So now I can't. They're gone, and we're having a baby. And there's something kind of—well, kind of fitting about that."

"Magazines for babies."

"Ba-*by,*" he says. "Singular. Right?"

"Yes. Oh, yes."

They're quiet a moment. Then she says, experimentally, "I'm afraid I've had some hard news."

"Hard news?" he says. "Are you feeling okay?"

"Well, yes. I mean, it's not about me. It's about my mom."

"Your mom?"

"Yes." For a moment she wishes she hadn't started in on this. His reactions are never the way she wants them to be. But she's come too far now to go back. "My mom—well, Soapie told me that she killed herself."

"She what?"

"She didn't die when a building fell on her."

"Oh," he says. "Wow."

"Yeah. Wow."

A beat of silence goes by, and she squeezes her eyes closed. "So that's kind of a surprise, huh?" he says.

"Yeah."

"That's bad, but I suppose we should have known. And it doesn't really matter, right? Not in the whole scheme of things. I mean, dead is dead. No matter the cause."

"I know, but it hit me pretty hard. It means she left me on purpose."

"You don't know what she was thinking," he says. "Also, Soapie is demented now. It might not even be true. Please don't let this bring you down. She was a person you didn't even know."

"Didn't I know her? I mean, back then I did. I think of what I missed, everything I didn't get—"

"Yeah, but that's not new news. It's okay. You made it through just fine."

"You think I made it through fine?"

He laughs. "Jesus in heaven, I can't think of what you want me to say. Yes, you made it through. You're smart and funny and people love you, and you're a good person, and you did all that without a mother. Give yourself some credit. Lots of people who had perfectly good moms aren't nearly as put-together as you. Me, for instance."

"Well, you," she says. "You're just a little bit obsessed with stuff, but you're okay. I don't think we can blame your mom for that."

"Oh, speaking of obsessions, I've been reading about pregnancy. And I learned that by the time you're at the stage or pregnancy you're in, you have fifty percent more blood in your body than you did when you started out. How's that? And also that your estrogen and prolactin levels have nearly tripled, and that if we were together, just being around you would mean that my testosterone would automatically start lowering. That's how nature gets men into daddy mode. Isn't that something?"

"Daddy mode? Are you kidding me?"

"Yeah, so we guys will help take care of the offspring, and not eat it or something."

"Very ingenious. I'd forgotten to worry about you possibly eating the baby."

"And so, what I was thinking was that just being around you at Christmas lowered my testosterone enough that I wanted to part with my *National Geographics* so I could buy a crib. I do not think this was a coincidence."

She laughs.

"Yeah, so there's that. Just so you know. I'm coming around."

"I know you are."

"I love you. Who knows? Maybe I'm going to go buy a baby name book tonight."

When she hangs up, she thinks it's lovely how hard he is trying, and that she'll be happy to see him again—just not yet. Not yet.

● ● ●

"Tony," she says later that night.

"Hmmm?" He's drowsing next to her in bed after painting her toenails, which she can no longer begin to reach. He made them a nice lavender color, he said. She insists she can't see them.

"Do you think we're having an affair?"

"Don't know."

"Because an affair usually means that one or both of the people is married. So I think we get off on a technicality, and we're not."

"But you're engaged," he says. "Wouldn't you say that counts?"

"Yeah." She sighs. "I guess it does."

"Do you want this to be an affair?"

"I don't know. The word is kind of sordid, isn't it?"

"Sorted? Sorted into what?"

She hauls herself up close to him on the pillow. "Also, Jonathan bought a crib. Sold one of his collections and bought a crib. So there's that."

"Wow. He's aces."

"I think if I have to fill out a questionnaire about whether I've had an affair, I'll say no, with an asterisk. And then if I have to explain, I'll say I enjoyed a Peace Corps of the heart."

He lifts his head up. "What kind of questionnaire makes you answer that?"

"You know. The kind you give yourself. When you think of all you did in life."

"I've never given myself a questionnaire."

"I know. I like that about you. You just do stuff. I've always got to think about it, analyze it, give it a name, and figure out why I did it."

"So, if I may ask you: what does the crib have to do with the affair?"

"Who said it did?"

"Well, you told me both at the same time. So I think it does."

"Hmmm. It makes it more . . . wicked?"

"It makes you feel guilty because a man is buying a crib for your baby, and you're here in bed with me."

"No!" she says. "Not at all. The guilt isn't in that direction. Amazingly enough. I'm feeling guilty because one day in about a week, I'm going to say good-bye to you, and it's going to be the hardest thing I ever did, because you are going to be here all alone, and I am at least going to have a man with a crib and then a new baby."

They lie there for a moment, looking at each other. Then he says, "I'll still have Milo, you know."

● ● ●

The next morning, she fixes Soapie her favorite breakfast: a cup of green tea and a poached egg, a cinnamon roll, and a glass of Coke—yes, it's the breakfast of somebody who doesn't care anymore what makes sense—and she takes it into the den, where Soapie is in her recliner, her fleece throw over her lap. She's staring out the window, watching the birds at the feeder.

"The cinnamon roll has all the sugar on one side, and none on the other," says Soapie slowly. She's staring at the roll as if it's a curiously defective piece of art, not something to eat.

"Huh. Want me to spread it around a bit?"

"No. I don't really care."

Later Rosie will both want to remember and want to forget this day, but for now she sits perched on the side of the couch watching her grandmother's face, and then looking down at the cinnamon roll, with its sugar perfectly centered all around the roll. Not defective. As soon as she gets Soapie fed, and when George comes down, she is going to go back upstairs and crawl back into bed with Tony.

"And the coffee is too hot."

"There isn't any coffee," Rosie says. "It's green tea, but I can put an ice cube in it."

"Do I even like green tea?"

"You do. At least you said you do."

"Green tea is a hoax. It's that stuff they pick up after— using that machine thing? The mower?"

Rosie laughs. "A hoax tea made of grass clippings? It does taste that way sometimes," she agrees. But Soapie is already looking at the cardinals at the feeder and tilting her head toward them, smiling. They talk about the birds— how the male and the female take turns pecking at the seeds, while the greedy squirrels sit on the ground, eating the husks that fall. Every now and then, one of the squirrels gets frustrated with waiting and figures a way to shimmy up the pole, using pure animal magic to scare the birds away and get the seeds.

The snow is crusted up on the pine tree branches. Soapie sees it. Then she says something Rosie can't really hear, about Ruth the editor. Then something about Serena's doll when she was a little girl. She loved that doll. A pair of sunglasses that Soapie used to have, with rhinestones in the corners. Cat glasses, someone called them.

"I don't . . . want . . . today. Not the grass apple; not cinnamon roll."

"Are you feeling okay?"

"Where's George?"

"He's upstairs."

"Coffee? And no hot." She puts a trembling hand to her head, squints.

"Sure. Do you want me to call George?"

Soapie doesn't answer. She stares out the window.

"I'll get him." Rosie goes to the stairs and calls up, "George? George, you decent?"

He doesn't answer right away, and then she hears the shower go on.

She goes back into the kitchen and calls back to Soapie, "I think he's in the shower. Did you want me to bring you an ice cube?" There's no answer, so she puts a piece of bread into the toaster for herself, and goes back into the den. Soapie is sitting in the same position as she was before, her head just slightly turned toward the window.

Rosie says, "He's in the shower," and goes over to her grandmother. "Soapie?"

There's no answer.

She reaches over and touches her. "Soapie?" and that's when she realizes that her grandmother is dead.

She puts her hand to her own chest.

Dead. Gone, just like that. Just sitting there in the chair, just the same as she was, only somehow . . . dead. So this can really happen, Rosie thinks, amazed: you can die suddenly, with no fanfare; as you're sitting watching the outside, you can just make your exit, your heart beating its last, your last breath coming without any warning. A stroke, a heart attack—some interior explosion had stopped everything, and she is sitting there with her head leaning back against the cushion, her hair flowing out from its bun, her blue eyes staring straight ahead, her mouth slightly open.

Rosie softly cries out, "Oh!" And starts to cry. It's a few

days before the scheduled nursing home move. That's what she thinks of first, and then once she finishes thinking that thought, she thinks, *Well, good for you, Soapie. You never did intend to go to the nursing home, did you? You beat that deadline.* Which is a crazy thing to think, but there you go.

It all went so fast. Wasn't that what Soapie had said, the night of the meltdown and the dancing?

It's over. The person who had stayed with her throughout is gone, and it all went so fast. She reaches over and strokes her grandmother's hand, holds it to her cheek and waits in that moment of in-between she knows so well, that moment when you wait just to see if the tears are going to come and how awful they're going to feel.

[twenty-nine]

Jonathan, as the fiancé of the bereaved, flies in the next evening, and she goes to pick him up at the airport. Outwardly, to the other passengers and their friends and families, she thinks that she probably doesn't look like someone who has just lost a whole part of herself. She has lost not only her grandmother, but she's lost the Peace Corps of the heart, and yet she probably looks like somebody who has everything to live for, heavy and careful with pregnancy. Her brown hair falls over her pale skin, and she is wearing light pink lipstick and a billowing maternity coat. She is waiting and then she is being spotted and kissed and hugged by a handsome man, a man who hurries toward her and tips her face up to his.

On the walk through the terminal, he tells her that January is one of the most common months for people to die. He Googled this fact. Then he tells her that, speaking just for himself, this death—regrettable but also inevitable, surely she will agree—is actually perfect timing because now she can come back with him before time runs out for her to be able to fly on an airplane. He tells her he misses her terribly and then says that San Diego is beautiful at this time of year. He bets she won't even miss Connecticut at all.

They are walking through the terminal at Bradley International Airport in Hartford, and she is thinking that the overheated air is too dry and thin, that it actually hurts on her skin. Jonathan keeps looking at her. And then even in public, he stops walking and hugs her.

"You're even bigger than you were three weeks ago," he says.

"Yes," she says. "That's the idea, I guess."

"Are you uncomfortable? All that extra blood volume weighing you down?" He says this while they're waiting to cross the street to get to her car in short-term parking. It's snowing lightly, and the flakes landing on his padded parka shoulders are like little stars. People are walking by, having conversations about their lives and where they parked the car and whether it will still be snowing when they get to Vermont, and all the ordinary things people talk about. Some people smile at her. They are thinking, *New baby*. They are thinking: *A couple reunited*.

But she is nearly eight months pregnant, and her story has come unraveled all of a sudden.

"What's the matter?" he says.

"I just miss her," she says.

"I thought we were talking pregnancy symptoms," he says.

"Those are okay. Manageable," she says. "It's Soapie."

"Look, she was a difficult woman, and just be glad you survived her," he says. The light changes, they cross the street. He hoists his duffel bag into the car trunk when they get there, and he comes around to the passenger side and asks her for the keys so he can let her in. He'll drive, he says.

She wonders what would happen if she just told him what's been going on. If she could make him understand what she's needed, and then what she's taken for herself. Maybe he even has a right to know. Maybe it's the kind of truth—like her mother's suicide—that hurts but that, even so, has to be known by all affected parties.

She waits to see if she says anything, but then she's not surprised to see that she doesn't mention it.

"If there's a silver lining," he's saying, "it's that this way now we can go back together. I can help you pack up the rest of the house, if needed, after the funeral, and then we can fly together. I was worried about you having to do all that packing and then flying by yourself."

She can't tell him. It would needlessly hurt him.

"Yeah, okay," she says. She closes her eyes and leans back against the seat. He turns on the radio after a while.

Tony told her this morning that he was going to go back to his apartment.

"Our two weeks," she had said.

"We had what we needed," he said. "Most people don't get that much."

When she gets back to the house, she knows George will be gone, too. It's as though everybody fled, knowing that Jonathan was coming back into the picture, as if they'd only been serving as a placeholder for him all along. The house will be huge and lonely with just her and Jonathan there to fill it up.

Here's where we made the spinach lasagna that time, here's where we stood when I found out I was pregnant, here's where I found Soapie on the floor for the first time, here's where Tony and I made meatball sub love . . .

That night at dinner, Jonathan takes her hand across the table and looks into her eyes. "I'm very sorry," he says. "If anything I've said has sounded like I don't know what a huge loss this is for you, I'm truly sorry. I know that you and Soapie loved each other."

She tears up.

"And I'm here to help you in any way I can," he says. "I shouldn't have rushed into talking about how you'll come back with me. I mean, I hope you will. But I know you've got a lot of stuff to process. This can't be easy."

She wipes her eyes on her napkin. "I just didn't see it coming," she says. "She was eating her breakfast and complaining about everything, and I went back into the kitchen, and when I came back in the living room, she was just . . . dead. Gone."

"It's probably a blessing, to go that way," he says.

"Please don't say it was a blessing," she says. "I hate when people say that about somebody dying." But what she really wants to say is, *Don't go being perfect at this stage. I've been so . . . so . . . not perfect.*

He holds her all night, his hands warm and soft on her body.

● ● ●

Surprise. Soapie had the funeral all planned: which songs were to be sung, which passages and poems were to be read. It was all written down on a piece of paper she left in her bedside table drawer, known only to George, of course. She liked a poem by Walt Whitman and something from "Self-Reliance" by Ralph Waldo Emerson. Nothing religious, she had written. And no talk about the hereafter or how she was now in God's hands. Also, the entire congregation was required to sing "I Get Along Without You Very Well," which made everybody laugh, even while they were sad.

Everybody came: Ruth, the editor, and Carlene, the publisher of the Dustcloth Diva series; Matt Lauer even came, showing up in a Lincoln Town Car, and leaving before the reception even began. He gave Rosie a kiss on the cheek and said he would always remember the day her grandmother came on his show and before she went on the air Matt told her there was nothing to be scared about, she was such a sweet old lady who at least wouldn't swear, and she'd said, "Fuck you, I'll swear if I want!" And laughed. They'd all laughed. And she'd come on three more times after that and made them laugh every time. Rosie has heard this story so many times, but she knows this might be the last time she hears it, and that is suddenly a huge loss. She'll have to be the one telling it from now on. How old will her daughter have to be before she can tell this story? Maybe she'll tell it to her the first day, in the hospital, and every year after.

People all come back to the house, and Jonathan builds a fire. A bunch of food materializes—everything from ham and turkey slices to bowls of macaroni salad and chips, slabs of cheese and bread. Someone makes coffee, and Jonathan opens a few bottles of wine and gets down the glasses from the high cabinet shelf. Greta's and Suzanne's kids walk around with trays of food with toothpicks in them. But who did all this?

Rosie can't imagine. She's so tired, and she sits on the stool in the kitchen, talking to first one group of people and then another. Whenever she looks up, she sees Jonathan, dressed in his dapper navy blue suit, presiding over everything, making sure people have drinks and that the older people find places to sit down. He brings her a plate of food, which is fortunate because she's just about to get that late-afternoon low blood sugar that makes her want to burst into tears so often. But how does Jonathan know that? Tony was the one who used to make sure she kept her blood sugar on track. But now it's Jonathan. He just seems to be everywhere at once, comforting people, being comforted by them, joining groups, watching out for how everyone's doing.

Tony's there, too—or an impression of him is, at least. He seems ghostly, almost wafting across the room like someone who is not quite there. Of course he must feel unwelcome, she thinks, with Jonathan there as the resident man of the house all of a sudden. Even George seems moved to the background. Jonathan and Rosie are the couple running this funeral. Nothing could be more clear. Frankly, Rosie thinks, it's a little intimidating. All this confident Jonathan-ness in a suit.

Much later, she sees Tony go upstairs to the bathroom, and she goes up and waits outside the door. When he comes out, she pushes him back in and goes in and closes and locks the door.

"Oh God, oh God, oh God," he says.

"I know. I came to see how you are."

"I'm okay. In shock."   .

"At me? Going?"

"No. I knew. The suddenality. Like a curtain came down."

"I know. I suppose I have to pick him," she says, and starts unbuttoning his shirt.

"No, no. You have to. He's the father. He's the guy. Look at how he's handling this funeral." He puts his hand over hers, stopping her from doing more.

"If we'd had our two full weeks, maybe we'd have been ready for this. We were robbed."

He tries to laugh. "Yeah, just another few days, and I totally would have been sick of you."

"Me, too, you," she says, and then realizes that that's what she and Jonathan always used to say to each other, and feels ashamed. Who is she the most disloyal to today?

"Look," he says. "Jonathan's going to be a good dad. He's come a long way. Look at him out there, running things. He looks like he's ready to coach the kid's soccer team or something."

"Yeah."

"And you—you're going to be a fantastic mom." He lifts

his hand up, about to stroke her cheek, and then hastily puts it back down again, remembering.

"Don't say that. I don't know what I'm doing. And anyway, this is getting too sentimental. I can't stand to be sentimental anymore today. I've had my quota of crying."

"Tough nuts. That's what funerals are for."

"Yeah, but this isn't the funeral," she says. "It's you and me in the bathroom doing a postmortem on our . . ." She leans against the wall and just looks at him, all dressed up in a suit, with his hair slicked down. So un-Tonylike, and yet she wants so badly to touch him.

He laughs. "Our what? We decided it wasn't an affair, remember?"

"On our stint in the Peace Corps."

"Sure," he says. "Okay."

"I'll write to Milo. I didn't get to say good-bye. And the two mommies. I'll write to them, too." She closes her eyes.

"And me?"

"I think you and I are going to have to take a little break, don't you? While I adjust."

"But you'll let me know when the baby comes!"

"Oh, sure, of course I will. God! Did you think I wouldn't tell you something like *that*?"

"No. You will. I know it." He gazes at her, and she can't help it, she starts rubbing his shoulder.

"Listen," she says. "I know we'll miss each other a lot, but I can't bear it if you don't move on. I know I was insanely jealous before, but I do know that you've got to find your own family. No more experiencing family only through the car window, okay? Please don't keep thinking of me."

He laughs a little. "You can't tell me how much to think of you," he says. He reaches over for her and she puts her head on his shoulder, but he shifts his body so they aren't touching all the way down. Then he moves his hands underneath her shirt and touches her rounded belly and caresses it. Then he bends down and kisses her abdomen all over, a trail of kisses.

"Be happy," he says, and she doesn't know if he's talking to her or to the baby inside. "Please, please be happy."

When it's time, she walks out of the bathroom first and joins Jonathan and the posse in the kitchen. Her knees are still shaky. Lots of people have left by now, and Joe and Hinton and Greg are washing the dishes, of all amazing things, and Greta and Suzanne are wrapping up the food. Everybody turns to see her, and for a moment she's sure they can tell everything she's feeling.

"Look at you," says Greta. "You've made it through, haven't you, honey?" She squeezes Rosie's shoulder.

"Let's go out to dinner!" says Joe. He throws his arms around Jonathan's and Greta's shoulders at the same time. "This time we'll see these two off right, so it'll take. We owe that to them, don't you think?"

"We're not leaving tonight," says Rosie, alarmed. "I have tons of things to do before I go."

Jonathan clears his throat. "Just the business with the real estate agent and signing the papers, and the will . . ."

"Yeah, yeah, yeah," says Joe. "I'm just saying we learned our lesson from last time. We're not dropping you off and assuming you leave together. *This* time I think I need to see all four of your legs walking through the terminal to get on that plane."

"Not a problem," says Jonathan. He comes and puts his arm around Rosie and smiles down at her. "We're ready for this."

[thirty]

"So when do you think we should get married?" Jonathan says at breakfast.

Ten days have passed, and they have already found another diner, their San Diego diner, although it's nothing like Ruby's. But that's okay. It's nice. Things are just different, that's all. It'll take forever, she thinks, before they know the cook. One thing that's missing is the downtrodden, slightly hopeless look that Ruby's had, the worn tiles on the floor, the peeling paint—all that ambiance that made you feel right at home.

But that may just be the way California is. Even their condo looks like it was manufactured at Disneyland and placed at the edge of a golf course, simply for their viewing pleasure. No polluted river outside their sliding door, no wooden boats, no restaurant across the water with braying karaoke singers belting out tunes all night long. Their condominium complex even has a name, Palm Desert Flower Estates— four words that she puts in a different wrong order every time—and it's made of blindingly white stucco and has smooth, even sidewalks, streetlights, and mailboxes in a respectable row, with names all uniformly typed out by a little label machine. There's even an office, with a manager and a full-time, smiling secretary, and a glittering turquoise pool in the back, with white plastic lounge chairs, always empty.

Their apartment—number 3295 B, one little box in such a huge number of apartments—has standard-issue white walls and tan carpet and drapes, a sliding glass door out to a little balcony overlooking the verdant golf course with its palm trees, sand traps, and a pond with a fountain. It all looks fake, of course, like a movie set. This is what can happen to a landscape when the sun shines on it all year long without letup. Even the air here is different: warm, dried out, too painfully bright. She hasn't seen a cloud yet.

She's pleased to see that their furniture makes it seem like home, or a reasonable facsimile, at least: the sofa bed, dining room table, their queen-sized bed. She'd missed their furniture, its old-fashioned, rounded, familiar edges—dear, dear end tables!—and the framed photographs of bluebirds hung over the couch. The butcher board table for the kitchen.

She feels as though she's spent the first few days there, taking score—ticking off the wins and the losses.

Jonathan wears polo shirts now and looks like a proud, golf-playing Republican: a loss. Beach in the wintertime: a win.

Frozen yogurt stands everywhere: a win.

He buys her gauzy summertime maternity clothes, even though it's January: a win.

She meets her new obstetrician, who is a guy and a stranger and not even remotely like Dr. Stinson: a loss.

Andres and Judith Schultz met them at the airport upon their arrival and Judith, who is very nice, said that Rosie can join her book group, if she'd like. A possible win.

Jonathan takes her to the museum to see the Lolitas, in all their show-offy glory, perched on pedestals like they've always wanted to be: okay, a win.

He talks nonstop about the museum in whole new categories now: the advertising budget, the need for social media exposure, the tweets, the blogs, the Facebook posts, the alarming fact that they still need *more* teacups. The Lolitas aren't even the point anymore. A *huge* loss, incalculable.

She misses rainy days, her students, her friends, her waistline, playing Scrabble, the river, cold air, Ruby's Diner, the color she painted the guest bathroom, Milo, and laughing about the diamond they made in the microwave. When Jonathan takes her on the eight-lane freeway, she misses the bucolic beauty of the Merritt Parkway with its shade trees and interesting overpasses.

She misses Soapie. George. Greta.

Tony. Oh my God, she misses Tony so much that sometimes the longing for him backs up in her throat and she can't speak.

She takes a sip of green tea as Jonathan says, "I know what. Let's just haul off and get married this weekend, make our baby legitimate. What do you say?"

"But I didn't bring my red cowboy boots," she says.

He looks pained. "Are those absolutely necessary, do you think?"

"I'm kidding."

He strives for a smile, but his face ends up looking even more pained, and she feels bad that she really has to try harder to remember to smile at him more and to quell her tendency to be sarcastic. They have to get used to each other all over again. It requires a kind of carefulness she's not used to. None of this is his fault.

"Well," he says in an annoyed voice, and folds up the *L.A. Times,* which they did not even attempt to share. "You think about it. Because I'd kind of like to make things official, before the baby comes. Call me old-fashioned, but I think it looks so nice on the birth certificate if the parents are married to each other."

"That does look nice," she says, "but on the other hand, I think it's sad to go get married in a courthouse with strangers. I want our friends there. Somebody, at least, who can say congratulations and mean it." She sees his face. "And preferably that person wouldn't be Andres Schultz, if you don't mind."

"Fine. Okay." He looks around the diner, mouth down-turned, but then fortunately for him his phone buzzes and he leaps up and heads out to take the call. He is actually happy and adjusted when he's not around her, she sees. Who knew he could turn into a Californian so easily? Or maybe it doesn't matter to him where he is, as long as he's got the teacups and a ringing cell phone.

She's just grieving, that's what this heaviness is. That's why she can't adjust as easily. Greta had said as much on the phone: "Look, you're nine months pregnant, you just lost your grandmother, and you've left the state you lived in your whole life, and you're away from all your friends, like *moi*. It's going to take some time."

And I found out my mother killed herself, and I've been sleeping with someone else who's not here with me. And . . . despite how it looks, it turns out I'm a terrible person.

She gives herself a stern talking-to and tries to rally by getting the apartment ready for the baby. They need things, after all. The crib is really the only piece of decent furniture, and she'd had to remind Jonathan that they'll need a changing table, too, and a dresser for the baby's clothes.

"Really?" he said, and he started getting that vague look he used to get, but then he remembered and covered it up. "Are you sure? Can't the baby get changed on our bed?"

She'd made a face at him. "Our *bed*? You do know what comes out of babies, don't you?"

"All right, all right. Well, then, we'll just have to go do more shopping. That's fine, it's fine." He smiles.

Two days later, they buy a little gliding rocking chair she found on Craigslist, and when they go pick the thing up, she gets to talking with the woman who's selling it. Tayari is her name, and she has a child who is a year old, a kid who apparently took so long to be born that industrial equipment almost needed to be called in, Tayari says. They were sending out for tanks and cranes and the kind of forceps that are used in factories, she tells them with a loud laugh.

She has bright red, curly hair and when she talks she moves her mouth to one side of her face, like everything she's going to say is ironic. Rosie and Tayari say they'll keep in touch. For good measure, Tayari throws in a folding changing table, which she said she used to use at her mother's house when they visited there.

Jonathan beams at her as they leave.

"See? This is going to be great for you," he says on the way out. "You've made a friend already."

She stops walking. "Look, I'm not a kindergartener on the first day of school," she says to him. "I'll find friends, don't you worry about it."

Then she has to apologize *again*. All he wants is for her to be happy. And she has no idea how to do that. Time, time, and more time. Isn't that what's supposed to heal you?

● ● ●

"I want to name the baby Serena Sophia," she tells him one morning. "I hope you won't mind, but I want to honor my mother and my grandmother."

"Seriously?" he says. "Isn't that kind of bad luck?"

"Why is it bad luck?"

"Well, if you ask me, it's two dead people's names. How good can that be?"

She points out that he really wasn't involved throughout

much of the pregnancy; that, in fact, she'd made the decision of what to name this child at a time when he wasn't even sure he was going to want anything to do with the whole business.

"Could she have a nickname?" he says finally.

"She was Serena the Bean in her ultrasound days," she says. "So . . . Beanie."

"Beanie it is," he says. "When she gets bigger and hates that name, though, we could switch to something of a real name. Something that isn't doomed. Like, I don't know, Patricia."

"No."

"Rosie, I was *kidding*."

● ● ●

Dear Milo, I am so sorry I didn't get to see you in person to tell you good-bye before I left for California.

~~I hope that sometime you can come and visit me here.~~ Maybe I will come back when my grandmother's house sells and you and I can see each other then. ~~If it sells.~~ I hope you are having a good time at school. I ~~love~~ miss you. ~~You are about the cutest kid I've ever had sleep in my yard.~~ Tell your mom and Dena hi for me. Love, Rosie.

P.S. Tell your dad hi, too.

● ● ●

"So let me get this straight," says Tayari. "You're *forty-four,* and this is your first baby?"

"Yes," says Rosie. "I'm a late bloomer."

They're at the playground, and Tayari is pushing her little one, Lulu, on the baby swing. She's invited Rosie there just so she can see where she'll probably spend many of her waking hours, in a month or two.

"Wow, that is seriously so brave of you! Forty-four! I just hope I'm still having *sex* when I'm that age!"

Rosie starts to say something and then can't continue. She wishes she could call Greta right this instant to report this conversation. Instead, she looks at Lulu, who is adorable and wearing a pink polka-dotted T-shirt and pants with purple lacy socks, and who has red ponytails springing from each side of her head and enormous blue eyes that look glazed over from the swinging motion. She's also sporting a gigantic yellow pacifier with a picture of a goldfish on it. She'd like to take a photo of this getup and send that along to Greta, too.

"Wow," says Tayari, and she shakes her red curls. "My mom is only forty-five," she says, and stops pushing Lulu's swing so she can check her phone, which has apparently just buzzed in her jeans pocket. She looks down at it for a moment and then says, "That is so weird."

"Yeah, I know, it's weird," says Rosie. "Two generations—"

"No, no, not you. My friend Lani just posted this thing on Facebook about what she ate for lunch," says Tayari.

"She posted a picture of her lunch?"

"Yeah. I mean, lots of people do that. But the thing is— whoa! Look at that wrap thingie she ate! I thought she was going on the paleo diet, but this wrap is so *not* on the diet." She starts tapping away at the keys on her phone with her thumbs. From the slowed-down swing, Lulu lets out a wail. "Give her a push, will you?" says Tayari, and so Rosie does. But then after a moment she says she has to get going, and thanks Tayari for showing her the playground. It looks like a fabulous place. She knows this will be her main hangout soon.

"Oh, sure. Yeah, I'm sure I'll see you around. This is like the place where everybody comes between naps. Sometimes the grandmothers come, too, ha ha! You'll like them."

● ● ●

"I'm old," she says to Jonathan that night. "I have it on good authority that no one this old has ever attempted to be a mother."

"What about Sarah from the Bible? Wasn't she ninety?"

"Forty-four *is* the new ninety," she says.

He doesn't answer. She knows why: there are no words. Also, he's staring at his phone. He is always staring at his phone.

"You know that we need to practice Lamaze," she tells him.

He looks up from whatever he'd been studying and frowns at her. "Does that stuff really work? I have to say, when I was there, I thought it sounded like wishful thinking to me."

"Jonathan, don't *say* that! We have to believe in it. It's all we have." She bursts into crazy tears. "If we don't believe in Lamaze, then we might as well just declare we're unfit parents right now!"

He looks at her steadily. "Okay, okay! I'm so sorry. I didn't know, honest."

After that, he gets down on the floor with her every night before bed and helps her practice the breathing, except he has to read from the faded mimeographed sheets that Starla Jones had handed out, and often he doesn't have his glasses because he left them at the museum, and, all in all, she'll be lucky to get through labor without being put in a strait-jacket, or whatever they do to women who can't do it.

One night he comes over to her side of the bed and wraps his arms around her and they just lie there together, feeling the baby doing her evening calisthenics.

"I'm sorry you've having such a hard time," he says in her ear. "But I just know you're going to end up loving it here. We're going to be okay. It's all going to work out."

"Thank you," she says.

"We just have to stick together," he says. "We're like two gears trying to meet and work together, to blend. And the trick is not to break off any of the teeth."

She laughs.

"Ohhh, Rosie," he says. "Oh, honey, it's so good to hear you laugh again. I can't believe it! You haven't laughed in weeks."

● ● ●

One day after she finishes painting the baby's room a light mossy green, which she did without even asking permission from the doctor—what the hell does he know about whether she can paint a room?—she goes into the kitchen to get a drink of water. Her cell phone is on the counter, and, after thinking about it for two-tenths of a nanosecond, she picks it up and punches in Tony's number. She'll just talk to him for a minute. It's her reward for all that painting. She should think of a question she needs to ask him. He's a painter, so is moss green a good color for a baby girl's room if you're not intending to go the bubble-gum pink route? That's what she'll say.

And then he answers. "Oh my God," he says in her ear.

"How are you? Let me guess. You're in labor, and you want to remember how to do the cleansing breaths."

She laughs.

"No, no," he says. "Really. How are you?"

"I'm . . . good," she says. And then she tells him that since she left Connecticut, she's found out that she's the oldest person ever contemplating giving birth and that another mom at the park thinks she'll get along better with the grandmothers than with the other new moms.

"Well . . . hell, *yeah*!" he says.

"Get this. Their idea of interesting is to photograph their lunch and put it on Facebook."

"Oh wow, do you think the world can handle a photo of my grilled cheese and arugula sandwich?"

Oh, she loves this. The sound of his voice, even the way he eats those stupid sandwiches. She'd forgotten about his unlikely sandwiches. Let's see, she says, there was the peanut butter and olive sandwich, and wasn't there something with tomato sauce and something else?

"Raw onion," he says. "As you well remember. And sometimes I added Spam."

"Please," she says. "I'm pregnant. I have a delicate constitution."

"How's Beanie the prizefighter fetus?"

"Still working out. Yesterday I'm positive she was doing lunges and squats. Today she's taking a break. She must know I'm painting her room."

She walks around the apartment while she talks to him, holding the phone close to her ear, laughing and talking. A half hour goes by. Forty-five minutes. She starts dinner, still on the phone. She tells him she's bigger than a house now, that her new doctor thinks she should be induced if she goes more than ten minutes beyond her due date, and also she can barely fit behind the wheel of the car anymore, and he insists she send him a photo of herself with her phone, and so she makes a face in the picture and pokes her belly out, and then he sends one of himself making the same face and with his flat belly thrust toward her.

Before they hang up, he says, "It's just good to talk to you. I'm glad you're fine. J-man okay?"

"He's good," she says. "Yeah, everything is great."

"That's wonderful."

They don't say they'll keep in touch. They just click off, and that's that.

• • •

"Okay, let me explain the importance to you of the cleansing breaths," he says the next day. He has called her. "Because I think you've taken this part of labor and delivery way too cavalantly."

"Too *what*?" She falls over, she is laughing so hard.

"I'll just wait until you're finished laughing at me."

"I'll *never* be finished laughing at you."

"Maybe a cleansing breath would be helpful to you right now."

• • •

Two days later:

"Milo told Annie he wants to live with me. I guess things aren't so great over there. He feels shut out."

"Jesus. What did Annie do?"

"Let's just say I'm looking for a bigger place."

"For you and him or for all of you together once again?"

Long silence. "Is it possible for you to go and wash out your mouth with dish deterrent? I am not living with those women ever again."

"Did you say dish *deterrent*?"

"See how nice I am to you? I give you these things just so you can use them to make fun of me."

"Yeah, you're a prince. Listen, I know this phone call is all about you and your problems and not about mine, but can you tell me one more time how to do the cleansing breaths?"

"What is *up* with you with this breathing? Am I going to have to fly out there and birth this baby with you?"

"Would you please?"

● ● ●

A week later:

"Tomorrow is the due date. So if I don't go into labor . . . yikes. I go to labor prison."

"You will."

"Can you promise?"

"Send me another picture of you, and I'll do a magic spell on it."

"Okay."

"Also, that woman at Edge of the Woods. The one you tried to fix me up with. She had her baby two days ago."

"Ah. Leila. How nice. So are you two dating, or what?"

"Yeah, that's right. We're getting married next week. Her goon of a boyfriend said if I can get the two mommies to join us, we can all make a nice happy family."

"Nice one."

"Oh. And I saw George. He's aged about a hundred years, but he says he's fine."

"Oh, Jonathan's coming in. Gotta go. I'll call you on the other side of the delivery."

"Yeah. And listen, good luck. Okay? Cleansing breaths . . . one, two, three . . . that's all there is to it. It centers you. That's why! Okay, I'll hang up. Bye. I . . . I love you!"

She says, "Yes. Good-bye."

thirty-one

She wakes up in a puddle, having dreamed that she was jumping in a lake. It's 4:33 in the morning, and she's not in a lake after all; her water has broken. She lies there, soggy, smiling in the darkness, feeling a thrill that she decides is 70 percent excited/happy and 28 percent terrified, and probably 2 percent undecided. It's her due date, and this is one prompt little baby.

She reaches over and nudges Jonathan. It's time, she tells him, and he instantly springs awake. He's done his reading, has crammed for the final exam, he told her last night. He's ready.

"Okayyyy," he says. "So she's decided to be a nocturnal sort. And a wet one! It's going to be this way, is it?" He leans over and turns on the lamp and gets his glasses and looks at her through his sleep-encrusted eyes. "So. You're really going to do this thing, huh?"

"I think at this point I don't have much choice." Then a contraction hits her, and she says, "Aaughhh."

"That's a funny look you just got on your face," he says.

"I think I have to breathe."

"Wait. I should get up and run around the room and pack a bag and stub my toe on the bed, shouldn't I? Isn't it my right as an almost-father?"

"Please," she says. "Don't make jokes, and don't do Dick Van Dyke. Can't we be calm? Where are the lollipops and tennis balls?"

Another contraction hits. Now she sees what she's up against, and this is just the early stage. She pulls herself up and remembers that there's a remedy for this pain. She takes a long, slow, deep breath—and after the contraction is over, she takes off her wet nightgown, and Jonathan pulls the mattress off the bed and removes the sheets. She breathes through the next contractions in the bathtub. He puts on the CD of Paul Cardall they'd chosen for its piano music, soothing and calm.

"Can you light some candles so we can—oh my God!"

"Breathe," he says. He's getting it. "So much better to breathe than to say *oh my God*."

"You have to help! You're supposed to be guiding me! Do you even know about the cleansing breaths?" she says, her eyes closed. The light is too bright, bright like the pain. "I have to do . . . cleansing breaths."

"Sure. Those are breaths you're doing in the bathtub," he says.

"Go stub your toe on the bed, why don't you?"

"That's not very nice."

● ● ●

When they get to the hospital, the nurse checks her and says she's four centimeters dilated—four out of ten. Best not to get in the bed at this stage, the nurse says. Why don't they walk? So she and Jonathan walk through the corridor on the labor and delivery floor, going back and forth again and again. The nurses seem to find them amusing, and Rosie can only imagine how they must seem—like the oldest couple giving birth ever to be seen in San Diego. She's bent over and moaning, and Jonathan, the befuddled labor coach, looks like an absentminded professor with his glasses on the end of his nose, and his graying buzz cut and polo shirt. He has to keep flipping through the cheat sheets, and she has to keep pointing things out to him between the contractions. He forgot, he says mournfully, to brush up on the stages of labor. "What's transition again?" he whispers to her.

Still, she's okay. She doesn't ask for an epidural, which seems to surprise the nurses. For a first-timer, they tell her, she's doing Very Well. And she's making progress. With each new exam, they tell her she's dilating more and more.

At about seven centimeters, though, her labor slows inexplicably. "What if the two of you get in the whirlpool bath?" the nurse asks, and Jonathan blanches. But he gets in with her, in his underwear, and Rosie lies back against him, breathing with him through the contractions. And sure enough, when she gets out, labor picks up in intensity.

She's in transition, the toughest part, the nurse tells Jonathan. Rosie, dazzled with pain, hears the nurse showing him how he could use the tennis balls to rub her back, and he's laughing as he says, "Oh, *this* is what those were for?" If she didn't hurt so much, she would ask him if he honestly thought they'd be playing catch in the labor room.

He turns on some music for her and gets her lollipops. But it's too late for those. She tells him she's scared, but she can barely get the words out because the contractions are coming so fast now. The edges of the room seem bright with shards of pain.

"You're doing great," he says, but he looks bewildered and overtired. They forgot to pack him anything to eat, and now it's way past lunchtime. The nurse urges him to go to the candy machine, but he won't go. Rosie closes her eyes, says, "Hee hee heee hee," to stop the world.

"I have to stay here," she hears him say. "I haven't been

much help during the pregnancy. I think that I didn't even see her enough that my testosterone levels went down enough. I probably still have, like, at least ninety-five percent of what I started with."

● ● ●

It's all crazy at the end, the way these things are. Pushing and urging and promises made, the calm voice of the doctor instructing her when to push and when to breathe, Jonathan mopping her forehead, someone else supporting her back. She refuses the mirror at first, doesn't want to see anything gory, even though the nurse says she shouldn't miss this. So she looks—this is a once-in-a-lifetime moment, after all— and she sees the baby's head emerging, little black squiggly lines of damp hair. Everything feels surreal, like the world is going in and out of focus.

The doctor says she's doing fine, just to give him one nice, steady push, and she does that, and then there is a whoosh, and suddenly he has a baby in his hands, a rosy-grayish baby with tiny little fists by her face and a circle of dark, damp hair and a bunch of white creamy stuff all over her. Then Rosie, who is shivering, can see him stroking the baby's back, and then the baby lets out a cry. A dim, lovely cry, not scared, just *I'm here.*

"An announcement from Beanie," says Jonathan in awe, and Rosie loves him for this, and she starts to cry and she sees that his eyes are filled with tears, too, as he takes her hand.

In fact, she loves everyone there. Tears are streaming down Rosie's face, and they hand her the baby, who is now beautiful and pink as can be with those wide, amazed eyes and little rosebud mouth, and she lies next to Rosie's bare skin, and Rosie cuddles her close, the damp warmth and weight of her, and she drinks in those big, curious, bottomless eyes that stare intelligently back into her own. She has all the required parts—the fingers and the toes, the sweet little arms and thighs. A tiny little butt, and amazing fingernails. Fingernails! She didn't know there would be fingernails, looking like they'd been freshly manicured.

"I'm your mommy," she says, and just saying that chokes her up.

"Aww," says the nurse. "Did you guys have to try for a long time to get pregnant?"

Jonathan and Rosie look at each other and smile. Rosie realizes she doesn't want to tell the story about the forgotten condom anymore. "Actually," she says, "we're fertility champions. One try."

Jonathan keeps his hands behind his back, leaning in to stare at the baby. His eyes are glassy.

"Look what we did," she says. "Are you happy?"

He nods and says that labor was just about ten hours, really good for a first baby. Pretty soon he's moved down to the end of the table and he's talking to the doctor about the Internet's information on lengths of labor and deliveries, and then somehow he veers into talking about the museum and how not nearly enough people know about it yet, and that's when a nurse interrupts and points Jonathan back up to Rosie, which is where he should have been all along. Rosie isn't mad; she laughs as he lumbers back up, and the nurse catches her eye and laughs, too.

"Men, in the delivery room," the nurse whispers to her later. "Mostly good, sometimes not. One guy we had to send over to fix the plumbing in the corner because he couldn't handle it."

But Rosie is in such a haze of love and relief and expansiveness. She is shaking with joy, with pleasure and relief, even as her eyes keep filling up with tears. Jonathan is just nervous, that's all, and she is slammed with love. That's what this is like.

"You should call your mother," she says to Jonathan. "Call your brothers. Oh, and Greta and Joe, so they can call the others! People have to be told."

"Can't she be just ours for a little longer?" he says.

"Yes," she says to him and smiles. "Yes, she can. Of course."

She wishes for a moment that she could put everyone in suspended animation, in some kind of bubble perhaps, and she could call Tony. He needs to know. But of course there is no way. Around her, the medical workers keep doing everything they're supposed to, getting her ready to be admitted to her room, and weighing and measuring and counting the parts on the baby, smiling and chatting and welcoming her and Jonathan to the world of parenthood. No, everything is going exactly as it should, and she has to be swept along in the flow. No looking back to Tony, who is the past.

● ● ●

They go home the next day, which seems insane. Rosie feels as though she has spent more time in line at the grocery store than she spent in this hospital.

"Can't I stay a little longer? Maybe I don't really know what I'm doing," she says.

"You're fine," says the nurse. "The baby's nursing, you're all peeing, and that means you're good to go."

"I can't believe they're letting us leave with her," Jonathan says. He spent the night in Rosie's room with her and the baby. "Please tell me that while I was sleeping they made you pass a test for this and that you qualified."

"None. Nothing," she says. "Apparently they give babies out to just anybody."

When he goes to use the bathroom, she can't help it: she takes out her cell phone and punches in Tony's number. It rings four times and then goes to voice mail, and she whispers, "Don't call me back. Baby's here. Leaving hospital. Everything's amazing." Which is all she has time for before Jonathan comes back into the room.

He sighs and says, "Well, I guess this is it, then. If they say we're authorized to be parents, then I guess we can't argue with them. We have to go home."

Actually, though, she thinks later, there were a few things they might have mentioned before they put the three of them out on the street.

They covered the belly button thing falling off and the fact that babies cry sometimes for no reason whatsoever, and that breast-feeding hurts at first but it doesn't mean you're inadequate or that you should stop. But could somebody—Greta? Anyone?—have taken a moment out to describe the crushing weight of the love she'd feel for this baby, the way her heart would almost hurt with all that love? Sometimes in the first days, sitting by the crib and watching little Serena sleeping, she tries to recall ever knowing this kind of gripping feeling, and no, there has been nothing like it. It's got to be dangerous, all this heart overload. No wonder Soapie tried to protect her from it. No wonder Greta wouldn't ever let her pick up the newborn Sandrine. She sits and strokes the little shell-like ear, the soft cheek, the little button of a nose. It's as though she's been born again herself, some new raw part of her emerging from the wreckage of her grief and her longing.

It makes her want to cry, how close she came to missing out on this.

She and Jonathan move through the first few days, sleep-deprived and stunned. He is excellent at keeping people away. He won't let Andres and Judith Schultz drop by with their baby gift, and he avoids the nice condo dwellers who smile at him in the bright sunny passageways and politely inquire about the new baby. Greta says this is a good thing and is exactly what he should be doing: using his handy Y chromosome to protect his woman and the baby from marauders, but she argues that he really does need to let Rosie talk to her old friends on the phone. She doesn't need to be deprived of *everyone*.

He also makes dinner, mostly his specialty items: hamburgers made with Worcestershire sauce, blueberry pancakes, grilled cheese sandwiches, and baked potatoes with broccoli and cheddar cheese. You can go a long way on that food, he tells her. Many, if not all, of the four food groups are represented there.

The baby, however, terrifies him. He gingerly holds her in his outstretched arms, as if she's made of the thin porcelain they used to make antique teacups out of, and when he gazes at her, he looks like someone who's fallen hopelessly in love but secretly hopes the authorities will come soon and tell him to cease and desist.

Mostly he tries to hand the baby back to Rosie. "I don't know how to do this," he says.

"Pretend she's a cup. Pretend her head is a thousand-year-old cup, and you'll be fine," she tells him, but he says the cups never look at him like he's incompetent, the way this baby does. She *knows*, he says.

One night after they've collapsed into bed, his disembodied

voice comes out of the darkness, rough and whispery: "So is this really what you wanted?"

"Yes," she says slowly.

"But are we doing it right? I mean—God, Rosie, she's going to need people who are competent. What's going to happen when she needs to learn to ride a bike, or when somebody doesn't take her to the prom, and she's crying? What about all that?"

"I think we have some time," she says, but then she thinks, *Yeah, what about all that?* And her heart starts beating so hard that it's like the time she took Sudafed and then drank two cups of coffee. And then she starts to cry—huge, great, gulping sobs, for Serena's bad luck in being born to them and for the prom date that won't materialize and the fact that they waited until they were beyond the age of competence for this stuff—holy God, they'll be in their *sixties* when the prom date doesn't show up! Senior citizens! How are they going to be able to fix anything for her and make it all right? She cannot stop crying.

Jonathan holds her, he says, "Shhh, shhh," and he says, "Do you want me to call someone?" and then he gets up and turns on the light and says, "Could I bring you an antihistamine or something so you can try to fall asleep?" She shakes her head, unable to even form words, and when she can't stop crying, he finally falls to his knees beside the bed and says, "Rosie, you are scaring me more than anything ever has. Are you going to be crazy from now on and leave me to raise this baby by myself? You have to tell me."

His expression is so dire that it actually makes her laugh. She's laughing and sobbing at the same time. Finally she's able to catch her breath enough to say to him, "It's okay, it's okay, I'm just postpartum." She tries to wipe the snot and tears off her face with her hands, and he stares at her in abject fear, so frozen he's unable even to get a tissue.

Then he whispers, "I can't do this. Please, for God's sake, tell me that you have some maternal instincts that are going to make this okay."

• • •

When Beanie is five days old, Jonathan goes back to work. Rosie can tell that he can't wait to get out of the house. He's *thrilled*. And as soon as he's out of the door, she walks around and around the apartment, holding Beanie on her shoulder and bouncing her, and then—what the hell—she grabs her cell phone and calls Tony.

"I can't believe you didn't call me before now," he says. "Have I been dying here, or what? I finally had to call Greta just to get the details."

"Well, good, I'm glad you did. I tried to call you from the hospital. You didn't pick up."

Silence. "I do occasionally get into the shower, but I was told I couldn't call back."

"Yes. Sorry about that."

"So it went well, I take it." His voice is still a little stiff. He's annoyed, she can tell.

"Really, Tony," she says, "how could you have ever thought I could get away to call you again? How was that going to work? Jonathan would have had a fit."

"Would he?"

"Yes. He's no dummy. He knows stuff is going on."

"But that's just it. Nothing *is* going on," says Tony. "Of *course* I'd be interested. It'd be weird if I didn't care, wouldn't it? I mean, I went through the whole pregnancy with you, didn't I? Would any reasoning person declaim that I wouldn't want to know the outcome?"

"You're right. I'm sorry. Don't make me start crying, okay? I feel guilty enough."

"All right. For God's sake, don't cry. Tell me everything. Every detail. What did you name her?"

"Beanie."

"You did *not* name that child Beanie."

"Okay. Serena Sophia."

"Beautiful," he says.

"Jonathan says it's two doomed names, so we call her Beanie."

"Eh. She'll refuge them."

"Thank you. That's what I thought, too. She'll take these names and cure them."

"The only better name would have been Toni, with an I. But I suppose you couldn't do that."

● ● ●

There are whole, long days she doesn't even get out of her room. Serena stays at her breast, happily bludgeoning one nipple at a time, while the other breast weeps and spurts milk out, in sympathy. But then there are the days—more and more frequently—when she gets up and, after some ninja bouts of concentration, manages to dress not only herself but the baby, too, and they go out into the world. They venture through the little lanes of the condo, Rosie pushing the stroller, staring down at the beatific face of her baby as she walks. She's now one of those moms, walking along with a baby carriage. She'd had no idea of the heroic effort it took.

They go to the playground, where she sees Tayari and

her friends. But Rosie doesn't have the energy to make her way across the asphalt to them, only to be seen for what she is: an old hag with a healing episiotomy and huge, leaky breasts and no clue of how to be in polite company anymore.

She calls Tony every day while she walks home. She has made fantastically funny stories out of the labor and delivery and even her postpartum tears, and yes, her discovery that she is now consigned to a life of abject fear and devotion. She tells him how she wanted to throttle a two-year-old who zoomed past Beanie's stroller and rattled it so violently that it startled the baby into tears.

"Blinding rage," she says, and he says, "I know. Oh, I know."

One day she puts potatoes on the stove to make mashed potatoes, and then she goes in and starts nursing the baby and falls asleep and doesn't wake up until she can smell the pan burning. She's horrified; she could have killed everybody in the entire building—but when she calls Tony, he thinks it's the funniest story ever. She wasn't going to kill anybody, he says. She killed one *pan*. And it's because she's not getting any sleep because she's been held hostage by somebody who weighs seven pounds, three ounces.

"Six ounces," she says.

"Ah, so the milk is working," he says. "Three ounces of weight gain."

"I'm not cut out for this."

"Awww, Rosie, you're doing fine."

• • •

The next time she calls him, his voice is worried, and when she makes him tell her what's going on, he says he didn't want to bother her, but that Milo isn't doing well in school, and Miss Minton called in the school social worker, who thinks that he's depressed.

"But, don't you see him, like, every week?" Rosie says.

"Yeah, but he's sad, they say."

"What does he say?"

"He says he doesn't know. He says that everything has changed."

"So what are you going to do?"

"Well, we're all going to sit down together and talk it through. Now that Dena's pregnant, she's really being kind of—"

"Wait. She's pregnant? You didn't tell me that!"

"Didn't I? Yeah, well, she found out just when you left, I guess."

"Wow. So is this a good thing or a bad thing?"

"Good, bad, who knows? It's made her more *intensive* in a way, but I also think that she might like some time away from Milo and his problems. Sad to say, but she's not the most clued-in person when it comes to the actual kid, you know."

"And now that she's having her own . . ."

"Exactly. That may be what he's feeling. She doesn't have the patience for his stuff anymore."

"Oh, poor Milo!"

"We're all sitting down next week with the mediators. I'm going to suggest I become the custodial parent, and they can have unlimited visitation."

"Wow."

"Yeah, I can't take this."

"I can't either," she says. "You have to get him."

"Yeah, well, I'll let you know. I may need you to write me a letter."

● ● ●

Andres Schultz and Judith invite Rosie and Jonathan to dinner one night. It's April, the baby is six weeks old by now, and they know of a very competent, good babysitter—actually their niece, Eliza, who's in college and is home on spring break. She's great with kids, Judith says, as though Serena needs someone who is "great with kids." What she needs is someone who has a lactating breast and a reasonable desire to walk her for hours on end. It also helps if that person knows the words to the Beatles song "Ob-La-Di, Ob-La-Da" and can read minds.

Jonathan thinks it will all be fine. "We have to go out sometime," he says. "Americans are allowed to leave their infants, if I'm not mistaken."

"But we don't know this girl."

So they meet Eliza in advance. She has a young, fresh face, a ponytail underneath a baseball cap, and a nice smile. She demonstrates that she knows how to hold a baby, how to administer a bottle, and how to walk a baby while supporting the head. She will call 911 at the first sign of any trouble. She will keep in touch with Rosie throughout the evening. She doesn't *know* "Ob-La-Di, Ob-La-Da," but she knows her university fight song, which might have the same spirit to it.

Rosie pumps breast milk into a bottle—a daylong project—which makes her feel like somebody's old, reluctant cow, but it gets the job done.

And then she and Jonathan actually leave the house and go out. Babyless.

They have dinner, wearing grown-up clothes. Judith turns out to be a sparkling dinner companion who doesn't mind hearing stories about new motherhood, even though it's nothing she ever wanted to experience herself. She sympathizes with Rosie's missing her students, and says that *of course* she'll help her find some students here, just as soon as she wants to return to work. Rosie can feel herself blanch: wait, she's expected to take care of this baby *and* work, too?

Naturally the men start their museum talk. Judith leans over and says to Rosie conspiratorially, "Have you ever seen such obsessive guys? They are just so incredibly lucky to have found each other. It's as though they were connected for many lifetimes."

This makes both women laugh, because the idea of these two balding, seriously wonky guys trudging together lifetime after lifetime hoarding their teacups is hilarious.

When the laughter dies down Judith says, "And lucky you! You got nearly a whole year off from it, didn't you?"

Rosie says, looking over at Jonathan fondly, "Well, but I'm glad to be back with him. I did miss him."

That's when the men look up from their talk. Andres has been on his BlackBerry and Jonathan on his iPhone, and their heads are nearly touching. And then Jonathan puts his phone down on the table and says, "That's it, then. We got it!"

Andres actually claps his hands.

"What's happening?" says Judith, and yawns.

"We just got a great collection that's become available— a dealer in Cincinnati is liquidating—and we won the bid," says Andres. Jonathan looks up at Rosie and smiles.

"Subject to our inspection," he says.

"In Cincinnati?" says Rosie.

"In Cincinnati." He turns back to Andres, who is calling up something else on his BlackBerry, and they bend their heads back together.

"Wait. You're going to Cincinnati?" Rosie says, but he's talking and doesn't answer.

"Obsessive," says Judith, tilting her head toward Rosie. She takes a sip of her wine and says, "You two never did get married, did you?"

When Rosie shakes her head, she says, "Yeah, Andres told me. We didn't either. I don't know why really. We just sort of forgot. It almost didn't make enough difference to go ahead and do it. It's funny how people say you have to do it, and then you realize you don't."

"Yeah," says Rosie. She keeps looking at Jonathan. He's going to Cincinnati, and she wonders if he'll remember to tell her.

The men get hauled back into the conversation after that, and after a suitable interval has gone by, Rosie says they really do have to get back to the baby. The truth is her breasts are filled with milk—and that might mean that Beanie has drunk all the milk that was pumped and is screaming in hunger. She can't believe she stayed out so long. She never meant to do this.

"I'm sure she's fine," Jonathan keeps saying. It takes forever for him and Andres to wrap up their plans.

"Eliza would call you if there's a problem," says Judith. "You can relax."

Rosie tries to smile at her. There's no point in trying to explain what this is like to someone who hasn't just given birth, how it feels to be so completely responsible for someone whose whole world depends upon you and your two breasts.

But when they get home, it turns out that everything really is all right. Beanie has been sleeping for four hours—like a miracle baby, Eliza says.

"See? What did I tell you? We have a miracle baby," Jonathan says.

Rosie smiles weakly, and once he leaves to take Eliza home, she goes in and stands by the bassinet and watches the baby sleep. Her little cheeks are so full and luscious, and her little rosebud lips are so sweetly pooched up. Rosie reaches over and touches those seashell ears, the sweep of fine brown hair, and tears spring into her eyes. It's all she can do not to scoop the baby up and nuzzle her.

She startles when Jonathan comes to the doorway. "Hey," he whispers. "Come in here, I have a surprise for you."

"Sssh. Come look at her. Tiptoe."

But he's already moved away from the door. After a moment, she goes into their bedroom, takes off her cardigan and her dress, and slips on her nightgown and sits down on the bed. He's in the bathroom, looking at his teeth in the mirror.

"Whew, I'm so tired, but wine keeps me awake now, I've noticed," she says. She takes her earrings off and looks over at him. "So what's this surprise you have for me? The fact that you're about to leave me and go on a business trip? Because I kind of figured that out with the context clues tonight."

He comes over to the bed and stretches out next to her and grins suggestively. "Nooo. I believe that six weeks are officially up, and things are back to normal . . . down there," he says, waggling his eyebrows and pointing toward her crotch. "I thought we'd . . ."

"Well, this is sort of out of the blue," she says. She stands up and puts her earrings on the dresser.

"Yep, I've been holding myself back," he says. "But tonight's the night. Come over here and let me reintroduce you to your old friend Mr. Happy."

"Jonathan, honestly? I'm kind of tired, and the baby is going to wake up in a minute and need to nurse, and also— as long as we're talking about surprises, I can't believe you didn't tell me about the Cincinnati trip."

"I didn't tell you because I just found out about the trip tonight. You were there with me when I heard we'd gotten the bid."

"But I didn't even know it was a possibility. Why are you still acquiring cups when you have so many? You said yourself that the museum isn't doing all that well—"

"People aren't going to keep coming to see the same old, same old," he says. "And look. Do you really want to get into a business discussion right now? Come on, I want you. Let's get naked and frisky."

"But I can't believe you're leaving me alone," she says. "You're taking off!"

"It's only for two days," he says. "You've never cared about me going away before."

"But we have a baby now," she says. "Can't you see how frightening it might be for me?"

"You're frightened of the baby?" He stares at her. "You, Rosie Kelley, are scared to be with the baby without me here? Me, who is pretty much useless since I know nothing about babies. I don't even hold her the right way. You're not scared, and you know it."

"Things could happen. And I'm all by myself here without my friends or anybody I can call on if something happens—"

"Call Judith. Call the doctor. What's going to happen?"

"Who knows what could happen? She could cry all night, she could stop breathing, I could fall down—"

"Rosie, Rosie, Rosie. It's fine. Come here and let's get into this bed together."

"No," she says, and starts to cry in earnest. "Jonathan, I can't do this. I'm so sad all the time, and I miss my friends and I feel bad when I have to try to make friends with other people, and you're the only person I have to depend on, and I'm trying so hard to get used to it here, but it's so weird, and I'm lonely. I'm just lonely."

"You're lonely?" he says. "Well, now that's ironic, isn't it? Here I am, right here, wanting to hold you, and this *could* be a good sexy, reuniting time, but instead you've picked this time to have a fight."

"But why is everything on your terms? Why are *you* picking the time for sex and then just telling me that's what we're going to do?"

"Why? Why am I picking this time for sex? Maybe because it's nighttime, and we had a nice evening out, and I *was* feeling good and relaxed, and feeling good about us and the fact that we could get away together for an evening—"

"See? Why is it all about getting away? *This* is where we're supposed to be, getting used to everything." She flings out her arms, in a gesture meant to take in the whole apartment.

"Playing house, you mean?"

"Maybe. Except for real. And now you can't even hide how excited you are about this trip to Cincinnati, too. You know, I don't know why you wanted me to come here in the first place."

He sighs and rubs his head and then looks away from her. "Okay, forget it," he says. "Forget I said anything about sex. I don't want it anymore. But I would just like to remind you that when I came to see you in Connecticut, *you* were the one who wanted sex all the time, *you* were the one who went batshit crazy when I didn't think it was the right thing to do. What happened to that woman, huh?"

"She had a baby."

"Yeah, she had a baby. And maybe she had something else, too." He gets up off the bed, walking with a heaviness she hasn't noticed in him before. He goes over to the desk in the corner, the bill-paying desk, which is covered with papers and letters and things for the museum. It takes him a moment of rifling through the papers, and then he picks up an envelope and brings it over to her. "A love letter for you from the cell phone company," he says.

Time starts to unspool so slowly.

"Open it," he says.

"I don't want to read it," she says. Something has gone cold in the pit of her stomach.

For a moment he just stands there and looks at her. And then he says, "You don't love me, do you? We can pretend some more, but it's really over, isn't it?"

"What do you mean, it's over? We're just starting with a new baby, it's always like this, it's a tough transition. I do love you, it's just—"

"No," he says. "It's not. I could have waited that out. But you're so unhappy, you're so distracted. You love him. You don't love me anymore."

"I do love you," she says dully, mechanically.

"But look at this," he says. He holds out the bill. "You talk to him *every day*. You called him from the hospital, even though I was there with you every single minute. How did you even manage to do that?"

She glances down at the line of numbers, Tony's cell phone number repeated over and over again, calls received, calls sent out, all dutifully recorded in their official capacity. She takes a deep breath; everything in the room has gone a little bit hazy, and she knows she needs to be sharp.

"Look," she says, making her voice sound reasonable, "he went through the pregnancy with me. We got to be friends.

I miss talking to him. Why shouldn't I? He was the one who went with me to the doctor's visits and who listened to me complain—you weren't there, remember?"

"That's bullshit," he says. "Life doesn't work that way. If it were just a friendship, you'd call him when I was around, wouldn't you? I know you. I see the signs. I tried to ignore it when I was there at Christmas, but I saw how you looked at each other."

She feels herself spiraling down. She doesn't have the stamina for this right now; she can't do it, it's too soon, she's too breakable, life is fragile, she needs time to think.

The baby starts to cry then, little piercing cries of hunger. Rosie gets up and goes in and picks her up from the bassinet. Beanie roots around, looking frantically for the breast, and Rosie sits down in the rocking glider and pulls open her nightgown, and Beanie clamps on as if for dear life, snuffling and sucking as hard as she can. Rosie winces at the sting of her breasts releasing the milk, and then she settles back in the glider in the dark, feeling both the pain and the relief.

She can hear Jonathan go into the bathroom and close the door. After a while, the door opens, and for a moment, she thinks maybe he'll come to see her and the baby. Maybe this talk went further than he meant it to, and he knows now he can't live without her and Beanie. He'll come in and say he wants her to stay with him.

But he doesn't come in. She hears him snap off the light in the bedroom and close the door against her, and for one tiny moment, she closes her eyes, consumed with guilt. Maybe she should take the baby and go into the bedroom and sit down on the bed with him and tell him how sorry she is for hurting him. She's not supposed to leave people; they've always gotten to leave her instead. Maybe she could promise to forget about Tony and to care more about the museum, to work harder at making friends here, to simply make herself *adjust*. She can be what he wants. She will just try harder and harder.

Then, rocking in the dark, she thinks of Tony—Tony, who wants the biggest Christmas tree, the funniest stories, the deepest kisses, the wackiest Scrabble words for Soapie, the most complicated tomato sauce, each and every ultrasound picture, the peanut butter diamonds. Tony, in Jonathan's place, would try to make things work. He would throw himself at love. He would say this is what the heart does, it can't help it. He'd be the one bringing apologies and promises and back rubs and love, he would come up with a theory, he would sit by her side all night long and watch the baby gulping milk. He would have come into the baby's room when he came home tonight, too. He would have stood beside Rosie, and nuzzled her neck, reached over and unbuttoned her dress, waltzed her to the bedroom, where he would have gently eased her down onto the bed, kissing every expanse of her.

He's a man who wants family so much that he's spent the last ten months experiencing parenthood through the windshield, and he loves her so much that he agreed to two weeks, and bowed out gracefully when it turned out to be only one.

Soapie said: *Pick one of those men, either one, just pick.* And: *Get you some joie de vivre.* And: *Don't sit around and let your whole life dribble away. Find what makes you happy, what gives you passion.*

And most devastating of all: *I know it was bad to lie to you. But I wanted to protect you, I guess.*

She looks out the window at the turquoise swimming pool, shining below like a fake jewel in the artificial lights.

A siren Dopplers itself down the street, and a door slams somewhere in the building. A woman laughs.

Life went by so fast, Soapie said. The whole damn eighty-eight years—you'd think it would be endless, but it flew by, she said. *Rosie, it goes so fast.*

Over the next few days she knows she and Jonathan will make all the necessary arrangements; they'll pack up her stuff and have the tough conversations. It'll be very civilized—he doesn't like messy scenes. It's a separation, they'll say to other people; she's going back home to take care of some things at her grandmother's house.

But to Jonathan, she has to be honest. She'll be her own caseworker again, leading herself gently through to where she's supposed to be. And it will be hard and messy and honest and ultimately glorious.

"Yes, I fell in love with Tony," she will say bravely. "I should have told you before. I thought it would just go away. But you deserve to know the truth."

All these years of trying to adjust the shape of herself into a square peg when what she needed was a round hole she could slip through.

He may seem upset at first, but he'll also be relieved in a way, at what wasn't asked of him, at what he escaped. He's happy here. After all, there are new teacups to be looked at in Cincinnati, there are new ways of attracting visitors to the museum, and there will always be more discoveries and fascinating facts for him.

He won't even miss the baby, not really. She thinks she should feel sad about this, and maybe later it will hit her harder—that there's yet another little girl whose father won't be present. But for right now, she hears Tony's voice in her head. He'd say love can swoop down anytime. And if Jonathan can't love the flesh-and-blood, messy, squalling and fragile little life in front of him, maybe he'll turn into the more "official" father, the kind of father who wants to read her school papers and discuss the best summer camps and arrangements, the guy who can't hear about the prom dates but who will care deeply about the SATs. Whatever level of involvement he'll choose, that will be fine.

She reaches down and strokes Beanie's cheek, and is surprised when a tear falls right on the baby's curled-up little fist. She didn't even know she was crying. Smiling and crying at the same time. So this is how it's going to be.

● ● ●

The airport is crowded for a weekday afternoon, she thinks. She straps the baby into the front pack, the funny one that ties all around and around, like the baby is an accessory you can just attach to yourself. It's good because your hands are free for the diaper bag and the purse. And even better, you can tip your face down and feel that velvety head next to your skin, like ripe peaches in the sunshine.

A week has gone by. Jonathan drives her and Beanie to the airport and unloads their stuff at the curbside. It reminds her of the night he left her at Soapie's. She feels that same sense of being freed from something, the same sense of the glorious unknown. And when he says to her, "I hope you know what you're doing," it feels all too familiar. Déjà vu all over again, she tells him.

This time, though, she reaches over and kisses him. He takes her hand and puts it next to his cheek.

"Call me when you get in," he says, and she promises that she will. He looks at her for a long moment, but she doesn't cry even when he looks as though he might. They're all cried out. Now it's time to simply take the first steps away.

She's all the way into the terminal, her red boots clicking as she hurries along the automatic moving walkway, before she realizes he didn't even lean down to look at the baby. Not even one last look.

• • •

Tony is in her ear on the phone while she waits for the flight to be called. When she told him she was coming back, he said he and Milo would meet the plane when she gets in, and if she wants, and if the baby thinks it's a good idea, they'll go get some dinner. "You'll be hungry," he said. "I hear they don't feed people on planes anymore."

"I might cry sometimes," she says. "I could be a bit of a wreck."

"That's okay. I've seen you eat and cry at the same time," Tony says.

"I might be insane to do this," she says. But even as she's saying it, she knows it's not true. She's planned it all out. She has the house to live in, and she can support herself by teaching. For now she can bring the baby along in a basket to her classes. Her students can pass her around.

"Actually, you seem kind of sane to me," he says. Which has always been one of the best things about him, she realizes: he always thinks things are falling into place. "Who knows what will happen? We'll take it a day at a time," he says.

It's not until she gets out in the middle of the country that she knows for sure it's going to be all right. Somewhere over the Mississippi River—that big crack in the middle of the United States—she has a moment. She'll ask Tony when she gets there, if he and Milo want to move in with her. Tony can paint houses, and she can keep the children and write. They'll cook together and set up the baby swing on the patio, and play catch in the grass when summer comes . . .

Is this crazy to dream like this? Or could it be that this is her story after all, rising up to meet her in midair?

Serena Sophia, who had been nursing peacefully, suddenly falls asleep and yanks her mouth off the breast and flings herself backward, arms outstretched and milk dribbling down her chin.

It's as if she's a drunken sailor on shore leave, absolutely inebriated with the abundance before her, smiling her toothless grin like somebody who just knows all the good things that are coming.

ACKNOWLEDGMENTS

I am so lucky to have people in my life who love to read early drafts and don't mind being asked—okay, forced—to give their opinions and constructive help. Alice Mattison, Kim Steffen, Leslie Connor, Nancy Hall, Allison Meade, Stephanie Shelton, Mary Rose Meade, Holly Robinson, Nancy Antle, Susanne Davis, Sharon Massoth, and Diane Cyr are among the very best readers and commenters a writer can have. Thank you for your love as well as your endless patience and humor, and for not hiding when you saw me coming.

Alice Smith, Lily Hamrick, Amy Kahn, Joan Levine, Peggy Allen, Deb Hare, Jennifer Smith, Marji Lipshez-Shapiro, Beth Levine, Nicole Wise, and Karen Pritzker Vlock offered undying friendship and diversions, cups of tea, long walks, green smoothies, hamburgers, wine, four-hour phone calls, and, in some cases when needed, full moon labyrinth treks. Thank you for everything.

I am fortunate to have Dr. Mary Jane Minkin in my life, a brilliant friend who was willing to devote a lot of thought to the phenomenon of late-in-life pregnancy and childbirth, and helped me know what Rosie was going through.

The Crown Publishing Group has been fantastic to work with. Thanks especially to the patient and wonderful Christine Kopprasch, who helped birth this book through her careful and wise editing and endless encouragement.

Thanks also to the people at Crown and Broadway who have been unfailingly kind and generous and helpful: Molly

Stern, Sheila O'Shea, Meagan Stacey, Catherine Cullen, and Jessica Prudhomme. Nancy Yost, my agent, is smart and funny and lively, and I couldn't do without her wisdom and great ideas.

My stepmother, Helen Myers, listened to plenty of drafts of this book via telephone and helped me shape the character of Soapie. Helen passed away before publication, and every day I have to remind myself that I can't just call her up anymore. I miss her more than words can say.

My children—Ben, Allie, Stephanie, Amy, and Mike—all bring me such laughter and love. They also brought me Charlie, Joshua, Miles, and Emma, for which I'm eternally grateful.

Thank you also to the women and men who gather around my dining room table for writing workshops and share their innermost thoughts and creative yearnings. You are truly a joy!

And last, a bigger-than-words-can-say thank you to Jim, who stands by me in love and every single day makes me laugh.

QUESTIONS FOR DISCUSSION

Please note: In order to provide reading groups with the most informed and thought-provoking questions possible, it is necessary to reveal important aspects of the plot of this novel—as well as the ending. If you have not finished reading *The Opposite of Maybe,* we respectfully suggest that you may want to wait before reviewing this guide.

1. When Rosie and Jonathan get interrupted while making love and he loses interest in continuing, Jonathan says this is just middle-aged life. Is Rosie's need for romance realistic after fifteen years?

2. Is Soapie accurate that Jonathan's love of the ancient, unusable, untouchable teacups says something about his personality? If he hadn't gotten the opportunity to move to California with the teacups and start a museum, do you think they would have stayed together?

3. What is the significance of the teasing their friends do—*The Jonathan and Rosie Show,* for instance?

4. When Soapie explains her philosophy of living the rest of her life to its utmost and not submitting to being cared for by people who will have authority

over her, Rosie can understand and support this decision, even though it means Soapie might be unsafe. How should we treat older people who resist nursing care and insist they have earned the right to take chances with their health?

5. Why is Tony so reluctant to challenge his former wife and her partner, and what eventually changes his mind? What is it that Rosie sees in Tony that he doesn't see in himself, and why does she eventually fall in love with him?

6. When Rosie finds out she's pregnant, her first reaction is to be shocked—and astonished—that her body could do this after so many years. But then this is quickly followed by her realistic sense that she isn't equipped for motherhood. What do you think really changes her mind and makes her decide to have the baby? Do you think Rosie will be a good mother even though she didn't have any real mothering herself?

7. Once Rosie hears the truth about her mother's death, she says she sees everything about her life in a different light. Everyone tells her it doesn't really change anything, but she doesn't agree. Is it just a matter of becoming accustomed to this new way of seeing her mother's short, tragic life and putting away the fantasy she had? How does her reaction color her relationships with Tony and Jonathan?

8. Rosie says that she and Tony are going to have a time of the "Peace Corps of the heart, where you get to be your own sweet caseworker, ministering to all the

hurt and ruined places, rebuilding the infrastructure and soothing the natives." Why does she think this will help her? Is it possible to give yourself that kind of uncommitted time from your real life?

9. Do you feel Rosie should have given life in California more of a chance, given that Jonathan is the baby's father?

10. Soapie always thought Rosie should go to Paris and write in a café, or go look at lions in Africa. But is there a way in which Rosie did end up doing exactly what Soapie advised her to do for her life?

11. Do you think Rosie and Tony will stay together? What do you expect Jonathan's role in Beanie's life will be? How did you feel about Rosie's decisions?

ABOUT THE AUTHOR

Maddie Dawson lives in Connecticut. She is the author of *The Stuff That Never Happened*. She's written for magazines and newspapers and has a website at www.maddiedawson.com.

ALSO BY
MADDIE DAWSON

"[A] deceptively bouncing, ultimately wrenching novel [that] will grab you at page one." —*People*

B\D\W\Y
Broadway Books

Available wherever books are sold